BUTTERFLIES BLUE

GLENNIS PAINE

PETALOOTHA PRESS

*This is for all the storytellers and story lovers…
and for those who fight injustices in the world.*

AUTHOR'S NOTE

This book is by an Australian author. Some of the spelling and punctuation may be unfamiliar but is nevertheless correct. There will also be words, phrases and concepts specific to the Australian dialect and setting. I hope you enjoy it!

Glennis Paine

PART I

1

———————

S wish!
The sound entered the space reserved for other things, then dissolved into the darkness.

Nebulous.

Nothing.

The sound shifted and sighed in Annalee's mind. It whispered, probed, attempted to draw out a memory, tried to pull her back. Important, this. How was it important?

Her mind in a fog. Body refusing to respond. Leaden limbs and a throbbing lower back added to the agony of the relentless pounding in her head.

She struggled to get comfortable, tossing and turning. Now her arm, numbed beneath her, clamoured for attention. At least the dreaded pins and needles didn't take hold as she squeezed and released her fingers.

Someone groaned. Was it her? This was all down to that exhausting double shift, followed by her date with Jamie, the delicious Jamie. Did she?

The memory eluded her, hidden in the haze. She had no recollection of the end of the shift or meeting Jamie. She didn't see herself there, in his car or hers, holding hands, a greeting kiss. Did they stroll along near the lake or the beach? Go to that favourite café? Jog along the river path? She screwed her face to focus, instantly regretting it as a fresh wave of pain hit behind her eyes. She forced one eye open. Much too dark. Back to sleep girl, it's too early to get up. Damn shift work.

Rolling over released another groan as the ache in her spine and the pounding in her head connected. She froze, willed it to stop and fought to relax the tension in her neck and shoulders. Maybe she was coming down with a virus. If she could get some water and paracetamol. She had to get up—needed a drink of water… needed to… sleep. Sleep the pain away.

"Wait. Wait for the light," whispered the darkness, drifting unheard in the space.

———

"HI, MRS T. HAVE YOU HEARD FROM ANNALEE?" LUCY resisted the urge to tap her fingers on the countertop and stuck her left hand in her pocket. She squashed down the niggling thoughts crowding into her mind to explain the whereabouts of her housemate and best friend, Annalee Tanaka.

"Oh, hello Lucy. What's that? You're looking for Annalee?"

"Yes, Mrs T, I haven't heard from her since yesterday lunchtime. I can't seem to get hold of her."

"Mm, why no, Lucy, I haven't heard from her since yesterday… er… lunchtime too. She sent a text. She's perhaps gone out with Jamie or one of her friends. I wasn't expecting to see her until tomorrow—we've got a lunch date."

Lucy grimaced at her mobile phone. "I'm a bit concerned, Mrs T. She was due home around four o'clock yesterday, but I'd left for my afternoon shift by then and didn't get in until after ten last night. Her car was there, and I didn't want to wake her, but this morning…" Lucy sucked in a long breath. "She wasn't there. Her bed hasn't been slept in."

"Oh… that *is* odd."

"And she had Impact group last night. She wouldn't miss that. I know it's only nine o'clock, but…"

"What can we do? Could she have gone somewhere with Jamie? Or be back at work? I get confused with the shifts."

"No, she wouldn't be at work after that extra shift she did yesterday." Anna had texted Lucy about the change. She'd been asked to cover for a colleague who couldn't make his morning shift due to a traffic accident. After working through her night shift, she had a short break before continuing on until 3.30 pm. Double shifts were not common but at times couldn't be avoided.

"Oh." Lucy waited for Heather to continue. "But she can't have gone far. I'll call her brother, Steve, or Meg and... er... what time is it now?"

Lucy bit her lip at the concern in Heather's voice. She didn't want to alarm her, but her own anxiety meter was registering in the red zone, and she didn't know what else to do. "It's just after nine." She glanced at the clock as the hour ticked over.

"Okay, er... should we wait a couple of hours longer? Can you call me back at... say, eleven, and we'll decide if... er... what to do next? Oh—and let me know straight away if she turns up."

"Absolutely, Mrs T. I'm sure it's just a misunderstanding. I've got my wires crossed somehow and forgotten what she told me." Lucy rang off, chewed at the inside of her cheek, and eyed the wall clock once more.

2

S wish!

That noise again. That odd, out-of-place noise punctuating the space between sleep and wakefulness. Did she or Lucy
forget to switch the TV off or was it the microwave or fridge? Did
microwaves swish? Fridges sometimes did—or did they click and
buzz? Thankfully, the pounding in her head had settled to a dull
ache. Forget the irritating noises.

After five months in the shared rental villa with Lucy, she should
be used to its night sounds. But compared to the twenty-odd years
back home in Bayswater, she must need longer to adapt. Sounds
playing tricks, a night-time aberration. It never happened during the
day. She groped around for the bedside light switch, but it eluded
her grasp. Come to think of it, her clock with its familiar red glow
was missing too.

She swallowed as she strained through the blackness. It was all
wrong. No lamp within reach—no bedside clock showing the time
—no fridge humming from the kitchen. And the surrounding air
seemed warm. The last few nights had been colder, autumn suddenly
making its presence felt. She had unpacked her cosy wool-filled
doona as defence against the fresh night air. Very few houses in

Australia were centrally heated, and with no heating in her bedroom, the doona was her only protection against the cold.

This darkness too—it was something else, so... thick. She resisted the urge to reach out and grab a handful of it and curled her fingers over the bedclothes. Her room was never this dark. There was invariably light coming from somewhere: the faint glow from the streetlights, or moonlight shining through the gaps where the curtains didn't quite reach. Hadn't it been nearing a full moon last night? Yes, she and Jamie had arranged a moonlit walk along the beach tonight, or was it tomorrow?

What was going on?

She wasn't afraid of the dark... Her heart thrummed against her rib cage, calling her a liar, and she wedged her hands under her armpits. The suffocating black air spiralled into her throat, threatening to suck the breath out. *Get a grip, Annalee. What are you afraid of?* Drawing in a deep breath and closing her mouth over it, she shrugged her shoulders and jerked her arm out from beneath the bedclothes. Maybe she had knocked her clock onto the floor.

As her fingers reached the edge of the bed, she gripped and swung over onto all fours. Not a brilliant move. Waves of nausea rippled up from her stomach, acrid bile searing her throat. A rush of heat and dizziness set her head thumping again. She slumped back into the mattress, gasping, and gulped down the bile, her throat raw. She loathed that feeling, but who didn't? No one in their right mind enjoyed throwing up. The virus theory was getting stronger by the minute.

The next attempt gave her some confidence as the dreaded nausea and dizziness stayed away. She figured she could live with the headache and back pain. She shuffled along the top of the mattress, feeling her way with hands outstretched—she wasn't ready to get off the bed yet.

Definitely a bigger bed than her double. It wasn't the dark playing tricks, magnifying the size of it. She edged to the side and sat, legs hanging. Her feet should touch the floor, toes sinking into the loop-pile carpet, if it was her bed and her room. Wrong size, wrong height, wrong bed! Where was she? She reached a big toe down, flinching when it met a cool, smooth surface.

Teeth gritted against the punishing pain in her spine, she scooted away from the edge and hugged her knees in tight. What was going on? The question hovered in the thick black air, its question mark looped white on the inside of her eyelids.

A dozen possibilities slammed in and spun off into the dark just as swiftly. Had she gone blind? Had an accident? Been kidnapped? What? Come on, Annalee Tanaka. You are—somewhere.

She clenched her eyes shut—they were of no benefit in the dark anyway—gripped her legs hard and squared her neck and shoulders. She hissed out a breath before taking a deep one in through her nose, then counted it out through her mouth. Those Pilates classes she'd taken earlier in the year were so worth it, if only for the breathing techniques. She worked her jaw and tightened and released her shoulders and fingers before working down her body, one muscle at a time. Peeling her legs away from her chest, she crossed them and gingerly straightened her spine.

Checklist time. What was real, and what wasn't? The room was pitch black, not a hint of light anywhere. Was she blind? Possible, but no. She would know—wouldn't she? Yet, isn't that what a newly blind person might believe? Smell: promising. A slight chemical odour, like bleach, drifted around the cotton-fragrance from the bed linen. At least the place didn't smell dank or mouldy.

Was that it? She was in a hospital. Had she taken ill or had an accident? Another and emphatic—NO—this time. It was absurd, hospitals were never this dark. There were always night-lights in the corridors, and they didn't hand out big, cushiony beds like this in any hospital she'd experienced. And the silence—it was as profound as the darkness—hospitals were not quiet either. How many patients complained about that?

She probed the achy and sore bits. Apart from her tender arm and back and the lingering headache, nothing else felt odd. No broken bones, no limbs covered in plaster or even—just as she thought 'sticking plasters' she found one. Her finger traced around the small patch above a tender spot on her wrist. It was the kind stuck on after removing IV drips. But why a drip if it wasn't a hospital?

"Lucy! Lucy! Are you there, Luce? Hello! Hello! Is anyone there?"

Her voice, thin and reedy, caught in her hair and around her throat, not piercing the cloying darkness. She sighed and settled into the mattress, gathering the covers around her like a cocoon. It was just her and the bed—her world for the moment. A moment she hoped would soon pass.

3

Lucy plugged her phone in to recharge, refusing to check again if she'd left it on silent. Her fingers itched to pick it up, but she resisted and turned her back, a frown puckering her forehead. She'd called all of their friends with no luck.

Empty silence echoed before her as she padded down the hallway. She stopped at Anna's room, her fingers gripping the door frame. A clue? A clue? She willed the room to give her something. It hadn't the past three times she'd looked. She went in—she had to.

Everything was in its place—the bed made to perfection, shoes and clothes out of sight in the drawers and wardrobe. A smile played on her lips as she sat on the edge of the bed. It was one reason they got on so well. They were both neat freaks. Some of their friends told horror stories of their flat-sharing experiences. Not fun. She shivered and eased onto her knees, fingers groping through the carpet and along the side of the bedside chest, searching for a fallen note. Nothing—besides, she knew perfectly well that Anna would have texted her or left a quick message on the kitchen bench.

As she settled back onto the edge of the bed, she swallowed a sigh and reached for Anna's teddy bear nestled in the middle of the pillows. Hugging him close, she drank in the essence of her friend—

the spicy smell of sandalwood and a hint of citrus, two of Anna's favourite fragrances.

To share a house or flat after they finished nursing studies had been their dream. They'd been lucky to find this small villa, built at the back of a 1950s bungalow after the large block was subdivided. Many of the original homes remained in the leafy tree-lined cul-de-sac, although a number of the owners were taking advantage of the changed planning laws and similarly subdividing. Set in the inner suburbs, their villa was conveniently within walking distance of a shopping centre. They were amazed to find it was in their rental budget, and had moved in almost six months ago.

Leaving their respective homes had been a mix of happy/sad. They were excited to taste independence—their parents supportive but less eager, voicing the usual parental concerns about their readiness for such a step. But when it became a reality, they couldn't do enough for them. Anna's mum bought a washing machine, her own mum and dad had been looking to buy a smaller fridge and gave them their old one. They only had to buy a table and chairs for the small dining room, as friends and family gave or loaned them the rest. They made their mark on the place with soft furnishings and had fun buying some blank canvases, attempting to create modern artworks with sample pots.

Lucy gazed at the pop art canvas adorning the wall opposite the bed. Anna's creation. She was proud of her hour's work, splashing paint about and splattering it with spots and splodges to finish. They had agreed any gallery would pay big money for such a masterpiece, before dissolving into a fit of giggles.

She gave Annalee's teddy a last squeeze and set him back in his spot, smoothing down his jacket. Her mobile's strident ring cut in. She bolted to the kitchen and snatched it up, half-disappointed to see Jamie's caller ID light up.

"Jamie. I've been trying to reach you. Is Anna with you?" She tightened her grip on the phone, willing him to say yes.

"Yeah, I saw all the missed calls. Anna? No, I haven't seen her since, uh… Monday—the day I flew in. We had dinner and a walk along the beach. I dropped her home around eight."

His good-natured reply sent Lucy's heart plummeting. He knew nothing about her concerns for Anna. "We can't contact her—she seems to have disappeared. Since yesterday, Jamie. I've called Mrs Tanaka, but no luck. Everyone's ringing around. Mrs T almost mentioned calling the police. I can't believe it. Jamie?"

"Wha… run that past me again, Lucy. Anna missing?"

"I… um, we can't think of anything else, anywhere else she might be. It doesn't make sense."

Annalee had been going out with Jamie for about three months and, although he was thirty to Annalee's twenty-two years, Lucy saw from the way he treated her that their relationship had the potential to be something special. She was happy for her, as Anna's ex-boyfriend, Dan, had seemed a bit of a loser. He never socialised with their crowd but spent his time watching TV or playing computer games—he was totally the opposite of Anna. She had been going out with Dan since high school so Lucy had kept her thoughts to herself. But she wasn't the only one relieved when Anna finally ended it.

"Can I come over, Lucy? I don't know what I can do, maybe we can think it through together. Two heads… and all that." She caught the strain in Jamie's voice, his attempt at levity falling flat in the air between them. He continued, "I've got three days before I fly out, and we were planning on spending the next couple of days together, anyhow."

Jamie Prince was a FIFO, a fly-in fly-out worker on an oil rig somewhere off the coast of Kalimantan, Indonesia. Anna had told her the details more than once, but it never registered. Mention exotic places, oil rigs, engineering and her eyes glazed over. Her family, from generations back, were all country folk—used to the land and holidaying in the same peppermint tree-lined caravan park next to a white sandy beach on the south coast at Augusta. Heck! they hadn't even ventured overseas to Rottnest—the popular holiday island, a ferry ride across the sea from Fremantle.

"Okay, sure. I'll be glad of the company, I've got so many stupid thoughts running through my head. I've been phoning or texting everyone I can think of. I'll try to think of a few more to call before you get here." She bit her lip at the inane drivel she was spouting, but this wasn't a situation that was in any way her experience. Friends, let alone housemates, didn't disappear in her world.

Not twenty minutes later, he arrived and insisted on having a look around for himself while Lucy made coffee. She raised an eyebrow—hadn't she searched the house more than once—but pressed her lips together over the 'But I…' she was about to voice. He just might pick up something she'd missed. And that was the aim, to find out where Anna was, not to make Lucy out to be incompetent.

But, apart from the dust bunnies he fished from under the fridge, no new clues materialised.

They perched on the kitchen stools, cradling their coffees, as Lucy related what little she knew. "I got home around ten-thirty last night. Anna's car was there, so I assumed she was home. She'd texted me earlier asking if I would buy the groceries because of the extra shift she did, so she could have a lie-down before going out again. She was keen to go to group last night—that's one reason I can't believe she would have gone somewhere else."

"I know. That shift cancelled our afternoon plans so I asked her to give the group thing a miss and come out with me, but no luck there."

A fleeting smile touched her lips. Jamie didn't understand Annalee's interest in exploring Christianity. Yet.

"What about her bike?" He set down his cup, his fingers brushing the back of her hand before he pushed back from the breakfast bar.

She turned away, the skin on her hand—along with her cheeks—burning. That was accidental, wasn't it? She followed him to the door, grateful his back was in her face. "I didn't think about that. I just presumed she'd driven her car."

The small shed—home to their bikes and a few garden tools—was missing one bike: Annalee's.

"Ahh, no bike—well that's one minor piece of the puzzle solved," he said.

4

The black silence was all-consuming. Her heart drumming, Annalee fanned the air in front of her nose. The thought of being encased in a tomb sent an icy shiver through her frame. She dismissed it just as quickly. It was ridiculous—on account of the large, plush bed she clung to. Whoever heard of such luxury in a place reserved for the dead?

She ran a finger over her dry lips. She couldn't ignore her scratchy throat and the tongue sticking to her teeth for much longer, and the relentless thud, thud, thudding in her head. She needed water. There had to be a bathroom close by. The adventurous, inquisitive Anna would be up, feeling her way around the room— not just for the bathroom, but to discover where on earth she was. But her sluggish limbs and foggy mind were winning.

If she could remember what happened, it might do the trick—or tricks, plural. Help her forget her woes. Plus help pass the time before morning and, just maybe, go partway to blocking the wild thoughts spinning through her head.

She'd cycled to the hospital and, with no rain forecast and a full moon, enjoyed the ride along the well-lit cycle paths skirting the city. Cycling under the tree canopy near King's Park always thrilled her with its soaring gum trees lining the path.

Her night shift had started at nine and she arrived, as planned, with thirty minutes to spare. Plenty of time to cool down from the ride and freshen up.

There were no dramas overnight, but she'd stayed to start the morning shift when Gervais hadn't turned up to take over. Forty-five minutes into it, Nurse Manager Val sought her out. Someone had driven through a red light and hit Gervais's car. Val wasn't sure of his injuries but he had called in himself which was a good sign. So Anna agreed to continue for the day. She'd done a couple of back-to-back shifts before, and although tiring it would mean at least twenty-four hours off before she had to work again.

Sleep had threatened as she sat in the canteen on her last break, but with only three hours left she'd settled for a double shot of coffee and some stretches in the restroom as a substitute.

She'd called her mum to confirm their lunch date for the following day, then Jamie rang, wanting to take her out that evening. Because of the extra shift, she'd texted him earlier to cancel their afternoon plans. He was persistent, but accepted her refusal in his usual sweet, good-natured way when she suggested a compromise— for him to pick her up after work for a coffee. Definitely a decaf, this time. She would be more than ready to fall into bed when she got home.

End-of-shift handover completed, she had hurried down the stairs and out, eager to see him. She could see herself outside C Block, hands on the handlebars. But she rode it so often. Was it another day? She sighed, rubbing her temple. She was waiting, scanning the carpark opposite and looking up and down the access road. What happened next?

Eyes searching through the darkness, she placed a palm on her forehead. It was hopeless.

No, no. That was wrong. She frowned and massaged the back of her neck. She had put Jamie off—the need for a king-sized nap before her evening group meeting winning out over even a few minutes with him. She remembered being annoyed at having to ride her bike home when she was so tired, and wrestling with her bike helmet straps. And that was it—nothing else. Her mind was blank.

Her foggy brain was still reluctant to engage fully with the need to remember… something. She gasped as the rumpled outline of the bedclothes slowly materialised. Morning, finally. Rolling onto her side, she stuck her elbow in the mattress and wedged her hand under her jaw. Her breath caught as she took in the room. Daylight? Not quite. The light was coming, somehow—from where the walls met the ceiling.

5

────────────────

Heather Tanaka hung up the phone and curled into the corner of the couch. Sparky, her beloved Jack Russell-cross, hopped up beside her and snuggled in close. She clutched a cushion to her chest and fondled his ear. Where could Annalee be? Her precious daughter, her youngest child. If Tony were here, he would know what to do.

She picked up the photo from the side table and ran her finger over the happy family group. The snap taken on their last holiday together a month before their son, Stephen, married Meg. Two missing faces: her husband, and now Anna. It couldn't be. She swiped at the tear trickling down her cheek. Sparky whined, pawing her skirt before he stood up, turned full-circle and settled again with his head on her knee, eyes locked onto hers.

"Good boy, Sparky. It'll be all right. You wait and see. Anna will be back with us soon." She sniffed and reached for a tissue.

His tail thumped at the words, but his eyes darted from her face to the photo and back again.

"What would I do without you, Sparky-boy? What would I do?" She circled his face with her hands and planted a kiss on the top of his head. "Don't let Anna see me doing that."

A smile ghosted as her daughter's lectures on germs, and dog germs in particular, brought back Anna's dedication to her chosen career.

"She can give me a million lectures—I won't complain a bit. Will I, Sparky? You see if I don't." He dropped his head to one side as Heather sighed, rubbed the edge of the photo frame, and eased back into the cushions.

The calendar pinned above her writing desk caught her gaze. Her eyes narrowed as she focused on the date. "Why, it can't be." She sucked in a breath and slapped the photo face down on the couch. Sparky leapt off and skipped around her feet as she crossed the room. She needed to check. If only it were wrong. Had she confused it with some other date? Her heart sank. She knew there was no mistake. That date was etched in her memory.

Her niece, Katie, had disappeared on the seventh of May four years ago and yesterday was the seventh of May. She poked at the calendar, as if it would magically transform the number into some other date—any other date.

"It can't be."

It would be laughable if she didn't feel like screaming right now. Her hands trembled as she rifled through the desk drawers under- neath. Where was that letter from her cousin, Barbara? Her finger- nails raked the surface of the tin hidden at the back of the bottom drawer.

She gritted her teeth and hissed out a breath, tugged out the tin and lowered herself onto the high-backed chair. Time stopped as she sat chewing her lip, only conscious of the cold metal seeping through her skirt, chilling her thighs. Then she sat back and eased off the lid, its squeal of protest sending a shiver down her spine. Old-tin odour caught her taste buds, souring her mouth, and she frowned at its contents.

A carefully folded letter, its envelope worn and limp at the edges, lay on top of a bunch of yellowing newspaper clippings. Barbara had written to her many times, but this letter had been the last one about Katie. Heather firmly believed her cousin had written it more for herself than for Heather. An attempt at laying out her heartbreak and pain, at making sense of her misery. A futile attempt at reaching some sort of closure.

She unfolded the pages, fingers stiff and fumbling, and read through the heartbreaking story of Katie's disappearance in England. She knew the letter inside-out, but there was no escaping. She had to read it again.

Katie—who wasn't really her niece, as Barbara was her cousin not her sister—missing without a trace at sixteen years of age. After setting off for school not three miles away from home, she was never seen again. The initial belief that she had run away soon dismissed, much to Barbara's relief. She'd known it wasn't possible, as any mother would. The endless search—not only by the police. Family, friends, even strangers scoured the town, the countryside. Then, after a suitable time, they scaled down the official search, and eventually called it off. It wasn't endless after all. Except for Barbara.

The days stretched into weeks and then months. The silence, the not knowing, not hearing anything from Katie or anyone connected with her. Her school friends didn't know where she was. They didn't know of any boyfriends or unusual behaviour. Her last known movements re-enacted on prime-time TV, with Barbara giving an impassioned plea at the end, husband John seated by her side, clutching her hand. The appeal for anyone who knew anything to come forward and, because the police insisted, the plea for Katie herself to get in touch and let them know she was safe. Nothing was so bad they couldn't resolve it.

Then, after a few weeks, things changed. Sympathies changed—first with the police, as they questioned the family and their movements, and then, as the media got a sniff, with the public. The trial by media, a relentless tide of sensationalism and insinuation. They seized on the minutest details and turned them into headlines. That John was Katie's stepfather, not her 'real' father, and that Barbara ran a market stall selling arts and crafts. They labelled her a bit of a hippie, a bit left-wing, someone who moved in less than desirable circles, mixed with hawkers, the homeless and so on. She became a prime target for the gutter press—not a normal, dedicated stay-at-home mum, as if there was such a thing anymore. And where was Hari, her mysterious Japanese ex-husband? Why wasn't he in their lives? They brought up mixed-race marriages, inevitable culture clashes and the effects on the children when marriages broke down. There was no end to it.

All the speculation, the assumptions and implications—aired endlessly, day after miserable day. Even neighbours and some Barbara had called friends appeared to avoid her and John. More than once, conversations faltered as she entered a room, guilty looks caught on faces.

The pages relating the family's harrowing journey poured out line by line in Barbara's precise and measured script. Heather shuddered. The tears trickled down her cheeks unrestrained, dripping onto her cotton blouse. But as one hit a page, daring to smudge the words, she pushed back, searching for the abandoned tissue box.

Surely this was nothing more than a weird coincidence. Heather pressed her lips together and blew her nose. But it was not something she would share with anyone yet, Barbara least of all. Nothing would come of it. It was all a big misunderstanding as Lucy had said. Anna had gone with one of her friends and forgotten to tell anyone. That was all, or she'd left a note and it had gone astray.

Heather stuffed the dread deep, deep down as she folded Barbara's letter, placed it carefully into the tin and pushed it back into the drawer.

6

———

 here on earth? Annalee frowned at the cold, clinical surrounds. Not that there was much to see. The comfort of the luxurious bed hadn't prepared her for this cave of a room, with its most noticeable missing feature: windows.

She scooped up her pillow and sandwiched it between her back and the grey-white leather-look headboard. Were the walls really clad in brushed metal? A stylish covering for white goods, but whole rooms? She ran her fingers over the surface next to the bedhead, her hand a ghostly image in the dull reflection.

The room screamed 'shipping container', yet, large as those could be, this must be the big brother. Her king-sized bed, in the centre of a long wall, was dwarfed by comparison. A couch with a low table before it stood against one of the narrow walls, and a small desk with a swivel chair at the opposite end. Couch and chair both matched the bedhead colour and material. The floor in one shade darker grey, a serviceable office or hospital type heavy-duty vinyl, was not out to win any home-beautiful awards.

With her preference for bold colours, the neutral shades in the room, along with the all-white bedding, would take some getting used to. And that wasn't something she wanted to do. She huffed out a breath.

Annalee's gaze jerked back towards the low table and she ran her dry tongue over still drier lips. An upturned tumbler and a glass jug full of water sat on a small tray. Liquid gold. The rest of her exploration could wait. She shuffled to the edge of the bed and went to stand only to land on her hands and knees.

"Ouch! What the…?"

Easing back, she rested her spinning head against the bed. How could one step result in that? Her muscles were weak and stiff, her balance all over the place.

She massaged her feet and calves and then, using the bed as a prop, urged her legs into action and shuffled around the bed a few times. The option of crawling across the floor didn't appeal, although the call of that water might change her mind.

Focusing on the couch, she took a deep breath and set off—arms held stiffly out sideways as if she was balancing on a tightrope. For someone who regularly ran ten kilometres, her slow progress across the room took on marathon proportions. She flopped onto the couch, wincing at the protest from her spine, legs shaking and head spinning once more.

There was a bluish tinge to her fingernails and an obvious tremor. Overall, she didn't feel cold, but that wasn't the only reason for a lack of healthy colour. She poured a glass of water and sipped. Pure ambrosia—water had never tasted so good. She savoured the next few mouthfuls before swallowing them, her raspy throat further soothed with each one. Holding up the glass, she resisted the urge to gulp the rest, not keen on losing it straightaway. Cleaning up after puking patients had never been her favourite job.

Midway through a second glass, her body and mind already responding to the hydration, she relaxed into the cushiony couch and scanned the room.

She hissed out a breath and jerked forward.

"Ouch!" *Remember the back!* She grimaced and rubbed the area in question. A door. There must be one somewhere. How had they done that? Windows was one thing, but no door? She eased to the edge of the couch as a flicker of movement caught her eye. A panel in the wall above the desk slid across, revealing a screen emblazoned with 'BATHE' in bold letters. As the panel slid back into place, a door-sized opening on the far side of the bed appeared.

Eyes wide, Anna gasped at the soft sound from the door. The noises she'd heard in the night weren't part of a dream, but doors opening or closing. Which begged the question: who was coming in or out, and why?

Her heart sped up a notch, and she pushed back into the couch, exhaling the breath she'd held onto. To 'bathe' at some unknown entity's demand didn't impress one iota. It presumed too much. They presumed too much. If they thought her a helpless victim ready to obey their every whim, they didn't know her. Yet.

She squeezed her lips together, picked up the jug, poured a full glass and resumed sipping.

Still, a good soak would ease the stiffness in her muscles, and that water intake was making its presence known on her bladder.

And—an open door was an opportunity. For what? Sitting here wouldn't answer the question. After another mouthful, she tested her legs and headed for the door. As she drew level with the bed a subtle blend of fragrances hit her nostrils, growing stronger the closer she got. Mm… cinnamon and possibly nutmeg, but with definite undertones of lavender and lemon? Other aromas in the mix were more elusive, but altogether they added up to a positive encouragement to 'bathe'.

She hesitated a step before the doorway, a tad breathless, but it was more than that. What would she find? Another disappointingly bland room or an end to this windowless confine with panoramic views to the outside world? She stepped into the doorway and gasped.

It was enormous. No windows, but what a bathroom. A low whistle of appreciation escaped at the luxury. Metallic-look walls as in the bedroom, but a marble floor? Still mostly grey toning, but with white and cream streaks that added warmth. Much more inviting than the 'bedroom'.

She traced a big toe across the floor's surface, savouring the earthy coolness, but the bathtub held her gaze. Some three metres away, the floor disappeared into a huge—large enough to have a spa party with four or five besties—oval-shaped sunken bath set in the middle of the room. An elegant silver spout poured steamy water into a mass of foamy bubbles, all jostling in her direction like a crowd let loose in the post-Christmas sales. A stack of white, fluffy towels sat along one side of the tub. A recessed shelf, just above the waterline, housed bottles of lotions, gels and a loofah.

At the far end of the room, a partition hid each corner, and a hand basin, complete with a wall mirror above it, was set midway between them. One must hide the toilet, surely? The other, an exit or shower? She would find out soon enough—that toilet was calling her name.

As she took a step, a sudden movement behind sent her spinning. The door finished slotting carefully back into place. She flung herself at it, her chest tightening as she pounded her fists on it. She dug her fingernails into the faint lines barely visible on the smooth expanse.

"Open up! Open it! What's going on? Who are you? What do you want with me? OPEN THIS DOOR! Let me out!"

Heather hung up the house phone. The call to the police station, though frustrating, had left her calm. The frustrating part was getting them to take her seriously, convincing them that Anna wasn't another runaway or sleeping it off at a friend's house. They'd finally arranged for someone to meet her at Lucy's at one o'clock. Strange how quickly her mind rearranged the status quo to call it Lucy's house, not Anna's.

She picked up the phone, set it down again and pulled out her address book. She hadn't needed to call Lucy before today. Luckily, Anna, always one to cross the T's and dot the I's, had insisted she copy it in when they first moved in together. She dialled the number —Lucy picking up at the first ring—and gave her the details.

She rang off and eased herself onto a kitchen stool, twisting her wedding ring and staring at the clock. What now? It was too early to get ready for Lucy's, and the thought of lunch sent her stomach flipping. Any more cups of tea and she would dissolve into a puddle, yet her mouth was so dry. She reached across the kitchen bench for a glass only to watch it slip through her fingers and shatter on the floor. Sparky rushed in from the garden, but skidded to a halt at her command to stop. He stood in the doorway, a front paw raised and head on one side.

"I know, I know, look what I've done. It's all gone wrong and…" She put her fingers over her mouth, tears pooling in her eyes.

"Drop, Sparky. Good boy. You stay there while I clean up this mess." She sent a thank you to Tony for encouraging her to persevere with obedience training, which didn't help the tears.

Between sniffles, she cleaned up and put the kettle on, settling for a coffee. The everyday activity was the signal Sparky needed to show normality reigned and he could resume garden patrol. He turned tail and headed for the doggy-door.

Coffee clasped in shaky hands, Heather went to call her son Stephen, before remembering he would be in the middle of a busy morning at the dental surgery. No need to disturb his wife Meg, either. It could wait. If Anna turned up, she would have worried them for nothing.

Oh, Tony, she sighed, glancing at his photo. She must turn up. Where is she? I know you're not here, my darling, but I wish you were. She reached for a tissue.

In the sixteen months since the freak accident which claimed his life, Heather was nowhere near coming to terms with it. Oh, she had some enjoyable days or parts of them, with Sparky or her beloved family and friends, but the grief was still raw and sometimes overwhelming. A train hit Tony after he cut through the flashing-light barriers, rushing to catch his connection. That was the official version—it had been a wet and windy night and, with no witnesses, not even the train driver realised he'd hit anyone. The police only pieced together what they could after finding traces of blood and hair on a train which had passed through the station.

A commuter found his still-warm body flung against the boundary fence and called the ambulance. So many questions remained unanswered for Heather and the family. Tony wasn't a risk-taker, nor absent-minded or so caught up in his research at Combined Security Systems that he couldn't take care of himself. He was down-to-earth and fully involved in all of their family, church and social activities. He was active, jogging most days or working out in the gym, and he rarely missed their daily dog walks.

Tony was or had been—Heather sniffed, setting her empty cup on the bench top—very close to the perfect husband and father. He was attentive and intuitive about her needs and moods and very involved with their kids from the moment they were born. His only flaw, if she had to name one, was his lack of physical affection in front of others. It didn't come naturally to him, but all his family were the same. Heather put it down to cultural differences, although only his father was Japanese, his mother, English. But he had worked on it with Heather's encouragement, and he was a sympathetic listener—ready with a hug at home or to come alongside whoever needed him. He… they both believed in encouraging and equipping their kids with the mental resources needed to survive the difficulties life would throw at them.

Heather always knew she and Tony were soul mates. She smiled, thinking of the times they finished each other's sentences. And they'd grown even closer in the years after the children grew up and moved out.

And then—he was gone. Heather trembled. The acrid taste of dread, her constant companion in the months following his death, crept back into her mouth and caught at her throat.

"I don't think I can bear it. Not again. Not Anna."

8

Annalee slumped against the bathroom door, a hiccupy-sob escaping her throat. She sagged onto her knees as hot tears salted her lips. It wasn't so much the door closing which rankled—after all, she was locked in the other room. It was the control. Sure, she would have a bath, but why lock the door? What was that about?

She squared her shoulders, turned and headed for the little room in the corner first.

As she returned to the tub, she eyed the tap, a couple of water drops escaping its elegant spout. Somehow it had turned itself off. She sat on the rim and dipped in a toe. She hadn't given her clothing a thought before, but as she shed the short-sleeved cotton top, matching elastic-waisted knee-length shorts and snug cotton briefs, she held them in front of her.

The top reminded her of a shorter version of the robes issued to hospital patients—wrap-around with thin fabric ties at one side. The simple white, waist-high cotton undies were something to behold. She hadn't seen or worn such a garment since primary school. A wry grin ghosted her face before disappearing, the thought of her unknown dresser sending a quiver through her spine.

She sighed and lowered herself into the bubbles, inhaling the fragrant steam and easing her head onto the towels. She rarely took a bath, a quick shower her preferred way to start or end the day. But the soft, velvety, perfumed liquid soon worked its magic, easing the tension in her muscles and going part way to soothing the aches and pains. Her eyes wandered around the room, observing faint outlines in the walls, rectangle and square shapes, the size of large drawers, or cupboards. The wall in front, though, appeared intact, its plain buffed-metal surface glowing softly in the low lighting, which, as in the bedroom, came from the top of the walls.

As she swallowed back a yawn, with the faintest of clicks two huge panels parted in the centre, exposing a wall-sized screen. She gasped at its size, relaxation forgotten, as the lights dimmed, and a 'show' started.

A rainforest setting appeared, verdant and tranquil. The camera eye meandered in and out, through towering trees, dangling vines and ground-dwelling ferns. Now it followed a slow-flowing stream snaking around rocks, tree roots and decaying branches. Then it shifted, chasing the silvery flickering lights piercing the canopy before it dropped dramatically, and faltered in the deep-green shadows. Sounds of the rainforest accompanied the sights, emphasising the calm. Birds called languorously, insects clicked and buzzed before settling, leaves and vines caught by the shifting air sighed or rustled their contentment. Unseen creatures scuffled in the undergrowth. The camera froze, searching for the culprit before shifting to examine water droplets dripping off a fern leaf into a stream to meet the quiet symphony played out by the moving water.

A minute or two into it and the room lighting changed. Coloured filters from the ceiling space played around the room, keeping pace with the journey through the rainforest, adding intensity to the light and shadows.

If she hadn't been where she was, she could imagine herself in a luxury boutique hotel relaxing in an outdoor jacuzzi somewhere deep in the rainforest. If she hadn't been who she was and aware of the subtle murmurings from inside her skin, she might have relaxed and enjoyed it. Instead, she straightened her back against the cool marble side of the tub, hugged her knees against her chest and toyed with her bottom lip.

None of it made sense. Her only comfort as she narrowed her

eyes and frowned at the screen was that whoever was behind this had gone to an awful lot of trouble and expense. At least she hadn't woken up shackled to a post in a dingy underground bunker or locked in a room in an isolated, tumbledown farmhouse. Her love of crime fiction conjured up the stereotypical places of confinement in which unwitting victims found themselves.

9

With two long hours stretching before her one o'clock meeting at Lucy's, Heather called Ruth, one of her oldest friends. She badly needed to talk to someone, and she could count on Ruth. They'd met not long after the Tanakas moved from England to Australia, eighteen years before, when Tony took up his research position. Looking for ways to connect into the community, Heather had taken Annalee to the local playgroup where Ruth was the leader.

They hit it off straight away as they shared the joys and demands of married life, raising toddlers and growing families. Ruth had a daughter, Esther, the same age as Heather's Stephen, and a son, Benjamin, two years younger. They soon discovered these three children attended the same primary school. Ruth also had two preschoolers, three-year-old twins Caleb and Levi, who came with her to the playgroup. Heather calculated that when the twins had been born, Ruth had four kids under four. What a struggle—but she appeared to take everything in her stride, handling the mischievous twins in a firm but patient manner.

When Ruth learned Heather and Tony had recently arrived in the country with no family support, she invited them to their first Aussie barbecue. They met Ruth's husband, Simon, and several local

33

families. Tony and Simon got along well and discovered a shared interest in keeping fit and bike riding. The entire Tanaka family soon felt connected in their adopted homeland and supported by this new extended family.

Heather came to know Ruth had a strong Christian faith, attending church on Sundays—a novel concept for her. She'd attended Sunday School as a child along with most of her peers but lost interest in organised religion in her teen years. Yet Ruth differed from Heather's skewed perception of a devoted churchgoer—a somewhat staid and inflexible person, inclined to look down their nose at anything resembling fun. Instead, she had an air of acceptance and ease, a lovely smile which signalled welcome and actions to back it up. She encouraged everyone she met, including Heather. And she had a wicked sense of humour. She knew how to have fun.

And the great thing was, Ruth never pressed her beliefs onto Heather or anybody else. It was her character, the way she showed love and included everyone, which piqued Heather's interest. She realised she had many misconceptions about religion and wanted to know more. After a time, Ruth invited her to a group she attended —women who met to explore Christianity and the Bible and discuss questions over afternoon tea. Heather enjoyed the spirited conversations, impressed with their openness to tackle issues she had battled with about aspects of Christianity and other faiths.

Heather picked up her phone. "Ruth, can you come over? I need to see you."

10

Mesmerising or relaxing, whatever the intent, Annalee ignored the rainforest wonders playing out on the screen and focused on her body. The soaking made peeling the sticking plaster off her wrist much simpler, exposing an IV cannula-shaped puncture wound with telltale bruising around it. More faint, yellowing bruises on the inside of both her elbows signified blood taken some days ago.

Days ago! Surely she had been at work then, but the evidence was there in front of her eyes. Fresh bruises were not that colour. Her heart sped up a notch. How long had she been here before she woke up? Suddenly eager to inspect her back, she resisted the urge to stand, none too comfortable with exposing her all in front of the mirror. Who knew what or who might be on the other side, watching her every move? No spooky mansion was complete without at least one double-sided mirror and an evil antagonist lurking behind it. This place was the least like a spooky mansion, but that mirror?

No, her eyes widened, and she squeezed her lips together. Whoever you are, you might have looked at me when I had no choice, but not now. She turned her head, eyeballed the mirror and stuck out her tongue.

Reaching behind, she worked her fingers towards her spine. Her searching fingertips hit the edge of another, larger, sticking plaster, covering that painful area on her lower back. She gasped, swallowed the lump threatening to close off her airways, and clutched her knees once more. A spinal tap or lumbar puncture? Why do that? Not an everyday procedure. It was a person's spinal cord, after all, and in this case, hers. The idea of someone fiddling about in her spine, her perfectly healthy spine, exposing it to any number of pathogens, or worse, sent tremors down the body part in question.

She lowered her head to her knees, watching the tiny soap bubbles as they scurried away from her hot breath. Tears pricked at her eyes. She snatched at the bubbles, scooping up handfuls and pushed them this way and that. Then she slowed and crafted a tower in front of her chest, up to her chin. If only it was strong enough to protect her from all this. She puffed her cheeks and blew at the bubbles, sending miniature snow flurries into the air and across the surface. Fighting to relax, she shrugged her shoulders, tried to refocus on the screen, and failed.

Her fingers found their way back to the plaster and teased away at its edges. Little by little, she loosened it. The surrounding tissue tingled a protest as the last bit came off. At least there was no trace of dirt or infection on it. Further probing around the spot helped as, despite its tenderness, it didn't feel swollen.

"Well, good Lord, what's to do here?"

The words her dear father had often said when confronted with a problem slipped out. Her eyes tracked a curled-up leaf drifting along a stream in the rainforest before misting over, and she gulped down a sob. As close as she was to her mother, she had been her daddy's little girl until he died so cruelly. She missed him—her protector, her strong tower. She missed him so much. Solid and reliable—no flighty collection of wash-down-the-drain bubbles. She swiped at the fragile tower peaks, their reflected rainbow hues under the coloured lights disappearing in the swathes.

He would have stopped this. They wouldn't have dared take her if he was alive.

She slapped at the water, gritted her teeth and whirled to face the closed door. Her face contorted, furious breaths punctuating her words. "Why? Why? How dare you do this to me!"

Palms outspread, she slapped at the surface over and over. Then bunched her fists, and began pounding at it—sending waterspouts and mini tsunamis over the sides of the tub and across the room in all directions.

Why was she here? Why take her? Why did her father have to die? She stopped, both fists raised, breaths convulsing from her throat. She closed her lips and slipped under the water, hair fanning around her head, the black silken tentacles teasing at her face.

But he did die. She counted to thirty before pushing up, sucked in a shuddering breath and slicked her hair back. She watched the last of the eddies snaking back into the tub. Bubble islands left behind on the marble tiles like so many clouds suspended in a sky unwilling to let them go… to freedom.

He. Did. Die.

Careering through the last crazy months of her nursing degree, Annalee had snatched a break before an evening tutorial and noticed several missed calls and a text from her mother.

'Can you come home straight away? Some sad family news.'

Her ever-considerate mother's way of preparing her for the worst. The night her father died was etched forever in her mind, a line drawn firmly in the sand of her existence. Her bitter awakening.

She sighed, rubbing at her eyes. The sour taste of helplessness and despair salted her tongue. The raw feelings her grief brought out back then had terrified her; it was the closest she'd come to giving up. Her world, safe, steady and predictable despite the stresses of looming final exams, had turned upside down.

No, more than that. It was destroyed. Nothing had ever been the same again.

Before his death, no one close to Annalee had died and for it to be her beloved father was beyond her comprehension. He was her rock, her place of safety and sometimes sanity from the pressures of study and exams, always ready with a cup of her favourite hot chocolate. They would sit together, chatting away about some inane subject or putting the world to rights. Even just content to sit in silence and sip their drinks. Dad knew when to speak and when to be silent. He didn't give unnecessary advice, telling her she should do this or that. They both knew he couldn't fix her world, but he supported and encouraged her, and she loved him for it. She had her mum's love and support too, but a girl's daddy has a special place in her heart, that maleness that was a vital part of the whole. The completeness that was, well, family.

Those first days, weeks, and months remained a blur. She saw fragments. Her mother, family, and friends standing in small groups, in freeze frames, as if the world stood still. Or them at home with the police, at the funeral directors, at the funeral itself and well-meaning gatherings after that. But that was it. Memories of what she had done, the ordinary everyday activities, the eating, sleeping or attending lectures, had all gone—sucked into the bottomless pit of despair which fugged her mind. How she got through her exams remained a mystery. She had grounds for a deferral but went ahead, not knowing nor caring about the outcome. Thankfully, the hard work she'd put in paid off, but the emotions she'd repressed exploded after the exams finished.

She'd prided herself on her self-control and a dispassionate approach to life, but the one thing that got her going was an injustice. Until her father died, injustice was out there in society: in marginalised individuals or groups, even kids on the outer at school or victims of bullying. There was someone responsible who must accept the consequences, and if it was within her capacity to do so, she would help put it right. Her ideal future saw her doing much more… one day. One day, her passion for the underdog would find the right path.

Yet, this other injustice—a random accident with no physical person to blame, no group responsible—was incomprehensible. Only fate, or destiny. Annalee eyed the closed door of her prison, bunching her fists. She was so angry he had died that way, well before his time. He was only fifty-nine and fit and healthy. She'd never imagined a future without him, expecting him to walk her down the aisle one day, to be a granddad for her children. He was the best grandfather to her nephew Matty, who followed him around with adoring eyes. The fun they had together playing cricket or constructing important things with pieces of wood in the shed. And he never got to see Matty's sister Jessica, born soon after his death, and he wouldn't be there for any children Annalee might have someday.

She winced at the memory of the explosive Annalee who slammed doors, tortured herself in the gym and pounded the pavements, who drove too fast and lost her temper too often. She'd had enough anger for the entire family. For Matty and Jessica, for Stephen and Meg, but most of all, for her mother—losing the love of her life, her companion and best friend. Anna saw how lost she was without him—so silent, so pale, so sad. As if her confidence and zest for life leaked away more with each new lonely day. Annalee felt helpless that she couldn't fix it for her mother as much as for herself. They were both bound up in their grief and for a time, lost touch with each other. Annalee found it difficult to articulate her feelings, imagining her unresponsive mother felt the same.

What was the purpose of life? What was the point if it disappeared in a split second? Why should you bother to make plans only to see them evaporate? Her mum and dad had made a start on retirement ideas. Although a few years off, they were planning a big trip to the UK and Europe to see the rellies. They'd also chatted about buying a caravan and travelling around Australia following the sun and avoiding the winter as many Aussie retirees did. All those plans and dreams vanished in the minutes it took the police to inform her mum about his death. Annalee knew her mother wouldn't do those things on her own. Her mum and dad were two halves of a whole, and half had gone.

Life, and the spectre of unavoidable death. Questions tormented her day after day, through the minutiae of life—her graduation, Jessica's birth, her successful job hunt and nursing life. They played a silent symphony, giving her no relief from the melancholy tune.

She didn't know what had sparked the turning point or when. Perhaps she had been dodging it. No, she knew she had. The unspoken, the things suppressed, coalesced and formed in front of that orchestra one night as if a conductor materialised where none was before. Ready to play a new song.

She had to find out more. If there was a God, a supreme deity, a creator of everything and responsible for all, then what was He doing? What was the reason for her father's death? Her childhood beliefs hadn't equipped her, but then, was it an area she had avoided as many people do? Life was for living, not for dwelling on what might happen, who may or may not die.

At work, she was no stranger to sickness and even death, but her patients were not her family. She had to disengage herself to a degree —had to discipline her mind to accept what would be an unavoidable part of her vocation.

Death had never been personal before. She hadn't experienced the crushing weight of its pain.

Why did God cause this or allow this to happen to her father, an outstanding person, one of His own? Why did he have to die and leave his loving family when so many other men misused or did worse to their wives and families and went on living? Was God really there? Was He a loving God who cared? Or was it all a farce with no rhyme nor reason behind anyone's existence and just blind fate or luck in charge?

She didn't want to add to her mother's grief by voicing her doubts, and Stephen and Meg were busy with the new baby. So she turned to Lucy, their friendship so strong that she could. Lucy was a supportive listener, and so patient with her, no matter if she was sad, angry, or full of questions. Lucy comforted her, didn't suggest she cheer up and get on with life, but encouraged her to pursue the answers she sought. Annalee invited herself to the group she knew Lucy attended. Her Christian friends who met to study the Bible together. Annalee was ready. She needed answers but didn't want to find them in a church. But a small group of contemporaries might be the starting point. Somewhere safe to explore and decide if her childhood faith could stand the scrutiny of adult intellect.

A bird's melancholy call to its mate from a corner of the room startled her. She shivered. The water in the tub had cooled, the bubbles all but dissolved. She inspected her prune-like fingers and reached back for a towel, draping herself in its ample folds as she rose.

The sound and light show faded, partitions sliding back into place to cover the screen. She jabbed at one of the square shapes in the wall until she freed an invisible catch, curbing the compulsion to fist pump the air. The drawer slid out to reveal neat piles of carbon-copy white cotton undies to those she'd discarded—all in her size. In other drawers there were toiletries, more towels, and the pastel-coloured cotton knee-length pants and tie-up tops. It was all very neat and tidy—all very boring. She was no fashion plate, but come on.

And there was no footwear—not a sock, shoe or even a slipper in sight, and no bras. Luckily, she was an AA cup—her eyes crinkled.

A double-sized outline exposed a chute. Dirty linen? She stood back and checked its dimensions. Would she fit? She reached an arm in and tried her shoulder, frowning as she withdrew. That wasn't going to be an escape route, even if she could tell where it led.

Turning back, she crossed the floor and scooped up her abandoned clothes before freezing, her fingers tightening on the pile. She tossed them down and turned to confront the mirror. "Stuff you!" she mouthed and strode to the door which swished open without objection.

12

———

Ruth fussed over an exuberant Sparky who'd pushed through the door to greet her as Heather opened it, then took one look at her friend's face and guided her to the couch. She sat next to her, held her hand, and waited. Her friend's tone in the phone call had spoken volumes. Heather wasn't a natural worrier, nor was she neurotic but confident and resourceful, accepting the trials which came her way with a stoic sense of optimism. The understandable exception being one which anyone would dread, the sudden and unexpected loss of someone close—such as Heather's husband.

"It's Annalee…" Heather broke off, tears welling, red-rimming her eyes. She swiped the corner of one with a tissue. "She didn't go home after work yesterday, and no one knows where she is."

Ruth squeezed Heather's hand, opened her mouth, then closed it again. Heather had been through so much already. Questions flooded in, but she held back as her friend relayed the scant details. Heather would have already asked herself every conceivable question countless times in the hours since she had known, which turned out to be the case.

"I'm sorry," Heather said, eyes on their hands, "I should have asked if you would like some tea?"

"Oh, Heather, don't worry about that, let me do it." Ruth led the way into her friend's kitchen, Sparky dancing circles around them, tail going nineteen to the dozen. She found the cups and saucers, tea, milk, and sugar as the kettle hummed away. Heather stood, staring out of the kitchen window, picking at her fingernails. The look of misery so profound on her face that Ruth's heart tightened. How would she feel if their situations were reversed? She stepped around the bench and hugged her friend.

"Let's pray together and afterwards I'll call the prayer chain." The group of ladies willing to pray from the church they attended was an excellent way to pass the word. Yet Ruth noticed the hesitation on Heather's face. "Heather?"

"I'm not sure about the prayer chain yet. I keep hope— er, thinking, that she'll turn up and after I get over being cross with her, we'll all have a big laugh. Let's just… you and me, pray together first."

"Okay, perhaps you can decide about the prayer chain after we finish." At Heather's nod, Ruth took a packet of biscuits from the pantry and arranged some on a plate. Sparky looked up at the rustling paper, but slumped, head back on his paws, when no treat materialised. Ruth placed the tea and biscuits on a tray and led the way back into the lounge.

They resumed their previous seats with Sparky draping himself across Heather's feet as they held each other's hands. Ruth prayed for Annalee's safety, wherever she was, and for God's peace for Heather. Heather added her desire for the situation to end soon, for Annalee to be free to contact someone and for protection from harm. Ruth saw the difference in Heather's face as they finished—the tension around her mouth and eyes easing. She poured the tea and passed Heather a cup and the biscuits.

They sat in silence, focussing on sipping the steaming brew, Heather scratching the top of Sparky's head pressed against her legs.

"He's been such a comfort to me since Tony died. Although he missed Annalee so much when she first moved out. And—he's supposed to be my dog." Heather smiled. "He would disappear for hours. I couldn't work out where he was until I found him sleeping in her room. But he's okay now. Aren't you, Sparky?"

Sparky sprang up at the mention of his name, cocked his head to one side and searched Heather's face before scampering off. He returned a few seconds later with a well-chewed tennis ball and dropped it at her feet.

"Any excuse to play ball, hey Sparky?" Heather rolled the ball across the carpet with the dog in hot pursuit. Although he favoured Heather, sometimes he dropped it at Ruth's feet, to include her in the game. After a few minutes, he tired of it, took the ball and disappeared. The rattle of the doggy door signalling his retreat into the garden.

"If only life were as uncomplicated for us as it is for Sparky," Heather said. "Nothing to worry about, satisfied with a little attention now and then, well-fed and able to take time out whenever you fancied."

Ruth followed Heather's eyes to the doorway. "Mm, might be a bit boring though."

"I could do with boring right now, Ruth. Predictable, secure, you-know-what-will-happen-next type of boring. That would suit me just fine."

"Oh, Heather." Ruth reached over and gave her another hug. They clung to each other for several minutes as Ruth searched for the words to say that would help, coming up blank.

Heather sighed, released her grip on Ruth and looked deep into her eyes. "Thank you for coming and for your support. Not just now, but over all the years we've known each other. Whenever I've needed someone you've always been ready and willing to be there for me."

"Hush now. You've done the same for me in the past. It's what friends are for."

Ruth searched Heather's eyes, saddened to see her tearing up before pulling back into the couch away from her. It was as if she was closing in on herself, trying to steel herself against what may come—and wanting to do it on her own. Ruth frowned as Heather eyed the clock.

"I'd better make myself presentable and get over to Lucy's. I want to talk to her before the police arrive."

Already knowing the answer, Ruth had to ask. "Would you like me to go with you?"

"No, I'll be okay with Lucy there. I'll call you as soon as I get back and let you know what they have to say."

13

Lucy scooped up her bowl of two-minute noodles and took it outside. Last resort, comfort food, but, hey. They always kept a few packets in the depths of the pantry for emergencies and today was the day.

She perched on the end of the sun lounge and angled her face toward the watery winter sun, fighting a losing battle against scudding grey clouds. Neither the sun's rays nor the lunch offering could shake off the chill coming from somewhere deep inside. As she forked through the bowl, each mouthful reminded her why the packets hadn't seen the light of day for months. It might as well be a bowlful of sodden cardboard. Imagine, only a few years ago she had almost lived on the stuff and savoured every mouthful. She scowled, contemplating the forkful of noodles, and replaced it in the bowl.

Jamie had left not long after the bike-shed revelation. But then she'd texted him after Mrs T arranged for the police to come, inviting him back. She was cursing herself—why did she do that? Should he even be here when they showed up? What did she know of police methods and missing persons, apart from those police shows Annalee was so fond of? They weren't real life. This was real life. Or surreal life.

People talked of the disconnect they felt when something huge happened, but it wasn't until it happened to you—like now—that you got it. She didn't know where to put herself, what to think, or do. How to solve it.

She dug her nails into her thighs, Jamie's face filling her mind. Did she want him here after the hand-touching incident? It was nothing. Her reaction was over the top, for sure. Anna's boyfriend. Anna's boyfriend who, until now… She'd never considered in that way and yet, the minute Anna wasn't around, she was experiencing feelings of—what? She couldn't even put words to it. What was the matter with her?

She didn't have a boyfriend, had never had a boyfriend, discounting the pre-pubescent crushes, and that was okay. It was her choice. She had plans for the future, and a man wasn't a part of them. Not that she didn't like men—she had two brothers and her dad was a wonderful role model. And the kids she'd grown up with in the small rural community down south were a close-knit group, all friends. Not boyfriends or girlfriends—just friends. She could still count most of them as that, slotting straight back in with them when she travelled home, despite the years she'd spent away studying and now, nursing.

No, her nursing career was her focus, and she planned to add to it in three or four years. A Masters, maybe add midwifery. Perhaps a doctorate somewhere down the track. Her eyes softened at the image of herself teaching other nurses the same skills she was applying now. Nurses from various cultures who would return to help their communities, even teach in turn. An ever-expanding legacy of health care for the most vulnerable. Her passion was for children. It broke her heart to hear of them going blind for want of a few dollars' worth of vitamins. Or dying because they had no access to immuni-sation, or from accidents western kids recovered from with no complications.

She'd taken an elective on tropical medicine as part of her degree, spending three months in Broome in the remote north of Western Australia. Many of the patients there were indigenous and suffering from ailments or deficiencies she hadn't encountered in the city.

She was open to exploring what God had in store for her, not discounting a stint as part of a missionary team one day. In a week or two, her church had missionaries coming to talk about the work they were doing. A couple from Scotland, distant relatives of her friend Amy, who were visiting support churches in Australia. They worked on a little island somewhere. Where was it now? Somewhere in the far reaches of Indonesia… or was it Malaysia? Lucy narrowed her eyes—Indonesia. Sulawesi, maybe. But there was a modest hospital there. She was looking forward to hearing the details, and perhaps in a year or two…

She sucked in a breath as she glimpsed her watch. Twenty minutes to go. Twenty minutes before the police, Mrs T and… Jamie. Maybe she should have checked with Mrs T first before inviting him. If the police wanted to see him, they would. Too late now—she couldn't very well un-invite him. What kind of idiot would he think she was?

And why was she concerned about what he thought of her, anyway? Her heart fluttered as her cheeks heated up, knowing it wasn't the sun. Hopefully, there wouldn't be a repeat of that the minute he arrived.

14

Food. The savoury aroma hit the second Anna swept through the door, setting her salivary glands dancing. Her stomach rumbled a welcome as she scooped the tray from the desk. Then she stopped, her eyes caught by the outline of another door in front of her. She tapped at it with her spare hand, the thunk of her knuckles sounding dead on its surface.

The room was clean and the bed made, a sumptuous bowl of fruit added to the coffee table next to the refilled water jug. Hence the bathroom door being locked—they didn't want her busting in on whoever had the pleasure of setting the room to rights. Why were they so shy about making themselves known?

Tucking her legs underneath, she balanced the tray on her knees and settled back into the couch—a light meal, like they offered to patients recovering from surgery or illness. Her eyes narrowed— from what was she recovering? Her stomach gave another impatient growl. Food now, think later. The eggs claimed first place, their savoury tang flaring her nostrils and delighting her taste buds with each bite.

Since when did scrambled eggs do that? The mundane had turned into the gourmet. Food rarely affected her that way, particularly breakfast, or was it lunch? Her mantra was food as fuel for the body—she was firmly in the 'eat to live' rather than the 'live to eat' camp.

The eggs went down well, along with the accompanying troop of toast soldiers—unfortunately, white bread—but standard fare for invalids. She sniffed. A bowl of porridge, stewed apple and yoghurt followed, washed down with a glass of tropical fruit juice and the contents of a pot of green tea.

Licking the corners of her mouth, she peered underneath the teapot, then upended each of the white porcelain plates and bowls. Not even a 'made in China' on any of them. Likewise, the linen tray cloths and serviette. As for the bath towels and clothing—she eyed the bathroom door—not a manufacturing label on any. Not a clue, however tenuous, to say where in the country, or the world for that matter, she was. Even the tea was loose leaf. She poked about in the teapot with the bamboo stirrer, placing it back next to the bamboo fork and spoons. Very now, but non-committal—no Royal Wiltshire silverware here, not that it would help if it were.

She ran her tongue around her mouth—her teeth needed a brush and her fingers were sticky. But this time the bathroom door refused to budge. She stepped backwards and tried again but stopped short of jumping up and down and waving her arms. It was a no-go. Bathroom cleaning time?

She pressed her ear to the door, not expecting to hear anything, and she wasn't disappointed. Bracing herself, she placed both palms on the door and pushed, before trying again with her shoulder. Not even the slightest creak or tremor registered, the moist outline of her fingers and hot breath fading fast into its polished surface.

What now? Her eyes raked the room. Although she still felt weak, the food had energised her, and she was ready to do... something. It might take a little time but, with a proper diet and exercise, she would be prepared for them. If only she knew who they were and what they wanted. Until they showed themselves, she had to make do, to work at strengthening herself in here—and at keeping sane. A flicker of tension caught the corner of her mouth. All she had were these two rooms, or it would be two if the bathroom door opened.

She returned to the couch and sank her teeth into a juicy pear, which didn't help the stickiness. Sucking her fingertips, she dipped the serviette edge in the water from the glass.

The bathroom door opened without protest the next time she tried, confirming the cleaning theory. She found the room in pristine condition and a door outline along the wall near the shower.

Having missed that one, and with nothing better to do, she examined both rooms slowly and carefully. The lines were so faint she studied each wall, not only from the front but from every other angle, even looking up from crouching on the floor.

The bedroom had one more secret to give up, though. She couldn't believe she'd missed it each time she'd walked past. A broad wardrobe-sized outline, opposite the foot of the bed, popped open from the middle to reveal shelves lined with books. A real hidden treasure. A smile played at the corners of her lips. Almost a library— and she loved to read.

She sat on the floor cross-legged and scanned the shelves, eyes darting from one book to the other, coming to rest on a title here, an author's name there. Her parents had fostered her love of books from birth, if not before. One of her mum's favourite stories was about the times she'd found Annalee so engrossed in 'baby's first books' in her cot or playpen that she grizzled if interrupted. As she'd mastered the words on the pages she had devoured everything readable in sight, which proved a significant source of frustration for anyone who wanted her attention.

With wide-ranging tastes she found reading relaxing, even more so after her father died. It was a way to unwind and escape life after the challenges of work or when emotions and thoughts about her father overwhelmed. She had a fondness for crime fiction, and biography or autobiography—'real' people's lives. The adage 'truth is stranger than fiction' rang true for her.

And the books here—she shuffled closer—were many of the books she would choose to stock her dream library. Classics such as *Wuthering Heights, Oliver Twist,* even Louisa May Alcott's *Little Women,* alongside more contemporary titles, some she recognised and had read, others not. A good assortment of non-fiction, including a shelf of biographies, filled a quarter of the library. If ever there was a list of a hundred books you must read before you die.

Nose almost resting on a shelf, she ran her finger over the ridges and indentations on the spines, the familiar mix of card, paper and ink somehow comforting. It gave a promise of stimulation and relaxation, even companionship, in this alien place. She sat back and shivered, looking over her shoulder at the doors—silent sentinels either side of the desk. Yet, how did they know the books she liked? How much of a coincidence was that? She pulled out a random volume and searched the inside cover, but her eyes refused to focus. Snapping the book shut, she tried the dust-jacket blurb, read it through twice, before giving up on the third attempt.

"Get a grip, Annalee," she murmured, not for the first time after waking up in this room—was it only this morning? How could she survive this when even the prospect of spending alone time with an enjoyable book did nothing for her?

She stood up and began pacing into the bathroom, around the bathtub, and repeating the process before coming to a stop where she'd started. About to select a book, she paused and stepped away, scanning the entire collection. One big omission. If they knew her so well and her tastes in literature, they would know its importance. There was no Bible. Why the oversight? A deliberate act to spite her, or an error? Or did religion have no meaning in their world?

Anna sighed. It was useless trying to work out the mind of an unknown entity, and they were doing an expert job of keeping it that way. Surely they had to show their hand soon. It would be impossible to keep this up—she looked from the food tray to the doors. She pressed her lips together and picked out *The Secret Garden*, a childhood favourite.

Focus on the positive, Annalee—this is, after all, close to literary heaven. If she could forget about being a prisoner and imagine herself in a luxury resort, then it would be the perfect place. To read, eat good food and relax. What more could a girl wish for?

15

Heather pulled up in her car, noticing Lucy waiting at the door. As they hugged, she felt the warmth of Lucy's breath on her neck, but fingers icy on her arms. What words could reassure Lucy when her heart was as cold as Lucy's fingers? She had nothing.

"Jamie's here. I hope you don't mind."

"Oh… I… er…" Heather had wanted Lucy to say everything was all right, that the communication mix-up she grasped at was a reality and Anna was inside. She didn't know Jamie that well yet. Not that she had anything against him, but this would be difficult enough without… "Sorry, Lucy, I'm feeling a bit wobbly. I still can't…" She gulped down the lump in her throat.

"Would you like me to ask him to leave?" Lucy's eyes were bright, her cheeks flushed but, given the circumstances, it was understandable.

Heather reached out and squeezed her hand. She was the mature mother-figure here, the one to offer encouragement and hope, although just now it was the last thing she felt like, entering her missing daughter's home as a guest.

"No, no. I didn't mean that. He must be as worried as we are. It's good of him to come. Where is he?" Jamie always seemed pleasant enough, and he clearly adored Anna. But then, who wouldn't? Heather dug her fingernails into her hand and rummaged in her bag for a tissue.

"He's inside, putting the kettle on. Come on in."

"No sign of the police yet?" Dumb thing to say, Heather. She squeezed her lips together as she followed Lucy into the kitchen.

"Not yet, no, but it's not quite one o'clock." Lucy looked up at the wall clock as she spoke, and Heather was grateful for her indulgence.

Jamie stepped forwards, arms outstretched, and she gripped his forearms before drawing him into a hug, the faint aroma of his after-shave reminding her of Tony. Not now. She squeezed her eyes shut. *I need your strength, Dear Lord. Help me—help us do this.* Taking in a deep breath, she drew back and looked into his eyes, noting the tension around his jaw and a slight twitch playing at the top of his cheekbone.

"I might have a glass of water instead of tea, if you don't mind."

"Sure." He looked comfortable in their kitchen. She watched him open the cupboard and select a glass. "Would you like to go through to the lounge and I'll bring it in?" She noticed Lucy watching him from the doorway until she caught Heather's look and turned away.

"Here they come." Lucy almost ran for the front door. Heather's eyes followed.

Detective Sergeant Elaine Troy introduced herself and her offsider, Detective Constable Jake Winters. She skilfully, yet empathetically questioned, listened and took mental notes, leaving the physical ones to Jake. She put them at ease straight away—it helped people to open up more than if they felt suspected or uncomfortable.

This case appeared potentially more serious than most missing persons' reports, which was why uniform had quickly passed it on to her team. People of Annalee's age usually turned up within a day or two after they disappeared. The majority left home after arguing with a parent or partner or following domestic violence; sometimes mental illness was a factor.

After ruling out the more obvious scenarios and getting a clearer picture of Annalee's character, Elaine massaged the back of her neck, that familiar tingle alerting her senses. She dug deeper, explaining the need to explore every possibility, no matter how foreign or far-fetched it sounded. Did any of them have any enemies? What about past relationships? She brought up the possibility of kidnapping—the surprised looks spoke volumes, their quiet protests and sideways glances noted. Had they noticed anyone around the neighbourhood or anything unusual in Annalee's behaviour? Anything out of character, in the past days, weeks, even months?

The mention of old relationships prompted a response from Lucy. Elaine noticed the way her eyes narrowed, how her mouth parted ever-so-slightly. She asked, "What is it Lucy? Even the smallest thing could be a help."

"I… I'm not sure if it's anything. But she had a boyfriend who—Her previous boyfriend was… quite possessive, and he took it rather badly when she broke off with him. But that was ages ago."

Lucy outlined what she knew about Dan with added input from Heather. Elaine noted Heather's view differed to Lucy's, understandable given their age difference and relationship to Annalee. Heather believed there was nothing in it, just a first love petering out as a natural course, and they had parted amicably.

"Sorry, Mrs Tanaka. Anna didn't want to worry you." Lucy detailed several incidents Annalee had shared with her. Dan's possessive nature getting worse to the point of him attempting to control what she did and who she saw. At the time, Anna had assured Lucy she could handle him and she would let him down gently.

Elaine affirmed, "It may be nothing, but we'll follow it up if needed."

"Do you have a contact number?" Jake added.

Lucy found the entry in her phone. "I have an address and mobile number, but I don't think it's current. I haven't had to use it since they broke up." She frowned and thrust the phone at Jake. "He lived in Bayswater but I heard through the grapevine that he shifted. I didn't pay attention to the details."

Elaine asked for a recent photo of Annalee, noting she favoured her father's Japanese heritage. She gazed intently at the girl standing next to her parents and smiling confidently for the camera, her even features and lively dark eyes set in an oval face framed with long, straight black hair. Heather had explained her husband Tony's death early in the discussion, the pain on her face clear as she related the events. Troy didn't press any further, vaguely remembering the accident because of its unusual nature. Not too many pedestrians died crossing railway lines in the suburbs of Perth. It had made the headlines and six o'clock news when it happened.

At the end of her profile enquiry, she asked Lucy to show them around. They spent some time in Annalee's room having Lucy check for missing items before they returned to the lounge. Elaine outlined what they would do next and then, if need be, what would follow. She assured them that her first stop would be the hospital as it was the last place Annalee was known to be. There should be good CCTV coverage of the hospital and grounds. She did her best to reassure them, but three pairs of eyes told her she had not succeeded.

"WHAT DO YOU THINK, SARGE?" JAKE AND ELAINE SAT IN THE car before moving off. He had his eyes on the house as she made a few extra notes.

"Hard to tell. It's early yet, but it's not your usual miss-per. More to the point, what do you think?" Elaine was mentoring Jake for his probationary period in the investigative team.

"Well, statistically a good percentage of missing persons turn up within forty-eight hours…"

"Hmm, but forget the stats for a minute, what is your gut telling you? What did you notice?"

He fell silent. Did he have a 'gut' yet? He had all the theoretical knowledge off pat and had gained his placement in the team on merit, but modern policing was more than that. He had worked with Elaine for two months and knew what she expected. She also liked to think outside the box, but that didn't include cutting corners. A mental and physical dynamo, she teased out every aspect of a case, even the most unlikely ones. And she didn't mind his input, encouraging him to challenge her ideas, to have something to say rather than agree with her every word.

"The mother, friend Lucy and boyfriend Jamie all seem regular, down-to-earth people. Middle-class, family-orientated, used to working for a living. All well dressed, clean clothes, nothing wild about them. Jamie had a small tattoo on his lower left arm. But these days that's common. Neat and tidy house, no sign of alcohol excesses. No bottles, either full or empty anywhere. Not even ashtrays or that stale nicotine odour you get in a smoker's house, which shows they're health conscious. The cars in the driveway were, again, average. And if one of them belongs to boyfriend Jamie, then he's not into muscle cars like many single FIFOs."

"Okay, I'm impressed—ordinary people living ordinary lives. Let's hope the outcome is ordinary too, and nurse Annalee will turn up alive and well. And soon." She rubbed at her neck. Unfortunately, that niggle at the base of her skull said otherwise. It wasn't often wrong.

16

Anna startled as the partitions above the desk clicked into life and slid apart.

It had been four days and three nights. Four long days marked by meals appearing and trays disappearing, doors locked or unlocked, and times of reading, naps and bouts of exercises. As each day passed she achieved more sit-ups, squats and jogs on the spot. On the third afternoon, in a sudden panic, she started to mark the days. She organised the books on the bottom shelf in a particular way, hoping they wouldn't note her apparent fussiness and rearrange them. The food, always fresh, remained light, but it helped her energy levels and her mood. She tried to catch them out delivering a meal, sitting at the desk until she could bear it no longer and had to visit the bathroom. They beat her each time, although, lately, her meals were lukewarm.

She took baths to break the monotony more than any need for cleanliness, and to hear something other than herself in the deathly quiet rooms. The background sounds and noises as the rainforest sequence played were more than the relaxing backdrop her captors no doubt intended. They provided sound. She didn't realise how much of it was in her day-to-day life until it was missing. In here.

One huge frustration was the absence of writing materials. Annalee voiced her exasperation to the unresponsive wall screen often in those first days.

"Could I have some paper and a pen, please?"

"A notebook. A pencil?"

"I would really like to communicate. With you. Draw a picture. Something. Writing things down is what I do."

"I would appreciate it if I could write down some of my thoughts about this place or write a letter to my mother letting her know that I'm alive."

She forced herself to always speak in a polite, calm and measured tone, despite the growing anger churning her insides.

There was no response. No writing materials appeared. What would be the harm in allowing her to journal or draw? Was it part of the plan to subjugate her and make her totally compliant? Were they attempting to brainwash her? To condition her by cutting off all human contact and preventing her from engaging in basic activities like writing or drawing or going for a walk in the fresh air. She didn't know much about brainwashing. Who did? It wasn't a subject taught in school or university. *Brainwashing 101*. It was archaic, surely? The stuff of history, in war time or old movies. She shuddered, and reached for a banana from the fruit bowl.

Writing was a big part of her life. She had journaled almost constantly from her early teens and not just with her thoughts and feelings. She copied down songs or poetry she enjoyed, wise or encouraging quotes or sayings she came across and, in the last few months, encouraging Bible verses she'd found or Lucy or her mum had pointed out to her. She sketched, decorated, doodled, call it what you will, on many of the pages, embellishing the words with little cartoons, lines and scrolls or stylised leaves on vines and flowers.

Four days. And three rough nights. Physically tired though she was from her weakened state, she slept fitfully, awake for hours in the blackness of the room, willing the light to return. When she managed to fall asleep, she would wake, drenched with sweat after what must surely be just a few minutes, panting for air, imagining the walls closing in on her. She would get up and shuffle around, one hand on the wall, from bed to couch, and back again—losing count of the times she did it. And when what passed for morning finally appeared, the promise faded with the dark. It all began again. *Groundhog Day* had nothing on this. At least Phil Connors could go out in the fresh air and connect with people.

She was commiserating with a young Jane Eyre as she endured the horrors of confinement in the red-room when she was interrupted by the screen slicking open. Its blunt message, EXIT, burned into her retinas.

The door near the desk opened. Her heart lurched as she strained forward to see through it from the safety of the couch, but the angle was too tight. The only thing to do was to get out there despite the compulsion to tell them where to stick their orders. And maybe this was her chance to do just that. She needed answers, and it was about time she faced her captors and got some about this elaborate setup and her place in it. Fisting her hands, she stalked across the room.

She hissed out a breath, working her mouth to unclench her jaw, and slumped against the doorframe. No one. The narrow, dimly lit tunnel outside the door was empty. It stretched to both left and right, metal-lustred surfaces reflecting muted strip lighting outlining the edges of a walkway. It looked for all the world like the innards of a gutted 747 waiting to have seats installed. She took off to the right, the way to take a no-brainer. Cabin crew directions on evacuation procedures echoed in her mind as she followed round, green downlights punctuating the single strip of roof lighting; red lights flashed a warning the other way.

The chill from the smooth floor pulsed through her toes and zinged into her tight calves as she stepped softly on the balls of her feet. She had to close her mouth more than once as her neck swivelled from side to side. Alice-like, she wanted to capture every detail as she moved through the green gloom in this less than magical version of Wonderland.

She paused, fingering the outline of the third door she passed on the same side as hers. There had also been two on the other side, spaced further apart. She turned to look back, but no longer saw her doorway, and the red glow had disappeared with it. Either the door had closed, or the tunnel was gradually curving. Her gut said the latter. The tunnel ended at a T-junction with the green lights showing left. But a scant three metres away, green changed to red in front of a lift. Its doors opened at her approach. Inside the lift, she searched for a keypad. There wasn't one. The lift doors swished shut. She leaned against the wall as it started a rapid ascent, that familiar drop in the pit of her stomach signifying the direction.

The lift opened to reveal a tunnel identical to the one she'd left. A short distance away, a door slid open in sync with the lift door closing behind her. Light spilled out of it at her feet, driving away the shadows. She took a step back, the cool metal of the lift door solid through her cotton top, her breath hot on her lips as she clenched and released her fingers. What could she do? She had little to no advantage over what or who was waiting in that room. But she was so ready to give them a piece of her mind. The whole notion of kidnapping someone, kidnapping her, was so bizarre it beggared belief. She shrugged her shoulders. The air cold on the back of her neck, she stepped through the doorway.

And staggered backwards, as if someone had struck her in the mid-section with a medicine ball.

It was a gym—nothing but a gym—and a gym devoid of people at that. She slid down the wall beside the door, palms on her knees, and dragged in a heavy breath.

"For pity's sake." Her cry went unheard in the sterile space. She counted in and out three slow breaths, then drew herself up to her full height. Eyes blazing, she scoured the room. A punching bag dangling from its frame caught her gaze. A substitute bad guy, if ever there was one. But not yet. She sighed—exercise was the last thing she felt like doing. She padded over and sat on the weight bench, kneading its smooth leather surface.

The gym was well-equipped for its size, with a range of the usual hardware: treadmill, exercise bike, rowing machine, and the weight bench complete with a collection of weights. One entire wall had a mirrored surface; the metal-look she was fast tiring of covered the other three. A small cubicle in a corner housed a toilet and wash-basin with the faint outlines of drawers and cupboards in the wall nearby. She explored their contents, finding towels and toiletries in one and smaller items—hand weights, skipping ropes, hand bindings and boxing gloves—in the others.

Picking out a skipping rope, she turned, then froze, her focus on the disk in the centre of the wall above the door. It was a timer rather than a clock, with sixty minutes marked off in five-minute increments. It showed four minutes past the zero, the solitary black spindle tipping over to the first marker as she stared.

She gasped. This place was timeless. So far, she'd accepted the time of day and measured it relative to going to bed, waking up or having meals. We wrap ordinary life in time, in keeping time, and the pressures or irritations of time constraints. Three minutes to boil an egg, I'll be there in five minutes, can you meet us at six and don't be late? But if someone had a mind to—she sucked in a breath—they could manipulate time.

Usually, sun-up and sundown dictated natural rhythms. We know what time of the day or year it is because of what came before and what followed. But how did she know if it was day or night? Just because it became lighter and they gave her breakfast didn't mean it was morning. It could be any time at all. Was an hour sixty minutes, or could it be fifty or less, or more if they chose? Anna shuddered, contemplating the timer. She'd lost another two minutes and suddenly didn't want to lose any more. It was time to exercise, and heaven knew when she would need to be fit to run, to fight, to escape this place.

She warmed up on the treadmill before switching to the stationary bike, followed by skipping and weights, leaving the boxing gloves and punch bag for the last ten minutes. The simple rhythm of each activity felt good; her increased heart rate and sweat reassured her that she was in some way preparing for what may come. On the downside, it confirmed she was not up to her usual form, muscles screaming for mercy after the first few minutes. She pounded the punch bag harder before collapsing onto it, gasping for breath.

How long had she been inactive for her body to be so weak? She had no recollection of events before waking the other day. A sob threatened as she shoved the punch bag away and peeled off the gloves. She watched as they dropped to the floor one by one. Out of the corner of her eye she saw the door slide open.

On her way out, she scooped up the discarded skipping rope and coiled it around her thumb and elbow. The timer above the door closed in on zero and hovered there as she passed under it. A silent arrow pointing to nothing.

The drive home was a blur. Heather turned the key in the lock as Sparky yipped a greeting.

"What am I going to do with you, mate?" She fussed over him and headed for the kitchen. "Now for a cuppa and some food. What do you say?"

Sparky skittered in front of her, sitting bolt upright as she made a sandwich and tea. The clinking lid of the cheese dish with its promise of a treat, his favourite sound, second only to the rattle of the lead signalling a walk.

Treat delivered, Heather picked up her sandwich and drink and headed for the dining room. She rarely dined in there unless there was company, but today she wanted to think things through, to process what had taken place at Lucy's without the TV's distraction. Lunchtime telly became her go-to companion after Tony died. Even though he worked on weekdays and she ate alone, it was different somehow, after... She closed her eyes and drew in a deep breath. It was all so different.

She concentrated on eating the cheese and salad sandwich, taking small bites and chewing them slowly. There had to be a rational explanation for Anna's disappearance. People didn't disappear for no reason, and the suggestion that someone made it happen was inconceivable.

"Kidnap." She let the word roll around her mouth. "Kidnap, kid… nap?" No, it was absurd. She… none of them was rich and definitely not famous. Other sick reasons for snatching Annalee, Heather dismissed. Anna wouldn't have gone without a struggle, and although she was slight, she was strong and very fit. Anyone trying to take her at the hospital, and in broad daylight, would be seen. Wouldn't they? She would have made a lot of noise about it too. Someone must have heard something.

Unless it was someone she knew. Perhaps if she knew them, they persuaded or deceived her into going with them. But, Heather sighed, picking up the crumbs which had eluded the plate, she would have let one of them know. It took her no time at all to send a text message. The replies to some of Heather's own laboriously configured texts came back almost before she set her phone down. If she could, she would have contacted her or Lucy. If she could.

The entire thing was so confusing. Heather replayed the events at Lucy's house over and over. Snippets of conversations with Lucy or Jamie or Lucy and Jamie, and then all of them with the police. She struggled to slow it down, to recall every word spoken by each one and visualise their expressions and body language as they contributed or questioned. She massaged her temples and sighed. It was turning into one tangled mess in her mind.

Heather frowned as Lucy's revelations about Anna's ex-boyfriend, Dan, came to mind. Surely it was nothing to do with him. She hadn't particularly liked him, and her dislike had increased in the months before Anna had broken it off, and from Lucy's response she was not alone in that. He wasn't rude, but he seemed to go out of his way to alienate her family and even their friends. Although now she thought about it, they were mostly Anna's friends.

He was an odd choice for a boyfriend, a quiet boy, never as outgoing as Anna. Heather always wondered if she took up with him for altruistic reasons, thinking he needed encouragement, but she never voiced that to her daughter. Anna was very much into psychology in senior high school and took up with some kids who didn't quite fit. Heather and Tony both admired her desire to help people, to treat everyone as equals. Dan just stayed around longer. What started as a friendship slowly changed into more—a first love? Heather was never certain. Only they were together a lot.

Anna revealed he was the only child of a single mother, who Heather never did get to meet. And Dan had been polite enough, happy to join in their birthday and Christmas celebrations at the start of their friendship. He wasn't used to their messy, noisy family gatherings, and Heather believed the experiences missing in his life drew him in. He was eager to want to belong but awkward in his attempts to fit in. They all worked hard to make him welcome and accepted him as readily as Anna did until he was just another member of the family, albeit a quiet one.

But of course, this changed over time, as Anna's study load grew and she made new friends at university. He became even quieter, retreated further and was a great deal moodier. If he came to visit of an evening, all he did was sit in front of the television with Anna by his side. He appeared to resent it when she needed to study, and if she had a break, didn't want to take her out or socialise much. If they invited him for a meal, he would find an excuse not to come or come with a face like thunder, looking as if Anna had drawn him into a trap. He hardly spoke and spent his time nibbling at the food or focusing on his mobile phone with a frown on his face.

As Heather looked back, she saw Lucy was right; there was more to it than Anna outgrowing him. She hadn't confided in her mother when she finished it beyond outlining the facts, merely stating that he was no longer a part of her life and she was ready to move on. No hint of anything darker. Heather secretly thought it embarrassed Anna that she had put up with him for so long, and tried not to let her relief show. She commiserated with her daughter and offered comfort, but Anna brushed it off as unnecessary. Heather had been relieved and happy to see Anna looking more like her old and lively self.

It's the quiet ones you have to watch, popped into her head. She frowned as Sparky stirred and jumped around her feet, reminding her it was time for a walk. Surely Dan hadn't harboured a grudge all this time and done something stupid.

18

Initial enquiries at the hospital were disappointing, if not downright perplexing. Annalee had finished her shift and left to go home. Her colleagues had noticed nothing out of the ordinary. She didn't mention to them what she was planning afterwards. They were all very concerned and effusive in their praises of her—both personally and professionally.

Nurse Manager, Craig Tulley, phoned ahead to security to arrange for DS Elaine Troy and DC Jake Winters to see the CCTV footage. It was standard black and white and limited to areas outside the main entrances, the car parks, around the lifts and high-traffic areas inside the building. It covered the waiting rooms, the corridors leading to the wards or clinics and the emergency department. They started with the likely exit that Annalee would have taken.

"There she is, leaving with her bicycle." Elaine poked at the screen. "Looks like she's waiting for someone, she's not in a hurry to ride off."

"Searching for her mobile phone. Someone's ringing her."

"A quick call though, finished already. Wait. She's looking behind, back through the glass door as if something's caught her attention. She's going back in. In a hurry too—the bike almost landed in the garden as she shoved it against the wall." Elaine turned to the security officer. "Do you have footage inside that entrance?"

She drummed her fingernails against the phone in her pocket as Rod, the security officer, set up the relevant recording. The footage covered the inside of the entrance from about twenty metres away. It revealed, none too clearly from that distance, Annalee hurrying to help with an emergency. Three people in hospital scrubs, gowned and masked, grouped around a mobile hospital bed. One pushing from its base, with the other two on either side near the top end, both trying to guide the bed and attend to the patient. They were struggling as he was thrashing his arms about, tearing at an oxygen mask on his face and at both of them. Annalee stepped in, picking up a position on the left side of the bed furthest away from the camera's field of vision, and moved in close behind that attendant. She and the attendant had a brief interaction before she used both hands to hold down something on the side of the patient's upper body, which freed him up to restrain those wildly swinging arms.

As they approached the lifts, several people waiting to enter stepped aside for them, the shock on their faces clear at the developing drama. The bird's-eye view they saw as the group passed under the camera above the lift showed an ominous stain on the patient's chest underneath Annalee's hands. Elaine squeezed her lips together —it would be next to impossible to identify the masked and gowned medicos beyond height and build. Likewise the patient, with the oxygen mask covering most of his face and a cap over his hair. The inferior quality recording didn't help.

"Do you have footage in the lift and the other floors where they exit?" Elaine asked Rod.

He frowned at the logbook. "Hmm, we have a slight problem there, the camera in that lift has no recorded footage. The maintenance log shows it running the day before. Yet there's nothing? It technically can't happen, but it has. And the other thing is…" He glanced away. "I had a quick look through while I was waiting, to see if I could see them coming out of the lift but so far haven't been able to spot them. I'll need time to go through more thoroughly. You can't tell which way the lift is going, but they should go up to a theatre. Only—"

Two pairs of eyes bored into his as he paused.

"These are not the lifts used to take patients to operating theatres or even to the wards. They're mainly for visitors going to the wards on Floors Two to Seven. Otherwise, they're used by maintenance, service or cleaning staff or medical staff. As you can see, it's quite a busy area." They studied the screen in silence for a few minutes as a steady stream of people entered and exited the lifts. Rod added, "It's that time of day. Peak visiting time."

"So, apart from the wards on Floors Two to—what was it?"

"Seven."

"Yeah, Seven. Where else do the lifts go?"

"There are two service-type floors below the ground floor. The first one is the kitchens, storerooms for food and cleaning equipment, some staff change rooms and the laundry. The next down is mainly plant, the engineers' and maintenance personnel's domain, although some medical staff use it for quick access from one side of the hospital to the other. It's a lot quicker than trying to dodge around the wards and people during the day. Above on One is clinics, doctors' offices and so on, then above the ward floors you've got administration offices and more doctors' or consultants' rooms on Eight and Nine."

"Okay, Rod, you choose which we look at first. Up or down?"

An hour and a half later and with most of the recordings exhausted, they reached the startling conclusion that Rod's earlier check was correct. There was no sign of the trolley, the medical staff or Annalee leaving the lift above or below the floor where they had entered.

19

She slipped into her room, a tempting aroma beckoning her to the tray set on the low table. Tossing the skipping rope onto the bed, she scrutinised the offering. Still on the boring stuff— a sniff at the soup bowl confirmed clear chicken broth. A salad bowl and sandwiches accompanied it, but she was surprisingly hungry after the gym session.

The rest of the day dragged. The gym outing had left her fidgety. Sitting around waiting for something to happen was her least favourite thing. Even on holiday breaks she packed in as many activities as possible, preferably outdoors. She moved the skipping rope from the bed to the desk. Maybe later. She picked up her book and settled on the bed, but despite her intention not to, she fell asleep.

The outer door sliding open jolted her awake, setting her heart racing. She snapped her eyes to the bare screen. No message. Her head dull from the fog of the extended daytime nap, she waited. Was someone coming in? Finally? She backed up against the bedhead and crossed her arms.

Nothing. She shuffled to the corner of the bed and counted twenty seconds before approaching the door.

A dinner tray sat neatly on the floor. That was a first.

A day of changes. First, the gym, and now dinners at the door.

Her world was expanding. She squeezed her lips together and stuck her head out, looking both ways. No one in sight. What else was new? She reached out her arm and studied her splayed fingers as they reflected the red from the tunnel's ceiling lights. The message was clear. She picked up the tray and withdrew, watching the door slide smugly into place.

Sleep beckoned again soon after dinner. Her eyelids grew heavy as she shared the pain and sense of injustice Jane Eyre felt at the situation thrust on her at Lowood. After the book dropped from her fingers a second time, Anna memorised the page number and set it to one side. Despite her earlier nap, or because of it, she was tired. Perhaps from her loss of form or the lack of mental stimulation. But again, peaceful sleep eluded her. She tossed and turned. Shadowy figures punctuated her dreams, passing through doors which swished open and shut at random. Shadowy, grey, faceless entities floated around the room and above her body in the inky blackness.

She woke with a jolt, gulping in air through her gasping throat, a nameless force panicking her awake. The pitch-black room, the bed itself, was swaying and roiling, threatening to tip her into an abyss which had opened in the floor at the foot of the bed. Her heart racing, her body soaked in sweat, she fought against the demons picking and snatching at the bedclothes. She swung her arms to drive away the horrors buzzing near her ears before drawing her knees up to her chest, gripping her hands around them and hiding her face.

"No. Go away. Get away from me. Who… Who's there?" Her voice reed-thin in the impenetrable blackness. Gulping back the sobs, she battled to tame her breathing and her mind and drive out the terrors with logic and reason. She was in her bed. She was a grown woman, a professional woman, and had nothing to fear. There were no demons. The bed was still. The room was quiet and spacious. There was air to breathe.

Yet the nightmare made her small and vulnerable again. It made her nine years old—the child she had been when it first started. A regular and repugnant night caller, it manifested itself once, often twice a week.

The nightmare always followed a similar sequence with just

enough variation to heighten the dread. Someone she didn't know was after her. Someone indescribable and unseen. She was alone, and her adversary, a shadowy spectre following her, was ever behind, never letting up. She only knew it was a malicious entity bent on her destruction. Sometimes she made headway, almost reaching safety, and then she would be lost, stuck, not knowing which path to take. Progress slowed, as if she were wading through thick yet invisible mud.

The nightmare always ended the same way. To escape, she had to jump from a considerable height. She stood, peering down, not able to see the bottom, yet knowing her nemesis was drawing ever closer and there was no other way out. She plunged. Down, down, down she plummeted, her terror growing as death approached. She knew she couldn't survive the fall. And then… nothing. She never hit the ground. Instead, she woke up screaming, terrified, her heart pounding and chest heaving as she struggled for breath and against the horrors, as she had tonight.

Her father or mother would be there to reassure her. It was only a dream. They would hug her, whisper soothing words, pray with her and encourage her that she could trust God to take care of her.

As she grew older, she reasoned with herself about dreams and reality but, in the middle of a dream, reasoning went out the window. Daylight hours were full of logic and truth, and each night she went to bed optimistic that the nightmare wouldn't reappear.

She endured it for years, at times afraid of going to bed until, one day, it ended as suddenly as it began, when she was fourteen years old. When it finally ended, she didn't realise for some weeks. She was just grateful it had.

But tonight it was back. And even more terrifying and vivid than she remembered. After eight years, it was back with a vengeance. Tremors coursed through her rigid frame, and the hot tears escaping her tightly squeezed eyelids dripped onto her fingers and knees. Her mouth and throat were dry as sandpaper, her tongue swollen. She needed a drink.

She grasped for the edge of the bed, waited for her heart to still, and wiped her cheeks with the sheet. Tracing her hand along the wall until she reached the couch, she sat on its edge and fumbled for the water jug.

The spectre in the nightmare had gone, but the other one, the one outside her door, would still have to be faced. How and when that would happen was out of her hands. She didn't have her parents to come running to save her. It was down to her. Who else was there?

God?

She had come partway in her spiritual quest with the support of Lucy and the others in the small group. Even her mum and her mum's friend Ruth had been helpful as she had grown more comfortable discussing it with them. The one-year goal she'd set had only two months to go. At times—most of the time, if she was honest—she felt she was no closer to what Lucy called a personal relationship with God.

And now this. What did this say about God and His care for her?

"God, are you there?" she whispered into the darkness. "Can you help me? You know where I am, even if I don't. What is going on? Why am I here? What do they want with me? Please tell me what to do. Show me a way out?"

She strained into the black space. The silence grew and took shape in the room, gathering substance as it circled her head before reverberating back. She recoiled against the back of the couch as if someone had slapped her, her fist to her mouth.

Nothing. No one.

The mocking silence weighed into the debate raging inside. *There is no one there. No one to help, to rescue, to comfort you. God, if there is such a phenomenon, is not remotely interested in you or what happens to you.*

Her questions shouted unspoken around her. How could a loving God allow this? What had she done wrong? Was she being punished? What had she done to deserve it?

And what about her mother? She must be going out of her mind with worry. Hadn't she already suffered enough after Dad's death? Annalee's heart ached at the anguish her mother would be feeling.

She dug her fingers into the couch, letting the hot tears fall
unhindered.

20

"It's ludicrous. They go into the lift, they must get out. Simple as that." DS Elaine Troy's eyes narrowed. "Can you help us here, Rod? What are we missing?"

The security officer said, "Beats me. I'm as baffled as you. The only thing I can suggest is that we get copies of theatre admissions and go through those. Then the orderlies' and the cleaners' logs to see who was on duty, what their movements were and so on. It'll take me a little time before I can get it together, though."

"Well, that's a start. See about the theatre admissions first and let us know. And we will need the CCTV recordings. If we can have all the recordings for that day with any connection to that area on any floor. There has to be a clue somewhere. A trolley bed can't dissolve into thin air, even if people can."

Elaine gave Rod Smithers her business card and urged him to call if he came across any more information. She would give him a follow-up call in any case if she didn't hear from him within twenty-four hours. But, from what she had learned of him in the few hours they had spent together, she believed he was reliable. Not just a hack sitting out his days waiting for payday who couldn't give a toss about the job.

Back at the station, she gave Jake the task of trawling through the footage. The mound of paperwork threatening to break out of her in-tray was her afternoon delight.

"Go through that first one with a fine-tooth comb, Jake. See if you can account for everyone entering and leaving those lifts, say, at least thirty minutes before the trolley goes in and up to an hour afterwards. Then you can start on the others—the later ones first and then backtrack through the day."

She saw the feigned smile Jake plastered on his face before he turned to his computer screen. The job wasn't all action and intrigue; some tasks were a tad more tedious than others. Focusing on a screen was not one of her favourite pastimes, and she imagined it to be the same for Jake. The TV might be an ideal way to unwind at home after a hard day, but faced with a few hours staring at black and white, poor quality footage, the soporific effect would soon kick in. Still, he had to do his time with the mundane stuff as they all did, and she was pleased with his progress overall. If anyone could track what was going on in that hospital, Jake would. As long as he could stay awake.

Elaine sank back into the chair and threw down her pen after she'd read the same lines for the third time. Annalee Tanaka's refined features with her sparkling eyes and playful smile interrupted her attempts to wade through case notes needing updates. She set them aside and picked up her budget, which needed a last review before tomorrow's deadline, and rifled through it before sighing and putting it down.

"Annalee, Annalee, Annalee, where are you?" She nudged her chair back and went in search of a coffee, hoping the brew would clear her head and help her refocus.

She made a slight detour on the way to the coffee machine to look in on her protégé. "Coffee, Jake?"

"Thanks, Sarge, an extra spoonful of sugar if you don't mind."

Balancing the paper cups in one hand, she pulled a chair in beside him and skimmed over his notes. Meticulous as always, he was noting time codes for various actions around the lifts. The screen was fixed on what looked to be a hospital employee.

"Who do you have there?"

"Twenty-five minutes before the lift incident, serviceman here with laundry hamper enters the same lift from the laundry service floor. Ten minutes before that, another two did the same. Differences are: they were female, he is male, and the two ladies entered together. He goes in ten minutes later and alone. The ladies get out at Floors Three and Four, respectively. He goes up further. Most likely to the sixth floor, as—surprise—the video cameras outside the lifts there were out of operation too."

Elaine's eyes narrowed as she focused on the worker. He had his head angled away from the camera, making it impossible to see his face.

"There's no trace of him on any of the other floors. None of the three come back down before Annalee and Co. go into the lift, unless they take another route and use different lifts. I'm about to check the next recording to see if I can track them returning."

"Interesting… So many cameras out of action in one day." She rapped the desk with her fingernails and pushed back her chair. "Okay, keep me posted."

21

Lucy swung the flyscreen door open, cursing the sensor light for failing to do its duty. She was positive she'd checked it was on yesterday before leaving for afternoon shift to avoid having to fumble in the dark for the right key as she was doing now. Fingers poised to insert it into the lock, she froze. Something was wrong. Pale splinters of raw wood were just discernible through the gloom near the bolt mechanism. She ran her fingers over them, gasping as the sharp edge caught her skin. The door gaped a little to reveal a black space where there shouldn't be one if the door were shut. She backed away, dropping her keys.

A break-in. Not something she needed right now. She was tired and cold, and the rain was starting up again. And her best friend was missing. Tears threatened as she scrabbled through the wind-blown leaves to salvage her keys, eyes fixed on the door. Should she go in? The question was answered for her as a muffled thud from inside sounded above the wind and rain spattering on the metal awning overhead.

She turned and fled back to the car, locked herself in and peered through the shadows around the door. There was no way to move the car quietly, but she couldn't stay in the middle of the driveway. Her hand trembled as she turned on the engine.

"No!" She clenched her teeth as her headlights illuminated the front of the house like a flare on a moonless night. She backed out and drove down the street, turned into a laneway and parked where she had an unobstructed view of her driveway. Fingers groping for her phone, she willed them to work and punched in the emergency number.

It was twenty agonising minutes before she saw the flashing lights. Thankfully, no sirens blared out to disturb her neighbours. She ran to the police car as it drew into her driveway. Another one squealed to a halt across the road seconds later, the sound setting her teeth on edge.

"Hi, I'm Lucy Roberts. I called you. I think there's someone still in the house."

At her words, the two officers raced to the house, torches flashing at the windows on their way to the front door. Another from the second car scaled the side gate into the backyard.

The driver of the second car approached Lucy. "Come back across the road and tell me what you know." Officer Jan Monks tapped Lucy's arm and introduced herself, her smile going some way to calming Lucy's wildly thumping heart. "They've got it. They shouldn't be too long." Despite the assurance, the officer didn't take her eyes off the driveway entrance.

"It'll probably be kids," she said as her radio crackled. "They take a punt that no one's home by the empty car space and hope they got it right. Maybe knocking on the door with some excuse in case they didn't. They'll be long gone."

"Kids, at this time of night?" Lucy shivered, longing to be safe and warm inside, despite knowing it was not likely to happen anytime soon.

"You'd be amazed at what they get up to. Some are out all night, either by choice or because they don't want to go home. Doesn't matter what day it is, or time of year." Jan glanced up at the threatening clouds. "Looks like it'll come down again soon. Do you want to wait in your car?"

"There's something you ought to know." Lucy wrapped her arms around herself, shivering uncontrollably. Was it shock or cold? She'd left her coat at home, thinking the dash from the warm car to the house didn't warrant taking it. "The police were here two days ago because my housemate has disappeared." Lucy bit her lip.

Jan reached her hand out, then withdrew it, but Lucy caught the warmth in her eyes. "We know. That's why you've got two cars here. Your call was red-flagged when your name and address came in. It may be just a coincidence, but we want to be on the safe side."

Jan's partner, Terry Banks, came back and looked from one to the other. "There's no one inside. Some scuff marks on the back fence, so he, or they, must have left that way. I'm sorry, but there's a bit of a mess in there, and we need to get forensics here to dust for fingerprints before we let you back in. When that's done, you can go in, have a look around and talk us through what's missing."

"Kids?" Jan raised an eyebrow at Terry.

He avoided eye contact with Lucy. "Yeah, it looks that way, with the mess and all, but we'll know more later after the sci-fi team has done its thing."

"The sci-fi team?" It was Lucy's turn to raise an eyebrow.

"Oh, don't mind him," Jan said. "He's all about putting silly labels on life, and he's nuts about *Star Wars*. But seriously, is there anywhere you can go for an hour or two while we do the necessary? What about the neighbours?" She eyed the curious few standing in their driveways, braving the weather.

Lucy glanced around, not realising they had an audience. Her cheeks burned. She didn't know most of them, beyond saying hello in passing if she was out for a jog or walk. "Maybe Mrs McCarthy, next door?" Lucy pictured the motherly, or rather grandmotherly, neighbour who walked her two Yorkies twice a day without fail. She had introduced herself when they moved in, holding out a basketful of cupcakes and a bottle of lemonade as welcome gifts. Since then, she often popped around with homemade goodies to share with 'you busy young ladies', as she called them. "It might be a little late for her, but I can see a light on. And her dogs are barking."

"Sounds like a plan." Terry turned to Jan. "Will you go with Lucy while I wait for the team? Stan and Ollie are about ready to roll."

"Plee-ase. It's getting too late for this." Jan punched Terry good naturedly on the arm. "Lead the way to Mrs McCarthy's please, Lucy."

"Oh, wait." Lucy stopped mid-step. "There's something else. I'd forgotten about it until now." The image of the car she'd passed as she turned in from the main road was firm in her mind.

22

Annalee grimaced, sweating through a series of ab-crunching sit-ups some fifteen minutes into her gym session. Until this place… this incarceration… this kidnapping… this torture, well mental torture anyway, her philosophy had been to make the best of circumstances. Whatever hurdles she faced: exams, the breakup with Dan, even her father's death—no, not that, that was still too raw— she could rise above the problems, and tough through the obligatory period of adjustment. But the yawning hours of forced isolation here tossed that idea out of the window.

The gym was her only reprieve. It was the highlight of her day. That one hour out of the room meant so much, and she could challenge herself, giving total focus to each exercise, going faster and extending her range each time. Almost forgetting where she was. Almost.

She liked a good challenge, something to sink her teeth into, whether it was physical exercise or her career. That was one of the things she missed the most. But stuck in here with little beyond exercise to stimulate her… She scowled, eyeing her reflection in the mirrored wall.

There was so much going on in the medical world, and she had only just got to the bottom rung. And now. Her lips twisted, picturing herself as a specimen in a lab under observation by a stern-faced man in a white coat armed with a notebook and pen. There had to be more to it than for whoever-it-was to watch her sweating through ab-crunches, sitting reading a book in her room or tossing and turning in the night. That's if they could see in the dark, which was more than she could.

Even lab specimens had a purpose.

Something out of place broke through her thoughts: a muted click, followed a split second later by the blank wall opposite the door flying out. Or so it seemed until her confused brain made sense of events and translated more accurately.

The gym wall had cantilevered outwards, tilting open like their old garage door at home. Only this was an entire wall. She froze mid-sit-up. The wall slid smoothly and swiftly, with just the faintest of whirring sounds. When it stopped moving, what had been the bottom half of the wall was now protruding outside at ceiling height, like a patio roof.

The outside swept in on an earthy, organic, spice-tinged waft of balmy air which encircled her, cooling the sweat on her skin. She choked on the breath caught in her throat as the pure light only nature could offer hit her eyes. As if she was viewing the scene through a vast picture frame, a myriad of colours, shades and sounds jostled for meaning, confusing her senses anew.

Mouth agape, she sat stunned, until her screaming stomach muscles forced her upright. She wrenched her hands from behind her neck and leant forward as if to stand, uncertain if her legs would hold her weight.

As her eyes adjusted, they were first drawn to a dense bank of trees beyond a low stone wall some metres away. Enormous, unfamiliar trees soared up from somewhere below, perhaps growing on a steep hillside. A tower of reds, browns, greys, and blacks, softened by countless foliage shades, with vines snaking through and around them, blocked out the sky. Some huge limbs and vines were draped here and there with pale grey-green petticoats of lacy grass, swaying gently in a light breeze. Other trees sported alien growths bulging from their trunks or branches, with vivid splashes of coloured flowers cascading from their centres. This side of the stone wall, lush green lawn swept up to a narrow paved area shaded by the cantilevered 'roof' created by the now-open wall.

She willed her frozen lower limbs into motion before the dream should dissolve and the wall reinstate itself. She stepped stiffly through the gap. A wave of dizziness stopped her. She put her hands on her knees and breathed in slowly, willing it to pass, as the delicious warm air drew her on.

Crossing the paving, she fell on her knees and sank into the grass's velvety surface. Her usual aversion to dirty fingernails forgotten, she dug her fingers deep through the grass and scraped at the soil beneath, before lifting her hand to study the black grains caught there. The sweet fragrance of the grass and the earthy, rich smell of the soil filled her nostrils. Resisting the urge to crawl on her hands and knees, she pushed up, crossed the lawn to the low stone wall, and sat on it for a moment, facing the building.

Her eyes narrowed at the long, dark strip of concrete and metal recessed into the hillside. It suggested a reclaimed gun emplacement left over from World War Two, obscured by a grassy, shrub-covered earth bank above. Grasses and ferns hanging over the edges made it look even more like a part of the landscape. The 'wall' she'd exited from swung back into place as she watched. She lifted a shoulder and turned away.

The slope beyond the stone wall fell away steeply, but as she leaned over, peering through the gloom, a distinct salty tanginess drifted upwards, mingled with the pungent vegetation. Her eyes widened—the sea. The ocean was below and there had to be a way down. She followed the low wall away from the building and found a gap opening to an inviting set of neat stone steps. They led to a narrower, grassed terrace running parallel to the wall. A short distance along and tell-tale stones intruding into the grass contours led to more steps.

And so it went: steps leading down through the giant trees to a terrace and on down to the next until she was totally surrounded by the immense forms, as if in a pale-green cathedral.

She stopped and squinted up, dizzied by the colossal giants, many of them skirted with huge protruding roots swathed in moss and vines. They created odd, fantastical shapes hiding among the dense understory of ferns, palms and other exotic vegetation.

Her eyes ached at the sheer expanse of the space after the limited dimensions of her rooms and the tunnels inside. She closed them and listened to the soft sigh of the breeze in the canopy above, to the rustles in the undergrowth as leaves brushed against bark or ferns rubbed one to another. This fascinating place whispered contentment somehow, even though strangers had violated it, carved out paths and made ways through. She dug her toes into the cool grass and spread her arms out wide, spinning a full circle. It was as if the trees and the warm air were embracing her, murmuring promises of hope and encouragement. To be outside again in a place like this… And to see the sea at the end would cap it off.

A few minutes more and there it was—not quite the ocean, but it would do. She shielded her eyes against the sun's glare and sucked in a breath.

23

"Lucy. Lucy. Earth to Lucy." Amy's hand came into focus, her finger and thumb poised to take the leaflet Lucy was gripping.

"I'm sorry. I shouldn't have come, but I needed to get out. And before…" Lucy's eyes misted, and she glanced away. "Before Anna disappeared, I was so looking forward to this."

The church auditorium was emptying fast after the mission-focused service. Lucy had scarcely heard a word of what Amy's great, or was it great-great, aunt and uncle had said about their work on exotic Vaui Island.

"No need to say sorry, after all you've been through. Come and have a coffee." Amy took her hand, pulling her to her feet. "Mrs Roberts has made her world-famous scones."

"I don't think I will. I'll just slip out quietly and go home. Maybe you can fill me in on the details another time." Lucy hugged Amy and turned to leave.

"Wait. You're not going home alone, are you? After the break-in and…" Amy almost had to jog to keep up with her. "At least let me walk you to your car."

Lucy turned and searched her friend's warm eyes. "No, it's okay.

I've moved back in with my aunt and uncle for a while. I was struggling to be there alone, and then… the break-in."

Lucy clicked the lock and reached for the car door handle. "I'm sorry, I'm not much fun to be with at the moment, and the thought of going into supper with everybody crowding around wanting to know… the latest…" A shiver ran up her spine.

"But you realise it's only because we love you. And I can defend you against the busybodies."

Lucy grinned at the image of five-foot-nothing Amy shielding her from the likes of Mrs Roberts, daunting in spite of the to-die-for scones she made in vast quantities nearly every week.

"Do you want to go for a coffee somewhere else? Just the two of us?"

"What about your parents, and Mr and Mrs Farleigh? I don't want to take you away from them."

"It's all good, they're staying with us for another week anyway, so I've plenty of time to spend with them before they go."

"Well, if you're sure…?" Lucy wasn't looking forward to going home so early and spending the night alone with her thoughts. Her aunt's busy household with boisterous eight-year-old twins, Alex and Adam, delightful as they were, wasn't the place to be for grown-up heart-to-hearts and sombre moods. Her aunt and uncle had challenging careers, their spare time taken up with the boys. Not the time or place to re-hash her troubles. They were concerned and supportive, of course, but it wasn't as if they could change anything.

"I'm sure," Amy said. "What about we go to the Greendoor? It's not too far away, and it's quiet there at this time of night. Just give me two minutes to tell my folks where I'm going. Can you drop me home afterwards?"

"Sure. And thanks, Amy." Lucy settled into the car to wait.

"Coffee or hot chocolate? My shout. It's the least I can do. I'm sorry—"

"Lucy. Will you stop apologising?" Amy shrugged off her jacket but didn't sit down. "Now sit, and I'll order. I know yours—a nice big mug of hot chocolate."

Lucy smiled, not able to meet Amy's smiling, wide eyes. "You know me well. Don't forget the marshmallows."

"It's a given." Amy lined up at the counter to place the order as Lucy texted her aunt about her plans. Not that she had to. She wasn't the teen student she'd been when she last stayed with her aunt and uncle. But, all the same, she'd promised to do it for the time being, and she did appreciate their concern.

Amy slipped in opposite Lucy. "They'll bring it over when it's ready, and I've ordered a mint slice to share. Not a patch on Mrs Robert's scones, but..." Amy reached across for Lucy's hand. "Do you want to talk or just sit?"

Lucy looked up as the waiter brought their order over. "There's not a lot to say, really. I don't know anything more—about Anna, and about the break-in. And that's the hard part. The not knowing, the thinking... all the rubbish things that go through my mind. Over and over." Once the words started, she found she wanted to talk, and she trusted Amy. She was a good friend; perhaps she could help her make sense of it. The Jamie part, she would keep to herself.

"Do the police think they're related?"

"They say it's improbable. They're still going with the opportunistic-kids theory." Lucy sighed and squished at her marshmallow before popping it into her mouth. "But I keep thinking, and it's driving me nuts, that they're keeping me in the dark. That's if they even know anything."

"Why would they keep you in the dark?"

"Well, I mean, not about the break-in, because it was our place, but about Anna. I'm in that awkward position of not being a close relative. We're... or she was... um... is, over twenty-one, but Mrs T is her closest relative." Lucy bit her lip at the past tense slip, hoping Amy would let it slide. Anna 'is'. No way can she be a 'was'. *Please, God.*

"Frustrating, huh?"

"Just a bit. Mrs T is great and passes on anything they tell her, which isn't much. But it's so hard for her. She's hurting—"

"You're hurting." Amy squeezed Lucy's hand. "Beats me how you can still go to work."

Lucy snorted, then put her hand over her mouth. "Sorry. But I have to. It's the only thing keeping me sane. Especially now."

"The break-in. So, they—the thieves, I mean. Did they take anything?"

"Didn't seem to, not that we have anything valuable. They emptied every drawer and cupboard in the place. Clothes, papers, everywhere. Rummaged through our junk jewellery—even emptied the fridge. Took some bread and a half chicken I bought the day before."

"That sounds like kids then. Hungry kids."

"Maybe, but… it seemed staged, somehow."

"Staged?"

"Some drawers weren't touched. And, our papers; they tipped accounts and receipts and so on out of the expander files we bought. If kids did it and they were after cash or jewellery, a quick look would show them there was nothing valuable there. Maybe I'm reading too much into it. With Anna…" Lucy's eyes teared up.

"Need a tissue?" Amy rummaged in her bag and passed the soft pack over.

"Thanks, I have a stash in my bag, but thanks." She selected one but held it on her lap, twisting it through her fingers before scowling. "The annoying thing is, I don't know what Anna had. Of value, I mean. You don't write up an inventory when you move in together, do you?"

"What about Anna's mum? Any help?"

"She came and looked around, helped us clean up too when the police let me back in. But no luck there—nothing missing that she could tell. Anna's important stuff, like her passport and birth certificate, were still at home. I mean, her mum's home."

"That's good—identity theft and all that. Perhaps that's why they went through your papers. I've heard of kids selling things like that on, to gangs—"

"In Perth?" Lucy raised an eyebrow. Perth might be the capital city in Western Australia, but it was hardly seething with organised crime syndicates.

"You'd better believe it. Why should we be immune?" Amy was working through a journalism degree and interested in all things connected to crime and justice. "I guess there are no rules for a break-in." She finished her drink and set the mug on the saucer. "Did they make a mess?"

"Not half as much mess as the police did with their fingerprint dust, stuff, whatever you call it." Lucy was grateful the thieves didn't trash the place, images of mashed food, graffitied walls and worse from TV news in her mind. "Mum and my sister, Vicky, came up from Albany and Aunt Karen helped clean up. And Anna's mum, as I said. It didn't take too long with everyone helping."

"Must've been good to have your mum there?"

"Sure was. I needed a hug or three and mum's good for that. Other things too, of course." Lucy laughed. The action felt strange, as if she hadn't laughed for a long time. "My sister, not so much. She's going through a stage. Never quite forgiven me for leaving home and coming to the big city."

"Not good when you needed the TLC."

"Oh, she's alright, but she's younger than me—just fourteen and going through all the teen-angst stuff. All the drama intrigued her though, what with Anna—" Lucy sucked in a breath, refusing to let those tears have their way.

Amy gripped her arm. "It's okay. If you want to cry, just go for it."

"Not a good look out here, and I've done enough crying lately." Lucy sniffed and took a mouthful of her chocolate drink, grimacing as she hit the sludge at the bottom. "I just want some answers. How can anyone disappear like that?"

24

---

*A*nna soaked in the sun's warmth, shielding her eyes as a clear blue sky dazzled, its brightness amplified in the mirror-image reflection in a rock-rimmed lagoon. Massive, black, dragon's teeth rocks encapsulated the semi-circular bay, with a profusion of stray 'teeth' lancing through the water close to the outer rim. The lagoon, easily the span of three Olympic-size pools, looked perfect for a decent swim if there were no menacing rocks under the surface.

As calm as the bay was, rhythmic thuds of powerful waves pounded the outside of the rocks, and spurts of spray forced their way through a couple of gaps near the centre. While the barrier rocks were commanding, they towered to twice the height on either side, before disappearing from view behind the thick vegetation on the slope.

An extinct volcano? Most likely, from the colour of the rocks and the beach sand, which was amazing. So... black. She'd only seen it in photos or travel documentaries before. She stepped onto its crunchy, coarse surface, savouring the warm particles rough under her feet and chafing through her toes. Such a contrast to the fine, white, often powdery sand of the beaches at home in Western Australia. She scooped up a handful, kneaded it on her palm, then raised her hand and let it trickle through her fingers, the sun spinning a kaleidoscope of colours through the falling grains.

Where was she? She couldn't think of any beaches in Australia with sand like this, and… she turned, looking back up the slope… there was that tropical 'jungle'. The far north of Western Australia? Queensland? The Northern Territory? They were all in the tropics and had rainforests, but black sand?

With a frown, she stepped into the water, letting out a gasp as the coolness of the water teased her warm skin. Identifying the strange location would have to wait. The water was calling her and she was struggling not to plunge straight in. But, those partly submerged rocks looked ominous. Although the water was clear, the sand was black, as were the rocks, and it would be difficult to see what lay under the surface.

She waded in up to her knees and gingerly felt her way along, heading for the nearest end. There, the trees, backed by the rock face, almost met the water, with just a narrow strip of leaf-litter-strewn sand and scree. She slowed as the sand underfoot gave way to rough stones and shale, and strained her neck to look up the almost-vertical barrier. There was no getting around it; the sharp rocks would cut her unprotected skin to pieces even if she could find a foothold. And the other end of the bay looked just as hazardous.

She back-tracked, treading carefully around some taller rock formations closest to the shore. Natural rock pools nestled in and between some of them. Seaweed, shells and tiny sea creatures inhabited many. She squatted next to one, delighted to find a community of thumbnail-sized crabs with distinctive red stripes. They scurried in and out of hidey-holes as she dipped her fingers in, curious to explore. Something alive, at least.

Once clear of the rocks, she zig-zagged from knee depth to above her waist and back again, finding the sandy floor relatively free from hidden hazards. Yet, her eyes were continually drawn to those water sprays. Maybe the gaps would be wide enough to squeeze through, or at least give her a glimpse of what lay beyond. Then, as the crystal clear water reached her shoulders, she kicked her feet out and sank to the bottom, pleased to see it free from hidden, razor-sharp rocks. With a slow exhalation, she watched the bubbles jostling to be free before she joined them and pushed up to the surface. She licked the familiar salty tanginess from her lips, slicked her hair back and sighed at the water's warm embrace.

She had loved the sea for as long as she could remember, her family frequenting the plentiful beaches near home most weekends. A powerful swimmer, she joined the school swimming squad as soon as she was old enough, and dabbled in surfing in her teen years.

She swam languorously across the lagoon and back, before angling towards those spray bursts. As she drew closer, she slowed and duck-dived, keeping a wary eye out for submerged rocks. The water was much deeper here, with some ridges and the start of the boundary rocks visible below and in the distance, but it was predominantly sandy seabed and shale. She caught glimpses of schools of tiny fish near the ridges, shimmering silver with rainbow-jewelled sides flashing as they flitted back and forth.

The water had a distinct push and pull to it now, which puzzled her—unless an underwater gap in the rocks was the answer. She coasted to a stop, rolled onto her back and stared into the deep-blue, cloudless sky, savouring the water's gentle tugs caressing her skin. She could be back home floating off the beach at Mullaloo or Watermans, gazing into the same sky, with the warmth of the same sun on her body. Perhaps friends of hers, even Lucy or Jamie, might be doing the same thing across the ocean. That's if it was the same ocean. Her lips thinned, and she squeezed her eyes shut.

A sound rang out across the water. She started and gulped in a mouthful of seawater. Arms and legs flailing, she fought to right herself, spluttering out the salty liquid burning her throat.

25

DS Elaine Troy frowned as she examined the case notes for the missing Annalee Tanaka. The investigative team had expanded as the mystery deepened. They were putting their all into finding this young woman. Yet, Elaine knew from the atmosphere in the incident room that few of them expected a positive outcome. Nobody voiced their opinions though, not wanting to say the words in case it summoned up the body they didn't want to find.

The trail at the hospital had run cold, ludicrous as it may seem. It shouldn't have, but it had. Annalee's removal was well-planned and meticulously implemented. The big question: was she the intended target or just someone in the wrong place at the wrong time? They clearly intended to snatch someone that day, but was it meant to be Annalee, or any nurse or medico? Did gender or age matter, or appearance, ethnicity?

It wasn't the only question. All their questions and theories, no matter how improbable, were noted on one end of the whiteboard in the incident room. 'Why take Annalee Tanaka?' topped the list. Elaine frowned as she considered that board. There were far too many questions on it for her liking and, what made it worse, they had answered very few.

What they knew supported the well-planned and well-executed

criteria. The kidnappers, for want of a better word, couldn't have chosen a better time and place. Tracing who went where in and around the lifts was proving difficult. It was hard to believe that what looked like a full-blown emergency with a distressed patient would have dissolved into finding an empty trolley bed abandoned in a corridor.

Two orderlies going about their duties came across it some hours later. Puzzled, they returned it to the holding area near Emergency, ready for cleaning and re-use. They assumed the bed was on its way there and somehow got abandoned by staff members, perhaps summoned away on more urgent business. Stranger things happened, they told the officers who questioned them; at least there was no patient left in it.

It was so busy in that area at the time that, typically, no one noticed a thing. Those who came forward after the grainy footage aired on prime time TV news had been so focused on their own affairs they had taken scant notice of the apparent emergency. It was a minute's drama played out for them in real-time by a cast of nondescript players clad in scrubs and masks. Indoctrinated by reality TV shows, they didn't consider it unusual to give way to the group who clearly needed the lift more than they did. Some of them described Annalee perfectly (helped by her face splashed all over the TV and newspapers), but as for the others around the trolley bed and the patient in it, they might have been Martians dressed up for all the useful information gleaned.

The mystery serviceman with the laundry hamper was definitely a person of interest. None of the staff or public recognised him from the video footage and the stills taken from it, and his physique and the cap he wore pulled over his eyes didn't help. Neither short nor exceptionally tall, he had short, darkish straight hair, and walked with no sign of an unusual gait. He kept his head down and avoided security cameras as he passed by, angling his head away from them. His uniform and cap were standard issue hospital gear, complete with the hospital logos. A check of the records confirmed his journey to be an unauthorised one, as regular service staff doing such work documented the times they exited and re-entered the service area. They also returned by alternative routes, including stairways, which engaged Jake and several other officers in many hours of viewing CCTV recordings.

She frowned. There were far too many people not accounted for. Nine men and fourteen women remained unidentified and untraced to date. The team discounted some of them, predominantly elderly and visitors who just hadn't seen the appeal to come forward; yet, that still left too many. And, unlike the trolley bed, no laundry hampers were reported missing or found in places they shouldn't be. The cameras, both inside the lift and outside on the sixth floor, were tampered with. No fingerprints, of course, which didn't help.

Nothing came up in the background checks on the family and friends. No ransom demands, no unusual contact with any family members so far. Elaine had received details on the disappearance of Anna's cousin some four years back, after Heather Tanaka mentioned it. While she discounted nothing, it appeared to be an unfortunate coincidence. However, the date thing was peculiar. Her UK contact, Detective Inspector Thomas Steele, who dealt with the case at the time before passing it to the unsolved cases team, agreed with her views. Elaine paused and scored another line underneath that date before she read on. The girl Katie's parents—rather, her mother and stepfather—were no longer suspects. Her birth father, Haruto Kimura, was estranged from the family and out of the country when his daughter went missing. He was eventually traced to Japan.

Annalee's ex-boyfriend, Daniel Wilmott, was proving to be elusive, as was the rest of his family. They hadn't—yet, Elaine corrected herself—traced his mother or other relatives, although there could be any number of reasons for that. His few friends said he left for Asia to find himself. They believed he was backpacking alone, and none of them knew his plans. Asia was a big place. He hadn't contacted any of them, and none counted him as a social media friend, citing that he wasn't into it, not his thing. Police departments from Indonesia to Northern India and beyond had been notified to help track him down.

The next on her list was the love interest, Jamie, aka, James Prince, the FIFO worker. While he appeared genuine and keen to cooperate, there was something about him that didn't gel. She might be reading too much into it. Still, she jotted down a note to look into his background and bring him in for a chat fairly soon. He was about to fly out to his oil-rig job and would be there for a month. He could keep. At least he'd had the good sense to notify her he was going. She rifled through her papers, noting the company details he'd given and the rig's location.

And there was that matter of the break-in at the girls' house. Another coincidence? Everything pointed to that. And Lucy thinking she had spotted Jamie's car leaving the area before she discovered the break-in—he had denied it, stating he was safely tucked up in bed at the time. His car was a common make, and grey. Lucy did say she wasn't sure, and it was dark and raining at the time.

Too many coincidences? Elaine frowned, shuffled the papers back into the file and steeled herself for this afternoon's meeting with Mrs Tanaka. Disliking the impotent feeling churning at her insides, she longed for a breakthrough so she would have something positive to tell her.

26

$\mathcal{A}$ sequence of melodious notes, like those pre-show chimes designed to get an audience's attention, floated across the water, reverberating off the rocks behind her. The unnatural sound was so out of place in this tranquil setting.

She spat out the rest of the seawater, scrubbed at her eyes and squinted at the shore. It was coming from somewhere along the tree line. She could see nothing, but the view of the slope from her vantage point halfway across the lagoon was magnificent. Prolific greenery camouflaged the building, but a subtle difference in depth and shading gave it away. It was about halfway up the mountain, or volcano. If all of this was in the crater of an ancient volcano, then it must have been huge. Above the building, the vegetation looked just as dense, only thinning a little nearer the top. A few areas of stark grey-black rock poked through in places toward the peak.

A shudder teased the base of her spine as she considered the building and all it represented, in contrast to the beauty and freedom out here. She froze as the musical series of five notes repeated its sequence.

What was it? The dinner gong? Time's up? Did they expect her to come back in? Her lips curled as she trod water, searching for its source. Another sequence began. The gaps between each set were getting shorter. Then, out of the corner of her eye, she saw a light, flashing green, showing through bushes a few metres away from the path she'd descended.

Interesting. They imprisoned her with no human contact—the brief messages on the screen didn't count. They directed every moment of her life to date and had now given her freedom. It was a beautiful day. She had just started out here, easily able to do another ten or more laps. Plus, she had those fingers of spray to explore. And a green light meant 'Go', didn't it?

She smirked, rolled onto her back and backstroked purposefully toward the nearest spray. Let them show themselves, come out and get her if they wanted. She was more than ready to negotiate, to see their faces.

The melodic notes' sequence was almost continuous now. She could live with the sound; it wasn't altogether unpleasant. She turned over, fishtailed into a crawl and matched her rhythm to the beat, on the lookout for submerged rocks with each downstroke. The small of her back tingled. Exhilarated by both the swim and her defiance, she ignored it, her excitement as she neared her goal reason enough for minor discomfort. Plus, it was a while since she'd had a decent swim, what with winter at home and the weeks of her confinement here. Twinges were on the cards.

The nerve endings at the base of her spine pulsed, as if in time with the musical notes. She faltered, gliding to a stop. Her shoulders tightened, and her neck goose-fleshed despite the warmth of the sun. The water was colder and deeper here, but she never felt the cold once she was swimming. She rubbed her lower back and trod water, eyeing the flashing green light. The notes sounded harsher now, more strident. As if they were reaching across the water and into her body, sending stronger and stronger surges through her spine.

All of her spine.

The needle-sharp shocks played up and down her spine before reaching out into her limbs, through her shoulders and buttocks, and up through her neck into her skull. Pins and needles gripped her fingertips and the soles of her feet and spread upwards to meet the shocks. A cold, creeping numbness claimed the left side of her body.

She snatched breaths of air, fighting to keep her mouth and nose above water as the spasms intensified. A groan escaped her clenched teeth as her back arched, sending her under. She kicked out with her right leg, came up spluttering out the acrid seawater, gagging as some trickled down her throat. With what little strength she could summon, she pushed onto one side. Her left arm and leg dragging uselessly, and jerking with each new shock, she inched towards the shore.

Half-dazed with the relentless spasms, she barely registered the rough sand in the shallows halting her progress. She lay there, her tongue working to push out the sand before nausea won and she retched. The shock-waves didn't let up. They coursed through her body as she purged the seawater. She was cold, so cold, her back arching convulsively as if a resident electric eel frantically fought to batter its way out through the top of her head. Dark spots appeared, grew and blurred her vision. Pain clamped a vice around her temples.

She could do nothing. She had nothing. Her body a twitching, writhing mass of unresponsive flesh.

"I get it." She forced through gritted teeth. "You win. You win."

If they heard her submission, she didn't know or care. Her voice sounded faint, as if coming from someone else lying on that beach. Someone far away. Yet, the shocks slowly subsided, leaving a numb, icy silence. The world stopped. All the sounds and movements and colours blended into a grey haze, thickly suspended in that time of exquisite relief. Through the slit of her eye, she saw the grey gradually fade. Flesh became visible. Her shoulder, sepulchral white against the black sand, still masked by a grey-flecked curtain. Was it her shoulder? The thing wouldn't respond to her brain's command to move, to shrug, to show it belonged. She squeezed the eyelid shut. Fingers, toes—the sum of the parts of her body were scattered, fragmented.

The chimes had stopped, yet the echo rang in her ears over the long silence before the world started up again. Sobs replaced the spasms and retching. She inched out of the water and pushed herself up the beach, toward the path. With the vines and tree roots as anchors, she managed to sit upright, resting her thumping head on scraped and bloodied knees. Waves of nausea and a black fog threatened as she fought to steady her breathing.

A note sounded out. Her head shot up and she winced, her jaw locked against what was to come as the chimes took up again. She pushed onto all fours, then up, wild eyes searching for that green light. She staggered along the beach, peering into the bushes until she saw it balefully blinking from the undergrowth. It pointed to a narrow foot-worn track winding between shrubs and ferns. She pushed past it and dragged herself along, clutching low branches and vines. All the while, those chimes rang out their relentless melody, the sound mocking and sinister as she entered the mountain through a jagged tear in its side.

27

Heather glanced at the clock as she filled the kettle. Three am. Sparky had raised an eyebrow when the light came on but stayed ensconced in his warm, rug-filled basket. The air had a bite to it. Heather yawned and fished her favourite mug out of the dishwasher before reaching for the drinking chocolate. Unfortunately, this was fast becoming her nightly routine, sleep proving elusive in the hours after midnight. Tense and exhausted with worry over Anna as she was, the fragmented sleep didn't help. She took her steaming mug and the packet of digestive biscuits and headed back to bed, hoping that reading her latest novel for half an hour might do the trick.

Ten minutes later, she set the book aside and picked up her journal but soon gave up on that as her pen hovered over the blank page for too long. She flipped through the pages and read over some of her recent entries. The entries made after Anna's disappearance. Her eyes misted and she reached for a tissue. And the phone.

One positive about being awake at this time of night: it was a good time to call the UK. Her cousin Barbara should be home and, she hoped, not too busy with her own life to resent Heather's frequent interruptions.

As difficult as the first phone call had been, her fears were unfounded. Barbara expressed nothing but compassion and understanding after the shocking news. Heather hadn't known how her cousin would take it after her own daughter's disappearance four years before. Would she slam down the phone? Or get angry at Heather because she felt guilty somehow about her own loss? Or fall apart because the awful coincidence was just too horrible to contemplate? All these thoughts flashed through Heather's mind when she dialled Barbara's number only three days after they'd reported Anna missing. She hadn't dared to leave it any longer, not wanting her to find out from the media reports as it was becoming big news in Australia. Anna's photo and the grainy CCTV footage from the hospital of Anna with the 'medical emergency' team entering the hospital lift aired over and over.

Since then, she and Barbara had spoken every few days. Heather was relieved that at least one person understood and wouldn't fill the air with useless platitudes and endless suggestions about where Anna might be. Or give advice, as too many of her friends had in the weeks since. Barbara listened and understood. They chatted comfortably about everything and nothing, relived the fun things they had done together as children and teens and the happy times spent together in the early days of their marriages. Nothing was off-limits. As they inevitably drew closer to the sad things each had faced, the conversation usually ended up with one or both of them dissolving into tears. And that was okay. The tears were therapeutic. They were at one with that belief.

She pressed the programmed number which worked away to dial Barb's number, and waited. It eventually clicked through as someone picked up.

"Barb, is that you?" Heather volunteered to the silence on the other end.

"Hello. Hello. Who's that?" John's voice finally cut in.

Heather sighed. Sometimes the connection wasn't all that clear, leaving them to resort to shouting to make themselves heard. Or giving up altogether and trying again in the hope of a better one.

"Hi, John, it's Heather. Is Barbara there?"

"Oh, Heather, good to hear from you. How are you going, love? Couldn't sleep, eh?"

She exhaled slowly and smiled at the recognition in his voice. "No, unfortunately, but I thought a chat with your lovely wife might do the trick." While Heather made light of it, she trusted John, knowing he was supportive of Barbara and the time she gave up for her. He knew how much it meant for them both.

"Ah, a word or two with my wife has been known to put anyone to sleep." He paused for effect before adding, "But not tonight, Heather, my dear, as she's not at home."

Heather's mouth dropped. "Oh, okay, thanks, John, I'll call another day."

"It won't do you any good. She's packed up and gone away."

"Away!" she gasped, puzzled by his cheery revelation. "She said nothing about going away. Is everything alright? Is someone ill or...?" Had she missed something in their last few conversations? Surely, she wasn't so preoccupied with all her woes that she'd missed something important happening in Barbara's life. Was her mum ill or someone else in her extended family? Had something happened to Fraser? Had he been in an accident or...?

"No, no, nothing like that. I guess you'll find out soon enough, so I'll tell you. She's on her way to see you. Left from London yesterday. She should land in Perth around noon, your time tomorrow. No, wait. Let me get my days right, noon today for you."

"She's what?" Heather struggled to make sense of what John was saying. How could she be arriving today? "Oh, no. She can't do that. She mustn't do that. Come all this way. No."

"Ah, Heather, love. It'll be alright. She thought you would say that, which is why she didn't tell you. She's on her way. Can't turn back now, can she?"

"Oh, John, I don't know what to say. And what about you— letting her go like that? I wish you'd asked me first. What can she do? What can we—I do? We can't do more than we are doing. If the police can't, we certainly can't. I just have to sit and wait—and hope. That's all I have left. Hope that they will find her..." She swiped away the tear trickling down her cheek.

"Listen, Heather. She realised all that you're saying. We discussed it over and over. She felt it was the right thing to do, and I fully agree. You have Stephen and Meg and your friends, but Barb has gone through this with Katie. She can't find Anna for you as she couldn't find Katie, but she can be there for you. That's what she wants, to be there for you for however long it takes. Now one more thing and I'll let you try to get some rest. You don't need to worry about her flight details or anything. Stephen knows all about it. He's going to pick her up and bring her to your house."

"Stephen!" Her stomach fluttered. Her son knew about this, and he hadn't let on. She clenched her teeth and then sighed. A sudden wave of utter weariness swept over her. She needed to get to bed desperately. Didn't want to think about any of it for a moment longer. She confirmed the details with John and just remembered to thank him before hanging up.

Long talks with Barbara over the phone might be one thing, but having her here for who knows how long? She wasn't sure that was such a good idea. For one thing, Barbara didn't share her beliefs. She had grown more cynical that a caring God even existed as the days of Katie's disappearance turned into years. Heather tried to talk to her about the underlying hope and peace in her life despite all this, but it seemed to fall on deaf ears. She sat on the edge of the bed, her mind whirling with too many scenarios, then slid between the sheets.

Guttural sounds from a distraught patient poked at Anna's consciousness. Someone needed her. It was her responsibility. Why hadn't they pushed their emergency buzzer for a nurse? She would go, but it was impossible; her head was stuck, caught in some kind of cloth. Bandages? Sheets?

Another groan. She forced grit-encrusted eyelids apart. She was the one who needed help, the one groaning. As she tugged the smothering cloths away from her face and neck, grains of black sand caught between her fingers came into focus. Images of the lagoon flooded back. The small of her back clenched and she cringed. She peered over her shoulder at the door, shut tight to the outside world, then at the stark, buffed walls with their dull, distorted view of her confinement. Her sorry, isolated, impossible world.

She inched to the edge of the bed, gritted her teeth, and eased herself upright. Her knees shook and gave way as she attempted to stand. She sagged back onto the bed, the accompanying groan sounding odd. More like a growl, as if she was one of those antique teddy bears that growled when you squeezed them. She didn't feel like a teddy bear—although being stuffed with cotton wool drew a parallel with the current state of her head. Her stomach cramped as she rolled her neck from side to side. Her entire body ached from the inside out, and muscles she didn't know she had were stiff and sore. As if she had run a marathon and then finished it with the Rottnest Island swim.

Tears threatened, but she refused to cry, sucked in a slow breath, counted to five and let it out again. She stared down at the salt lines staining her top and shorts, at the stiff folds where the cloth had compressed underneath her. Suddenly, the black beach sand and dried salt made its presence felt all over her body and in every orifice imaginable—she ran her tongue over her teeth and gums—including her mouth. The salty, chemical taste almost made her gag. She needed a hot bath, to rid herself of the grime and, with any luck, it would soothe away the aches—as long as her legs cooperated.

She ran the bath and edged herself in, grimacing as the water bit into the raw skin on her knees and hands. The doors to the wall screen opened. She scowled as one of the shows started. She had seen it only once before and had delighted in the scenes of gorgeous beaches, the camera tracking the wind along cliff tops and craggy outcrops to the next golden bay, before it paused to focus on waves crashing onto the shore. She had imagined herself there. Ready to dive into the surf after a run along the beach.

But now, what was this? A deliberate tactic to rub in her 'lesson' at the lagoon? She sighed and squeezed her eyes shut, sinking as far down into the water as possible. But it was no use. Closing her eyes checked the visual, but she couldn't stop her ears to the sounds of waves crashing and the music reverberating around the room. She cut her soak short and dried herself, for once thankful that the video stopped automatically when she emerged from the tub.

As she walked through the doorway, towelling her hair dry, she froze. The perfectly made-up room greeted her. Not a single grain of sand in sight. As if nothing out of the ordinary had happened.

"You bastards." She threw her towel down and yanked the bedclothes off the bed. "Who do you think you are? You can't do this. You can't keep me here. You CANNOT. I am NOT..."

She snatched up a pillow and dashed it against the bed again and again before tossing it across the room. Raging through both rooms, she tore the contents out of drawers and cupboards. She plucked a spoon from the meal tray left on the desk, whirled around and jabbed at the faint edges outlining the outer door. As it splintered, she repeated the exercise with the remaining bamboo utensils, launching each one across the room as it broke. She picked a bread roll off the tray and aimed it at the wall screen, watching it bounce off, crumbs spraying across the desk.

About to launch a plate of skilfully arranged smoked salmon and cheese morsels at the screen, she stopped short, hot tears coursing down her cheeks, her breath coming in gulps. The smoky tanginess of the wafer-thin slices of fish and the salty, rich aroma of golden cubes of cheese caught her nostrils. It was enough. She placed the plate carefully back onto its tray, inched away and slid down the wall, pulling her limbs in tight and rocking backwards and forwards.

They could keep her here and control her every move with whatever that thing was, implanted in her spine. She had no choice in when and where she could go and for how long. And she COULD. DO. NOTHING. ABOUT. IT. NOT A THING. She was POWERLESS.

Time stood still. It was as if she was looking down at herself, curled up on the floor. At the girl in the room—at Annalee, staring wide-eyed into the incomprehensible void of the days and weeks to come.

29

*L*ucy's phone buzzed. "Jamie?" Her heart leapt off the starting block and took off without her as she waited, not trusting herself to say another word. What did he want?

"Hi, Lucy. Can we meet up? I'm flying out tomorrow and would like to touch base with you before I go."

"Tomorrow? Meet up?" Words wouldn't come. The capacity to create full sentences was gone. She stood, opening and closing her mouth like a goldfish. What the—? And did he say touch base? She loathed that term. She glared down at the phone. Say something, Lucy. Speak.

"Sorry, Jamie, I'm not at home. I'm staying with my aunt for a while. You heard about the break-in?" Did he know about the break-in? Of course he did. He was there, wasn't he?

"Yes—about that. The police came around and asked me—." He paused.

She waited, hearing his even breaths clear on the line.

"Anyway, that's one thing I wanted to talk about. And just catch up generally… See how you're travelling before I go."

"Um, no. I mean, it's tricky." Definitely, no. He couldn't come to her aunt and uncle's place. The twins' curiosity knew no bounds, and there would be nowhere to talk uninterrupted. And besides, he was the last person she wanted to have a conversation with right now, even if it was about Anna's disappearance. She had nothing new to disclose. Any developments were all over the TV before she got to hear about them, and sadly, there had been precious few of those of late.

She heard the catch in his breath and instantly regretted her negativity. He was Anna's boyfriend, after all, and had appeared besotted with her from the minute they met. Up to her disappearance, Lucy believed he was Mr Right for Anna.

How rapidly that had changed, along with her feelings for him. She felt the colour rise in her cheeks and bit her lip. Then, thinking she had seen his car near her house on the night of the break-in. It may well have been another car, a similar make and colour, and it was an atrocious night. Surely it was inconceivable that he had anything to do with it, and now he wanted to explain.

To hear him out was the least she could do.

"Let me think. I finish work at seven tonight. I could meet you at, say, eight, for coffee somewhere."

"What about dinner? Say—seven-thirty?" His tone sounded natural enough.

What was wrong with two friends meeting for dinner to catch up, the night before one of them flew out for a month's hard slog on an oil rig? No, there was a whole lot of difference between the intimacy of a dinner together and a cappuccino. She narrowed her eyes —and the circumstances were far from ordinary.

"Thanks for the offer, but I have something to do on the way home. It'll be a push for me to get there before eight."

He hesitated before he said, "No worries." Despite the pause, Lucy still detected no tension in his voice.

"What say we meet in the car park behind the Oxford Street strip in Leederville? There's a range of coffee shops and restaurants along there. You can change your mind about dinner then, if you like. The offer's still open."

Lucy grimaced at her phone. "Sure, I'll see you then." She scowled at the squeak in her voice, and cleared her throat.

While he seemed to be taking the conversation in his stride, she sure wasn't. And she'd make sure she ate more than the obligatory apple on her afternoon break, so she wasn't hungry enough to change her mind about dinner. Her planned stop at the Joondanna house to check for mail didn't really justify her delay. She dropped by every two or three days, and another one wouldn't hurt. But right now it was a handy excuse to avoid the idea of a dinner date. Plus, she could grab a quick shower after her long day at the hospital. She should be able to dig something out to wear—half of her wardrobe was still there.

The afternoon dragged, despite the busyness in the wards, Lucy having to release the tension building in her muscles more than once as the hours ticked by. Why did he want to see her? Would he confront her about informing the police of her suspicions? Why did she do that, anyway? Her memory of the car was even hazier now. Her cheeks burned at the thought. It seemed the right thing to do then, but maybe she should have thought it through, even rung and asked him. No—what if it was him? She really didn't want to see him, not confident at masking her emotions, and she hated deceit.

There was still time to phone and cancel. Sorry, Jamie, I'm suffering from an attack of not-wanting-to-see-you-itis. Or send a text? No, that wouldn't be appropriate when she'd agreed to meet up.

Her stomach turning somersaults, she drew into the car park and, grateful it was well lit, headed for a bay close to one of the overhead lights. She checked her watch. Seven minutes to go. Her fingers reaching to turn off the engine, she hesitated. There was still time to make an escape. "Courage, Lucy." She sighed into the rear-vision mirror, "What are you so afraid of?" then turned the key and pulled on the handbrake. Eyeing the wildly swaying treetops silhouetted against the dark night sky, she stayed in the car. The cold southerly wind had intensified.

It had felt good to return to the house tonight. With no trace of the break-in left, the house was warm and welcoming, despite its unlived-in status. She should move back in soon. Until tonight, she knew she had avoided thinking about it.

She couldn't stay at her aunt's indefinitely, not wanting to take their hospitality for granted. They hadn't suggested she pay board, yet, but if they did, she couldn't afford both. Now that Anna was gone, she was paying the full rent herself and that was a stretch, but what were the options? Move out and get a one-bedroom flat or small unit for herself. But Lucy couldn't bear the thought of Anna returning with nowhere to go, all her stuff packed up and stored away. Or she could try to get someone else to share with her, but when Anna came back, what then?

Her watch showed five past eight. Either Jamie was late or…? She scanned the rear-view and side mirrors. She had an excellent view of most of the car park, but perhaps he was standing around the corner out of the wind. Zipping her jacket, she slipped out of the car and headed that way. A backward glance confirmed the car doors locking as she depressed the button. She hesitated at the intersection. No one in sight, and if she walked the block to the street front, she might miss him.

Her phone pinged a message:

'Hi Lucy. So sorry I have to cancel tonight. Something unavoidable came up. Jamie.'

30

The nightmare returned with the dark. She was falling, face down, the blood flooding to her head. Falling, falling through the air in the darkness, eyes searching desperately for the ground.

She woke drenched with sweat, heart pounding, her muscles tensed against the impact. She pressed back against the headboard, its solid surface offering little solace in the engulfing blackness. The air in the room was cold and clammy, nightmare beings reaching towards her, teasing the goosebumps on her arms and legs. Malevolent fingers glided over her shoulders and around her waist. The small of her back tingled.

It was only the sweat cooling her skin. That was all. Gulping in lungfuls of air, she shrank down into the bed, willing the excruciating punishment she'd experienced earlier that day not to return.

For the first time in her life, she was alone—utterly and desperately alone; and not an 'I like to be alone' time, or the 'I don't mind my own company' time she valued when the clamour of life got too much. She could opt in and out of those, comfortably able to join in again whenever she wanted. Echoes of 'you are never alone'—from Lucy, her mother and voices from the past—surrounded her. She reached her arm upward in the dark, fingers pointing at the ceiling.

How to start? A half-remembered conversation with her father drifted in. She'd asked him how to pray, not thinking she was doing it right, and she did so want to get things right back then. What was new? She grimaced. But he sat beside her and took both of her hands in his, folding her fingers into his firm hands as he spoke.

"Just speak to God as you would to anyone. To your mum or me. No special formula will make God listen to you more or less. He doesn't expect big fancy prayers, nor lengthy ones. Normal speech is fine. Ask what you want. Say what you feel. God is big enough for all of your questions and problems."

Simple and clear. Then why was it so tough to do? She shoved down all the 'buts' demanding to interrupt—all the times when she had prayed, and nothing had happened, or nothing that she wanted—and concentrated on her father's words again. They were as distinct to her now as when he said them.

Was it possible? What did she have to lose? She took a slow, deep breath.

"Father God, if you are there, if you care for me, can you help me? I'm not sure how much of this I can take. I'm not sure if I can do it on my own. I need someone. I need you." She waited as the seconds and then the minutes ticked by until, almost imperceptibly at first, something shifted. Her limbs started to warm, her muscles relaxing as the tension melted away. The pleasant warmth gradually replaced the icy dread in her bones from the nightmare.

It was enough. She slept.

<hr>

The water jug was empty. It was never empty, but the image woke her.

She licked dry lips and rolled onto her side, wincing as tight and aching muscles brought back yesterday's trial. The room pitch black, she slipped out of bed and, with one hand on the wall, traced her way to the couch. She slowed, avoided a collision with its arm and eased down, patting the table until her fingers discovered the jug and the tumbler. The jug was relatively light, but thankfully not empty as in the dream, and with one hand encircling the top of the glass she poured in the jug's contents and took a sip.

Her stomach rumbled, and she reached for the fruit bowl. It wasn't there.

It was in place when she went to bed, wasn't it? She pictured the banana and nashi pear in situ after dinner the night before. The fruit bowl was always on the table, and she always left at least one piece of fruit for the morning. Whether or not she ate it, it was there until they restocked the bowl when she was at the gym.

She settled back into the couch. But why was she hungry and so very wide awake? She didn't usually go in for midnight snacks and, while yesterday had been an exceptionally different day, it wasn't like her or her stomach to react this way. There was nothing for it but to go back to bed and wait for morning. Yet the missing fruit bowl niggled.

Something was wrong. It was dark, she was hungry, the fruit bowl had disappeared.

It should be light. That was it. She was sure it was daytime, or what signified as daytime in this underground bunker. Her heart sped up a notch. She felt for the glass and raised it to her lips.

Wait. If it was daytime and they were keeping her in the dark, and without food—

She had to find out.

Water gushed into the basin then slowed to a dribble before stopping altogether. The promising spurt of water had duped her into complacency, and she only cupped her hand under the basin tap the second before the flow stopped.

"Damn." She swallowed the meagre mouthful and sagged forward, her forehead resting on the cool of the mirror. Not a gleam of light reflected at her through the glass; only its soft-polished surface spoke of its substance. She turned and edged forward towards the bathtub before stopping and made her way back to the couch for the tumbler.

This time, she caught the water left in the bathtub spout—which still didn't fill her glass, but it was better than nothing.

No water or food. Was this further punishment for her disobedience at the beach yesterday? As if the torture from that 'thing' wasn't enough. Now she was to be held in the dark, with no food and water. And for how long?

Her lips tightened as she clutched the tap. She could do this. It would be okay. She had water in the glass; an occasional sip would see her through. They couldn't keep it up for too long. Could they? Her stomach growled its disapproval.

31

Tears flowing freely, Heather welcomed her cousin Barbara at the door with a hug. Stephen hovered behind, grinning broadly. Heather had spent the previous hour pacing to and from the window overlooking the driveway, but missed the moment because Sparky demanded her attention in the back garden. He'd spotted the cat next door on a tree branch, and his non-stop barks of protest had drawn her there to sort him out.

Steve had texted from the airport to say the plane had landed, but something had delayed the luggage removal and he had to wait. Not one to send progress reports every few minutes, Stephen kept Heather guessing after his initial text. She'd just had to wait it out, her tension rising with every passing minute.

As she hugged Barbara in the doorway, she shot him an 'I'll deal with you later' look through her teary eyes. He flashed back a grin and shrugged his shoulders before returning to the car to retrieve Barbara's suitcases.

Steve's, "Where do you want these, Mum?" followed by rapid-fire, "Down, Sparky! Look out, you'll get squished," brought a smile to Heather's lips. Sparky was making up for his neglect of policing the front door by bowling into the legs of one of his favourite people. He jumped up and down, sniffing at Steve to make sure it was him, before transferring his attention to the suitcases covered in glorious aromas from exotic places.

"In your old room, please, Steve love," she called out before turning to Barbara. "It's the guest room now. Funny how it's always still Stephen's room or Annal—" She swallowed down the rising lump in her throat and looked away.

"It's okay, you need to let it out, to talk about her like that. Never let go of all that she is, all that she will be, despite what others may put into your mind," Barbara whispered and drew her into another hug. "Come on, let's make a cuppa, I've been sitting down for so long I need to move my legs for a while."

And with that, Heather led the way, both of them soon engaged in the intricacies of tea making.

Heather laid out the sandwiches she'd made earlier, not knowing if Barbara would be hungry after her flight. It had given her something to do to take her mind off the imminent arrival, and she guessed, rightly, that Stephen wouldn't have had lunch with the plane due in close to noon.

"Can you spare time to stay and eat with us, Stephen? Or do you have to get back to the surgery?" Heather noticed the lines deepening around his eyes and the grey hairs appearing on his temples. He looked a little tired, too, or perhaps a little tense? Was it because of Annalee or the busyness of his dental practice and family life? It would be nice if he could stay.

"Not a problem, Mum. I've taken the afternoon off. And I can't go past your curried egg sandwiches." He chuckled as he lifted one to his nose, took a deep sniff, then squashed the delicate triangle into his mouth.

Lunch was light; their conversation to match. Heather was grateful for that, but her eyes kept returning to her son's face. There was a pinched look around his eyes and mouth—and the way he teased the ends of his thumbnails. She couldn't recall the last time she had spent time alone with him. They met up for dinner at least once a week, but with Meg and the children. Not a time for in-depth conversations; plus, he was so like his father in that respect, playing his cards close to his chest.

He had been through a lot, losing his father, having babies, busy at work, and now——. She dug her fingernails into her palm. Right now she wanted to focus on him, and Barbara, not herself. It would be a welcome distraction from the negative thoughts constantly filling her head. She made a mental note to see him on his own, and soon, to find out how he was truly feeling.

32

Annalee had no way of knowing how long the dark lasted, only that it was interminable, the minutes ticking silently away into hours. The irony of that was not lost—if only something were ticking. Any sound beyond herself, however irritating, would have been welcome. The dead silence and the black air entombing her lay heavy on her chest, on her face. It pressed against her mouth and nose, her heartbeats soughing faintly in her ears like ancient dried grasses stirred by a desultory easterly wind.

It seemed as if days had passed since that last drop of water left her tumbler. One day, two? One night, two? Ten hours, twenty—more? She pressed her eyelids together once, twice, three times, but the tears wouldn't come. There were none left to moisten the dryness. She was hot and thirsty, yet, surprisingly, no longer hungry. Despite the cramping pains gnawing at her abdomen, the urgent need for water had long ago transcended the desire for food.

As the water dried up and disappeared, she'd taken to chewing on the corner of her cotton pillowcase to stimulate saliva, until her jaw ached and she had to stop. Hot shallow breaths hissed their way between cracked and tender lips. Her swollen lump-of-meat tongue, no longer capable of moistening anything, rested heavily at the back of her teeth. She lay motionless, save for the occasional twitch from some desperate muscle or sinew protesting its plight. Her sunken eyes—molten orbs heavy in her skull, covered with leaden eyelid blankets—could not distinguish between the inner and outer darkness.

"Lucy? Oh, Lucy. Where have you been?" She reached out as the fragrance of her friend teased her nostrils.

"It's okay, I'm here now." Lucy sat beside her on the bed and laid a cool palm on her cheek.

"Why is it still dark, Luce? I can't see you." Anna had so many questions to ask, but her swollen lips and dry tongue stumbled over the words. It didn't matter. At least she was here. It would be alright now. Lucy would help her. They were a wonderful team. Two was better than one. Two was—

"Lucy? Water. I… I need water."

"Shh, it will be alright. Soon. Soon you can have water." Lucy's fingers brushed her lips and teased the hair away from her face and neck, arranging it carefully around her head on the pillow.

"Lucy, how is Mum? Have you seen my mum? She must be so worried. I can't… And Jamie?"

"Shh, don't talk. Good news, Jamie is here too. We came together. We came to take you home."

"Jamie? Jamie…" Her fingers clutched at the bedclothes.

"No, it's Mick. Micky is here." Lucy's sweet brother. He was the one; he would save her. Like he did that time in Albany when she and Lucy almost got swept off a rock by a king wave. Despite her strength she had been no match for the unexpected drenching and the power of the wave as it sucked back into the sea, gathering their fishing rods and bait buckets with it. She felt his strong grip now as he pulled her and Lucy back to safety, one hand on her wrist, the other on Lucy's. Safe. Back from the darkness.

"Micky."

"Jamie."

It no longer mattered. He no longer…

She floated away from the heat, the dryness, the twitching in her body. Lifted, becoming lost—to herself and what was real in the room: her breathing, her slow, steady heartbeats, the bed, the people she loved. Lucy, Jamie, Mum, Dad, Mick. They were there.

Not there.

There.

Watching her go—sad faces illuminating the dark. Upturned faces watching her drift in her black velvet cocoon. Weightless. A slow giggle floated beside her. Was it from her mouth, or Lucy's? It didn't matter.

Peaceful, this floating, her mind letting go of the minutiae of life. Letting go of the myriads of thoughts jostling for attention every nanosecond of a day. Letting go of loves. Perfect freedom. Retreating, fading away from sorrow, wickedness and worries. Loves.

Others spoke of moving towards light in the moments before death. It wasn't true. The dark called. She simply had to let go. Give herself to the peace. The darkness beckoned—calling, crying; carrying her away.

33

Annalee slicked back her hair and wiped the dripping water from her face. The swim had been exhilarating; it was the first day she'd had the strength to do it, and the third time they'd let her out since—that night.

The first time had been a struggle, despite three days having passed since the lights came on and the water jug sat full on the table. Even the trek down to the lagoon had been an effort. She arrived on the bottom step hot and panting, the idea of a swim unthinkable. It was all she could manage to dip a toe in before retreating to the step where she sat in the shade, glad when the chimes sounded out. The second time, two days later, showed an improvement, but she still hadn't gone in past her knees.

She sat cross-legged, the smooth black rock warm against her back, and peered across the lagoon. Energised, yet still panting from the laps she'd swum, her eyes combed the waterline at the base of the rocks, locking on to the sea spray pumping its thin misty stream through that elusive fissure. The ocean, unreachable today as it had been that first torturous day.

She shuddered and dropped her eyes to the rock pool. She didn't want to recall the agonising pain inflicted on her, or its aftermath, but neither did she want to forget. It was still raw but her body was already downplaying the effects. Which was a positive thing, wasn't it? The body's unique capacity to bounce back given time, care and rest. And she had an abundance of that looming before her—as long as she toed the line.

Her skin tightened as it dried, nerve endings twitching a reminder of what over-stimulation did when someone else had the power to control your body. She sighed and squeezed her eyes shut.

Back to the rock pool—focus on the pond life instead of her own 'pond' life—the life of isolation and confinement imposed by her captors. While the creatures in the pool had their boundaries, they, at least, had each other. They had a community, which, from where she sat, appeared content and quiet, although some larger crabs looked a little battle-weary with nicks in their shells, and one or two missed an entire limb. Perhaps not such a safe place, after all. Her eyes flicked around the cove. Was anywhere safe in this life?

"Enough negativity, Annalee." She pursed her lips together, before forcing a smile at the tiny crabs' antics as she disturbed them by gently swirling her fingers around the top of the pool.

"What's on the schedule for today, Mr B?" She'd called the largest of the tiny crabs Mr B, for Mr Big, or perhaps Mr Boss. But he didn't respond, not that she wanted him to; she valued her sanity. However, she needed to use her voice, and if her mum's favourite movie star, Tom Hanks, could talk to a volleyball for four years when stranded on an island then she could talk to a pond full of crabs. At least they were alive.

"I know it was only a movie, but I don't want to be here for four months, let alone four years." She plucked a tiny, fingernail-shaped shell from the edge of the pool, turned it over and set it adrift on the water, watching it bob up and down as it floated to the centre. The crabs didn't respond. They grew excited when she dipped her fingers or toes in but seemed to know when the object sailing overhead was inanimate, although to be fair if she found a fragment of seaweed in the lagoon and introduced that it was as if all their Christmases had come at once. The entire community scuttled out to pick and prod and explore the prize.

"No seaweed today, I hope you don't mind. The bigger pond was delightful, though. I had a fabulous swim. Maybe you should all try it sometime. Expand your world, see things from another perspective." Her eyes wandered to the far side of the lagoon, and she frowned. She had to stay positive, but it was a battle.

For heaven's sake, she was chatting to crabs. Her 'can do' attitude had taken a king hit, and her other cautious attempts at testing the boundaries had come to nothing. Whenever she approached a barrier, they were either inaccessible, or threatening tingles started in her fingers and then her spine, sending her hastily in the opposite direction. Today she'd tried to approach the sea spray from the surface, resulting in tingles and a speedy retreat. Then from a deep dive and underwater trajectory, with almost the same result. That time, only her fingers felt the electricity, and she turned straight away.

Despite its serenity and beauty, this little cove and the tropical paradise behind her may as well be surrounded by five-metre high steel-grey bars topped with razor-wire. They had every base covered. Not only could they control her with the implant but, somehow, there were invisible electrified boundaries in areas she was obviously forbidden to go.

She focused on the small pile of shells she'd collected and started arranging and rearranging them in various shapes. If there was no way to escape from the cove, then her other alternatives were to find a way through the tunnels inside somehow, or up and over the mountain. She leant forward, twisted her neck and flicked her eyes up to the summit just visible from her position behind the rock. Inside seemed out of the question; there were likely cameras everywhere. How else did they know if she was going the right way down a tunnel, or entering the lift and not walking past it?

There must be cameras out here too, although she'd never spotted any, but it was worth a try. But then, if she reached the top what would she find? She supposed this was an island, but it might also be an isolated spot on a greater landmass. If so, she might find someone to help her. If not, if it was an island, the other side could be as unoccupied as this side. But all that setup inside the mountain: the floors, the lifts, the gym, her 'suite', it wasn't just cobbled together. It took serious money to produce and maintain all that.

She sighed. But. But. But. Too many buts. But—a smile played around the corners of her mouth—she had to try something.

The chimes rang out, startling her. Would she ever get used to that sound? She pushed up to her feet and moved into the open and faced the ocean once more, waited for two sequences of tones to finish then trudged up the beach. As she neared the tree-line, she turned again, her eyes drawn to the jagged outline of rocks stark against the azure-blue sky, before continuing her steady-paced walk along the pathway and into the mountainside.

34

"Mick, oh Micky, are you busy?" Lucy sat back on the couch and grabbed her wrist, steadying the phone at her ear. The tremble in her hands that seemed to dog her lately had returned. She bit her lip, eyeing the darkness through the window across the room. Thin, twiggy branches encouraged by the wind scratched against the metal frames. She'd meant to close the drapes earlier.

Perhaps coming back to an empty house wasn't such a good idea after all. She was jumpy. Every noise had her on edge. Her urge to check and recheck everything was locked was driving her crazy.

"Me, no. Always here for you, Luce. What's up?" Her big brother's calm—always calm and mellow voice had the desired effect, instantly lowering the tension in her body.

"I just needed a friendly voice to tell me the world is still a safe place." She hugged a cushion to her chest and stretched her legs across the couch as she pictured Mick in their family home in Albany. The home where her mum and dad and little sister, Vicky, and Mick still lived. Happily. Safely. No pressure. No fears. "It's so quiet without Anna. I'm not sure if I can stay here on my own." She sighed, releasing her grip on the cushion, and stretched each finger in turn. Thankfully, the tremor had disappeared.

"Talk me through it, Luce. That might help. Always good to share the load."

She and Mick had been close growing up. Although he and Troy, the eldest of the four, teased her mercilessly at times, he hadn't been the kind of big brother who thought his little sister was a constant pain and to be avoided at all costs. He often let her tag along with him and his friends at weekends or during school holidays. And when Troy moved up to Perth to go to university, they had grown even closer.

"I'm not sure what to do. Keep this place going for when Anna comes back, or…?" She blinked back threatening tears.

"Or nothing, Luce. Sorry to butt in, but I think you know that's a given."

"I do." She tried on a watery smile. He knew her so well, and despite his laid-back attitude to life, he was no dummy. He'd given voice to the confirmation she was seeking. "I've worked through the alternatives, and it's the only logical solution. But…"

"But?"

"It's hard, really hard, Mick. I think it was the break-in. I mean, Anna and I were often on different shifts, and I never had a problem staying here by myself then. Since I moved back in, I've been jumping at any little noise and waking up half a dozen times a night." She must get up and close the drapes, imagining eyes peering through the bushes, watching her every move. The tap, tap, tapping on the window… not the wind harassing a wayward branch, but the 'someone' shifting his weight as he tried to get a better view. She shuddered and clung to the comfort of her brother's love and care for her conveyed through his steady tone.

"That's understandable. None of us has experienced that before."

True. Though there was crime in Albany, their family home had never experienced a break-in. It was only in the last ten years or so that people even locked their doors. Lucy stifled a yawn.

"You'd have to be some kind of freak if it didn't affect you. No one likes the thought of someone pawing through their stuff."

"Don't remind me. I washed our clothes three times before I could face wearing anything. Luckily, Amy leant me a couple of outfits, and it's cold, so a thick jumper can hide a lot." Her friend,

Amy, was two sizes bigger than Lucy and half a head shorter. Lucy didn't go for designer labels but with Amy still at university, her clothes budget was definitely op-shop chic.

"*Our* clothes?"

"I had to do Anna's as well. What was I supposed to do? Leave them in a heap on the floor, or give them to Mrs T to wash?"

"Mm. Anything back from the police?"

Lucy had told her mum, but maybe the news hadn't filtered through. "Only that they think it was kids."

"Have you seen anything of the boyfriend?"

Where had that come from? "What boyfriend? Why would I?" Her stomach flipped. That had come out too fast, her voice too high and squeaky. Maybe he wouldn't notice.

"Lucy?"

Damn. He'd noticed. His choice of 'Lucy' confirmed it. Her family, mostly her mother, only used that name when she had some explaining to do. She tried a little deflecting.

"Sorry, big gust of wind outside, blew a pot over on the patio. Made me jump." She sucked in a breath, holding the phone away from her face. "Jamie. No, I haven't seen him for ages." That was true, at least, since his no-show for coffee last week. "And I think he's away offshore at the moment. I call him if I have any news. When he's here, I mean. I don't call him when he's away."

She stopped. Over-explaining wasn't her style, and Micky was well aware of that. If she kept going, he would get suspicious. Not that there was any reason for him to be suspicious. She frowned.

"Anyway, back to you. You need someone with you, even if only for a short time."

"Yes, but someone who wouldn't mind moving out when Anna comes back." Lucy refused to consider that Anna wouldn't be back, hugging the cushion tight again. "I still can't believe it. Every time I walk past her room, I expect to see her in there or a note left for me or... Then, after the break-in, I had to pack it all up. It seemed like a good time... to... put it in her room and close the door. But..."

"But?"

She could see the quizzical look on Mick's face. That way he held his head on one side, his left eye narrowed.

"But it's been almost seven weeks, and now it's all dying down. It's as if everybody is forgetting Anna and getting on with their lives. I don't know what to do. Where can she be? I can't bear to think that she's… that she…"

"Don't even think it, Luce. She is going to be found. We have to keep believing that. But in the meantime, who's supporting you?"

"Well… realistically, there's many people I can talk to. The guys at Impact group, and Amy will come over any time, but she's full-on with her studies. Then churchies—a few go out of their way to catch up with me, phone me and so on. Even the hospital chaplain has been great, came to find me a couple of days after… We've had some good chats, but she's busy with the patients and their parents." Lucy sat up and swung her legs to the floor, her eyes fixed on the window.

"And I'm no fun to be around. I keep zoning out of conversations, going into the messy space in my mind, the 'Anna, where are you?' questions filling my brain…"

"Ah, Luce, you can't do that…"

"Don't I know it, Mick; it's eating me up. I'm working on it, believe me. Giving it all to God. I know I should be, and I am to a certain extent, but then it crowds back in. I'm playing music, listening to podcasts, and praying, praying, praying. Anything to stop the questions and the solutions I don't want to know. Anyway, I'm sorry I've chewed your ear off, rambling on. I'll let you get to bed. Thanks for being there for me, Micky. Love you, big brother."

"Wait, wait. Apart from the platitudes of that's what big brothers are for and all that. I've got an idea."

"Oh, no! A lightbulb moment. How bright?" Lucy chuckled at the familiar one-liner their grandfather introduced into family lore. She and her siblings had taken it up with delight and used it on each other for as long as she could remember.

"Yeah, yeah, I know. No, seriously, I'll come up and stay with you. If you'll have me?"

"Have you? I'd love to have you, but what about your job? And youth group?"

"Nah, it'll be fine. Just give me a few days to sort it and then I'll be there. It's quietish at work. They owe me some time off anyway, and youth group… the other leaders can manage there. It'll only be for a couple of weeks. She'll be back by then. A holiday in the big city. I can handle that. I think."

"Oh Mick, it would be great if you could, but you hate it here."

"Luce, no sacrifice is too great for you—and Anna, of course. Besides, there's something I want to look into. Something I've been putting off for some time."

35

There was a thin line of tension that began every time Annalee woke up. It thickened and formed dark bands around her chest as the door slipped open to invite her to the gym. Each morning, she fought against it and scolded herself for her lack of self-control. She'd thought herself mentally more robust and ready to do battle against their control, even if they knew nothing about her internal struggle.

As each day passed, her confidence grew that the door would open today and she could escape the room for an hour, but the other —the freedom to go outside—wasn't an everyday occurrence. Sometimes two or three days passed before the wall opened up and paradise swarmed in to whisk her away. By the time she was twenty minutes into a gym session, she was fit to explode with anticipation. Would it or wouldn't it?

Annalee set her cup down and eyed the empty breakfast tray. She had a good while before her gym time. What to do first? A little reading, some stretches and skipping, a shower or perhaps a bath? She lifted an eyebrow. If she had a quick shower after skipping, it would only leave more time to kill. If she took a bath instead, she could make it last almost until it was time to leave. She liked to mix it up. It helped break the monotony. The humdrum. The routine.

She wanted to think it distracted her from the building tension, but she knew it didn't. A yawn threatened, and she picked up her book, found the page she was up to, but soon lowered it again.

Going outside was her lifeline to get through the rest of her existence here. Before that first opening, she would have said it was the gym sessions that got her through. But the freedom to wander the gardens, explore the pathways between the majestic trees, and swim in the lagoon was living. There was life all around to wonder at and discover. A Garden of Eden but, like the original, it came complete with its version of an evil serpent.

She grimaced and squeezed her eyes together. No, her time on the outside was her canvas to fill with beauty and treasured experiences, and with no way to record anything, her mind was her journal. Each time the gym wall didn't open, it was like a physical blow, not that she let it show. She hoped. She didn't want to give them the satisfaction, didn't want them to see her as weak and afraid, despite that being exactly how she felt.

Her hopes of finding a way up the mountain the previous week had been dashed when the force field kicked in. She'd tried to gain a foothold in the dense bank of vegetation along from the building but, each time she reached out, her fingers tingled and she had to back off. The terrain there was a lot steeper and wilder than the slope below, but she had climbed worse in the past, and the vegetation, low tree branches and protruding roots would provide good foot- and hand-holds. If only she could get past her controller.

A cursory examination of the other end of the building, which was tucked tightly beneath a steep rocky outcrop, had proved equally disappointing. It was hard to see where the construction ended and the solid rock began. Only the hardiest of climbers with all the right gear could make any progress there. And that wasn't her, with her bare feet and light cotton clothes. To escape that way was out of the question.

The idea of finding her way through the mountain seemed equally impossible. Nothing was ever out of place. There was never an open door, a green light where a red one should be or even a light on the blink. Nothing to suggest the slightest lapse in their observation of where she was at all times. Besides, there were no handles on any doors along the tunnels. She'd pushed against several of them at random, but they wouldn't budge. If she took more than two steps into a red-lit zone, the buzz started in her spine.

Another yawn. She eyed the skipping rope and put the book on the table. Her eyelids were so heavy; she could hardly keep them open. A brisk bout of skipping on the spot might help. She always brought a rope back from the gym. They didn't like her having one in the room and would take it out when she was absent. There wasn't much she could control, but the cat-and-mouse game with the skipping rope amused her. It was irritating when she forgot, but that only happened the first few times when the outside wall opened. Now she would pick one up as soon as she got into the gym and place it on that side of the room, ready to scoop up on her way out. Why they didn't leave it in her room, she couldn't fathom. Did they think she was going to hang herself or tie someone up? If only there was someone to try that theory out on.

She ran her fingers through her hair, linked both hands at the back of her neck and pushed her head back hard into them before leaning forward and rotating her shoulders forward and then backward. She stifled another yawn and reached for her book. No skipping; her legs felt leaden and uncooperative. Maybe a chapter of the book first. She settled back into the couch cushions, but the words blurred on the page. The book slid from her grasp and slipped to the floor. She reached forward, trying to push herself up, but nothing would cooperate, and she slumped back again.

A delicious warm feeling rose from the pit of her stomach, spread across her chest and neck and heated her face. A cuddly warm cottonwool blanket smothering her thoughts, her need to move, to escape. The sensation reminded her of something. What was it? What did she have to do? Where could she go? The walls in the room were fading red now, black clouds hovered at the edges. Blood rhythmically pulsing through her ears slowed and quietened. The faint swish as the door to the corridor opened, a distant sound in her memory.

36

"What about we try this fish recipe tonight?" Barbara was leafing through one of Heather's cookbooks as they finished their morning coffee. "We'll need to buy the fish when we're out this afternoon."

"That looks tasty. I've never been very good at cooking white fish. I don't seem to get the timing right; it turns out underdone or too dry."

"Ah, well, let's give it a go. You'll have to help me with the fish; they all seem to be different down here. I'm used to plaice and cod, sometimes trout, but snapper and barra are a mystery to me," Barbara said as she reached for a notepad.

Heather's misgivings about Barbara's surprise appearance had dissolved with each passing day. Her cousin was nothing but supportive and, with Heather's permission, encouraged her to do the things she had been neglecting. Heather had struggled to get back into daily exercise and healthy eating after the sudden death of her husband, Tony, and it had all gone by the board again with Anna's disappearance. Barbara eased her into something like a routine, having regular mealtimes instead of the snatched mouthfuls of toast or sandwiches she'd taken to eating when she could be bothered to eat at all. She was also a skilled cook and prepared tasty, nutritious meals, involving Heather in planning the daily menu and talking through their favourite recipes, some from their childhood and more contemporary styles each had tried in later years. Heather knew Barbara was distracting her, but it was a welcome relief from the mental torment she constantly battled.

"Oh, wait." Heather jumped up, drawing a yip from Sparky, who skittered to the doorway in front of her. She returned, diary in hand. "I'd forgotten that tonight is the night we're going to Ruth and Simon's for dinner. Do you remember me telling you last week they'd invited us?"

Barbara frowned, replacing the cookbook on the shelf. "Yes, of course, your friends from church. You did say. I'd forgotten too."

"Are you alright to go?" Heather took in Barbara's expression. "You remember me saying that Ruth and Simon are easygoing, not pushy at all."

"Yes, yes, of course. I'm looking forward to meeting them. It's just that... Well, you know how I feel about all that now. But I understand how important your beliefs are to you. I envy you in a way, I... I..."

Heather reached for Barbara's arm, squeezing it. "It's alright. I know how difficult it is to hang on to the belief that God has everything in hand when your world falls apart. Honestly." She sighed. "I'm struggling myself. Sometimes for a few moments, other times for hours, even days. It all seems so bleak. How can it all work together for good? Especially so soon after Tony...." She sniffed as tears pooled. "But I have to believe that Annalee will be okay. That she *is* okay. Sometimes I feel a real peace about it, but I'm a gibbering mess most of the time. I just know in my heart that she's not dead. I would know if she was. I'm sure I would." *Please God, don't let her be dead.* Heather shuddered, not looking at Barbara, yet comforted by the arms slipping around her shoulders and the ready hug.

Barbara's voice was soft in Heather's ear. "I still feel that about Katie, that she's still alive somewhere, somehow. A mother knows. The maternal connection is so strong, even after all this time. I would know if her spirit was no longer on this earthly plane. I'm sure I would." Heather straightened and stretched across the bench top to reach the tissue box. Barbara hadn't moved. Heather turned, catching the lost look on Barbara's face, her sad eyes staring at a spot beyond them both before she shook her head.

"But then, maybe I'm deluding myself…" Heather stiffened at the words and the look of resignation on Barbara's face. "I'm sorry. I shouldn't have said that. It isn't fair to you. And here I am trying to make things better for you."

Heather sighed. "While we haven't heard anything, I'm going with the 'no news is good news' mantra. I have to cling to that." She felt suddenly guilty at cutting Barbara off, not allowing her to voice her feelings at her own daughter's disappearance. Did Barbara want to? She didn't know. They hadn't discussed it since her arrival. In fact, Barbara hadn't brought it up when they'd talked on the phone, not for a long time.

But not today, not now. The time wasn't right. Not for her, at least. Heather looked across at Barbara. It would be unbearable to compare notes.

"Anyway, dinner with your friends, Ruth and Simon." Colour was returning to Barbara's face and a smile playing around her lips. "The not-pushy Christians."

"No, it'll be fine. They might say grace before dinner, but they won't whisk us off into a prayer huddle or anything like that. Ruth has been a great support to me since… And we do, or did, meet and pray together once or twice a week. Only, she knows you're here, of course, and is giving us time."

"Does she, or rather, do they, know about Katie?"

"Yes, I've told her most of it over the years. The good and the bad. She knows how close we were growing up. How close we are, I should say. She helped me so much when Tony died."

Barbara got up to clear the dishes, her expression blank. "You can meet up with her for prayer while I'm here, you know. I wouldn't mind in the least. I… I might even join you. It's been a long time. But I'll draw the line at going to church, just in case you or they ask. And no need to be embarrassed if they bring it up. I'm comfortable discussing or debating, if you like, where I stand in my beliefs. But if you want to go to church, don't feel awkward about it. I can find plenty to do here."

Heather stared at her cousin's back before reaching for a tea towel and joining her at the sink.

37

The brain fog refused to shift. It wasn't the nightmare, but something else. Her mouth felt dry and metallic, her teeth sharp against the inside of her cheeks. Blood?

Where was she? Home, her mother in the next room? No, she'd moved in with Lucy.

No.

Not the dark again. The blackness. Not the punishment. She hadn't known. Not meant to do it. She wouldn't do it again.

Please, no.

Rolling onto her side hurt. Moving back was worse. She was stiff and sore all over. Her head pounded. When the pounding settled into a dull ache, she eased to a sitting position and dangled her legs over the edge of the bed. Not a good move. She clutched at the bedclothes, waiting for the dizziness to subside, desperate for the toilet and a drink of water.

Water. There had to be water. The torments of the long punishing night after she'd disobeyed the call to come in from the lagoon flooded back. Her cheeks heated and her palms felt wet. She wiped her hands on the bedclothes and swayed as acrid bile filled her throat. But her full bladder demanded attention, so she tottered on cotton wool legs around the room to the bathroom, using the bed and walls as props.

Thigh muscles screaming, she lowered herself and sat, pressing her hands to her temples. Despite the desperate urge, she struggled to squeeze out any drops of urine. When it came, it burned. Her breath caught as waves of nausea sent her skin from icy cold to soaring heat within seconds. She put her hand over her mouth, willing the contents of her stomach to stay put. Cursing the dark, the nausea, and the monster who was behind it all.

What had they done?

Her last memory was finishing breakfast and the overwhelming tiredness, and now it was—what? The middle of the night? She willed her reluctant fingers to move along her arms first. Her left wrist was tender and sported a small round adhesive dressing. The crook of her right elbow was tender. She teased at the small of her back next but exhaled a long slow breath, as it was neither sore nor covered with a dressing.

The next bit had to be done. She gritted her teeth, leaned back and parted her legs, gently working her fingers up the insides of her thighs. The tenderness she'd suspected but not wanted to find was there. She whipped both hands away, tucked them under her arms and rocked back and forth, her breath panting out in low moans, tears forced out through tight eyelids.

Somehow she made it to the basin, splashed water on her face and rinsed her mouth.

Somehow she made it to the bed, curled into a foetal position, and willed her mind to focus on something beyond herself. Anything but herself.

She fixed her mind on the outdoors, counting on the tranquil world outside to work its magic and bring her comfort. The beauty of the lagoon with its flashing fish darting as one; the tiny crabs in the pools scurrying about, waving their pincers in alarm at her; the lush ferns and flowers under the gigantic trees teeming with ants and beetles calmly going about their chores.

But tonight, it didn't help. Didn't bring the comfort she was desperate for. The images of their safe little habitats, unspoilt by interference from shadowy malevolent forces, only brought hot tears to her eyes. She was helpless to prevent their escape as they trickled slowly down her cheeks. She stuffed her fist into her mouth, turned her face into the pillows, and wept.

WHAT KIND OF MONSTROUS EXCUSE FOR A HUMAN BEING snatches someone off the street and keeps them for weeks before…? More to the point, what kind of sicko has sex with someone who is drugged, unresponsive—a lump of meat?

Her stomach roiled, and she clamped her hand to her mouth and bolted to the bathroom, reaching the toilet bowl just in time.

Annalee searched her reflection in the mirror as she dabbed at her cheeks with a damp cloth. A grim, pale face framed with dishevelled, lifeless hair stared back, her eyes dull, rimmed with deep shadows. Angry red blotches on each cheek, the only colour.

Why yesterday? She'd been here for weeks. Why now? She shuddered, gulping in air as her stomach threatened to divest itself of more of her breakfast. She had eaten little. There must be very little left to purge. What kind of pervert was doing this? What perverse pleasure did he or they get from keeping her in this isolation, denying her one of the most fundamental needs—being with people, having some human contact with others? And then—. Heat burned her cheeks again. She unclenched her jaw and flung more water at her face. She had to stop. Stop thinking about it. Distract herself somehow. But it was hopeless. She returned to the couch, but the sight of the tray with cold globs of scrambled eggs left on the plate threatened to goad her insides into further action.

Was she part of some weird scientific experiment, to be kept here as a guinea pig for goodness knows what purpose? The image of the white-coated figure writing notes on a clipboard returned. But why choose her? Was she just randomly plucked from all that she knew and held dear, or was it deliberate? Had they chosen her specifically for something she had, or for who she was?

There was nothing special about her. An ordinary girl, nurse, sister, daughter, friend. No wealthy family, just average middle-class folks, no rich spinster great-aunt in the background. They were an average Australian family who went to work, saved for what they needed and put a little aside for the future. No strange affiliations with radical political groups or any other individuals or groups. She'd had no significant diseases, illnesses or operations in her past, apart from a broken collarbone when she was nine and the odd bout of tonsillitis. That was about it. AB blood type—not that common, but not rare either.

She drew in a deep breath and hugged a cushion to her chest. She had been a virgin. Her eyes pooled, the urge to resume the foetal position tightening her stomach. Blinking away the tears, she searched the room for answers, but there was no sense in any of it. This place didn't match up with any notions she had about kidnapping or sex slavery.

Sex slavery: the act of depriving someone (predominantly a female) of their freedom to gratify the needs of the captor. Or forcing the 'slave' to make herself available to men for a fee, of which the sum went to the 'owner'.

Somehow that definition wrote itself across her brain. She couldn't even remember reading it. Gender studies or perhaps justice? Year three of nursing studies. What did it matter? Now, she was living it, but it made little sense. None of that fitted.

Her virginity had been a vital part of her identity. The 'had been' another stab to her chest. She valued that part of her womanhood and held the firm belief that casual sex weakened relationships rather than strengthened them. Maybe it was the Christian influence from her family and church teaching, the belief that sexual purity before marriage from both parties paved the way for a solid marriage. Nothing in either's past to cast a shadow on the new union. Maybe, but she was confident in her decision to wait for 'Mr Right', and most of her previous boyfriends had respected that, with those who didn't soon moving on.

She knew she wasn't perfect and had struggled, particularly with Dan, her first crush. She'd thought him devastatingly handsome at first, if in a broody, little-boy-lost kind of way, but as time went on, his dark moods dominated their every meeting. His efforts to control what she did, where they went, and who they hung out with increased. She'd known she had to end it. The final straw came when he set up a 'surprise' for her birthday. She'd thought they were going out on a day trip with a sunset picnic in the hills until the car conveniently broke down close to a quaint B&B. There was one room available; he would sleep on the floor or go back to the car, he said. She noticed the owner give Dan an odd look as she handed him the keys. He clutched Annalee's hand, opened the door and there it was, a cosy room lit with candles, champagne on ice, and rose petals on the bed. The door was as far as she got. She spent the night on the couch in the lobby, not noticing or caring where Dan went.

There were two or three dates with others, but she'd been happy to focus on her studies, and then Jamie. It was just a few short months since they'd met at a workmate's birthday party. But he'd soon become a part of her life. Easygoing, dependable, caring, and mature, all she could wish for in a friend, let alone someone she dared think of spending her future with. Jamie, his powerful arms wrapped around her, the warmth of his breath tickling the side of her neck, the way he held her hand. The funny texts she would wake up to. The contentment she felt as they jogged along the beach side-by-side or walked under the stars together.

She sighed. An almost unbearable wave of sadness washed through her frame. She felt crushed, battered and bruised, and not just physically; the pain in her heart and psyche was so much greater.

She'd wanted him or someone like him to be the first, to be the one she gave herself to, not some nameless entity who took from her without her consent.

Despite her desire to zone out, to disappear, she couldn't escape her torment by sleeping. But neither did she have the energy to move, to exercise. The skipping rope was nowhere in sight. As usual, they'd removed it from the room, but it didn't matter. Exerting herself was the last thing she felt like doing. The morning dragged, and it wasn't until the door opened to reveal a meal tray that she realised her gym session time had come and gone without an invitation.

She picked up the tray and placed it on the desk behind her, but lingered in the open doorway. What if she walked out right now? Defied the red lights, turning her skin blood red under their sinister glow, and walked away? She peered into the red distance as it dulled into thick blackness until the colours spun and whirled, a ghoulish dance at the back of her eyes.

38

It was two days before the green lights in the tunnel invited Anna back to the gym. It may have been longer. The only difference between the days and the nights was the absence of light, and there had been two periods of that, she was sure. Or was it three? It didn't matter. She drifted between the bed and the couch, curling into a foetal position on each one, willing the minutes and the hours to pass. Times of torpor sandwiched between bursts of terrifying clarity filled with panic-stricken, restless anxiety marked the passing hours.

She didn't know if she was awake or asleep when the manic episodes hit: images of her being taken, carried out, hands reaching for her, touching her, pulling her this way and that flashed through her mind. Her skin crawled, her stomach contracted. Imaginings. Nightmares. They couldn't be real. Surely.

She had to escape. Adrenalin coursed through her body, feeding her anxiety. She needed to run, fight, to scream at what they had done to her and the injustice of it all. But there was nowhere to run and no one to fight. No one to hear her angry outbursts. It was hopeless. Reading didn't provide any relief from the torment, and the food on offer took on the consistency of stodgy porridge, sticking to her teeth and gums and provoking her throat into spasms. She tried every strategy she knew to settle her mind, to dissociate herself from the black thoughts. She was desperate to pull the old Anna back. The Anna who was full of fun and laughter, ready to encourage others when they faced their predicaments and the Anna who was above all in control of her thoughts and feelings.

When the door opened, despite her disinclination to move from the couch, she forced herself up. Getting out of that room even for an hour had to be better than staying in it. As she stumbled along the tunnel, her spirits lifted. By the time she reached the lift, something had shifted a little, and her mind felt clearer. She almost fancied she could smell the fresh sea air through the gym door as it opened. But would that translate into reality? Would they give her time outside?

The minutes on the timer taunted, each one taking an age to tick over to the next. Each plodding step she took, each measured minute on the treadmill seemed to whisper, *No, not today.* The gym equipment joined in the taunts, growing bony fingers and toes designed to trip her up or catch at her clothes to pull her back as she moved from one activity to the next.

"Ouch!" She bent down to inspect the fresh bruise spreading on her shin just as the change in air pressure and light behind her signalled what she'd hoped for.

With a sharp intake of breath, she blinked at the intensity of the day, tears flooding her eyes in defence. The bright daylight seemed even more intense than the first time she'd been let outside. All the smells and sights were larger than life, almost overwhelming as she took in the familiarity yet somehow difference of the day. The air was as fragrant as ever, but more so, the heady mix of perfume and spices of the flowers and wood filled her nostrils with fragrances she couldn't remember smelling before. They drew her onto the grass and carried her down, down through the towering trees, the soft grass caressing the soles of her feet. It was as if she were floating above the ground, her legs and feet moving of their own accord, her mind still entranced with the aromas, the colours of the foliage, the feel of the air on her skin. And then she was on the sand, the coarse black grains crunching underfoot before she sank to her knees, her fingers and toes digging into its warm, rich surface.

She fell back and sat cross-legged, and turned her face to the sky, drinking in the sun as it warmed her skin, soaking it in as if she could store it deep inside. To keep it in reserve for the days they denied her access. The breeze caressed her hair, teasing the fresh growth as she stepped into the water and began a leisurely swim up and then back along the lagoon. She stopped halfway back, returning to the spot where she'd entered, and sat in the shallows. She drew her knees to her chest, feeling the cool water lap at her thighs.

Fixing her eyes on the far side of the lagoon, she dug her fingers into the wet sand, fisted a handful and rubbed it into the skin on her feet, pressing her fingertips down and around in small circles, scrubbing the sand into her skin. She repeated the exercise with both hands, beginning on her ankles before moving up her legs, grabbing more sand as the pain subsided. She'd started slowly, methodically scooping up the sand, but as she reached her thighs and torso, her fingers moved faster and more vigorously, until jerking across her chest, up her neck to her chin, she stopped. Hot tears gathered and fell as she gritted her teeth, fighting to stop the thin, keening cries escaping between them.

Swiping at her eyes, she got up and stumbled into the water, gasping as the salt bit into her raw skin before she gulped in a breath and dove to the bottom. Pushing off, she struck out in a fast crawl across the lagoon. Once, twice across, she kept going until her lungs were screaming and black spots threatened her eyes. She flung herself onto the beach near the rock pool and lay panting, her eyes closed. The pain from her scourging burred her skin, yet somehow its warm numbness brought comfort.

As her heart rate returned to normal, she pushed onto her elbows and peered into the pool. The crabs were hardly visible, most hiding from the sun under the rock ledges except for a group of three or four picking at a patch of weed. She frowned. Something about it looked odd. She leant in closer, trying to make out what it was they were picking at. It wasn't seaweed, but something else; something darker. Something with a more refined shape. Shooing them gently away with her fingers, she teased at the object half-buried under a small rock, prised it free and nestled it in her cupped hand.

It was circular, in the shape of a ring, barely big enough to fit her pinkie finger. Yet, it was no band of silver or gold. She prodded at it, seeing it flex. It couldn't be possible, but she knew it was as she picked it up between her thumb and forefinger and squeezed. A ring of hair, delicately woven or plaited, with the centre of the band worked in criss-cross diamond shapes between edges of tightly pulled loops. It was so neatly and finely crafted, with only a few loose ends sticking out, probably where the crabs had worked at it.

The hair was dark, almost black, so like her own. Obviously human hair. Her eyes narrowed at the thought that its creator had most likely sat in this very spot. She looked over her shoulder, closing her fist over the ring, suddenly wary of watching eyes.

Of course, she knew she wasn't the only one imprisoned here. What with the other doors, and not having access outside every day —but this was the first proof of another person beside herself who was alive in this place. And as she studied the ring, as improbable as it was, it made perfect sense for its creator to craft something from her hair. There was nothing else available to use. They had no access to pen and paper. The mountain slope and beach had never shown the slightest sign of another soul having been in it until today. She pictured an army of workers scurrying around, tidying up after her, erasing signs of her excursions outside—and anyone else's. But they didn't count. She felt the soft strength of the ring against her skin. She wasn't alone. Somewhere inside the mountain, there was someone else doing the best she could to survive.

Anna tucked the ring carefully between her finger and thumb and, straightening her face as the warning chimes started up, carried her precious cargo inside. Somehow, she would send a message back.

39

*L*ucy frowned at the lumpy mess of Mick and his doona, in imminent danger of parting company. Mick's bare leg hung off the couch, his foot about to touch down, his right elbow at an awkward angle against the back support, a hand covering his eyes. His couple of weeks' stay had turned into three, then four; the couch his bed the first night and every other since. Lucy couldn't bring herself to suggest he sleep in Anna's room, and he never asked.

He was such a sweet big brother, but this was impossible. It wouldn't be doing his back any good. Retreating to the kitchen, she punched in Heather's number before she changed her mind. Thankfully, Heather agreed with her plan to store Anna's things, both emphasising it would only be a temporary solution until her return.

LUCY TOOK IN HEATHER'S PALE, DRAWN FACE AND BARBARA'S lips pressed tightly together as she opened the front door. She said nothing, only offering a half-smile of welcome before showing them in. There was nothing to say that would make it any easier, and besides, she didn't trust her emotions. As she'd waited for them to come, she hadn't been able to settle down to anything. Mick glanced her way more than once, but she'd refused to meet his eyes, looking blankly down at the crossword puzzle in her hands.

The three women worked methodically, emptying drawers and the wardrobe and folding the clothes neatly into cardboard boxes. Nobody spoke until Heather let out a quiet sob. Barbara reached her first, and then the three of them locked arms tightly as the two older women collapsed onto the bed. Lucy sank to the floor at their feet, tears dripping from her cheeks onto Heather's jeans. Mick appeared in the doorway proffering a box of tissues, his own eyes moist before he stepped back, murmuring about putting the kettle on.

Tea and biscuits helped restore their spirits, and they finished the task without a repeat of their earlier tears. Most of the boxes fitted in Heather's car, with the rest stowed in Mick's ute. He would follow her home and help unpack the boxes at the other end. Lucy opted to stay, giving the excuse of housework to be done before she prepared for her evening shift.

Lucy stood in Anna's bedroom doorway, the sudden silence overwhelming. All of her best friend's material possessions had gone, and soon there would be no trace of her left in the house. In her life. Anna's presence had been stripped bare along with the bed, leaving only the mattress and pillows behind. Her eyes welled as she scanned the bedside table and chest of drawers, cleared of photos and Anna's knick-knacks. She remembered the day they moved in, before they'd unpacked and arranged those special mementos, turning the bones of still-echoing rooms into a home. It had been a day full of joy and laughter, as they each took turns explaining the significance of an item which, to anyone else, might easily be a piece of junk.

"It's as if she's never been here." Lucy spoke to the empty walls, tears spilling over onto her cheeks.

She started as Mick came up behind and wrapped his arms around her waist. "It'll be okay, Luce. We'll find her. I know we will."

"I thought you'd gone." Lucy stiffened, her cheeks heating. It was all she could do not to scream at him. How could it be okay after all this time? And as for 'we'll find her', if the police hadn't managed it, how could 'we'? Glad her back was to him, she forced out, "You'd better get going, Mrs T must be waiting."

"Won't you come?" She heard the plea in his voice and knew he didn't want to leave her alone.

"No, they don't need me there. I'll stay here if you don't mind." It was enough to pack it all up. She didn't want to see the remnants of Anna's life piled in the corner of some dark room.

He turned her around, his eyes searching her face. She saw her sorrow reflected in his eyes before he drew her close in a hug. Despite her annoyance, she cherished the warmth of his body, feeling a sudden chill when he let go and made for the door.

"It will be okay," he said, and left, shutting it quietly.

"How do you know that?" She spoke into the space he'd vacated and turned back to face Anna's empty room.

* * *

"Wha— What's going on?" Mick's eyes widened on his return as he surveyed the mess. "Did a tornado hit while I was away?"

"Well, you could say that. I hope you don't mind, but I think I'll feel better if I take Anna's room and you have mine."

Within minutes of his departure, the idea had sparked and rapidly grown. She would move in rather than Mick, and he could have her room. Somehow, it was the right thing to do. If she couldn't bring Anna back—yet—maybe she would feel closer to her. It was more caring, somehow, and not as if she was giving the room away to a complete stranger. Not that Mick was a stranger, far from it. Besides, it wouldn't matter to him.

By the time he returned, she was halfway through the transition, with piles of clothes stacked on her stripped bed, and a trail of shoes littering the hallway. She was making up the bed in Anna's—no— her room with fresh sheets, and arranging her favourite doona.

"No, it's fine by me. But are you sure? It won't bring you too many memories in the middle of the night?"

"No, I think it will help, if anything. Besides, you know I sleep like a baby." Most of the time. She avoided Mick's eyes, discounting the many nights after Anna's disappearance and then the break-in when she'd lain awake, her mind caught in an ever-tightening loop of despair or anxiety, wondering if Jamie had anything to do with some or all of it. Thinking over and over of the conversation she would have with him, rehearsing and rehashing the ways to confront him, to get to the truth. Then, just as suddenly, discounting the ideas as absurd. He had been nothing but kind and sincere in his interactions with her. And Anna had loved him, hadn't she? Lucy sniffed and rubbed her nose.

"Dust," she said. "Now, help me move my stuff. If you dump my clothes onto the bed, I'll put them away, then you can move in there, not that you have much stuff." She smiled at the image of Mick's hold-all containing just about his entire wardrobe from Albany.

"What does a bloke need?" He grinned and shrugged.

"It's good to have the couch back." Lucy surveyed the tidy room as they sat together drinking coffee. "Not that I minded you sleeping on it, but I don't think I wanted to face the fact that... this... that it would come to this. You know. That Anna would still be missing. I was just letting each day go by, not wanting to acknowledge the days turning into weeks and now... months." She gulped and set down her cup.

Placing his hand on hers, Mick gave a gentle squeeze. She was glad he said nothing and didn't repeat his earlier assertion that Anna would turn up, that all would be okay. It was something she desperately wanted to believe herself, or had done. When did that change? When did she give up? Had she given up? Or was it just today, having to pack up Anna's things? It had been a raw day all round. She sighed and looked away.

"Mick, just say the word. You can go back to Albany anytime. I don't want you to put your life on hold for me. For this." She held her breath, hoping he would stay for at least a few weeks more. He was a great encouragement to her just by being there, but it wasn't a permanent solution. He would never willingly leave Albany for city-life for any length of time.

"Let's leave it for a bit Luce. A couple more weeks to get over this, then we'll rethink it. Besides, I just got a room, I don't want to lose it again."

Lucy's shoulders relaxed with his answer, but she wasn't ready to let it go. "But you've given up so much and put up with my moods. Don't you want to get back to normal?"

"Shh." He put a finger on her lips. "This is only for a time. It won't last and then I'll go back. I believe I'm meant to be here just now. Truth be told, it's been good for me too. I've had time away from my comfort zone to think about my life. And I needed to get away to do it—been drifting for way too long, putting off what I believe the Lord has put on my mind. What he wants me to do."

"Which is?" Leaning forward, she searched his eyes.

"Bible college." His eyes widened with the words and she saw the wonder and excitement in equal measure. "I believe I'm meant to go to Bible college to study theology."

"Theo college. Wow, that's huge. What… when… how…? Tell me all, big brother." A broad smile lit up her face. She was genuinely pleased for him. She, along with her mum and dad, had long believed it was something he would do one day. They had been patiently waiting for Mick to come to that realisation himself.

40

Pregnant!

The word started as a whisper a couple of days ago. Now it was shouting in her ear.

Anna studied her reflection in the bathroom mirror, searching for a tangible sign of this... this... miracle of new life. This possibility.

Was it true? Could it be?

Somehow, she knew it was. Despite the glaring absence of a handy chemist to pop into, to purchase the home pregnancy test. A sharp pain twisted in her side at the thought of 'home'. She winced and rubbed her ribs, glaring at the mirror. But the subtle differences in her body were making their presence felt. Every meal lately looked and smelled like cardboard, and she'd been queasy in the mornings for the past few days. Her breasts were definitely tender, and she was feeling more tired than usual.

A woman knows. She echoed her sister-in-law Meg's assertion, four years ago when she was pregnant with Matthew. Anna and her mother had been sceptical that she could tell, especially as it was her first baby, but she was adamant and proven right when a pregnancy test confirmed it some days later.

The miracle of a new life beginning. It should be a time for joy.

A miracle born from the love of a man and his wife. What was this, then? Miracle or misfortune? A child conceived in deception and perversity. Not a time for anyone to celebrate. A tear escaped as she slunk back to the couch.

When Megan and Stephen found they were expecting Matthew, and again two years later with Jessica on the way, everyone was thrilled. All so excited and so involved. Anna had been ecstatic that she was to be an auntie and shopped for tiny clothes at every chance. She and her mum and dad helped Steve and Meg paint and decorate the nursery and they went shopping together—after much debate about the best quality and safety features—to buy the cot, pram, change table, and car capsule. Annalee saved up what seemed a fortune at the time and bought them a beautifully crafted rocking chair which fitted perfectly in the nursery.

When Matthew arrived, there was no shortage of willing helpers and babysitters to aid the happy but exhausted couple. He was a good weight but rather colicky at first, so Anna and Heather did night shift, once a week each, to give the tired parents a break. That rocking chair came in handy as they whiled away the dark night hours trying to settle little Matty.

Jessica was entirely different, a perfect little cherub with a mop of dark hair. She settled straight away and the rocking chair was perfect for feeding or baby watching. Anna loved to watch Matthew and then Jessica sleeping, their tiny lips pursing, noses wrinkling or fingers curling as they dreamt about milk and mum and dad or whatever else it was that babies dream about. She loved holding them, breathing in that perfect baby smell as their tiny heads rested on her shoulder while she rocked or walked the floor in the night.

She'd contemplated paediatric nursing early in her studies but decided against it as she didn't like to think of such tiny humans facing illness and suffering. She didn't envy Lucy working at the children's hospital, and they'd agreed not to discuss distressing cases they came across. Anna couldn't bear the thought that anything similar might happen to either Matty or Jess.

Sighing, she settled back into the couch and reached for her book. The contrast between the past joys shared with her family and her present reality was huge. If only she could lose herself in the book, put it all out of her mind. After all, she might be wrong. Maybe feeling a bit off because she'd eaten something bad or had forgotten to wash her hands. Maybe after picking those flowers she'd scattered on the beach some days ago.

Who was she kidding? If she was pregnant, then… Her stomach lurched, and she raced for the bathroom, bile searing her throat. How could she have a baby all by herself? What about medical care during the pregnancy? Would they finally show themselves and give her the care and the things she would need? What would they do about it if they found out? And the bigger question: what would she want them to do?

Having a baby was impossible. A child conceived in, conceived in… what? Well, it certainly wasn't a loving relationship, or any kind of relationship, for that matter. Who was the other party? What unimaginable defects or diseases did they carry and pass on to her and the child? Her throat constricted as vomit threatened once more. She took several slow, deep breaths and splashed water on her face before sipping some from her cupped hand.

What would they do? What did she want? Her head throbbed. And what choice did she have?

Pregnancy, unless halted in some way, led to life. The alternative, abortion, led to death.

Anna had always hated the idea of it. It went against everything she believed in. Firm in her convictions, she yet dared to think it was nothing to do with her family's Christian beliefs. A woman was especially designed or created, call it what you will, to have a baby. In the right circumstances. Her body, on conception, went into 'baby' mode, everything working to prepare for the months ahead, to nurture and grow the unique life within.

It was a hard, hard decision for any woman to end that life. To deliberately end it. To go on with life as if the child had never existed.

Experiences partly coloured her view on abortion. She was fourteen when a girl in their class had an abortion. They had rallied around Sarah when she told them she was pregnant, with opinion divided over what she should do. She was too young to have a baby. Her life would be over. Some would label her a skank when everybody saw the bulge. The boys would think she was easy. The girls, a slut. No, the positive ones tried to reason. She could do it. They would all be there for her. Help her through it. They believed in her. She wasn't a slut, far from it; just a shy, sensitive girl who had fallen for the first boy who asked her out. Her parents weren't even aware she was dating someone. Anna and the others vowed to help her in any way they could. Help her catch up with schoolwork, and definitely help her with the baby, all ready and eager to babysit.

The dream baby never materialised as the school nurse became involved, and Sarah's family, Anna believed, convinced her to have an abortion. Sarah was never the same after that, often breaking down in tears, then not wanting to hang around with them. She missed a lot of school and, during the Christmas school holidays, gravitated to another group. A group who all dressed alike, in tight black jeans and T-shirts or sweaters, their eyes thickly made up to match the clothes. When Anna or others in their circle tried to message Sarah, she said little and soon stopped responding. The following school year she'd changed schools, and around May they heard she'd become pregnant again and left home, moving in with her boyfriend and his mother.

Anna had known others who had had abortions. At the time it had seemed to her that none of them had realised the impact it would have on them, even those with strong pro-choice views. All had good reasons for not having a baby. One had just secured her dream job, another's boyfriend would leave her if she had the baby, a uni friend had got drunk one night and didn't remember who she had slept with. None of their circumstances were right for having a baby; who could argue with that?

In the right circumstances. The phrase echoed through her mind. Circumstances were not always right, and this was far from it. She sighed. It was all too much. The baby was the innocent party. But… what about her? Did she still have those strong convictions she'd held as a teenager? She had never judged Sarah or the others for having an abortion. Had she? When you were the outsider looking in, it was different. Easier to make a decision when it was someone else. But now?

41

Heather sagged, her shoulder wedged against the door frame as she surveyed her backyard. Bright morning sunlight filtered through the leafy-green, lemon-scented gum she and Tony had planted when they first moved in. It never should have been planted there, of course. It was much too big for a suburban backyard, but they had been naïve about such trees back then, only wanting instant shade from the relentless Australian sun. They wanted shade for the children to play under safely, and some shelter over the roof for those hot, hot days when a sea breeze failed to materialise three days in a row.

But it was a beautiful tree and the bonus lemon fragrance which filled the air whenever Tony mowed the lawn, crushing the dropped leaves, had never failed to delight her.

She did the mowing herself now. Now he was gone. Her heart twisted, and she felt her chest rise ready to exhale a sigh, but didn't hear it. The scene set before her played out like a silent movie, only in slow motion.

She watched Barbara sitting with a sun beam haloing her head and shoulders. Always a sun lover, she moved around as the sun did, her chair in a different position every half hour. Heather would laugh as Barbara shoved and scraped the wooden patio chair around

159

in search of the perfect spot. She usually wanted sun on her legs, but not this morning. She was waiting for Heather to return with their coffee, and would, no doubt, have heard the phone ring inside. But there was no hint of curiosity on her face.

Heather's eyes followed as Barbara leant forward to read something in the magazine more carefully. Watched as her hand drifted to the top of the page, ready to turn it, but then twisted her head to look up at the tree before returning to the page.

Heather strained to see what had distracted Barbara, but she wasn't at the right angle, the patio roof obscuring her view. She had to take the tray out to the table and Barbara before the coffee got cold, but her legs wouldn't move. She was frozen. Lifting a foot would cause her remaining leg to buckle and she and the tray would end up in a crashing mess on the ground. She'd made it to the doorway but could go no further.

Sparky, comfortable in his own sunny spot near Barbara's feet, suddenly sat up, looked at her near the door and whimpered. Barbara looked down and reached out to pat him before following his eyeline. Heather saw Barbara's eyes widen as she took in her expression. Then the world seemed to start up again as Barbara jumped up, magazine tossed aside, and dashed over with hands outstretched. The sounds of the birds and the breeze in the trees crashed back in, along with the contents of the tray rattling their consternation should her trembling fingers fail.

"Heather, whatever is it? Here, let me take that. Stay there and I'll come back for you."

Barbara set the tray down and led Heather to a chair, pulling hers closer, still gripping her arm above the wrist. Heather was grateful for the warmth of another person's touch seeping into her skin. It didn't penetrate, though. The inside of her was deathly cold. Pinpricks of blackness threatened her vision, and a sudden wave of nausea filled her stomach. She put her free hand under her breast as if to keep it down and gulped.

"Was it the phone call?" Barbara said.

She nodded, opening her mouth to explain, but no words came.

"Okay, take your time. Sip some coffee. Get your hands around the mug to warm them." Barbara passed the mug, and the plate of biscuits at which she shook her head.

"You're still trembling. Let me get the rug." Barbara reached behind her and shook out the wrap before arranging it around Heather's shoulders and back. "There, how's that?"

Heather shot her a thin smile and took another sip. How to start? There was no way to soften the news.

"They've found a body." She focused on the brown liquid in her cup, unsure if the words had made it from her mouth. Repeating them was out of the question, but if she looked at Barbara for confirmation, that would be the end. She felt Barbara stiffen and pull away.

"No!"

"Yes." She inhaled a long breath. "Someone was out walking on a bush track north of Wanneroo and their dog disturbed what appeared to be a shallow grave." The words came out exactly as Detective Sergeant Elaine Troy had relayed them to her, not five minutes before. She had said more, of course, but those words seemed to be in bold and edged in black and gold. A bit like some of the condolence cards she had received after Tony's death.

"It doesn't mean that…" Barbara paused, patting at her knee. Heather grimaced at Barbara's face, now pale, her dark eyes even darker. With the shock, Heather supposed. She had known the effect this news would have on Barbara and would give anything to spare her. To spare them both.

"I know. That's what Sergeant Troy said." She sat back against the cushion and took in the deep breath she badly needed. Her chest was a tight band, as if her ribs had solidified and refused to allow any more of the sweet, fresh air in to warm her inside.

"She said she called me as soon as they got the news—before I heard it on the radio or TV. It only happened a few hours ago and they—she—don't have any details yet. She doesn't know if it—the body, I mean, is even male or female. No age or anything or how long—the person…" It seemed important for Heather to acknowledge that. "Has been there."

"Oh, Heather. I…"

Heather clutched at Barbara's hand, her eyes wide. "Did this happen to you?" She imagined police officers and detectives all over Australia—the world even—reaching for telephones and warning parents of missing children to be ready. For what? Good news that it wasn't their son or daughter found there, lying in that shallow grave waiting for a curious dog to find. Or was it bad news? If it wasn't their child, and the waiting continued, day after day. Waiting until they found the next one.

Yet they had found one. One out of the hundreds, if not thousands, reported missing every year. One set of parents who would find the answer they had been searching for. One... She heard Barbara's voice even as she knew what she would say. Of course it had happened to her, more than once. She'd told her each time. Each time, the pain had come through over the telephone line. What was she thinking?

"I'm sorry," she cut in. "I'm sorry. That was a stupid question."

"It's alright," Barbara said, although Heather saw her pinched look. What could she do to right this terrible injustice? They were in the same nightmare club that nobody wanted to be a member of, and there was no way to cancel their membership.

"What do we do now?" Heather said, knowing the answer to that one, too.

We wait.

PART II

42

"I'm going to try to see Koh again," David Wilson said to his wife.

Jenni looked up, her eyes searching his as she groped for the spoon and popped it back on the highchair tray. Liam's chubby fingers grasped for it, a wicked chuckle escaping his cherubic lips.

"What's the point?" she said. "That man won't let anyone set foot on his island without an invitation. Particularly you." She swiped at Liam's chin with the soft bib, deftly catching the banana-laced dribble about to launch.

David held her gaze, but he'd noticed the sharpness in her tone. "I know, but Adela is insisting that we do something about Jimi. She wants to see her grandson."

"But what can we do? You've tried enough times. She should go to the police again. Surely they would listen to her now."

Jenni lifted Liam out of the highchair. He toddled off, chubby legs building speed, hands outstretched in front of him, no doubt in search of some new mischief. Oh, how David envied his son's innocence and confidence. That all was well in his world, with a little care and love from the people around him.

Jenni turned toward David again and wrapped her arms around his neck, her face upturned, her blue eyes steady, but he saw the quiver at the corner of her mouth. Did she need reassurance as much as he did that this blight on their almost idyllic island life would disappear? If only he could make it disappear. But with a swift peck on his cheek, she slid her hands down his back and squeezed his arms before backing away.

"Anyway, I must get to morning clinic. Let's discuss it later. You're on Liam watch." She added, "And where's Miranda?"

"Still curled up with Mrs Chook on the verandah, reading her a story."

"Good man." Jenni whirled around, pausing in the doorway. "I do love you, David Wilson. We'll think of something."

"I love you too," he called through the empty doorway, a frown creasing his brow. Something had to be done.

David and Jenni Wilson, along with five-year-old Miranda and fifteen-month-old Liam, had taken up the missionary post on the small island of Vaui eleven months before. They were replacing Peter and Marion Farleigh, who were transitioning into retirement after almost twenty years. Currently, the Farleighs were midway through a six-month break, visiting their home country of Scotland and several support churches in England, Australia, and New Zealand. Peter was a doctor and honorary elder supporting the indigenous pastor, Jean-Paul, and Marion was the head teacher in the village school. They had both encouraged and mentored the islanders to value education and, with financial aid from support churches who provided scholarships, keen students continued on to teacher's college or university on the mainland. The Wilsons were a good fit to take over, although the roles were reversed with David a pastor and teacher, and Jenni the doctor.

David caught up with Liam, who was sitting on his haunches staring up at Mrs Chook, safely cradled in Miranda's arms. He was clearly entranced and quiet for once, his fingers alternately bunching into fists and loosening as he switched his gaze from the chicken's beady eyes to his adored older sister.

Miranda closed the picture book with a resounding, "The end." And handed it down to Liam.

Liam flopped onto his bottom, his face serious as he tried to prise open the pages.

"Da-adda," he said, holding the book out and fixing David with his dark-blue eyes. Jenni's eyes. His own and Miranda's were hazel, and both had chestnut curls to match. Jenni and Liam had white-blond straight hair, although Liam's hadn't quite settled into 'straight' yet, sticking out every which way, particularly after a sleep.

"Storwy." Liam's bottom lip jutted out, and he drummed his heels on the wooden floorboards.

David smiled as he sat cross-legged beside his son, drew him onto his lap, and opened the cover. Liam didn't know too many words, but 'storwy' was one of them.

"After the story, we can see the boats." It was almost time for the fishermen to return. They would have completed their morning trip to the mainland to sell the bulk of the catch, the rest kept for family or bartered with villagers who farmed.

"Boats! Fishies!" Liam squirmed out of his father's arms, thrusting the book to one side and pointing toward the small cove, Vaui Island's only access point to the outside world.

"Soon, Liam. Soon." David grabbed his hand, easing him back onto his lap, but it wasn't to be. Liam had no interest in the book nor sitting still after the magical word 'boats' had escaped.

"I think it's now, Dad." Miranda gently set Mrs Chook down. The chicken stayed where she was for a few seconds before ruffling her feathers, letting out a large squawk and hopping off the veran-dah, running to join her mates foraging beneath the bushes.

"I think you're right, Mims." He ruffled her curls and took hold of Liam's hand. "Liam, hold Miranda's hand too." The toddler shook his head and tucked his hand into his side, then thrust it out just as quickly, giggling as Miranda tickled him under the arm.

Small fishing boats were pulled up onto the beach with their owners unloading their catch, baskets of supplies or nets ready to dry and mend. Wooden jetties framed each side of the cove, with half-a-dozen runabouts taking up the space in the middle. Two larger boats were tied up to one jetty. The crews, made up of extended families who had clubbed together to widen their range and catch bigger fish, were engaged in doing the same as those of the smaller boats.

David raised his hand to shade his eyes, watching the last boat, which would take up its station at the opposite jetty, skimming across the water from Koh's Island. It was the only one permitted a stop there but, while they supplied seafood, that was all they would say about Mr Koh and what they saw over there. David couldn't blame them. He saw the trepidation in their eyes when he or others tried to glean any information. They no doubt feared they would lose what must be a considerable portion of their trade. Despite the friendliness of all the fishermen, there was healthy competition between them and the two families opposite would be glad to step in at the chance of a guaranteed income.

He scanned the view from the cove, across turquoise-blue sea dotted with islands small and large. Few were habitable, some mere rocks poking a few craggy tips through the surface. Peiho, or Koh's Island as it became known after the wealthy businessman bought it twelve years before, was their nearest neighbour, and by far the largest after their own. Most of its low-lying area at fifteen kilometres or eight nautical miles distance was a low smudge on the horizon, but its trademark conical-shaped extinct volcano, almost identical to their own, speared upwards, as if desperate to escape the ocean. Swathed in darkness from the black volcanic rock daubed with rich, dark green vegetation, it stood out in stark relief against the cloudless blue sky.

David's eyes lighted on a compact figure striding along the beach towards the empty jetty. Adela did this every day, waiting for the launch to return to ask if they had seen her grandson, Jimi, on Koh's Island.

"It's Mama Adela." Miranda touched his arm. David hadn't realised Miranda was following his gaze.

"I know, Mims. She's waiting for the boat. Waiting to talk to the Pakaris."

"Daddy?" David heard the catch in her voice.

"Yes, chicken."

"Daddy, Mama Adela is so sad. Why can't God bring Jimi back? He can do anything, right?"

"He can, Mims, but sometimes people have other ideas and want different things."

With a low groan, Annalee rolled over, struggling to find a comfortable position, but the ache in her lower back still nagged. She must have slept awkwardly. The last few nights her growing baby bump and the child's penchant for nocturnal callisthenics had made it difficult to sleep as soundly as she would like. Rearranging her pillow, she put her head down. It was no use. She eased onto one elbow and peered across the room through heavy eyelids. It couldn't be morning, but the room was showing signs of what passed for daylight in this windowless bunker, not its usual pitch black. What was going on?

A jolt of electricity shot through her spine, sending her bolt upright. Suddenly wide awake, she shoved her heels into the mattress and pushed back, the solid bedhead halting her progress. She sucked in a mouthful of air, fixing her eyes on the door open wide to the tunnel, the green glow from its roof lights spilling into the room.

What the—? Where did they want her to go in the middle of the night? Was she finally about to face her captors? But why pick now, unless they wanted to catch her off guard? They'd certainly achieved that. Her heart racing, she gulped in a few deep breaths and crossed the room, thankful the pain in her spine had stopped.

She stood in the doorway and peered along the tunnel, letting out a slow breath. Green lights were only glowing one way and for a short distance, with solid red fading to black beyond. There were doors along there, just like her own. How many between her and the no-go area, she couldn't tell. As her eyes and sleep-fogged brain adjusted to what she was seeing, the green light appeared to glow golden and swell in the distance. It blotted out the darkness on the other side, as if the tunnel were a test tube and the Bunsen burner had been turned up, heating its contents to boiling point.

A door had opened. Whatever was in there, it was for her, and her alone, to investigate. A quick glance in the opposite direction confirmed she was the only one 'invited' out tonight. All was red, dark and quiet. Squaring her shoulders, she paced along, passing one door, then two. The third was open, but she slowed to a stop two metres from it, her heart thudding, breaths coming in shallow pants. Her muscles quivered from the tension, and she hunched forward, placed her hands on her thighs before straightening up slowly, drawing in a slow, deep breath. It helped for a beat, then an unearthly sound escaped the room, echoing past her head down the tunnel, as if something or someone in there was caught in a trap.

No! She almost leapt at the door, her eyes widening as she focused on the bed.

It was a carbon-copy of the one in her room, positioned in exactly the same place along the wall, and it contained a figure. A woman. A female form, at least. Annalee could see she was small. A child. No. Please God, no.

Her anger flared as she tore across the room to the bedside, her eyes appraising, taking in her patient. She was, after all, her patient. They had demanded that of her tonight.

Why? shot through her mind, but now wasn't the time for questions. Someone needed her care desperately, and she would do what she could. A searching look showed she wasn't a child, but it was hard to tell her age, dwarfed as she was by the size of the bed. She looked no bigger than a twelve or thirteen-year-old, but could be anything from late teens to mid-thirties. Anna swallowed the gasp threatening to escape.

What had happened to her? She was an apparition, more skeleton than woman. Shorter by far than Annalee, who was no great height, but her arms and shoulders, the parts of her protruding from the bedclothes, looked emaciated, sharp bony knees two points under it. Anna grasped the nearest hand, halting the thin fingers fluttering across the cover, but jagged nails bit into her palm. She flinched but swallowed down a cry of pain and gently eased the fingers loose, working her own up to grasp the thin wrist, feeling for a pulse.

"It's okay. It'll be okay. I'm Anna. I'm here to help you. What's your name?"

The response was another anguished, gut-wrenching scream, the sound hissing through lips stretched taught over blood-flecked teeth.

Anna flinched, willing it to stop, seeing the tense muscles in the woman's neck finally relax.

"What's your name? Can you tell me your name?"

Nothing. Stale hot breaths puffed between sunken cheeks. The woman's small oval face, framed with dark wispy unkempt hair, was sallow and pale, apart from small angry red blotches staining each cheek. Her enormous dark eyes stared vacantly at the ceiling. Then tears glittered, and they darted around the room, looking everywhere but at Anna. Her fingers clutched at the bedclothes as her body tensed, and another keening scream rang out.

Anna lifted the cover with her free hand to confirm what she dreaded to see. The woman's drawn-up knees hid her distended belly, taut with the contraction coursing through it. It was the only thing big about her. An amazing spectacle to behold in normal circumstances. Anna's heart shuddered. But not now. Not this. There was blood. Too much blood. The bedding underneath soaked. And it was bright red. Not a good sign. Red for danger. Her patient was haemorrhaging. Without urgent specialised medical treatment, she would die.

Anna looked wildly around the room, her eyes flitting to the still-open door before coming back to the woman's face. She wanted to give reassurance. An ambulance was on its way. Doctors, rather than a lone nurse with nothing, were about to rush into the room shouting instructions. There were trays full of equipment, a drip stand holding fluids and litres of blood, and a trolley bed waiting to rush her to surgery.

This time, the large black eyes locked onto hers.

"I'm Anna." She pointed to herself, willing her voice to sound calm and confident. "What's your name?"

"Is it you? Is it really you?"

The words squeezed out over dry vocal cords. Anna's heart lurched, but she smiled and tried again, squeezing the icy fingers gently. What could she mean? Who was she expecting to see? But there was still no response to her question. She didn't even know if those dark eyes boring into hers were seeing her. Perhaps she didn't understand English. Her strange response showed she did, but was there a trace of an accent? She hadn't spoken enough words for Anna to work that one out.

But then her eyes flooded with tears and she gasped out, "Help me!"

"I will help you. Can you tell me what happened?" Nothing this time, only the fear in the woman's eyes as another contraction began. Anna grimaced. She had to do something, but what?

"I'm going to get some things to help. Help you—and the baby." She hated to let go of the hand clutching hers, but the brief time between contractions spurred her on. That, and the bleeding. She squeezed her eyes shut before looking away, then crossed the room, heading for the bathroom. About to pass the blank wall screen, she stopped short. Someone must be watching. They had to help. What were they thinking? She sucked in a breath, and tried a calm, clear voice, not the one screaming at her inside. The last thing the woman needed was to hear the person sent to help her lose it. She must be terrified enough.

"This woman needs medical help. She needs a doctor. She's going to bleed to death." Her heart sank even as she clipped out the words. After all this time with nothing and no one, why would tonight be any different? Why would they rush in and help when they had dragged her out of bed? She stuffed her fist in her mouth, glanced back at the bed, and raced into the bathroom, grabbing an armful of towels. She stopped at the basin, moistening the end of one, and glared at the mirror. Cameras behind the screen in the other room, two-way mirror in here or not? They had to get the message.

"I can't help her. I'm not a doctor. Something is wrong. Get someone in here. Please." That 'please' wasn't for them or for her. It was for the woman on the bed. She turned and raced back to the bedside.

44

*L*ucy slowed the car to a walking pace, frowning at the unfamiliar car parked too close to her driveway entrance. She had to make an awkward wide-angle turn to negotiate around it. Tricky in the dark, moonless night. She parked and watched through her rear-view mirror as the figure of a man emerged from it.

"Jamie," she gasped, her heart betraying her, pounding so loud she was sure he must hear it. It couldn't be. His name sounded strange, squeaked out through her rapidly drying throat. She grabbed her bag and swung out of her seat. It was him.

"Lucy," he said, his voice pleasant, his steps confident as he approached.

"Jamie. What are you doing here?" She took a step backwards towards her front door, stopping as the sensor light triggered and flooded the doorway and half the driveway with light. He looked a little thinner, but still tanned, clean-shaven and fit, his hair longer than before, stray curls escaping from behind his ears tousled by the last efforts of the sea breeze.

"How are you?" he said, a half-smile on his lips, and raised one arm in a sweeping gesture as if he included the house in his question.

She didn't answer. What did he want? And why come here after no contact for so long? His last message to her had been the night he'd asked her to meet for coffee just weeks after Anna went missing. He'd stood her up, his brief text saying something had come up and he couldn't make it. And then nothing.

As if he'd read her thoughts, he said, "I'm in town for a week. I wanted to explain what happened—that last time." He paused, looked toward his car, and then at the door behind her. "I knocked on your door and your… uh… friend told me you were out, so I thought I'd wait."

"Friend. Oh, you mean, Mick. He's—" She stopped, turned, and put her key in the lock. "Come in, I'll introduce you properly." She was glad that Mick was home tonight. He worked some evenings, re-stocking shelves at their local supermarket, a casual job to support his studies at theological college.

"Hi Mick. I'm home. Are you decent?" She called, swallowing the chuckle wanting to bubble from her throat. Happiness or hysteria? A little of both, perhaps. Focus on Mick, forget the tall hand-some man about to explain his disappearing act behind her. She bit the inside of her cheek. Not such a good association. He was or had been, after all, Anna's boyfriend.

"In here." His closed bedroom door muffled Mick's voice. He was no doubt immersed in books at the desk set up in there. "Decent?" he said, followed by, "Oh." As his head poked through the door, a puzzled look was rapidly replaced by a wary smile as he spotted Jamie.

"Coffee?" Lucy included them both and led the way to the kitchen. Putting the kettle on, she rummaged in the cupboards looking for biscuits and sugar—did Jamie take sugar? Probably not, but it gave her space to tame her breathing and hope her drumming heartbeat would slow enough to not be visible when she turned around.

She looked up to see both males focused on her, striking almost identical poses, legs spaced out and arms a measured distance from their sides as if they were cowboys ready to draw guns. They were standing about as far from each other as they could get in the not too spacious kitchen-diner.

"Oh, sorry," she said, trying a smile. "Mick, this is Jamie, Anna's

—friend." Boyfriend didn't seem right somehow. "And Jamie, this is Mick, my brother." She watched as their expressions changed in the nanosecond before they smiled and shook hands. Jamie's, from surprise to… was it relief? And Mick's, still a little wary, but with a growing realisation of who Jamie was.

"You should have said," Mick said. "At the door, I mean, who you were."

Jamie shrugged. "It's fine. It's been—too long, and I didn't want to leave a message. I owe Lucy an explanation and felt I needed to do it face to face."

That was the understatement of the year. Lucy pushed the tray across the countertop to Mick. "Let's go sit," she said. "You two go ahead. I'll get some nibbles." Mick dutifully took the tray laden with three mugs of steaming coffee. Lucy didn't trust her shaking hands to make it safely.

What was Jamie up to? He wouldn't have news of Anna, surely. Not before her, certainly not before Anna's mum. Heather would be on the phone to Lucy straight away if there was news. Perhaps he was coming to tell her he'd met someone else. Moving on with his life. He was a good-looking guy, earned plenty of money with his oil-rig job, and he had only been going out with Anna for about three months before she— Lucy bit her lip. Delaying tactics by staying in here wouldn't find out. Get in there, Lucy Roberts.

Mick and Jamie were doing a great job of pretending each was the only occupant of the room, their heads bent, intent on examining the rug. Or was it their shoes? Both sets of eyes, hopeful and expectant, swivelled to search hers as she entered. She almost heard sighs of relief but, unwilling to make the first move, she fixed her eyes on the two snack bowls in her hands, taking her time to arrange them carefully on the coffee table. The smile she'd plastered on her face was beginning to feel ridiculous, and she felt a twinge of annoyance at Mick as she sat beside him on the couch. It wasn't like her chatty brother to miss an opportunity to engage anyone in conversation. She watched Jamie's hand as he lifted his mug to take a sip, willing her eyes to go no further. She could wait. She'd been waiting all this time, after all.

"Look," he said, "I'm really sorry about my sudden departure.

We had a family emergency, and I had to leave for Brisbane straight away. It was so—unexpected. It was all… I was on the phone, you know, arranging flights, trying to get more information from…"

He blinked slowly and wrapped both hands around his mug. Lucy had a million questions, mainly to do with him filling in the blanks. She opened her mouth and then closed it again. Was he about to cry? But? Her eyes narrowed. Nothing for almost four months? What kind of family emergency prevents a quick phone call or text in all that time? She tried to read his expression, but he looked at ease, a little pinched around his eyes but nothing shifty or evasive there. And he had come tonight, finally. He didn't really owe her an explanation. Unless—

"I'm not explaining very well," he said. "It's difficult. Still raw. But my sister was in a car accident, seriously injured. It was touch and go at first. Sadly, her best friend died. I'd known her too, since they were little. Both our families were close."

She and Mick let out matching huffs of air. Her own left her chest deflated, her ribs aching, as if she would never fill her lungs again. Her mouth in a perfect O.

"How awful," she said when she could muster the words. "How is she now? Your sister?"

"Slowly improving. She had head and spinal injuries. They put her in a coma initially. We didn't know how much damage. But now, it's looking more hopeful. She's learning to—basically everything. Talk, walk. Now she can walk with two sticks, but is in a wheelchair most of the time. She tires easily."

Lucy wanted to pull him into a hug. No wonder he hadn't communicated. This was huge. It must have been all-consuming. She looked at Mick and thought of her own little sister, Vicki. And her brothers. But, even so, a simple text. How hard was that? She dug her fingernails into the palm of her hands. Suspicions danced around the edges, sending nasty barbs through her mind. He had gone through so much. First Anna, and now this. What kind of person was she, thinking only the worst of him? She cleared her throat and focused on what he was saying.

Their parents were elderly. He was the only sibling. He'd moved back to Queensland to help, support. Had come back briefly to finalise selling his apartment here, pack up the rest of his stuff, and send it over.

Lucy's head screamed all the questions she wanted answers to. What about Anna? Then 'what about me?' slammed in behind. She picked up her coffee cup, and held it to her cheek to hide the rising heat, glad of the cooler night and high collar covering her neck. No. This was about Jamie, and all he was going through, not about her. There was not a Lucy and Jamie, never was and never would be.

Jamie held out a card. She didn't trust herself to reach for it. If their fingers met? The self-loathing at her wayward thoughts crashed in waves through her mind. This wasn't the way a so-called friend should think, let alone feel.

"Here's my address and phone number, email too. If you hear anything about Anna, I mean. I… don't know what to say…" He trailed off, his eyes distinctly red-rimmed now.

45

*A*nnalee had very little experience with midwifery, just a few weeks in the second year of her nursing degree. The outer-suburbs hospital was small by city standards, with a six bed obstetric wing where she'd attended three or four deliveries. As a trainee, her role had been to observe and make notes for an assessment. Nothing hands-on was required, and they were straightforward births. This was far from it.

"It's okay. You're going to be okay," Anna lied as she wiped the feverish face and patted the moist towel on chapped, dry lips. Those enormous eyes locked onto hers, and she saw the despair and truth reflected there before they misted over as another strong contraction took hold.

Anna pushed down the covers, draping one of the soft towels over the woman's shoulders and chest before manoeuvring herself down the bed. Her eyes narrowed, her heart ramping up again at the sight of all the blood, but there was a small dark circle visible.

"Your baby's almost here. I can see its head." Along with the rivulets of blood pulsing from the force of the contraction. Anna covered the red-stained sheets with layers of towels and drew as close as she could. How many more contractions it would take, she didn't know. Neither did she count them, not daring to suggest an end to it, although desperately willing it to happen. Willing the woman to keep going. Willing her to have enough blood to last. There was surely more on the bed than her slight frame contained, yet it still kept coming.

Her knowledge of what to expect was hazy. She searched her memory of those few births she had attended. Midwife, nurses and then doctors hovering around, ready with sterile equipment, forceps if needed, scalpel and sutures to prevent a tear. She had none of them. She bit her lip, tasting her blood. The acrid saltiness of it, while the stench of the woman's blood pooling beneath her knees assaulted her nostrils.

When? When? How would she know when was the right time? Was that small crown of black getting bigger, or was it her imagination? And then something changed. In the contraction's nature? In the woman's body? The difference in her scream? It was time. Somehow Anna knew, and as the next contraction began, she reached up and squeezed the icy fingers clutching the towel.

"You must push really, really hard now. Your baby is almost here." She gulped in a breath and risked a look at the woman's face. It was grey, almost translucent, the red in her cheeks gone. Her upper body was still. Her eyes closed, mouth no longer straining. Anna couldn't see any sign of breathing from her mouth or nose, any rise or fall from her rib cage under the towel.

"No!" She slapped the thigh next to her chin. "Push. You must push." She held her breath as she waited, watching for movement, and then there it was. The smallest twitch of her lips. The slightest rise from her chest.

"You can do it." You have to. Please don't die before—. Her head swam. Tears pooled, blurring her vision. She couldn't do this. She wasn't capable. Waves of heat suffused her neck and flooded her cheeks. She forced some air in between clenched teeth, and worked her jaw, blinking the tears away. It's down to you, Annalee Tanaka. Who else was there?

"Come on. Come on, one more big push."

From somewhere deep within the woman, a low, guttural growl stirred and sighed between her lips. A hideous grimace contorted her face as her head rose from the pillow, almost meeting her knees, before she sank back. It was enough. The baby's head and shoulders were out. Then Anna could ease the tiny torso free and lay the child on a clean towel.

"You have a baby girl." Anna blinked. "You have a perfect little girl." Her words were clear and confident, belying what she felt as she gazed at the unresponsive scrap.

The tiny form with translucent grey skin, the patches not covered with blood showing cotton threads of dark blood vessels. An apple-sized perfect face, eyes tight shut, button nose and rosebud lips pursed in a surprised pout. Surprised at her birth? Too soon and too violent. Anna couldn't take her eyes off those lips. Perfectly formed, ready to speak a million words, ready to stake her claim on the world. To say her piece, speak up for herself. But they were not pink rosebuds, ready to bloom. They were blue, a mere shade darker than her skin.

Anna let out a long breath. "Oh!" escaped her lips. She too had such a miracle within. Growing steadily. Only waiting for the chance to… A surge of intense longing and… love? Yes, love, for her child coursed through her. Up until that moment, she'd done her best to dissociate from the reality of her pregnancy. Uncertain, even as she felt her baby's tentative movements growing stronger over the past weeks, how she should feel about something forced upon her. But now… Tears pooled in her eyes.

She blinked hard and picked up the baby, cradled her in her palm and stroked her back, limbs, and chest with one finger. She didn't know how premature she was, but she fitted into Anna's hand, tiny knees just coming past her wrist. She blew gently across her face.

"Breathe for me. Breathe," she whispered, her tears spilling unchecked onto the baby's cheek. "Oh, God. If you are there, if you can see this. If you care. Help this little one. Help her live." Seconds and minutes stretched around her and the baby as she urged her on to take a breath. Her own breath locked tight in her chest as she waited, as if letting it out would signal defeat. The only sound, her blood throbbing in her temples, her heart drumming fast, too fast.

It was no use. She exhaled a sob. She had to do what she could for the baby's mother. If she could save one of them? With a gentle kiss on the baby's cheek, she placed her down on the towel and wrapped her, taking care to leave her face uncovered. Her mother could still see her child. Should still see her. She could say goodbye.

Anna didn't want to say goodbye to both of them, her heart heavy as she lifted the precious bundle up to place her on the woman's chest. As she did, there was a tiny movement of the baby's lips, the ghost of a twitch of one eyelid. Anna blinked the tears away. Did she imagine it? And then the faintest of sounds came out of that perfect little mouth. An infinitesimal flaring of pin-head sized nostrils. Anna gasped, drew her close and puffed air across her face again, rewarded as skin started to pink, the little chest heaving with stronger cries.

Anna shuffled up the bed, her thighs screaming, and placed the baby under the towel across her mother's chest. She lifted the woman's thin, flaccid arm and cradled it around the bundle.

"Your beautiful baby girl. Hold her tight. She needs you," Anna said, bile burning her throat at the ashen, goose-fleshed skin. Muscles twitched around the woman's face and neck, her eyes were rolling back. Shallow panting breaths forced their way through thinned lips, trembling over chattering teeth. She was going into shock. There wasn't much time left.

She eased one hand under the woman's sweat-slicked neck and leaned in close, willing the warmth from her body to transfer to the other.

"She's a little fighter, your baby daughter." Anna swallowed the scream rising from her belly. "Can you tell me your name? What is your name?" She had to know who she was. Something for her to cling onto, to remember when all this was over.

There was no response at first, but then the woman's eyes fluttered open and she worked to loosen her jaw. "K… Kay…" the barely audible word sounded out. Anna leaned in closer.

46

"Barb?" Heather hesitated, unsure if the silence on the line meant a connection or not. You could never tell, what with answering machine messages tricking you into thinking you were talking to a real person or the vagaries of magical places phone calls travelled through with Wi-Fi. 'The Cloud.' What was that all about? Her son Stephen and his wife Meg had explained it to her more than once, but...? She shrugged and wrapped her dressing gown more tightly around her. "Barb, can you hear me?"

"Hello, Heather. Yes, yes, I can. Loud and clear. How are you?"

"Is now a good time, or will I call back later?" Heather's fingers tightened around the new iPhone Barbara had helped her to buy just before she returned to the UK.

"Heather, what is it? Yes, it's fine. A good time, although not so good for you. What time is it over there? Couldn't you sleep? Has something happened? Have they..."

Heather eyed the bedside clock, ticking over to 3.16 am. She hoped this was a one-off. Her old sleep pattern of a solid seven hours, the one she had before Annalee went missing, had settled back in over the past few weeks. Until tonight.

"No. No, nothing like that. But it is something to do with the case." Why did she say that? Annalee wasn't a 'case', she was her missing daughter, gone now since the seventh of May: six months, one week and three days ago.

"I mean—Oh, where to start?" She put a fist to her mouth, stifling a yawn, grateful for Barbara's steady presence on the other end. Her cousin was the one person Heather could turn to after a day like today, when all the what ifs, maybes and should haves, were dredged up by some new 'development'. If that was what this was.

She could turn to Ruth, her best friend at church, her spiritual sister, and she did most of the time. They met regularly, sometimes just the two of them, at other times with a dedicated group of friends, to pray for Anna and other issues of concern. But three in the morning was not the best time to wake any of them, and Barbara had firsthand knowledge of what she was going through.

"Do you want to FaceTime?" Barbara said.

She had stayed with Heather for three months after the nightmare of Anna's disappearance, but eventually returned to England and her own life. They had argued over a date for her to go back, Barbara wanting to stay for as long as Heather needed her and Heather torn between that need and consideration for the strain she knew Barbara was under. With the spectre of Barbara's own daughter, Katie, missing without a trace for over four years, ever hovering over them. In the end, they sat together at the computer and booked the flight. Neither of them willing to acknowledge that it may be years, if ever, before they would find Anna.

"FaceTime. No." This brought a shudder and then a smile to Heather's lips. "You don't want to see what I look like in the middle of the night." She knew Barbara wouldn't care and they FaceTimed often now that Heather had the fancy phone. Barbara and her husband John were way ahead of her in the technology stakes and had often FaceTimed each other when she was staying with Heather.

"A features journalist called me today. They want to put Anna in an article about missing persons—in the lead up to Christmas." Heather's stomach lurched. The mention of Christmas filled her with terror. It was a time to celebrate. Particularly for her as a Christian, to celebrate an amazing time remembering when Christ came to earth. But leaving that aside, she frowned, a time to get together with family. How could she face that again? It had been bad enough after Tony died. And now this year—her eyes filled, and she reached for a tissue.

She swallowed the lump in her throat and tried a normal voice, not wanting Barbara to hear her sorrow yet again. "It's not just Anna, but they want a big focus on her. 'Call home', it's going to be called, or something like that. Apparently they do it about this time every year."

Heather vaguely recalled similar articles. She'd always felt so sorry for the families as she studied the images. Each one with the brief details splashed across the bottom of the black and white grainy photos of those 'lucky' enough to have only been missing a short time. Most of them depicted happy smiling men or women enjoying life, above a short paragraph outlining their name, age, place where they were last seen, and other information designed to jog the public's memory. Perhaps even the missing person's conscience, assuming they had chosen to disappear. Heather dabbed at her eyes. But Anna wasn't one of those. She would never manufacture her own disappearance without a word to her mother or anyone she loved. She would make that phone call if she could.

Barbara said, "Oh… wow. And you're thinking…? A million and one things, I'm guessing."

"Exactly that. My head's buzzing."

"Poor you. Do you have a choice?"

She did. Her immediate reaction was to shout "No!" and hang up the phone, but she'd bitten her tongue and listened to the softly spoken, very nice research assistant. Valerie something-or-other stepped her through the newspaper's plan and purpose for the article. But being the centre of attention once more filled her with dread. People she barely knew ringing or stopping her to ask—sometimes the most insensitive questions. Or to offer suggestions for Heather or the police to try, or where Anna might be, as if they hadn't thought of all of that to the nth degree. Then Valerie dangled the carrot, outlining several cases—there was that word again—that were solved, directly linked to similar campaigns. And that, above all, was what she, what they all wanted. It wasn't all about her. She would do anything to bring Anna back.

Detective Troy's face flashed into Heather's mind. She hadn't heard from her for such a long time, not since that last time when a body turned up. Thankfully, it hadn't been Anna. Was Elaine aware of this newspaper feature? Should Heather contact her to ask if it was a good idea? Heather sniffed. But then, what would be the point of calling? The police were so busy, and she did trust Elaine. She'd promised to contact her first thing if anything came up.

Heather realised Barbara was talking. "Oh, Barb, I'm sorry. What were you saying?"

"Nothing really. Just tossing through my mind what I would do. We don't do it here. Probably too many—" Barbara broke off.

No! Heather should have realised. It had been alright when they were here together to talk about Barbara's experiences after the disappearance of Katie but now, with the distance between them, she should be more sensitive.

"I'm sorry, Barb." Here she was thinking about how insensitive people were to her and she was doing the same thing to Barbara.

"No. Don't apologise, Heather. We've talked about this. You don't have to tread softly with me. You know that. It's something you never get used to, but, if it can help…"

Heather bit her lip. She knew it, but that didn't make it any easier. Nothing had helped Barbara find Katie. And she, they, weren't the only ones. So many families had gone through this. Waiting year after year. Hoping their son or daughter was still alive somewhere and would turn up at the door, happy and unharmed. To dwell on the alternative was unbearable. Yet they knew in their hearts, as Heather and Barbara did, that their child wouldn't do that. Would never leave them without a word.

"All in all," Barbara said, "I believe it will be worthwhile. Some people have turned up. Some families no longer have to go through what we're going through."

47

"Fishies!" Liam strained at David's hand.

"Okay, mate." David hoisted Liam onto his shoulders, feeling the familiar warmth of his little body and the hands clamped around his forehead as he walked towards the row of runabouts. Miranda skipped alongside, joining hands with two of her classmates as they ran up to her, wide smiles turning into giggles and shouts of laughter, her concern for Adela forgotten. They joined the gathering crowd of islanders, most of whom were from the main village, but a number he recognised from the other two villages further inland.

David moved comfortably through the throng, people stopping him to pat his or Liam's arm, sharing a smile or pointing out something he must see. This time of day at the cove was important in the social life of the people as they caught up with family and friends from near and far.

Everything stopped for the hour after the boats came in. The Wilsons had followed the Farleighs' lead and continued their practice of closing the school and medical clinic and joining the merry crowd heading down to the cove. Time not spent inspecting and bartering for goods was used to discuss the latest news: who was having the next celebration, what it was for, how the preparations were going, and so on. David—and Jenni, whenever she could make it—enjoyed joining in and found it a valuable time to get to know more of the islanders and their culture.

Tranquil Vaui Island with its natural freshwater springs was large enough to support three villages. The original inhabitants had made it their home so long ago that no one could remember when. Stories passed down told of escape from aggressive war-lords on the mainland who constantly raided their villages for plantation slaves or recruits to make up for the warriors decimated by tribal conflicts. The islanders' ancestors wanted peace and freedom from oppression and welcomed the Christian missionaries spreading the gospel of peace, as it fitted in well with their traditional beliefs and values.

"Liam. Miranda."

David turned as Jenni slipped her arm into his. "You made it then?"

"Yes, fairly quiet at the clinic this morning." Jenni reached for Liam, who was swaying precariously towards her across David's neck, chubby fingers straining.

As David, now kilograms lighter, straightened up, he caught sight of Adela again. She stood next to the boat now tied up at the jetty, her arms waving in all directions. Snatches of her high-pitched tone cut across the surface of the water between them. She was far from happy.

"We have to do what we can for Adela," he said softly to Jenni, her eyes tracking at his words to the scene playing out across the water.

"But David, you've tried three times to speak to the mysterious Mr Koh, and each time that great motorboat comes out to warn you off."

And that wasn't the half of it. What Jenni didn't know, because he had sworn Bim and Jon to secrecy, was that the last time they tried, Koh's army of thugs very nearly capsized their small runabout. The men on the powerful motor-launch laughed and jeered, waving sub-machine guns at them as they roared past metres away.

David had reported the incident to the police at Kepolo the next time they visited, but it fell on deaf ears. The sergeant-in-charge

smiled genially and insisted that Mr Koh was a good fella and enti-
tled to his privacy. He didn't want to be bothered by no missionary
man. He had his own gods and needed no more. David got the
message. Corruption was widespread in these parts and Koh had
plenty of money to splash about.

"Why don't we take Adela to the mainland with us next time?
You can go with her to the police station and help her explain.
Maybe with you to support her, they might listen and finally investi-
gate what's going on over there."

"We can but try," David said, although he wasn't optimistic
about the outcome. Jimi wasn't the only one who had disappeared.
The villagers told many stories about the island, but the truth was
over half a dozen families had children or grandchildren supposedly
working for Koh and all had lost contact with them. Money was the
attraction, yet despite the warnings from village elders, Pastor Jean-
Paul, and David and Jenni, the villagers succumbed to the promises
of good pay and job training for their kids.

As if Jenni read his mind, she said. "They're so poor and fishing
doesn't bring in what it used to. It's no wonder they see Koh as the
answer to their problems."

"Until the money stops and they can't contact their children.
And with Sergeant Vanuai insisting that they have gone to the mainland to spend up big before going on to other cities to work or back
to Koh's Island, there's nothing they can say."

Jenni snorted, her cheeks flushing red. "It's so ridiculous,
suggesting that not one of them cares enough for their folks here to
even call them. He thinks that if he keeps telling the same old
stories, they'll believe them and forget about their children."

"Well, Adela is made of stronger stuff than that. She won't give
up so easily."

"And with you and the good Lord on her side, what can go
wrong?" Jenni squeezed his arm.

David raised an eyebrow at his wife's last words. He certainly had
that faith in God, and he would be by Adela's side fighting in her
corner, but trying to raise questions about Koh and the workers he
recruited was like running into a brick wall.

Perhaps they should go further afield than the small town of

Kepolo on the mainland. He made a mental note to do just that if they got the same run-around next time.

48

"Kay? Are you Kay?" Annalee squeezed the woman's arm gently and bit down the questions she desperately wanted answers to. About her. About this place. How long had she been here? Where did she come from? How old was she? Had she ever seen anyone? What were they like? What did they want?

Kay was the first living soul Anna had met since her captivity, and she was watching her die. Anna's face and neck grew hot, tears blurring her eyes. She sniffed them away. She had to be strong. In her job, death wasn't a stranger, but it was never easy, and not like this. It shouldn't be like this. Why was this woman so emaciated, left in such poor condition when she was pregnant? Nothing could justify that. As if in perfect agreement, Anna's own baby began kicking, tapping out a little dance inside her skin. That surge of love she'd felt earlier shot through her again, a flutter in her heart causing a hiccup to catch in her throat. But Kay was her priority right now. Her eyes had become still, barely slits, the black pupils fully dilated. Anna, mesmerised, felt drawn deep, deep down into the dark abyss Kay was inexorably being sucked into.

"Kay. Kay. Can you hear me? What will you name your baby? What will you call your daughter?"

191

She felt Kay's hand around the baby tense. Saw a tear slide out of one eye and lips moving to shape words.

"C… care… my… babe sss." The monosyllables slipped out, the last hissing on her final breath. The eyes locked onto Anna's dimmed, her features smoothed, and her head became heavy in Anna's hand.

Anna gently lowered Kay's head to the pillow, checked the snuffling baby wasn't in danger of slipping, and eased herself upright. She was stiff, sick and sore, her muscles cramping, screaming for rest, but most of all, she was deathly tired. She wanted to run, to get out of this room. Away from all the blood. Go back to her room and crawl into bed. But there was more to be done. She couldn't leave Kay this way. Her training dictated she give dignity to the dead by presenting them well for the next stage of their journey. Her hands and feet worked of their own accord, moving from one side of the bed to the other, straightening Kay's body and the thin top cover. The swaddled baby was still on Kay's chest. She would leave her close to her mother until it was time to go.

After checking the baby's colour and breathing, she risked a visit to the bathroom. She pulled off her soiled clothes and scrubbed at her hands and arms, and found a clean top and shorts in the drawers. The blood clinging to her legs and torso, she would deal with later. Her dry mouth and burning throat demanded a drink, so she greedily gulped a few handfuls of water and headed back, with a wetted facecloth.

As she washed Kay's waxen face and smoothed her hair, images of the patients she'd cared for after death came back one by one. There weren't many. Each face, enshrined in sepulchral white sheets, paraded before her, until the final one. Not a patient, but her beloved father, lying in his coffin at the family viewing. A sob escaped her throat, unleashing tears which spilled unchecked this time, dripping onto Kay's cheeks, her eyes and mouth, as if in a futile attempt at revival.

Lifting the sleeping baby carefully into her arms, she burrowed her face into the thick towel swaddle, waiting for the tears to stop. Already, the unmistakable baby smell which promised so much to a mother infused the towel. Anna forced herself to study Kay's face. She had to imprint every contour and curve into her memory. Imagine how she once would have been, youthful and vibrant. Full of life and joy after birthing her daughter. She must do this for the baby. For herself.

Kay had been beautiful, with fine features and high cheekbones. No wrinkles around the corners of her eyes or mouth, no skin blemishes or even tiny pock-marks from teen pimples or chicken-pox. It was difficult to tell her age, anything from mid-teens to late twenties, her size and features masking that. Her hair, despite the lack of condition, showed signs of former strength and lustre. Anna thought about the hair ring from the cove; it was the same dark colour and coarse texture. It seemed unlikely that Kay had fashioned it, given the state she was in. But, like herself, she was of Asian origin by her hair colour, looks and those large eyes.

Who was she? Herself in the future? Anna shuddered. Her head was throbbing, her eyes hot orbs, and not just from crying. She was spent, her thoughts fuddled, but couldn't look away from Kay. Were all the captives here from a similar background? Although Anna was of mixed race, with a part-Japanese father and an English mother, it was difficult to tell with Kay. Was that part of the perverse selection criteria of their captors?

The baby snuffled, and she looked down, tracing her finger around the tiny hand escaping the towel. She would do what she could to honour Kay's last wishes. She frowned, looking at the doorway. How she would take care of a baby was beyond her, even if the child survived her premature birth without specialist care. She needed a humidicrib, a paediatrician and... so much more. Still, Anna had heard some amazing survival stories in the past when nothing but willingness to help and the baby's will to live were available.

The placenta had birthed, so Anna wrapped it in a separate towel and hitched it under the baby. She had no sterile clamps and scissors to cut the tough cord attaching it to the child, but would cross that bridge later. When her brother and Meg were expecting Matthew, they'd debated the merits of leaving the placenta attached to the baby until nature took its course. It would detach naturally after three to ten days. Termed a 'lotus' birth, it was gaining traction in some circles, but there was a risk of infection, so Steve and Meg discounted it. Anna had little choice; cutting or sawing through it with anything she could come up with would probably be worse.

"Let's go, little one." She kissed the top of the baby's head and started for the door, which swished shut as she neared.

"What the…?" She didn't need this. The door had remained open the entire time, and now it closed. She turned to the bed, her eyes wide, heart racing. What was going on? The answer buzzed at the base of her spine.

No. They had to open the door.

"Let me out. Open this door." She took two steps toward it, her eyes fixed on the screen above the desk. A burst of electricity radiated down her thighs, sending her staggering. Clutching her abdomen with her free hand, she fought to regain balance. The baby mewled weakly but settled again. She tried a step backward, and the intensity of the current died down. She retreated to the bed and sat on its edge, gulping in air and rubbing the small of her back. The door slid open once more.

She had no strength to play games, but knew this was no game as her second attempt brought the same punishing result. She stood her ground, refusing to retreat, and gritted her teeth against the shock-waves pulsing through every nerve.

Her "What do you want from me?" died in her throat. She knew exactly what they wanted. For her to give up the baby and leave. Red fiery rage rose from her chest even as steel blades of pain forced their way into every joint and muscle.

"No! No! I can't leave her here. I won't…." Had she said the words aloud over her numbing tongue and lips? Her head was ready to explode, yet under her skin, ice cold needles were lancing through her as the punishing voltage increased. Black and purple swirls clouded the corners of her vision.

"What are you going to do with her? I promised to… care…"

Someone was sobbing. Anna didn't look at the bed. It couldn't be Kay. She was dead, wasn't she? The next heaving sob from her chest surprised her, but spurred her on. She shuffled half a step, and then another, clenching her jaw against the pain. Her feet were solid, wet sandbags dragging across the floor, but she made it. The cool metal of the door seemed somehow soft against her forehead as she slid to her knees. Her only thought was to cushion the baby, both babies, as the blackness swelled and took over.

49

'B there in 5.'

Amy's text pinged through as Lucy finished her tea and rinsed the cup. Amy had talked her into Christmas shopping, sealing the invitation with a catch up lunch when Lucy tried to decline. Shopping was not her favourite thing, but they hadn't seen each other for weeks, if not months. It had been too long, what with her long hours at the hospital and Amy's full-on commitment to gaining a distinction in her second-last year of a journalism degree. Lucy admired her discipline in foregoing all extra-curricular activities to focus.

Study hadn't come easily to Amy, and she'd taken a gap year off after high school to decide if she should go to university at all. But writing was her passion and she'd surprised everyone, including herself, by getting the score she needed for the course, then promptly deferring for the year, surprising everyone again. She'd confessed to Lucy how much of a struggle that final year of high school had been. Not only with the coursework, but with a bad bout of teenage acne, and ridicule from some of her peers about said acne and her size 14 body. It didn't help that she was the shortest in her cohort. Her year off did the trick though, as she spent part of the time at Youth With A Mission, and got to know a group who were far removed from the judgemental and unkind Year 12s from her school.

"Who do you have to buy for?" Amy said as Lucy settled into her friend's battered Mazda. Typical student car—cheap but reliable. It had belonged to Amy's cousin before her parents helped her buy it when she left school.

"Only my sister, but she's the hardest to buy for. And, naturally, whatever I get will be wrong. I can see the disappointment on her face already." Lucy caught the grimace of sympathy on Amy's face, her eyes glued to the busy road. Lucy had pumped her mum for clues as to what fifteen-year-old Vicky wanted, which changed every few days. They'd shared a few chuckles at some items on the fridge list, which ranged from a puppy to an easel and paints. The puppy wasn't an option, with three dogs already in the family. The easel and paints had been a short-lived addition after a local artist visited her school art-class. The many rapid sketches she did in class had impressed Vicky. Unfortunately, her attempts only produced frustration, and the easel left the list. Nothing practical or in Lucy's price range seemed to make it.

"It looks like everyone else is going to Karrinyup, too." Amy risked a glance at Lucy as she drew into the long queue leading to the underground carpark. No doubt everyone hoping for a spot out of the hot December sun. "Sorry."

"It's okay. I need to do it and can't wait to catch up with you. What about you, how many presents?" Lucy crossed her mental fingers that there would be few, and they wouldn't have to battle the crowds for hours.

"Just Mum and Dad, and Gramps." Amy was an only child. Lucy had alternated for years between envying her friend the limelight the position gave her with her parents, and feeling sorry that she didn't have the chance to experience the delights—mostly—of belonging to a happy, if boisterous, group of siblings.

"What about Vicky's art interest you were telling me about? You could get her something from the art shop. I love going in there. I'm going to buy my mum some watercolours and paper. She's been hinting at it, but when I pin her down she tells me she's always too busy and will do it 'one day'. Apparently, she wasn't too bad an artist in school, but of course, back then, it wasn't considered a suitable career. The aim was to marry, be a good wife and all that."

Lucy filled her in on Vicky's swift turnabout from a wannabe world-famous artist. "But I'm glad your mum is finding the time to paint."

"Well, I'm hoping she will." Amy grinned. "If I buy her the stuff, then it might be the incentive she needs. But then again, maybe it's not such a good idea, if she just puts it in the cupboard and doesn't use it."

"Presents are so hard sometimes." Who wants clothes that don't fit or you hate the colour or style, or perfume that gives you a headache? Lucy thought back to the disappointments she'd had over the years. Most people got it right, but some things her brothers in particular had given her were cringe-worthy, to say the least.

"Where to for lunch?" Amy said.

They had completed their purchases before noon, pleasing Lucy no end. She'd never liked crowds. Something she put down to growing up in a smaller country town, but her unease seemed to be getting worse lately. "Somewhere quiet, maybe Knox Box?" Lucy liked the franchise for its simple, healthy fare, and the one nearby usually had room to spare.

"Fine by me. You lead the way. I have no idea where we are or which way to go." Amy's poor sense of direction was legendary.

"Do you want to hold my hand?" Lucy laughed.

"Ha-ha. Cruel, you are." But her warm brown eyes twinkled at the jibe.

"But you still love me." Lucy pointed to a table along the back wall. "What about there? You order yours and I'll sit."

"Have you seen the article?" Amy returned, waving a newspaper she'd picked up from the rack near the counter.

"Sort of." Lucy barely glanced at the front page colour photo of Anna standing solemnly in her graduation gown under the bold headline 'Call Home'. Passport-sized photos of other faces framed the large image, with bold type pointing to page four for more detail. Amy went to open the paper, but Lucy put her hand out.

"Don't." She withdrew her hand and put it to her mouth. "Sorry.

I…" A throb started at the back of her head and she fumbled in her bag for her water bottle.

"Okay." Amy folded the paper and placed it on the empty seat beside her. "Do you want to talk about it?"

Lucy stayed silent. No. Maybe. Which part of 'it' did she want to talk about? The article? She'd seen the front page. Everywhere. It had been screaming at her from every direction since it came out yesterday. Even today, as they shopped, she must have seen it at least half a dozen times. Every newsagent, every café, even a couple of copies left on tables in the food hall as they passed through. And it wasn't just in print, but out on all possible social media platforms to maximise the exposure. Her social media connections were busy liking or sad-facing it and sharing with the world.

She'd bought a newspaper on her way home last night but hadn't been able to open it. Mrs Tanaka had told her back in November that it was going to happen and messaged the day before it came out, but Lucy still wasn't prepared for her reaction when it did. When she held that paper in her hand and placed it on the coffee table, where she'd sat staring at it, suddenly not hungry after her long day at work.

"Lucy?" Amy leant towards her, reaching for her hand.

She forced herself to meet her friend's gaze. "It's not the right time for it. Not the week before Christmas," was all she could come up with. No time was the right time. "Everybody is too busy, concerned about shopping, presents, parties, and food." She broke off, looking away.

"Yeah, I know, but there really isn't any right time, is there? Especially for you, and Mrs Tanaka, her brother…" Amy lifted the paper and stared at the images before putting it down again. "The other families." She was silent, but Lucy could feel her eyes searching her face. "You know it's got to be a good thing, doing a focus like this, don't you? Many people—"

"Many?" Lucy stiffened and sat upright. Amy had to go down that track. She knew journalism was her passion, but that statement wasn't true.

"No. Listen." Her voice was soft, but firm. "I wasn't about to say they've found many people, rather that many people offer useful information."

"Sorry, Amy, I shouldn't have interrupted." She sighed. "But either way, it still opens it all up again." Lucy's eyes pooled, but she ignored the threatening tears. In the months since Anna's disappearance, she'd learned to let them have their way. They would either fall or not, and she no longer cared if anyone saw her.

"It brings it all back. It's too hard. Wondering what happened, and… all the thoughts that go through your head." Lucy was grateful Amy stayed silent, the sorrow clear in her eyes. "I miss her so much."

Lucy shrugged, suddenly feeling the chill in the air-conditioned space. "Anyway, can we change the subject? Tell me about your holiday plans."

"Sure. But if you want to talk about… this"—she gestured at the newspaper—"you know I'm here for you. And with the long summer break before uni starts again, I can come over anytime. Just say the word. Is Mick still at yours?"

"No, he left a few days after his exams." Lucy saw Amy's eyes narrow and heard the sharp intake of breath. "It's okay, he didn't abandon me. I practically had to force him to go. I've been fine, a lot more settled, for weeks, and I wanted to see how I'd go on my own."

"But, at night?"

Lucy smiled. "All good. I've been sleeping better, not afraid to go home. I think the longer days and warmer weather help. And… I've met more of my neighbours since the break-in, who all say they're looking out for me. Given me their numbers and so on." She knew she was talking too fast, and why had she brought that up? She glanced at Amy, hoping she hadn't noticed. Amy's eyes were darting around, fixing on a face across the room, then on someone else walking past. For once, she was happy that Amy was distracted. The police seemed satisfied that it was kids who'd broken in, telling her they'd found fingerprints matching another break-in a few streets away that night and several more around that time. Lucy was working hard to put it behind her.

With Amy's eyes back on hers, she said, "And, after Boxing Day it's my ten days break. I'll be heading down home too."

Lucy had volunteered to work on Christmas and Boxing Day to allow other staff with children the time at home. She didn't mind. There were fewer patients, as the hospital sent as many as they could home, even if it was just for a few precious hours with their families. The remaining staff made it a special time for the children who had to stay, a day full of fun activities and treats.

"That's great. You deserve a break." Amy checked her watch. "Have we had enough?"

"Sure." Lucy reached for her bags. "But what about your plans? We never got to you." She put her hand on Amy's arm, suddenly feeling guilty that the entire conversation had been about her and all her woes. Amy hadn't got a look in.

"Not much to tell, really. I'll fill you in on the way home."

50

Annalee reached for the clock to switch off the alarm, but her straining fingers couldn't find it. She groaned and attempted to sit, her body awkward, muscles screaming their protest. She gave up and sank back into bed. It was always the same after a week of night shifts. She licked her dry lips and swallowed past the lump in her throat. Putting a hand to her foggy head, she brushed past wet tears on her cheek and stiffened.

"No." She pushed herself to the edge of the bed and sat, waiting for the swirls of blackness to settle. The room was in semi-darkness, which was odd, but strangely welcome. The full-on brightness which passed for daylight in here would have grated on her already severely depleted energy and nerves.

Her fingers explored the bottom edge of her cotton top, expecting to feel the fabric stiff with dried blood. But her clothes were clean. She scrunched her shoulder up and sniffed—smelled fresh, too. She'd definitely changed after Kay died, but there was still so much blood left behind. Exposing her swelling belly, she cupped it in her hands. Not only was her outfit clean, but her skin, too. All the blood on her torso and legs she hadn't got to in Kay's bathroom was gone. Kay's blood. She retreated up the bed and hugged her pillow, squeezing her eyes shut. The stench of it remained, though, clinging to her nostrils.

She had no memory of coming back here, of getting cleaned up and changed. Had she done it? And what did it matter? Kay was dead, and the baby? That poor, defenceless tiny scrap of a girl. She stuffed her fist in her mouth. What had they done with her? Left her alone with a dead mother to die from neglect?

Her head pounded. Thinking about it made it worse. Once again, the bed became her refuge as the hours passed. The strange half-light prevailed, and she drifted in and out of sleep, the events in Kay's room swirling and replaying in blood-soaked nightmares. Baby Kay's eyes bored into hers, followed by Kay's, imploring Anna to help them, to save them, before they faded and became lifeless. More dreams brought back the blood, so vivid and red. It covered her. She was slipping in it, unable to reach the bed to help Kay or find the baby, who was crying piteously somewhere out of sight. She would wake tear-stained and sweating, her muscles tight, jaw clenching, fighting for breath.

In periods of wakefulness, she dragged herself to the bathroom or the water jug on the little table, desperately tired, barely able to lift it to pour a drink. Then she would crawl back to bed and stare dully at the wall or ceiling, willing her mind to be blank.

Food trays came and went, marking the hours passing with the repetitious swish of the door as it opened or closed. She ignored them. The idea of food made her retch. The physical heaviness of her body defied explanation as if gravity itself had magnified its pull on her extremities. Even her eyelids seemed reluctant to part—unfortunately failing to close out the vivid images replaying on a continuous loop.

Jolting upright after another blood-bathed nightmare, she sat sweating and gasping for breath. What was it? Something different. An impression of someone leaning over her, a delicate puff of sweet breath on her cheek, something cool dabbing her face and the backs of her hands. She had tried to reach out, but the faceless form retreated, its shadow disappearing from her sight.

Her mouth was dry and her stomach rumbled, but she turned her face to the pillow. She should eat for her baby's sake? But was it too late? Despite her desire to blot out the anguish of what happened, she'd been acutely aware there had been no movement in her womb. Not a single flutter or kick since that night in Kay's room. Had she harmed, even killed her own child by trying to leave with Kay's? She drew her knees up to her chest and wrapped her arms around her stomach and legs, letting the tears slide unhindered onto the pillow.

What was she to do? What would they do with her if she had lost her baby?

Her baby.

A wave of longing washed through her frame and she spread her fingers over her stomach.

What had she done? She'd never felt lower, not even when her father died. At least then she had her mother, brother, and friends around her. Now she had no one. No one to walk with her through the dark days ahead. No one to comfort her grief.

And God. Wasn't He meant to be the origin of all comfort and peace? Didn't it say so in the Bible? Scraps of verses came to mind— she should draw near to Him and He would draw near to her and He would never leave her nor forsake her; God so loved... She sighed. It was elusive, this promised presence, this promised love and peace from God. Was it real? Had it ever been? She felt so alone, so wretched. Where was He? Where had He been for Kay? Had He cared what happened to the baby? To her? To any of them in this place? She tried to form words into another question. Or was it a prayer? But nothing came. No words. No comfort. No peace.

51

Jenni watched David guide Adela through the crowd as they disembarked the ferry in Kepolo, his shoulder tilted low, obviously attentive to something she was saying. He was so much taller—the top of Adela's head barely came up to his waist. Jenni found it hard to drag her eyes away. The excitement the monthly trip to the mainland usually brought was missing. The futility of the task had sobered them all. Jenni frowned. 'Futility.' Where did that come from? Anything was possible, and she firmly believed in miracles. But from all their efforts so far to find out what had happened to Adela's grandson, this would need a big one.

"Mam-ma." Liam was drumming his feet on the stroller's footrest, leaning forward and pointing. She'd better move before he wanted out. Sitting was not his preferred state of being. If he had to be confined to the stroller, it should be in motion, not stationary. There were places to explore, exciting things to see, feel, and taste. He didn't mind what they did as long as movement was involved.

"Okay, let's go," she said, pleased to see him relax back into the seat with the first push. Miranda gripped one handle of the stroller, and Jenni covered the small hand with her own, pleased to see the lessons in staying safe in Kepolo were paying off. It wasn't a huge city, a small town really, but a lot busier than Vaui where they knew most of the islanders and Miranda could wander freely in safety.

Their first stop was the general store, where Jenni tracked down most items on her list. School supplies for David, stationery, the medical supplies she needed, and perhaps a few cans or jars of things they didn't grow or preserve on the island. She knew a slow walk around shelves brimming with many weird and wonderful items jammed in tightly together would keep both children entranced, at least for a short while. Vaui didn't have the luxury of a store, and Jenni enjoyed watching Miranda's eyes grow wider and wider, her mouth agape as she took in the plethora of goods. Jenni found the shop fascinating too, but came away with tired eyes, sore from flitting from one item to the next, trying to spot the things she wanted. She smiled, ever hopeful of finding a jar of Vegemite one day, but that exotic treat wasn't too palatable to the uninitiated, so they had to rely on the occasional visitor from Australia for their supply. Luckily, a little went a long way.

Basket full, they made their way to the long, partitioned counter at the side of the store. She stopped at the pharmacy section to collect her order, backed out of the lane partitioned from the next by a plastic chain to repeat the process in the queue for the post office counter. It always amused her when the same assistant on the other side of the counter neatly side-stepped to serve her, but she never complained or questioned the practice, figuring the quirky reasoning behind it was long-embedded in the store's history. The owner, Mr Lwa, or sometimes his daughter, occupied the last section near the door. Jenni watched, fascinated, as Mr Lwa deftly calculated the cost of the items in her basket and added the price on the pharmacy slip with a few brief squiggles on his notepad.

The markets were next, where colourful stalls sold everything from fresh produce to household furniture to vehicles—mainly bicycles. Exotic-smelling spices filled the air, mixed with the sweetness of sugar dust when a vendor emptied a sack into his huge metal bowl as they passed. He was about to concoct one of his garishly coloured sweet treats. Jenni tapped Miranda's shoulder to move her on. She could almost see her salivating at the sight.

But Miranda wouldn't budge. "May I watch, please?" She looked up at her, enormous eyes pleading.

"Not today, Mims." Jenni was after fabric to make the children more play clothes, and they were yet to run the gauntlet of Miranda's favourite area. That part would take some time to get through before they met up with David and Adela. Vendors selling live creatures of every imaginable kind took up almost a quarter of the market's area. Not Jenni's idea of fun, seeing animals and birds kept in cages, the fish or crabs slowly moving about in buckets or, if they were lucky, bigger containers, awaiting their fate. But she couldn't deny Miranda the experience, or pretend it wasn't there. The animal and bird sounds were an ever-present backdrop above the crowd. Jenni would, as always, plaster a smile on her face as Miranda clucked over a brightly coloured bird or stopped to stroke a turtle, a pig, or a goat. She dreaded the day her daughter realised it was not a giant pet shop, with animals waiting to be welcomed into loving homes. Jenni's one consolation was that Miranda understood the no-purchase rule; it was important to keep the animals on Vaui safe from outside disease.

They'd planned to meet David and Adela under some shady trees in a corner of the markets. Not knowing how long it would take at the police station, Jenni was sharing lunch with Miranda and Liam when she spotted David's tall figure. He was searching the crowd, his head slowly swivelling from side to side. She waved wildly and saw the smile of recognition as he threaded his way towards them. As the crowd parted, Adela came into view. Her hair was wild, framing her angry red face. She was holding her headcloth close to one eye. Jenni sighed and got to her feet as they drew closer. She wrapped her arms around Adela and helped her sit down.

"That sergeant say my Jimi's gone to the city. He say he come by here three months ago. And with a girl." Adela snorted the last word out before continuing rapidly. "He say he saw them get on the bus hisself!" She swiped at her eyes, stared into the crowd, and seemed to shrink into herself as Jenni watched.

David stayed silent for a minute, his jaw working, before he sat on the other side of Adela, lifted an insistent Liam onto his knee and kissed the top of his head.

"He has all the answers, won't listen to anything we have to say. It's so frustrating," he said finally. Jenni looked into his face, seeing the sorrow pinching at the corners of his eyes and mouth, the tension in his upper jaw.

"I know that sergeant lying. Why, he doesn't know what my Jimi look like. How can he see him get on a bus? My Jimi want to be a doctor, like Pastor Farleigh 'n' you, Missus Wilson. He only work for that Mr Koh to save money for college. He wouldn't run away from that, from me and the family." She threw her arm in a wide arc. "That's why he want to be a doctor. You know that. So he can help the people."

"Mm, we know, Adela." David put his arm around her shoulders and drew her in close. "And he will make a fine doctor, too. Mrs Farleigh said he was one of the best pupils she ever taught in the school, and Dr Farleigh found him a great help in the clinic. He was already learning so much about medicine."

"You have to find him, Pastor David. You just have to." She tugged at his sleeve, tears coursing down her cheeks.

David looked over Adela's head at Jenni. They joined hands around Adela and the children. David said a prayer for wisdom to know what to do next and for Jimi's safe return.

52

"Anything useful?" his boss said.

Detective Constable Jake Winters was scrolling through the 'shortlist' of responses to the 'Come Home' article released ten days before Christmas. It had provoked more than the usual number of calls and emails. Christmas had that effect on people, which was, of course, their goal. No one liked to think that their loved one would be missing from the table on the big day. His shortlist held well over two hundred entries. All relating to Annalee Tanaka's unusual disappearance, which had provoked the state's, if not the nation's, collective interest.

Responses relating to the other missing persons in the feature had come in, but their combined number altogether was less than this one. And, thankfully, those responses had gone off to other teams.

He watched as another email appeared at the top of the screen. In the week following Christmas, responses had slowed, but in no way stopped. After the excitement of the big day, people had time to catch up on back news or spotted links to the article or heard word of mouth.

"Annalee's been seen everywhere from Donnybrook picking

apples, to a sex worker in Kal, to a…" He frowned. Detective Sergeant Troy wouldn't want to know that.

"Sorry." He drew his mouth into a taut line. "I've just had the once-through. I'm about to highlight a few to focus on." He would backtrack on the others. You could never tell when even the most obscure piece of information would be the key they had been waiting for. Jake felt a breath warm on his neck, the faintest trace of lemon reaching his nostrils, but despite her proximity he wasn't annoyed that Elaine was peering over his shoulder. She wouldn't be there long, and he was comfortable knowing she had complete confidence in his ability to spot the more promising items.

"What about that one?" Her neatly manicured fingernail hovered above #44 on the list.

So much for her complete confidence. He resisted the sudden urge to roll his eyes and relaxed his shoulders. This case was important to her. He'd felt her growing frustration as the months passed and Annalee Tanaka's disappearance met dead end after dead end. Hell, he felt it himself, but wasn't sure if it was rubbing off from her or it was his own. It was, after all, the first big missing person's case he'd been directly involved with in his relatively brief career as a DC. "Yes, that one caught my eye, too."

"Good. Good." The changed tone behind his ear signified she was moving on, even if reluctantly. Her busy schedule pulling her away from what he knew she would prefer to do. Sit beside him and point out responses of interest. "I'm about to head off. Meeting. Back at 12.30."

"Okay. Should be clearer when you get back." He swivelled his chair and watched her leave, also taking in the sparsely occupied incident room. Some of the team were on leave and the only other two occupants were working on investigations not related to Annalee Tanaka.

In the months since she had disappeared, the packed incident room had gradually divested itself of the extra staff brought in for the initial full-scale, leave-no-stone-unturned investigation. As time passed, the ebb and flow of other crimes took precedence until solved, dropped, or put on hold. Annalee's face no longer looked accusingly at him from the board each time he passed to and from his desk. Yet, he only had to shut his eyes to see every minute detail of that elfin, refined face with those large, dark eyes. At night, he'd woken up more than once, the ghost of a dream featuring her leaving him shaken or sad. Her eyes haunted him. They were not angry, nor imploring, but sadly despairing of her situation and coolly appraising. The look suggesting that if only he noticed this or went after that, he would finally get it, and come for her. No, he didn't need the photo printout of Annalee, currently filed into the compact mobile system in the back room. He had a much larger one playing on repeat, ready at his disposal.

***

"Has this name come up before?"

"No, there's no record of an interview, or any contact from her before today." Jake had done his homework on the top six responses in the hours that his boss was at her meeting.

"She went to high school with Anna and remembers the boyfriend well, she states. Then the family moved, and she lost touch…" Elaine broke off, scanning through the information until she got to the literal bottom line. Jake saw her pupils dilate and the smile play on her lips.

"She saw him at a party," Jake said. "Spoke to him, even. They sat together, and he filled her in on what he'd been doing since he left school, his time in India and Malaysia and so on."

"So, definitely him."

"Looks like it."

"How did she know we were interested in him?"

Jake traced up through the response, his finger stopping at the relevant sentences. "A friend of a friend remembered it from our initial enquiries, and when she said she'd seen Dan Wilmott at the party…"

"Thank heavens for civic-minded citizens." Elaine sat back in her chair. Jake watched her fingers make their way to the back of her neck to begin the habitual massage.

She leant forward, scanning the response again. "Hmm. Wondering why we didn't get an alert that he was back in the country… Anyway, schedule a time to see this… Sarah Lovett, and we'll see what else they shared in their deep and meaningful. Would it be too much to hope for a phone number?" She pushed back her chair and half rose. "Did we ever contact his mother?"

"No. If she exists, she must have another name. She didn't come forward and we couldn't trace her."

"If she exists. She, or rather, they seem keen to keep a low profile. Maybe I'm reading too much into it. Many reasons for that these days. Of course, she could live overseas or… be dead."

Jake frowned. "We checked for the latter. Even there we drew a blank with the name."

"Right, let me know when you have a time to meet Ms Sarah Lovett."

53

Annalee sat on the stone steps, peering into the gloom below. The sultry, cloud-covered day echoed her mood. It was the first time she'd set foot outside since that night in Kay's room, and now it was dark and foreboding, as if a storm was about to break. This was a first.

The familiar cool breeze drifting up from the sea was missing, replaced by hot fetid air, ripe with decay from rotting vegetation. Surely it had been there before, but she'd never noticed, the thrill of exploration and the lure of the ocean with its tangy salt air spurring her on down to the cove.

She longed to be on the beach, but the thought of traversing the oppressive looking slope had her beat. She was tired, desperately tired, after what happened in Kay's room just days before. It was the shock, the trauma—her body reacting sluggishly, her mind fuddled, no doubt trying to protect her from the horrors.

Plus, she was afraid. Desperately afraid that the baby in her womb had died that night too. Two days on and there had still been no movement. She'd tried to reason with herself that it wasn't out of the ordinary. In the weeks since she had first felt movement it had been sporadic. The odd flutter and then nothing for several days, but... She sighed, deep down she knew that the tiny movements had increased as she grew more accustomed to what was baby and what was her.

Swallowing another sigh, she wrapped her arms around her chest. She had a precious hour of freedom and though she longed to crawl back into bed she needed to move.

Perhaps, down there, the water would work its magic, and wash away the lethargy enveloping her. She stood up, stretched her calf muscles, took a deep breath and set off.

The unaccustomed cloud cover and resultant humidity had changed things. Darkened things she'd thought were familiar to her, as if she was suddenly plunged into a new and alien environment. Unfamiliar shapes loomed, creaks from the tree branches and rustles in the undergrowth startled her more than once. The moist, still air closed around her mouth and nose the further she descended, as if blocking her next breath and holding the stale one hostage in her throat.

Her heartbeat pulsed ever louder in her ears, thrumming in tune to the cicadas' rhythm. Were there cicadas? Another thing she hadn't noticed before.

Her nostrils flared with the pungency rising from the under-growth and flowers. Usually delightful, today it was sickeningly cloying, threatening to turn her stomach. Everything had changed. It was as if, despite her tiredness, all her senses were on high alert, her nerves zinging with anticipation. Of what? She had no idea, but if the last days had taught her anything at all, it couldn't be good.

Halfway down, she stopped. Frozen in place, her eyes wide, she wrapped trembling fingers around her body. It was too much.

She looked back up the path she'd taken, then down at her toes, disappearing into the grey-green grasses tufting the pathway. She inhaled several deep, slow breaths, trying to swallow the rising nausea and threatening light-headedness. If only she could follow her toes and disappear into the ground, now certain that if she didn't she would overbalance and fall, anyway.

But this was nonsense. There was nothing for her if she stopped here, and she refused to go back. She squeezed her eyelids together and shook her shoulders. It did the trick, but she emerged from the trees onto the beach shaking and bathed in sweat.

The welcome coolness of the water sent a shiver up her spine. This, at least, hadn't changed, although the cloud cover had stolen the aqua-blue lagoon, replacing it with a steel grey sheet, only now fragmenting with ripples from her entry. The black jagged rocks on the perimeter and those close to shore loomed even more menacingly, silent sentinels watching for their signal to march up the beach to attack. That thought brought a half-smile. As long as they were on her side. She would lead the charge and together they would storm the evil castle and defeat the dragon and its minions.

And set the captives free.

If only. Anna sighed and waded along to the rocks near the shore, lowering herself to sit waist deep, her back against the familiar smooth base of one. More than anything, she wished the water's cleansing saltiness could work its magic inside her head to drive away the clouds. She tried focusing on points on the distant rocks, then close by as she slowly breathed in and out, but peace was elusive. The events of that night flooded back. The questions. Other if-onlys clamoured for attention.

What could she have done differently? To stop Kay's haemorrhage? To prevent her death? And what about Kay's baby? Was she alive? Dead? Anna should have been stronger, stood up to them more fiercely, fought harder for the baby. She cupped water in her palms and splashed it in her face, allowing the drips to fall like tears around her bowed head. Salt teased at the corners of her mouth, its sting pricking her eyes. The answers were obvious. Her constant analysis of every micro-second spent in that room told her that. Except for the baby's fate.

She scrubbed at her eyes, stifling a sob. There was nothing she could have done to make a difference. Her only consolation was that Kay was not alone when she died. Someone was with her who cared if she lived or not.

The why question was harder, more inexplicable. Why her? Why had they summoned her to Kay's room that night? Was it some sort of test? They went to such lengths to conceal what they were doing. In her time here, she hadn't caught so much as a glimpse of another person—except for that impression of someone standing over her the other morning. Yet, even that was hazy, the details fading. Was it real or a dream? What had been going on for them to call on her?

The glaringly obvious fact was preposterous: Anna, Kay, and who knows how many others were here to produce babies. It was beyond belief, in her world. She'd discounted her earlier idea that she was a sex slave, as they'd only taken her away once. Somehow, they had impregnated her. She shuddered, flicking a look at the bushes hiding the path back into the mountain. But if their purpose was to make babies for whatever reason, they had to be prepared for medical emergencies. Even straightforward births required some help. Surely they couldn't expect the women, herself even, to deliver their own. And then? What happened to the babies?

Kay's was not a normal delivery. Did they call on her because it *was* an emergency? And she wasn't anywhere near full-term. Was no doctor available in the middle of the night? They had some sophisticated medical technology here: the spinal device, the undetectable drug put in her food or drink. Not to mention the money spent on this place. Perhaps they only brought in doctors when needed or when the babies were due.

It was still more than a little strange. Babies were unpredictable. They could come two or three weeks early or one to two weeks late. And the ante-natal care was non-existent. Pregnant mothers usually had monthly check-ups at first and then more often towards the due date. They had blood and urine tests, blood pressure checks, and at least a couple of ultra-sounds to make sure all was well in the womb. Megan and Steve had taken great delight in showing everyone their pre-birth 'photos' of her nephew and niece, Matty and Jess. Tears filled her eyes again as those joy-filled moments flooded in.

She sniffed and dragged her hand across her face. How could she escape? To think of her family and friends was excruciating, yet all she had to block those memories was much worse. The night in Kay's room. That tiny, exquisite child cupped in her hands. It made little sense. If a baby was the goal for these people, then it seemed strange to neglect the care needed. How could they be sure of a safe birth and healthy mother and child?

And then, what could they want babies for? Adoption? If so, it was an expensive way to go about it. She forced herself to think, to focus. If not adoption, then what? Designer babies? Designed for what? And for whom? There had been a tremendous fuss some years back when a family had another child to provide stem cells or possibly organ donation for a sick older sibling. She shuddered.

Maybe surrogacy? Surrogate mothers for women who couldn't have their own? But commercial surrogacy was available in many countries. If these babies were destined for people with money, then why the kidnapping? Why the isolation? There were many willing women who entered commercial surrogacy agreements without resorting to taking someone against their will.

Was there something about herself and Kay that made the babies special? Not for the first time, she thought about the cultural resemblance. Japanese or Asian, part-Asian? The hair in the ring matched too, with the same dark colour and unique coarse texture. But Kay's few words had been in English, and Anna hadn't picked up anything about the way she spoke. She replayed them in her mind. It was perhaps a slightly more refined English than the Australian accent. A slight difference in the way she pronounced 'you' when she said, "Is it you? Is it really you?"

Anna sighed, squeezing her eyes against the tears. She was getting nowhere. Did Kay mean anything by that question? Or was she just rambling in her pain and distress, relieved that someone was there to help at all? Thinking of the 'help' she had given sent shudders through Anna's frame as waves of grief and guilt washed over her once more.

The idea of cloning, of babies genetically altered, sparked in her mind. She snorted. It was the stuff of movies, of science fiction. Suddenly she drew in a sharp breath, her eyes narrowing.

Babies!

Babies! Kay had said 'babies'. "Take care of my babies." Annalee clearly heard the plurality now. Why hadn't she before? It had been Kay's last word.

Wide-eyed, her heart pounding against her rib cage under the water, she went through it again. Was she mistaken? Had Kay meant it that way? She was dying and could have been confused, her mind weakened by blood loss. Did she think she had given birth to more than one baby that day?

No. She meant what she said. She'd had at least one baby before and was entreating Anna to look after them both.

She staggered to her feet and pushed through the water to the shore, barely conscious that the chimes had begun. What happened to the first baby? Or the others? How long had Kay been here? How long had they subjected her to this—this—?

As she reached the beach, Anna fell to her knees, tears coursing down her cheeks, sobs choking her throat. She saw the years stretching out before her. No wonder Kay had been so thin, so wasted. Had she just given up, not wanting to keep churning out babies, only to have them ripped away before the process repeated itself?

She looked up and down the black shoreline. What was this place? No paradise here, only hell on earth.

Terror froze the hairs on the back of her neck as the threatening bile burnt her throat. The wind picked up across the water, sending several huge raindrops slamming into her back. She eyed the green light blinking balefully through the undergrowth, and placed a hand on her still, quiet abdomen. "Whatever happens, I have to get out of here, and soon, or die trying."

$\mathcal{H}$eather settled into the couch opposite her good friend Ruth. Their regular get-together had passed the cuppa and catchup-chat phase and now they were planning to pray. Heather reached for her notebook and pen. Ruth had hers ready on her lap. Sparky was lying on the mat under the window, eyes closed, content in the knowledge that it was a good time for a nap.

"Can I ask you a question?" Heather paused, her mouth suddenly dry. She knew she could ask Ruth anything, but should she? Sometimes she felt much less than the mature Christian woman she ought to be at her age, whereas Ruth's steady faith radiated from her pores. She exuded confidence and wisdom and knowledge of all things related to 'the way' she had followed since childhood.

"Sure, go for it." Ruth put her pen down and gave Heather her full attention.

"Hmm, where to start?" Heather fought to order her inner turmoil. She had a question, but what did it boil down to? She was convinced that what she believed was true. She and Tony had carefully investigated the validity of Christianity and the veracity of its holy book, the Bible, in the first few years after they came to Australia, soon after they had met and become friends with Ruth and her husband, Simon.

Yet, despite her assurances, niggling doubts crept in at times. Like now. Vague thoughts she didn't even want to admit to herself, let alone anyone else.

"I'll just come out with it… not sure if it will even make sense." Heather leaned back in her chair, closing her eyes.

"Do you ever think this…" She opened her eyes and lifted her notebook to reveal her Bible on the side table beside her. "That it may not be true?"

"You mean all of it?"

"Yes. No. I don't know." Heather shrugged her shoulders, grateful for the look in Ruth's eyes, which was neither incredulous nor condemning, but curious. "Do you remember Pamela Treloar?" Heather said.

"Yes, she moved to the country after she retired, near Bunbury, I think. About ten years ago, wasn't it?"

Heather nodded. "I remember something she said to me once. I can't remember what topic we were studying, it was so long ago. But I hadn't been in the study group long—maybe a couple of years— and she always seemed to me to be one of the wise women of faith in the church. She used to lead the studies with… Jill, I think."

Ruth nodded for Heather to go on.

"She said, 'Sometimes, I wonder if heaven will be all it's cracked up to be when we get there.' I remember the shock I felt. And she said it so quietly. I wasn't sure if she meant for me to hear, or whether she put her thoughts into words and didn't realise anyone had heard. But there I was lapping up all the studies and enjoying church for the first time in my life, and then a woman I admired and respected was having doubts about heaven. That the promise of an end to our life of suffering—not that it's all suffering, but you know what I mean…?" Heather huffed out a breath. There, she'd said it. Voiced the deepest reservation she'd kept hidden inside for all these years. Maybe even from herself. She'd never allowed it airtime before.

Ruth nodded again but stayed quiet. Heather was ever grateful for her friend's willingness to listen and not jump in with a quick-fix Bible verse, or bristle with indignation that anyone could so much as dare voice a doubt about Christianity. She knew Ruth would take her thought seriously. That's what it was, just a thought niggling away and trying to destabilise her when she was already struggling to stay sane.

Heather grimaced before smiling at Ruth and continuing. "That… it might not be the *utopia* that is promised in the Bible. Anyway, I remember wanting to ask her what she meant, wanting to know why she'd said that, but I never did, of course."

"Why not?" Ruth's tone was gentle, her voice low.

"Ah, now. You know I'm a slow learner in all this." She gestured at the Bible again, noticing Ruth sit up straighter in her seat. "Well, I was in those days. I wanted to be sure that it was all true. That I could place my trust, my life really"—Heather could feel the moisture gathering in her eyes—"in this book." She picked up her Bible and laid it on her lap. Her fingers caressed the familiar indentations of the letters etched into its leather-covered surface.

"I didn't want to think that anyone like a *'leader'*"—Heather made air quotes with her fingers—"would voice doubts. I think I didn't want to go into it, so I kept it to myself, not wanting anything to burst my new faith bubble."

This time, Heather groaned inside. This wasn't even making sense to her. She knew none of them were perfect, and she certainly wasn't. Maybe she should let it go, stuff it back inside where it belonged. She was taking up valuable time when they could be, should be, writing down their prayer points. The pages of her notebook came to mind with her daughter Anna's name featured heavily at the top of every page. She sighed and looked across at the peacefully sleeping Sparky, envying his contentment and simple pleasures.

"I'd mostly forgotten about Pam's words over the years as I grew more confident that God's Word is trustworthy, but sometimes, lately…" She searched Ruth's face for signs of understanding. "… it comes back to me. I can still see her face as she spoke, and the sadness in her eyes.

"So I think my question is: is God real? Is there this ultimate being who is pure love, who cares, who listens to our prayers? Who gives a damn whether we live or die? Whether my daughter lives or dies…" She broke off, slapping her hand to her mouth as her cheeks grew hot.

That hadn't meant to come out, but there it was. This was all about Anna.

55

DS Elaine Troy knocked again, a little more forcefully this time. She'd rung the bell twice but hadn't heard any chimes through the thin wooden door. The battery was most likely flat or missing altogether.

It had taken forty-eight hours after Sarah Lovett's interview to track Dan Wilmott to this address. It was in a suburb known for having more than its fair share of police call-outs—investigations for criminal activity more of nuisance value rather than serious crime. Let's say you wouldn't want your favourite mother-in-law to live here.

She eyed the two-metre high double-panel gate blocking the view to the backyard. The sheen on the taupe-grey Colorbond metal surface revealed it to be fairly new. Expensive, too. It looked out of place against the tired cream brickwork typical of the 1970s three bedroom, one bathroom house, cheaply built to accommodate blue-collar workers lucky enough to score a mortgage. Those were the days before banks considered a wife's income. Or building societies. Did they have building societies back then? Elaine tried to recall her older brother's struggles back in the day and came up blank. She wouldn't even have got a look-in, being young, single, on a police constable's wage and, of course, female.

Jake moved to the gate at her gesture. He bent to peer through the small gap not blocked by a thick chain wound several times around the central column. A heavy-duty padlock designed to thwart all but the hardiest attempts to gain entry was securely locked. He pointed up. But she'd already spotted the shards of broken glass some enterprising soul had glued along the top of the gate. Talk about broadcasting there was something to hide. Most likely drugs, but their prior check had raised no red flags. It was a rental, with the owner living interstate. Must be a none-too-particular property manager, by the state of the unkempt front garden. Likely only interested in the rent coming in on time.

She stepped to the side of the door and rapped on the window. Flakes of dull, yellow paint from its sun-worn wooden frame floated into the weed-infested garden bed beneath.

"Hello," she called out, then rapped again and listened.

Someone was inside. The curtain twitched as she moved back to the door and gestured for Jake to stay where he was. It was an advantage to be a woman and wearing plain clothes at times. The occupier often felt less threatened. This was one of those times.

The door scraped open just enough to show a sallow-skinned man, his head crowned by wild tufts of red hair. The tufts on the near side reached through the opening as if they were desperate to escape. She struggled not to wrinkle her nose and step back as his body odour and foul breath made it through, slapping her full in the face. He had the familiar look of a long-term user.

"Dan Wilmott? Are you Dan Wilmott?"

His eyes shifted to one side before flicking back to land somewhere beneath her chin. "Nah."

"I'm looking for Dan Wilmott. Are you Dan?" She knew he wasn't unless he'd cut and dyed his hair and chopped a good chunk off both his legs. Sarah Lovett described Dan as 'tall as', which they'd confirmed to be a little over six feet. Elaine was conscious of Jake taking a step closer.

"Who?" The man shuffled back a step, half-disappearing into the gloom behind him.

She waved her badge, holding it close and steady so he could take a good look.

"Dan Wilmott," she repeated. "He lives here."

"Nah." He shuffled back further, the door beginning to close.

"Wait." Elaine wasn't about to stick her foot in the gap, hoping the command would do the trick.

It did. He stopped, but the door gap stayed open a mere three centimetres. She could barely see him now. Just one dull green eye glaring at her.

"Does... Dan... Wilmott... live... here?" She kept her voice steady, but hoped the steely tone and emphasis on each word would do the trick. There was no response. At least he hadn't shut the door. The eye blinked slowly at her.

"Look... we can do this now, or..."—she gestured towards the heavily fortified gate—"...later. I can come back with a warrant and a whole lot of investigators you might not want here just now."

She continued, "And just in case you thought that would give you time to tidy up, or go visit your ailing aunt, my colleague here will wait outside while I make those arrangements." She gestured at Jake, now at her side and holding his own card for scrutiny.

The door scraped back to its initial position. "No Dan here." He raised his hand in a gesture of resignation.

"Okay. What about a tall guy, about your age, sun-tanned and fit, with bleached brown dreadlocks?" She saw the spark of recognition in his eyes and the ghost of a smile lifting the corner of his mouth.

"That's Sam. Sammy. Not Dan."

"Is..."

"Nah," he cut in. "He's not here. Looking for a place, he said." The man scratched the side of his neck, then under his arm, a wince turning his mouth into a grimace.

"Look. I gotta go." He dropped his hand to his side, trembling fingers searching for an elusive pocket in his cargo pants.

"Two minutes." Elaine held two fingers up, but despite the number of questions she asked to clarify Dan 'Sam' Wilmott's movements, they gleaned nothing useful. He said he didn't even know 'Sam's' last name.

"Get Dan, er, Sam, to call us when he comes back." She held out her card and pushed it into his hand when he didn't reach for it.

She waved her fingers towards the side gate as she turned. "Don't forget!"

56

Annalee gasped at the fluttery sensation just above her belly button. It stopped for a beat, started again a little stronger, then settled into a rhythmic pulse under her skin. Her heart soared.

She was sitting on the warm dark sand at the water's edge, her legs stretched out in front, ankles teased by the cool water. Droplets of salty tang shrank and dried on her skin, leaving faint patches of white. The swim had been exhilarating, chasing the cobwebs of confinement away, reminding her of how much she missed the freedom of taking herself to the beach whenever she liked. The white sandy beach at home.

She shook her head and focused on a thin finger of spray released by the rocks arching across the water in the distance. And now—a grin spread across her face as she carefully placed her palm on her stomach. It was the first time she had felt her baby move since Kay's death three nights ago.

Tension fell from her shoulders as she drew in a sweet, warm breath. Salt on the air, mixed with spicy aromas from the undergrowth behind her, teased her nose. She'd been so afraid her baby hadn't survived as she'd fought against the electric current at Kay's door that night. Since then, every time her stomach gurgled or twitched she had frozen and waited. Was it, or wasn't it? She'd tried to compare the movements to what she'd felt before, but the memory of what was baby kicks and what was normal bodily functions had eluded her. The torment had been almost as crippling as the grief engulfing her from watching Kay die.

But now, how could she have forgotten? There was no doubt it was the baby kicking. Now, she had something beside herself to fight for.

Her heart still racing, she stood up and with both hands on the gentle swelling above her pubic bone lifted her face towards the sun across the golden lagoon. Tiny wavelets rippling across the water caught the light and sparkled like diamonds. The familiar scene was suddenly fresh—richer and brighter somehow, warm and welcoming, as if sharing her joy. The warmth of the sun on her skin, the cool breeze kissing her cheeks and playing with her hair, the watery diamonds, all combined as if in a renewed welcome to her baby.

She caught a flash of movement from the corner of her eye. Two of the amazing blue butterflies she'd occasionally glimpsed under the tree canopy were fluttering into the breeze, following the shoreline. She twisted her neck as they flew above her and followed their progress as they turned toward the centre of the lagoon. They spiralled around each other, engaged in a graceful, intricate dance of their own design. One would fly high, the other follow, then they would twirl rapidly around each other while dropping slowly, before separating to begin the sequence again. Anna held her breath each time they descended, fearful they would hit the surface and drown. She cheered them on when they rose again. Finally, they hovered for what seemed like several minutes before soaring higher than ever before and beginning a long, twirling arc toward her. They came so close she almost reached her hands out for them to land, but she didn't dare, too afraid to move a muscle in case she broke the spell and frightened them away.

They landed on the sand instead, not a metre away. Close together, but not touching, their iridescent azure-blue wings opening and closing slowly. The colours seemed to harness both the sunlight and the reflection of the water, as if two precious jewels had suddenly sprouted through the rich black sand. Anna hardly dared breathe, mesmerised by their shimmering beauty. Suddenly, a third butterfly flew from behind her. It didn't touch down. It was as if it had an urgent message for the courting couple.

They lifted off, moving in synchronised flight with their new chum, the three making for the shelter of the trees, no doubt to seek nectar in the flowers below. But no, Anna watched as they rose vertically. She strained to follow, but lost sight of them as they merged into the colours of the sun-dappled canopy. Transfixed, she couldn't move, only her eyes following the trees up the steep slope to its summit.

'I lift up my eyes to the mountains—where does my help come from? My help comes from the Lord, the Maker of heaven and earth'.

The words from the opening of Psalm 121 floated down towards her, growing in volume and clarity the closer they got. Her confusion gave way to delight as they resonated clearly in her ears. Echoes of the words circled around her, as the butterflies had with each other. She spread her arms out, fingers splayed as if, this time, these precious words and phrases would land and she could gather them close.

There was no confusion. No doubt that they hadn't come from inside her head. And they were familiar. The soft, golden sound of each syllable drew closer and enveloped her with a deep peace. A feeling of warmth spread gently, yet firmly, through her skin, reaching into the core of her being. She started to shake, and with legs no longer able to support herself, sank to her knees.

Tears pouring down her cheeks, she closed her eyes and whispered, "Thank you, thank you!" She bowed her head and cupped her belly. "It's going to be all right. We're going to get out of here."

Familiar words along with a melody came to her lips. This time from her memory. She sang, quietly at first, then her voice growing with confidence as it came back. The Psalm had been adapted and put to music. It was a favourite in her early teen years, in the days before she'd been so caught up with her studies and putting the world right her way.

It was enough. After all this time, the silence, the not knowing, the doubting that God existed or cared anything about her disappeared in an instant. She was sobbing and gasping through the tears, not in pain and despair any longer, but with overwhelming joy and happiness over such an experience. That God had heard her, and He had acknowledged it in such a tangible way.

The audible voice was a first. She had some friends who said God spoke to them, but she never quite got it when they tried to explain. Each one was different and even her dear friend Lucy had difficulty. Lucy believed it to be true but, for her, it was through reading the Bible. She explained that sometimes words or sentences fairly jumped off the page as if it was a message just for her. But also that sometimes she'd heard a quiet whisper in her mind.

Anna had always had doubts. How could you know it wasn't your own thoughts? Something you wanted to hear? Lucy just said that when it happened, you knew, and now, she did. It was unbelievable—God knew where she was. He cared about her and was showing the way out.

But now what? She bit her lip, eyes drawn once more to the tree-tops and mountain peak. What was she to do with the message? Wait for someone to come over the mountain and rescue her, or did she have to do it herself? Climb that slope? And if so, when? How? There was, after all, the small matter of the electronic device control-ling her every move.

She breathed in slowly and shook her head. She had to stop her incessant questioning and relinquish the need for control. Despite all the barriers to an escape, she had to trust there would be a way.

"Wait!" the breeze whispered in her ear.

ucy stretched, working to ease the tension in her muscles. It was constantly there, a physical reminder of her unease. She rolled to her side and breathed deeply, taking in the fresh 'home' smell. There was nothing like it. This break away, brief as it was, would work its magic. She hoped. She needed renewal, refreshing, a break from… everything. The sun streaming through the dormer window warmed her face, teasing at her closed eyelids, but she wasn't ready to open them yet.

She strained to hear signs of life below. Was everybody sleeping in? That would be a first. They were a family of early risers. Her dad out fishing at dawn if he wasn't working, Mum swimming or with Dad in the tinny. Mick catching a wave, or the wind if he'd taken his kite board. Brad far away. She squeezed her eyelids tighter. And Vicky? No longer the cute little sister bouncing in to wake her up, eager to cajole her into the 'fun' things she'd dreamed up for the day. Lucy missed that, but this morning was thankful for a sister growing up, and likely sleeping-in too, giving her much-needed peace and space. She had been so tired last night, after the long drive down from Perth. That and working extra hours as the holiday season ramped up.

She swiped her hand across her eyes. Who was she kidding?

Behind it all lurked the ever-present spectre of her anxiety about Annalee.

It was impossible to ignore, to stuff inside, to forget for even one day. It was a nightmare. She did her best to put on a brave face, or if not a brave face, then a pleasant one at least. She could do her job efficiently and professionally, but something was not quite right there, too. Nursing didn't bring quite the same joy and satisfaction as it had before Anna disappeared. Her friends, home, church all lacked the ability to switch her on, to engage her heart and mind as they had before. Not that it was their responsibility. God? Even that relationship seemed strained, distant in a way. She sighed. It was as if the surrounding air had thickened somehow, distorting everything which used to be so clear, filming it all with a layer of grime.

There was a soft tap at the door before her mother's face appeared, sending a delicious waft of frying bacon in. "Just checking if you want breakfast and how far away you are from getting up?"

"Thanks, Mum. I was awake. Bacon smells great. Two minutes." Lucy hoped her response came out normal. She swung her feet off the bed and looked around for her shorts.

"Scrambled eggs okay?" Her mother asked, but didn't wait for a reply. Lucy heard the slap of her thongs on the polished wooden staircase. *I guess it's scrambled then.* Not that she minded. Having someone cook her breakfast was a treat. Lately, her own efforts stretched as far as a bowl of cereal or a piece or two of toast. She sighed again, hating the threatening gloom, and this slow descent into self-absorption. It was the last thing she wanted, with ten days surrounded by her beloved family in front of her. Was Anna eating eggs this morning?

"Where is everyone?" Lucy sat at the wooden table, the comfortable centre-piece of the large kitchen-dining room. Cupboards, plus a six-burner stove, a large fridge and the entrance to a walk-in pantry took up two of the four walls. The kitchen sink sat under the window where the view looked down at the Southern Ocean, dotted with craggy islands in the distance. There was never an argument about washing or drying dishes when you could look out there and watch the day unfold.

Her mother smiled as she passed a laden plate across and sat down opposite. "Nothing's changed." She nodded towards the window. "Fishing, surfing. Although, I tell a lie. Mick's been out fishing with Dad a few times since he's been back."

Lucy lifted an eyebrow. "That's new." Neither she nor Mick had caught their father's passion for sitting in a boat or on a jetty for hours on end, waiting for a nibble. Her eldest brother, Brad, had always been the fisherman's apprentice. Since he was old enough to hold a rod or line, he had shadowed Dad. Probably something to do with being the first child.

Her big brother, Brad. She'd barely spared him a thought. For… how long? She frowned. "Have you heard from Brad?"

"Yes." Her mum nodded. "He phoned Christmas Day. He's okay, having a great time. Can you imagine? A white Christmas."

Lucy looked out the window at the cloudless blue sky, the sun already high with promise. Brad was in Finland, invited by his new friend, Leon, to spend time with his family over the Christmas break. They'd met at UWA doing the same post-grad course. Leon had been in Australia on a twelve month overseas study grant. Suddenly, remembering this was important. She'd never really been close to Brad, not as close as she was to Mick, but she could have tried. He was studying in Perth, living in student accommodation, probably less than ten kilometres from her place, but they never met up. Never even texted, or hardly ever. Why was that?

Her mother was looking at her, expecting some kind of response. "That would be something. A white Christmas." It could get cold in Albany in the winter, and on very rare occasions they might have a flurry of snow, but it didn't last. "But I don't think I could stand the cold for months at a time. And the dark." Lucy grimaced. "How much daylight do they get now?"

"Five hours." The voice from the doorway ushered in Vicky, clad in cutesie, koala-print summer PJs, hair mussed on one side, but with headphones firmly clamped over her ears.

Lucy marvelled at how she'd heard the question over the noise-cancelling headphones she'd given Vicky for Christmas. They were a bit over her budget, but her sister's delight at opening the gift had been well worth it. It touched Lucy that her family waited for her to arrive the day after Boxing Day before they traded gifts. Almost.

Vicky couldn't wait and opened a couple of hers on Christmas Day, then felt pleased with herself at having the strength to resist opening the rest. After dinner last night they'd sat around the big tree taking pride of place in the living room and pretended it was still Christmas Day.

"Five?" Lucy swallowed her mouthful of egg and got up to give Vicky a hug. So far, Vicky was showing no signs of the petulant, abrasive teen monster she'd turned into a couple of years ago. But then Lucy had only arrived sixteen hours before.

"That means nineteen hours of darkness. How boring! I'd die." Vicky took off the headphones, wrapped them around her neck and spooned scrambled eggs onto toast.

Lucy and her mum exchanged a smile.

"I suppose they get used to it. Just like we get used to the long summer days," her mum said, reaching for her phone and scrolling. "Brad sent a few photos. Here."

Lucy knew her parents were a little put out by Brad's decision to go to Finland, particularly with a growing student loan to pay off one day. But they were equally supporting of his sense of adventure and the opportunity. They jokingly blamed Leon for enticing him away with talk of the wonders of Finland and Christmas celebrated the traditional way. In the snow and not the heat of an Australian summer.

She took in the family scene with her brother's face closest and distorted in the classic selfie-shot look. "Love those sweaters." She scrolled through the other images. "Brad has one on, too." She laughed. The entire group, apart from her brother, was clearly related, and wearing matching dark-green sweaters with a large, stylised reindeer head on the front, complete with red antlers and Rudolph-red noses.

"Family bonding." Lucy turned the phone around to show them. "Who's that next to Brad?"

"Hmm." Her mother's eyes twinkled. "The little sister. Cosying up to him. She'd better not get any ideas."

"She's beautiful." And not so little. Lucy's stomach lurched at the thought of her brother bringing home a Finnish bride.

"Her name is Eva," Vicky added. "I got to talk to her when Brad had to go get some drink. Glooggi or something? That drink. See, there, in that one. It's a special warm drink they have at Christmas. Anyway, Eva. She's nice, but she's only eighteen and mad keen on skiing, ice skating and snowboarding. She wants to be in the Olympics."

Lucy saw her mother's face relax even as she let out a breath. If Brad were to fall in love with someone from overseas, they would likely not see him much unless his girl was happy to leave her country and stay here. Although, realistically, Brad's studies in Ecosystems Ecology may well involve jobs in other countries. And she was already losing touch with whatever closeness she'd had with him. Suddenly, Lucy couldn't bear the thought of anyone else going away. Looking down at her congealing bacon rind, she squeezed away the threatening tears.

Warm fingers enveloped hers and she looked up. Both her mother and Vicky were staring at her.

"What? Do I have egg on my face?" Lucy tried a smile, but her chin wobbled and the tears swelled.

"I'm…" She wanted to say 'okay', but the word wouldn't come. "I'm just tired, with work and everything, but give me a few days and… I need…" She could no longer stop the tears as her mother and sister reached for her at the same time. One hugging, the other tucking a tissue into her hand.

58

Ruth blinked, resisting the urge to cross the room and envelop Heather in a hug. A thousand answers to Heather's question were ready to trip off her tongue. But this wasn't about the question, it was about Heather's misery, her grief at losing her daughter, and so soon after losing her husband. And what right did she have with her near-perfect life to spout words of wisdom to her dear friend? She had a brilliant marriage, adult children doing all the right things. Her eldest, Esther, was about to produce a third grandchild. She, Ruth Kingsley, had no experience of one such devastating loss, let alone two.

Ruth took a deep breath and searched Heather's face.

"Heather, what you're going through is so hard, it's… unimaginable to me. I've never had to cope with anything like what you're facing." Then Ruth crossed the room, sat beside Heather, and put her arms around her. Heather didn't look at her but rested her head on Ruth's shoulder. That was reassuring.

"I guess in the end, beyond our experiences here, we will only know if God is real when we die. Will we meet nothing or be swept up into the greatest relief imaginable from all our sadnesses and pain?" Ruth heard Heather sniff and passed her a tissue.

"There are so many passages or verses in the Bible I could quote, but that's not what you need." Ruth felt Heather's shoulders relax a little at her words. Sometimes words were more of a weapon than a comfort. She waited, releasing her hug, but stayed next to Heather. She was grateful Heather trusted her enough to voice her doubts. Most people bottled them up, not wanting to allow even their closest friends to think they might be weak. Had she ever done that?

"We've seen a lot over the years, you and I." Ruth held up her notebook. "Seen answers to prayer when we knew things were humanly impossible. Could they just be coincidences? Some of them perhaps, but others… no. We've seen God work in the most unlikely situations and change things completely around." She took another deep breath. "If there is nothing… afterwards, as some people believe… if it turns out they are right, then I can emphatically state that my life has been better for believing that there is a God."

Heather swiped at her nose with the tissue. "In my heart of hearts, I know God is who He says He is, that His word can be trusted. I know I will see Tony again, and Anna…" Ruth pressed her hand as she paused. "Hopefully in this life. But if not…" Ruth held her breath as Heather struggled with the words. "…then in the next. We'll be together again. I have to have that hope."

"And how did little Tim behave?" asked Mrs Cratchit, when she had rallied Bob on his credulity, and Bob had hugged his daughter to his heart's content.

"As good as gold," said Bob, "and better. Somehow he gets thoughtful, sitting by himself so much, and thinks the strangest things you ever heard. He told me, coming home, that he hoped the people saw him in the church, because he was a cripple, and it might be pleasant to them to remember upon Christmas Day, who made lame beggars walk, and blind men see."

Anna stopped reading aloud and snapped the book shut. This part of Charles Dickens' *A Christmas Carol* always got to her, and there was only more sadness to come. She had avoided the book for weeks, glancing at it and selecting another, but inevitably her fingers lingered there and finally drew it out. She resolved to read it, knowing the story would move her. Tears were not far away, anyway. It was likely the pregnancy hormones. She squashed the idea it was growing anxiety at the weeks passing with no sign of rescue.

From calculating the marks she'd made in the current book, it must be close to Christmas. Reality said it could have come and gone weeks ago, with the obvious gaps in her ability to record the days accurately. The major one being the unknown chunk of time between her kidnap at the hospital and arrival here.

Her mind was a complete blank until she woke in the dark in this room. No nebulous memories, no flashbacks of—anything— came back to her. And then there were those nightmare times when they'd drugged and impregnated her, and then when Kay… She chewed her lip, willing the replay of events in Kay's room not to repeat. There had been many days after both events when she hadn't even thought of reading a book, let alone making a mark in one.

Her neck and cheeks warmed, and she fumbled to re-open the novel. But the words blurred through pooling tears, the heaviness in her chest telling her something else. She also had avoided the book yet longed to read it because it reminded her so much of home. The family Christmases she'd shared with her mum, dad, and brother, and later Meg, and her dear nephew and niece. They would sit squashed up on the couch, lazy and full after the big dinner, and watch various film adaptations of the story year after year. Then *The Muppet Christmas Carol* came out and blew them away. Her brother bought a copy of the DVD, and after that it was the only one they viewed. They all loved it, not just the kids.

"I'm sorry, Mr Dickens, I can't do it. You'll have to go back on the shelf." She clutched a hand to her chest, willing the pain away, and slid the book into its spot. Her family and friends were all going on without her. Lucy. Jamie. She stifled a sob, sank to the floor, and began pulling books off the shelves. She flipped through some, scrolled down the pages of others and made neat stacks on the floor beside her.

She needed a distraction, and this was one small thing she did to refocus her thoughts away from the past. Her other life. And it was three days since she'd made a mark. Sometimes she left it for four, or shortened it to two, also picking a different time of the day. All her strategies, she hoped, worked to hide what she was doing. They could think what they liked. That she was just quirky, or doing it to pass the time, maybe to scratch an itch for the need to do some- thing, have some control in her life. But all in all, they could assume she was going loopy for all she cared, as long as they didn't discover the marks and take away the books. So far, no one had touched the bookshelf, neither exchanging any books, nor rearranging her ordering. The bookshelf remained the same, which in one sense caused some anxiety—she was fast running out of new material to read—but on the other hand, was comforting. She knew roughly how long she had been here. She also believed she was close to being seven months pregnant.

Doubts about her experience on the beach niggled, the tension building as each day passed. Had she really heard God speak? Maybe her excitement at feeling the baby move again triggered an emotional response, bringing out her need to escape. The clear voice she'd heard was fading, and the butterflies' dance enhancing the scene. Just a lucky coincidence? The words came back many times throughout the quiet days and nights, but only as part of the song. She had known it, liked it in her teens. Could that be all it was? Her deep longing as she followed the butterflies' progress? Her deep longing to follow them, to be somewhere else. Away from here.

After all, how would she get up there with the force field on the slope, the device in her spine? Soon it would be too late for her to physically manage such a wild, steep climb, and then what? And even if she could, what would she find? What or who would be on the other side? Would it be as deserted as here, or would she walk straight into the arms of her kidnappers? Doubts and questions darted through her mind like angry hornets, buzzing and stinging, unsettling the deep desire for her mind and body to be strong and healthy. Not only for the possibility of escape, but for her growing baby.

He or she—she rubbed her hand across the top of her growing stomach—was a constant source of wonder in this otherwise foreboding place. Someone other than herself who was alive, rather than artificial or contrived. She saw it all as that now. Even the wonder of the paradise garden and lagoon was losing its appeal as she focused on the changes her pregnancy made. She never tired of feeling the little kicks and pushes at her skin and, lately, her rib cage.

Her hands strayed there, cupping the swelling. Despite its size, she wasn't huge as some women were, not even a decent-sized watermelon yet. She smiled at the image. If she was at work or home, few people would even notice. Her smile quickly faded as a wave of despair rolled up from her stomach.

Her time outside today hadn't helped. Each day lately seemed to be gloomy, and uncomfortably humid. It must be the rainy season, only it never rained when she was out, but stayed oppressive and hot —thick, dark clouds banking up beyond the ridge, blotting out the sun. She craved the rain. Better, a wind-tossed storm to vary the same, same sameness of her days. She'd never seen evidence of one, no broken branches or debris littering the shore, and she'd certainly never heard one inside the mountain. A few drops of rain were the closest she'd got.

A flash of light had caught the corner of her eye today. Lightning? It was so fleeting and far away it could have been imagination. She'd shuffled around to focus on the sky, listening hard for thunder, which didn't come. A swim cooled her off, but the heat undid all that soon after she emerged and headed for the rock pool.

Even its tiny inhabitants had been elusive, just one or two pincer-claw tips poking out from under rocks and seaweed, slowly waving in time with the current. Perhaps they were expecting the coming storm, too. She willed it to break, and soon. She would so enjoy watching its wildness and fury.

When she was little, her mum and dad had sometimes taken her and Steve to the coast when a storm was brewing. Safely in the car, they watched the unrestrained electricity divest its energy over the restless, violent ocean. Lightning raked the black clouds, flinging bolts from one side to the other as if opposing armies were battling it out. Sometimes, spectacular spears exploded as they struck the surface, sending up plumes of spray. The roaring wind and crashing waves fought to outdo the thunder in a futile bid to show who was master.

Once, they'd even seen a waterspout. As tall as a skyscraper, it moved purposefully towards the coast from several kilometres away. She and Steve sat frozen, holding their breath, as they waited for the car to be snatched up like Dorothy's house in *The Wizard of Oz*— except they would all drown because they would end up in the sea for sure. At the edge of the breakers, though, it turned away, slowly tracking north parallel to the shoreline before disappearing from their sight, just as Dad had predicted. Anna was secretly relieved and, studying her brother's pale face, knew he had been too.

But as ever, she'd missed the storm today. Hot wind and a few fat raindrops followed her up the beach as the chimes sounded out. She turned to take one last look, watching sheets of rain advancing toward the cove, the smell of petrichor filling her nostrils as the raindrops hit the hot sand and leaf litter.

She'd carried that smell to her room. Was it universal? She could swear it was the same wherever she'd travelled, but more so at home. It belonged to her childhood, walking to school with her brother, dashing into shelter if they could. Welcome rain after long dry spells. Freshness and hope.

But now. She put the books slowly back on the shelves. Where was the hope?

60

"We have him," his boss said as she slid the strap of her shoulder bag into position and beckoned Jake.

Jake didn't need too many guesses at who 'him' might be. Dan or Sam Wilmott was way top of the list. Plus, the DS's face was beaming after days of scowls and furrowed brows since they'd first tracked him to the drug house on Meriweather Way. They'd passed their suspicions about the house and its fortifications on. The drug squad divulged they already had an interest, but were happy to keep a lookout for a certain individual.

"Where to?" Jake indicated left as they exited the carpark.

"The airport. International." Elaine tapped her fingers on her bag. Jake felt the tension radiating from her.

His eyes widened as he adjusted his mental roadmap and turned towards the highway leading to the airports. So, Dan wasn't at the house.

As if reading his mind, Elaine explained. "Surveillance of the house was ramped up after our visit. Photos of everyone going in and out, but no Dan. Probably our friend Rufus White tipped him off. I went in too softly there. Should've pushed it."

Jake saw her frown, knowing how much she would be kicking herself. But their approach had seemed the right one to him, too.

She hadn't wanted to alarm the guy at Number 37, who'd reluctantly confirmed his identity as Rufus White before they left. She wanted to give the impression they were only interested in Dan. Should she have gone in harder? Swings and roundabouts. It didn't matter if…

"They picked him up, waiting to board a plane to Bali." Elaine's face had softened. No smile, but she must have got past her self-castigation. Jake had been around long enough now to appreciate her optimistic nature. If she got angry or disappointed, it didn't last long. She shook it off and reset to her usual positive demeanour. That was one big plus for Jake, as far as he was concerned. Dwelling on the negatives and the what-ifs did little for your psyche. If you made a mistake, then you had to 'fess up and wear the consequences. He'd known too many people who'd let life's challenges wear them down. His own father, for instance. He frowned and looked in the rear-view mirror.

"Was it the dreadlocks?" Couldn't be too many men boarding planes fitting the description Sarah Lovett had given them. Dreadies were still around, but a lot less common these days.

"No, funnily enough. He'd cut them off and tidied himself up. Quite the clean-cut junior executive. Glasses, smart jacket and all. His hair was darker, but a sharp-eyed desk clerk got suspicious when he showed his ID at the counter. Sent an alert through and they double checked before he could board.

"He also said he was going for a holiday which didn't match the persona he was trying for, plus he had a scruffy backpack, no laptop, and no check-in luggage. It set off alarm bells in all the right places."

"Good for us." Dan had more brains than that, surely. If he'd worn a t-shirt and shorts to go with his backpack, they probably wouldn't have looked at him twice. Jake indicated left for the airport turnoff and slowed to the obligatory 60 kph. After the fast-paced run up the freeway, it felt as if he could have got out and jogged to the terminal if he hadn't been behind the wheel. "Did they say what name he was using?"

"Yes." Elaine made a strange noise in her throat. Jake tried to catch her expression from the corner of his eye, but missed it as he negotiated the traffic to manoeuvre into the narrow laneway leading to airport security. It was busy this morning, and trying to dodge all the cars and taxis vying for spaces in front of arrivals took concentration. Must be a big one coming in.

"Sam." She paused. "Sam Worthing."

"Worthington?"

"No, Worthing, but it was close enough to spark the desk clerk's suspicious nature."

"O…kay." Jake raised an eyebrow. "There's a lot we could do with Avatars, or maybe Titans, right now."

"Don't go there." Elaine was already opening her door as he parked. "But sometimes you have to wonder."

<hr>

Elaine opened her mouth and closed it again, her fingernails, short as they were, biting into her palm. It was all she could do not to spit in his face and slam out of the room.

"You'll just have to…" Her superior, Detective Inspector Ross Martin, waved his hand in the air and picked up his phone, avoiding her gaze.

She was dismissed to go and suck it up, the unspoken words echoing through her brain.

They had returned empty-handed from the airport. What little she got from the officer in charge of security sent her back to the station and straight into Ross's office. Sims, at the airport, would only say that, yes, they were holding Sam Worthing, and yes, they had informed her earlier that he was there, but things had changed. No, she could not take him with her and neither could she question him onsite, nor even see him at the present time. Sims met her demands about the sudden turnaround and who was responsible with stony silence.

Ross knew what it was about, she was sure. She'd caught the fleeting look of sympathy as she opened his door before his eyes darkened into the stony, cold, nothing-to-see-here look she knew well. Her hand was reaching for the door handle on her way out when she spun around instead and marched back to his desk.

"Can you at least tell me if there are any links to Annalee's disappearance?"

He stared at her for a long time and then he sighed. "Look. It's out of our hands. But..."

"But?" Elaine prompted.

"For what it's worth, it looks as if Dan has played more of a role in bringing in a big shipment of drugs than the drug squad first thought. And it's not the first time."

"Annalee?"

"No. Her name hasn't come up so far. There doesn't appear to be any connection to her disappearance."

"So far?" She struggled to keep the exasperation from her tone. Were they even bothered? "But, why not let me question him?"

"It seems as if they are in the middle of something. Dan is about halfway up the food chain. They're keeping him under wraps, hoping he'll give them more."

"Look, boss..."

"No, Elaine. No. I've already said more than I should. You need to leave this. Leave it with me. You'll be the first to know if Annalee's name comes up."

Still seething, Elaine left. Dammit! It wasn't good enough. What was bigger than solving the mystery of Annalee's disappearance? She ignored the obvious. Her priority was Annalee, and if Dan knew anything about it, she wanted to know. The ache started at the base of her skull and she stretched her neck.

She needed this. She needed something. Dan was the only promising lead they'd had in months, and he'd been whisked away, practically in front of her nose.

PART III

arm air swept in as always when the gym wall slid up, but a pungent odour hit her nostrils and caught in her throat. Hesitating for a beat, she forced her legs to move before the powers that be changed their minds and shut it again. Something was happening. Something radically different. Her heart raced ahead of her as she crossed the narrow stretch of grass, searching what little she could see of the sky under the looming canopy.

Smoke. Something was burning, and it was more than a backyard burn-off.

She couldn't place the odour yet; not burning vegetation, and there was no sign of even a wisp of smoke from below. The slightest of breezes ruffled the treetops, no cool sea air meandering up from the cove today. A whiff of smoke from gums and brush burning sent alarm bells, if not panic, through communities back home. Fresh sea breezes or land-heated hot winds might whip a small flame into an angry, fast-moving furnace within minutes in the dry Australian summer.

She sniffed again. It wasn't from household or industrial refuse either. No man-made plastics or rubber in the mix. It was an odd smell, acidic and somehow familiar. She searched her memory as she descended the path through the understorey, eyes alert for any changes in the surrounding gloom. The odour wasn't as strong here, but it was filtering through, all the same. Just as she reached the water's edge, it came back. She spun around, her eyes widening at the plume of dark greyish-blue smoke rising skyward beyond the mountain peak.

Her breath hitched, but she forced herself not to stare. Instead, she turned away and walked the length of the beach. There would be a much better view when she returned.

An active volcano. The acidic, sulfuric odour made sense. Its metallic zing coated her tongue and caught at the back of her throat, bringing back memories of their family holiday in New Zealand when she was twelve. A holiday which wouldn't be complete without visiting Rotorua with its many hot springs, boiling mud pools, and geysers spouting steam. The sulphurous atmosphere was very strong in parts of the town. She and her brother Steve had covered their noses as they sat in the back of the hire car or walked the paths around the tourist spots.

But an even greater highlight had been their visit to White Island, off the coast of Whakatane. This was long before it was closed to the public due to a catastrophic eruption which killed more than twenty tourists. When her family had booked the tour the probability of an eruption was explained as unlikely in the light of constant seismic activity recordings. Their tour guide took them through such an alien landscape, Annalee thought herself on the surface of the moon. It was eerily quiet as they walked carefully on the narrow paths marked out for them, with steaming fissures and boiling mud pits bubbling ominously all around. There was no vegetation, just white-grey rock formations, with areas coloured mustard yellow, sometimes pale green, signalling the chemical mix oozing to the surface.

They were guided to a barrier at the edge of the crater, where they stared down into its very core. Only they didn't. Anna had strained to see anything through the thick steam cloud obscuring the view. She had been expecting churning red molten lava like in the documentaries. As compensation, she was thrilled when a slight shower of what their tour guide called acid rain caught them on the way back to the tourist boat. Minute droplets of sea mist carried by the wind picked up the chemicals in the steam, stinging any uncovered skin. It wasn't enough to burn, but the thrill of it was a topic of conversation for days. As the years went by, thoughts of her exciting visit there was tempered by the deep sadness she felt for the families left behind after the later tragic eruption.

Now, she was careful to look straight ahead on the way back along the water's edge, with only the occasional glance at the smoke spreading in an ever-widening circle. The day was sunny and cloudless. Perfect, except for that giant inkblot. And that blot was the key to her rescue. There was no doubt in her mind. It was perfectly placed behind the mountain's peak. The very spot the words had come from on the day of the butterflies.

As if in agreement, the smoke column ballooned to twice its width, reaching feathery fingers ever upward. The ground trembled beneath her feet.

62

The jolt broke into her dream. But this was no dream. The bed was a live thing, bucking and swaying on the floor. Sleep fog fled as she grabbed at the bedsheets, trying to claw herself upright. Metal screamed and shrieked as the building resisted the intrusion. Primordial rumbling bellows punctuated the cacophony. The sounds assaulted her ears, penetrating through to her brain and setting her teeth on edge. If her hands had been free to do so, she would have stuffed her fingers in her ears.

She fought for the edge of the bed, untangling from the warm bedsheet, and slid to the floor. "Ouch!" The dancing bed hit her spine. She shuffled forward. What was it she'd read about best practice during an earthquake? Something about staying away from windows or standing in solid doorways.

No problems with shattering glass in a windowless room, and her door frame was not likely to offer any protection, clamped shut as it was.

Or was it? The room was tinged red, not the usual nightly blackout conditions. Even if she felt the need to go to the toilet in the night, which was often more than once with the baby pressing on her bladder, she had to feel her way around.

As she shuffled further away from the bed, the door came into view. The tunnel's dull red lights leaked through a small gap. She crab-walked forward, hands steadying from behind, her toes leading the way. Strong tremors ran like waves underneath, as if the building had a bad dose of the chills. Sudden jolts sent her sliding on the shiny floor.

She gripped the doorframe and hauled herself upright, legs braced against the shaking and pitching room. The gap wasn't huge, but she had nothing to lose. She wouldn't stay and wait for help or for the door to suddenly close and shut her in. She turned sideways and eased through.

"Lucky you're not sumo size, baby-mine," she said, as she carefully kneaded her stomach in for the final few centimetres.

The tunnel lights glowed red both ways. An occasional flicker from one, and sometimes all together, showed how fragile even this emergency lighting was. Without thinking, she turned along the tunnel leading to the beach. There were no lifts to negotiate. It was all on this level. It had a spiralling slope, downwards in this case, near the exit. The only hurdle might be the door to the outside. It was always open when she returned from the cove, swishing shut behind her when she was a few paces in. Would it be open tonight? It had to be. It would take her out of this mountain, into fresh air and safety.

A strong shudder from the depths knocked her sideways into the wall. She groaned, waiting for the pain in her shoulder to subside, her eyes searching the way forward. The red lights flickered and suddenly flared before fading to nothing. She was in total darkness. But there had been a sound. Something out of place, piercing through the roaring, screeching, jangling clamour beating at her senses.

"Tasu…"

It was nothing. Surely. Just her imagination. There was so much noise. She desperately wanted to move on before the whole place collapsed around her. But she forced herself to wait and strained to listen.

"Tasukete!"

A garbled sound, but stronger this time, despite the terror in the words. Anna looked back towards her room. It came from that way.

Someone else trapped. She knew she wasn't the only one imprisoned here, but with no human contact for so long, she'd tried, not always successfully, to shut off that part of her. The part that craved companionship, the touch of another. Yet, why should her door be the only one open?

"Tasukete!"

The syllables sparked a memory. Her basic knowledge of high-school Japanese registered the word for 'help'.

"I'm here. Hello. Hello."

There was nothing she wanted to do less than go back, but there was no question about it. She had to help if possible. Her breath caught as she gingerly worked her way upright. Her head spun in the pitch-blackness. She put a steadying hand on the tunnel wall, as if it were a lifeline, and waited for the threatening nausea to settle. The fears she'd lived with night after night as she lay awake in the darkness, willing sleep or the next day to come, fought for attention.

But there was no choice. There was no way she would leave another woman trapped in here. She steadied her breathing until her stomach settled and she was sure her trembling legs would hold her up. She inched back along the tunnel, her fingers feeling their way along the smooth wall. As she reached the gap in her door, she stopped and called out.

"Hello. Hello. Are you there?"

"Yes. Yes. Help." The quick reply came from not too far away. Anna knew the limitations of her faltering Japanese and was grateful it was in English. She moved along more confidently now, or as much as the swaying, rolling passage would allow. Her fingertips registered the tiny indentations marking two more closed doors as she passed by. Suddenly, they slid around a gap just as the other woman called out. Anna's fingers contacted something soft and warm and she huffed out a breath and skittered back, as a shriek of fright escaped the space. Then they were grasping for each other and clinging on, both talking at once.

"I'm Anna. Who are you?"

"Help me. Yes." A breathless, "I am Mishtko."

"Mishtko?" Anna tried the unfamiliar sounds against her tongue.

"Mishtko. Yes. I am prisoner here. What is happening? I think earthquake. Please help me."

"Can you get through the door?" Anna tasted bile in her throat, the answer already plain. There wasn't enough room for her hand to fit through, let alone a body. She swallowed hard.

"No, no. It stuck."

"We must try to open the door, Mishtko." Anna pulled back a little, but Mishtko wouldn't let go of her fingers. "Oh Mishtko—this is hard, but we have to do it together."

Anna used her other hand to loosen Mishtko's fingers, wincing as pain shot through her sore shoulder. It did the trick, though, and she put Mishtko's fingers on the door's edge.

"We must push the door back. Push together."

"Okay, I will push with you. I understand."

"Okay, push now." The solid door didn't even squeak. Annalee's heart sank. She looked into the darkness. Every second here meant the difference between freedom and…?

"Let's try again. One, two, three, push. Push really hard." It was no use. She heard her newfound friend groaning through gritted teeth even as she did the same.

"Stop, stop. It isn't budging. What can we do? Mishtko, is there anything in your room we can use for a lever?"

"Lever? What is… lever?"

"Umm, like a chair or…" *A handy iron bar*, she thought. But Mishtko's room would be like hers. Nothing in it strong enough to use.

"I will get chair." Anna's fingers felt empty and cold after Mishtko's warm hand and sweet breath disappeared. The sound of scraping signalled her effort to get at least one leg of the chair into the gap. Annalee reached down, feeling for the end of the chair leg and easing it through.

"Okay, let's go. You pull one side and I will push the other." She pressed on Mishtko's fingers to emphasise which way to try. "One, two, three, go." They strained and tugged until both were panting and breathless.

"One more time, Anna. You help me. Okay?"

Anna marvelled at the resolve in her voice. She hoped her own response was as strong.

"Okay." This time Mishtko did the count, and they gave it their all, Anna sliding to the floor with her head against the edge of the door, panting and hot.

"I'm sorry, Mishtko, it's no use," Anna said. "The door is stuck. I must get help. Get someone…."

"No. No. Don't leave me. You must…" Her voice trailed off into a sob, the despair in it wrenching at Anna's heart.

"I have to go, Mishtko. I'm sorry." Her voice sounded thin and reedy in her ears as she forced the words out. She didn't know how long she had been at Mishtko's door, but her anxiety was growing by the second. She would be no use to either of them if she stayed here and was caught.

"I'm sorry, Mishtko," she said, "but I promise I will come back for you. I promise."

"Wait." Mishtko withdrew her fingers and disappeared once more. Then she was back and pressing something soft into Anna's hand.

She knew instantly it was a woven ring of hair.

"Oh, Mishtko. It was you. Thank you." Tears flooded her eyes, and she was glad of the dark. "You gave me hope. I will come back for you. I promise I will." With a last squeeze of her fingers, she left, Mishtko's sobs echoing along the groaning tunnel around her.

Tears streaming down her face, she stumbled on. The ground beneath her feet continued to tremble, the random lurches throwing her off-balance. The tunnel walls devoid of handrails did little to aid in the inky blackness. Each time her fingertips detected another door's fine outline, she flinched, imagining the terrified occupant of the room.

A powerful jolt sent her sprawling and knocked the air from her lungs. She squeezed her eyes shut and lay still, her head spinning, lungs begging for air. Pinpricks of light danced at the corners of her eyes. The air was thick, cloying. As if all the oxygen was being sucked out of the tunnel and replaced by a dense, black, velvet curtain. She didn't know which way to go. Had she spun around when she fell? The wall wasn't much, but at least it gave her a reference point. At last, her searching fingers found it. She eased back against it, drew her legs in close and clutched her knees, tears dripping onto them. She was done.

If only it wasn't so dark. She shook her head and stretched her neck, rotating her shoulders in turn. The one she'd hurt earlier was tender, but not too bad. She had to fight the fear and summon the old Annalee. Fear was just an emotion. It had no basis in fact. There was air. She breathed. In. Out. In. Out. It was warm, but there was plenty of air. You can do this, Annalee Tanaka, despite the dark and noises of the heaving building and the niggling voices whispering negative thoughts. All the what-ifs crowding her mind.

"No," she cried out, not even sure she'd said it aloud. She had to go on. Fight her fears. For Mishtko. For her baby and the others. She pushed up, grateful for the wall cool against her spine, and forced her legs to move. One step and then the next. Each step taking her closer to freedom.

63

A faint orange glow gradually pushed away the inky blackness. She breathed in a deep, jagged breath, her whole body relaxing as its warmth grew and reflected off the tunnel walls. The barrier door must be open. As she rounded the last curve, she stopped to take in this unaccustomed view of the entrance from the beach.

Each time she had been summoned inside after her precious minutes of freedom in the cove, she had rarely looked behind her once inside the tunnel. She would hear the mechanical swish of a sliding door moving into place but, after the first few times, refused to look back. But now, that barrier was gone, and the air, although laced with acidic, sulphurous odours, felt sweet on her face. It beckoned her forward.

She paused inside the rocky overhang of the entrance, straining to hear anything to suggest someone might be there. It was impossible. As the ground shifted and groaned, trees and branches were cracking and grinding against each other. But this could work to her advantage. With any luck, her captors had also been blind-sided by tonight's upheaval and would have enough to occupy them elsewhere.

Slipping along the well-trodden path, dodging fern fronds and branches swaying on either side, she was still unprepared for the full force of the wild night as she emerged on the beach. Wild was an understatement. The rumbles and snarls from the eruption had masked the weather's fury. Sudden wind gusts snatched at her clothes, her hair flew up and snagged in the bushes. She teased it out and twisted her hair at the nape of her neck. Sand particles caught by the wind stung her eyes, blurring the surreal scene in the cove. The orange-yellow night sky painted everything in a garish light, the trees casting dancing shadows as they battled, not only the pitching ground, but a punishing wind. They moaned and creaked in their struggles, the wind shrieking high-pitched whistles as it streaked towards them and on up the slope. A huge branch crashed onto the sand not three metres from where she stood, sending her reeling backwards into the bushes.

The normally calm lagoon was dumping metre high, orange-pink, foam-flecked waves onto the black sand. Foam collecting around the rocks and indentations on the beach looked like snow. Only it wasn't cold. Cotton candy lumps tore off these and tumbled up the beach, disappearing as they bounced along the coarse sand. Anna watched one of the larger ones tumble into the tree line and glue itself around the protruding roots of a soaring tree, its tiny bubbles glistening myriad rainbows in the light.

Beyond the breakers, the water swelled and sank in great oily mounds as if undecided at which direction to turn—to join the frenzied waves and dash onto the beach or stay safely where it was. She blinked, then blinked again at the glistening black rocks surrounding the lagoon. It was as if they were living things, the waves below flicking orange-red phosphorescent fingers up and onto them. It looked as if hundreds of imps were dancing and cavorting along the edges.

She wanted to move on, but her feet weren't paying attention. Then a burst of spray hit her face, and sand particles loosed from the beach stung at her bare legs and ankles, breaking the spell.

She shivered and crossed her arms, turning her back. Her eyes adjusted to the gloom as she scanned for the nearest pathway. How different it was from her usual refuge of peace and beauty. She'd never been out here at night. And in this madness. The hairs on the back of her neck rose as she found the path. It was barely visible, ferns and vines buffeted by the wind barring the way, leaf litter and splintered tree branches hiding the manicured surface. But there was no other way. She had no hope of rescue from this isolated cove, even if anyone, or the right sort of 'anyone', knew where she was. She couldn't stay on the beach, just as there had been no option to stay inside the mountain. This was the way to freedom. It had to be.

***

SHE CROUCHED LOW BEHIND THE STONE WALL ACROSS FROM the gym, waiting for her breathing to slow. The climb had taken longer than she'd wanted. It had been slow going in the dark, her nerves zinging at every odd sound or looming shadowy shape. Plus, she'd had to backtrack and find another path more than once because of fallen branches. And that was the straightforward part. She stifled a grin at the absurdity. The reality loomed in front of her across the terrace. Dark and foreboding, shadowed from the light cast by the eruption, the slope above appeared as solid as a sheer rock face.

But first she had to get across the grass unseen, and then there was the small matter of the force field. She looked down at her dirt-streaked pale-blue top. As camouflage, it was woeful. It shone even brighter under the orange glow of the volcano.

Her route had brought her to the middle of the three sets of steps, about halfway along the terrace and a good four metres away from the gym. She knew that straight ahead of her, if she could have seen it, was the dense undergrowth, tree roots and bushes which signified the steep upper slope. Her vantage point made it difficult to see if the gym's wall panel was open, shaded as it was under the over-hang. The alternative was to backtrack and cross from the furthest set of steps which were closest to the mountain. The terrace sharp-ened to a point at that end, but she knew the slope was even steeper there. She licked her lips, working her tongue to moisten her mouth. A sip of water would be heaven right now. She hadn't given it a thought before, but her mouth, her entire body, was crying out for it.

A sudden flicker of light from below the overhang caught her eye. She shrank back down the steps, chest hammering. Minutes passed as she strained to hear anything above the sound of the wind and eruption. It was impossible so she risked another look. The light still flickered intermittently showing that the gym wall was half open. She watched until she was sure it wasn't torchlight. Maybe overhead lighting trying to reconnect. Which was not good. If the electricity reconnected, all the internal doors would work. And then there was the force field. If it was off, it wouldn't be for long.

It was now or never. She sucked in a deep breath and bolted across the terrace. With a split-second of hesitation, she flattened against the bushes on the other side. There was a slight tingle in her knees and fingers, but it was tolerable. She'd never got this close to the upper slope before. It would work. She could do it. A weak current radiated from her fingers to her elbows as she reached up, but after she'd climbed a few metres, it faded and then was gone.

64

Buoyed by the lack of force field, she clawed her way up through the dense undergrowth. Branches and roots rustled and snapped. It seemed as if she was making a racket far noisier than the fury of nature and, if anyone was out looking, they would find her straight away. But right now, she didn't care. Gaining distance from that building was all she cared about.

It was tough going. She had to feel the way with her fingers to gain purchase in the slippery, loose, leaf litter, her toes searching for anything strong enough to hold her weight. As she hauled herself from one tree root or branch up to the next, every muscle burned. Her shoulder was aching a little, but it was bearable. Even so, nothing prepared her for the climb, particularly the lack of protective clothing and boots. Rocks and sharp sticks cut into her bare skin, thorns snagged, and whip-sharp fern tendrils sliced, and shed their irritating fronds into her wounds.

Time lost all meaning as she dragged herself, inch by painful inch, upwards. An overwhelming need to stop and rest taunted her, but she dared not. Who knew how long it would be before she was missed, or from which direction searchers might come. Her arms felt as if they didn't belong to her, her hands and feet soon numbed by the pain. The humidity and extra weight she was carrying didn't help. Sweat coursed down her face and neck.

One push around the roots of a solid tree bravely clinging to the slope, and she sank into the damp and mildewy leaf litter gathered in a root-lined hollow. Any resident creepy-crawlies were the least of her worries. Her skin was smarting so badly she wouldn't know if she'd been stung or bitten. She hissed a breath in through her clenched teeth and looked up the slope.

She knew from the mental notes she'd made that there were patches of clear ground nearer the top. Was she getting close? Was she even going in the right direction? She was climbing, but which way? At least she was going up and not down. It was impossible to see too far ahead under the trees, and it didn't help that her eyes were streaming, everything blurring into one big red-black haze.

Her mouth was so dry she was tempted to lie down and suck the moisture from the leaves and damp earth. With a sigh, she nestled closer into the hollow. Tired. Too tired. Surely a few minutes' rest wouldn't hurt? Just enough to get her breath back and ease her aching body. It would give her the energy to go on. Heavy eyelids drooped and fell. Night sounds faded. The trembling earth lulled her to sleep.

The baby was kicking again. Why did they always do that in the night? Just when you were in the deepest, most peaceful sleep. It was as if there was a serious soccer game going on.

Anna's eyes flew open. The drama of the night and then the pain from a thousand cuts and scratches swooped in as if a swarm of hornets had attacked. She scrambled to her knees. Had she slept for minutes? Or hours? She had no idea. At least it was still dark. Why had she allowed herself to sleep? Wasting precious time. Then the baby kicked again, stopping her self-recriminations. She placed her hand on the spot.

"Thank you, baby-mine. Thank you for waking me, for reminding me about you. About us. We can do this. We will do it."

An overwhelming flood of warmth coursed through her as she climbed from her woody cocoon. Something was different. The wind had slowed, reduced to gently whispering up the slope through the ferns and branches. She took in a deep breath. No more creaking and grinding, branches splintering and dropping, smothering possible noises from human sources she didn't want to hear. The ground still rumbled, but the crazy lurching seemed to have slowed too.

The vegetation thinned, finally. It was a relief to move faster, to avoid most of the tangles and snares intent on finding every area of raw skin. She still kept close to the trees, though, not daring to risk crossing any of the larger open spaces. The glow from the volcano lit up the clearings brighter than a full moon.

About to step from a clump of trees, the faint sound of a twig snapping halted her. She spun around, eyes searching back through the gloom. It was from below, she was almost certain—but noise was deceptive on a slope. Heart thrumming against her sternum, she shrank back into the undergrowth and waited.

Then, her peripheral vision caught something which sent her already rapid heartbeat into overdrive.

65

Flickering lights. They were higher up the slope and to the left of her position. At least two, possibly three, lights, flashing back and forth through the trees.

Another snap from below. And a... grunt? Her rapid heart rate didn't let up, the pounding fit to burst through her throat. If she wasn't careful, they would catch her in the middle.

The three above—she counted three distinct lights now—were about halfway between the peak and the large clearing ahead. She would have to backtrack to go to the right of it, bringing her closer to whoever was climbing up behind. Risky, but her previous intention of following the trees to the left would present a greater threat. She was scanning through the murk of the alternative route when a fiery red plume shot high into the sky. A volley of blazing shooting stars, which crackled through the air in every direction, accompanied it. Seconds later, the ground bucked and rolled. Anna grabbed at a solid tree root and just managed to stay upright.

The sky boomed and cracked with this new eruption. She covered her ears, easing her jaw from side-to-side to relieve the effects of a sudden change in air pressure. Her temples throbbed as the noise rolled in waves above her before fading into the sea behind.

Panicked shouts and shrieks came from both directions. This

confirmed at least two behind her and, unfortunately, they were much closer, and directly below. She had to move, hoping the mayhem created by the volcano's outburst was enough of a distraction. Head down, she wound through the trees and shrubs, the jolting ground continually throwing her off-balance. But she didn't stop. She'd come so far and wasn't about to give up now.

The bright red glow from the eruption started to fade. The fiery plume was no longer visible, although deep groans and rumbles still carried through the air. Was it her eyes adjusting or did the sky seem lighter than before, more gold than orange? She bit her lip. There was still some ground to cover to reach the top, but then what?

Maybe it would be a better idea to hunker down somewhere and hope for the best. Hope the search parties would miss her altogether. A sudden constriction at the back of her throat answered the question. She needed water. Desperately. She tried to focus on what she was doing instead of her dry mouth. Focus on the leaves, twigs or dirt on the soles of her feet, the texture of each branch or vine, but her heavy head hampered the clarity she craved. She was desperately tired. And where were those guys with the torches? The new eruption had masked their progress.

Climbing over knee-high aerial roots, she settled her back against the massive tree trunk and inched her way around it just as torch-light swept by. She clamped her hand over the gasp about to erupt and dropped to the ground. But her glance had shown her searchers crossing the open patch not six metres away.

Listening to the even tones in their voices as they scuffled along reassured her she hadn't been spotted. Then, as if they'd read her thoughts somehow, the voices rose in volume; strident calls and excited exchanges echoed around the trees. Her heart sank. She braced against the tree trunk, expecting a hand to reach for her at any moment, the appearance of torch-lit faces.

Nothing happened. She let out a slow breath, realising why they were so excited. The two groups had connected.

Loud and animated conversation, interspersed with grunts and groans and outbursts of laughter and, presumably, what sounded like back slapping, followed. She couldn't make out what they were saying, but imagined them sharing information about their exploits and probably about the trail she'd left. As if to confirm her suspicions, a torch beam swept through the trees before receding. She crept further into a denser patch of undergrowth and tried to make herself as small as possible. Their voices became muted, leaves and twigs scuffled occasionally and torchlight flickered in random sweeps.

Then leaves crunched and twigs snapped so close that Anna startled and pushed her mouth into her shoulder to stop a scream. She ducked her head, shrinking even further into herself and the ground, not daring to breathe. Someone was shining a torch from the other side of the tree she'd stood behind moments before. The sharp beam of light zig-zagged all around before it slowed and rested on the fern tops above her head. It was an age before it moved off again. The surrounding leaves rustled as she shook, sweat oozing from her pores. He must have seen her, must be able to hear her now.

Just as quickly as they'd come, the footsteps crunched away. The torchlight gone. Was he toying with her? Or had he left to get reinforcements, not wanting to risk losing her? Were they even now circling the tree, waiting for her to move? She stayed frozen, ears straining for any clues. Besides, her limbs had turned to quivering jelly. Forget about fight or flight. She was sure she could do neither.

As the seconds ticked by into long minutes, the noises of the night around her and the voices merged. She strained to hear what was real, or only imagined. But the passing time gave her breathing-space. They were not crashing around the tree, shouting and flushing her out. The voices, if they were voices, were low and calm. Perhaps they had gone? No. She would have heard them. Maybe the one who came near hadn't seen her after all.

Then there was the distinct sound of a match being struck, followed by the acrid yet slightly sweet odour of cigarette smoke filtering through the leaves. She stifled a groan. No. Surely they weren't settling in for the long haul? Her left leg was cramping and the need for water was all-consuming. She would have to risk changing positions soon, stretch out her leg and massage it. Only a few minutes more, and they would go. Please God, make them go.

The crackle of a walkie-talkie punctuated the night. A few terse, undecipherable words from someone with a deep voice. Then it clicked off. The group all began talking at once, and there were sounds of movement. She held her breath, but exhaled as footsteps crunched away.

She eased onto her back, resting her head against a fern's lumpy trunk, and wiped the back of her hand across her sweating forehead. Every movement from her cramped limbs brought waves of pins and needles. Through clenched teeth, she reached for a foot, just as a gripping sensation crept up from her pubic bone, growing to encase her belly. A needle-thin pain raked her left side. Her entire abdomen felt as hard as rock before the sensation eased.

No! Not a contraction. It was too early. She couldn't be having contractions. Not here and not now. She fanned her face with her hand. Hopefully, it was just the cramped position she'd been forced into. She pushed herself to stand, head spinning. Too bad if someone was there. She was coming out. Thankfully, all was quiet, and the movement helped, her legs strengthening as she walked on the spot and scanned around. She saw the occasional flicker from torchlight in the distance. They were now quite close to the summit.

She cupped her abdomen and felt gentle repositioning under her fingers as something sparked in her tired brain. Braxton Hicks. Her sister-in-law Megan had Braxton Hicks contractions during her pregnancy. They occurred occasionally in late pregnancy and most pregnant women had them. It wasn't real labour and one of the likely causes was not drinking enough water. That must be it. Surely.

Something caught the corner of her eye as she changed position. At the base of the tree. It was a small bottle, and almost three-quarters full of liquid. Was it water? How did it get there? It was standing upright and in plain view, as if placed there deliberately. Was it meant for her, or just dumped? Odd to be discarded and standing upright, though.

What did it mean? Dared she think someone put it there for her? That someone, the guy who came near the tree, knew she was there and left it for her. Was it possible she had someone on her side?

She picked it up and retreated into the shadows, studying its contents. With shaking hands, she swished the liquid and then uncapped the bottle, sniffing slowly. It might be a trick or even contain something to knock her out. But it wasn't likely. The guy could have raised the alarm and captured her easily enough when he had the chance. She wiped her grubby finger on her top, placed it on the bottle's mouth and tilted it to wet her fingertip. It tasted like water. Taking a sip, she rolled it across her dry tongue and teeth. Amazing. Although quite warm, it was beyond delicious. She drank half the bottle, checking her urge to guzzle the lot, and screwed the cap back on.

"Thank you. Thank you. Whoever you are," she said, her eyes tearing up.

66

He smiled again as he thought of the girl and what he had done. Just a little thing, but he remembered Sissy telling him the girl would need water. There were no bottles in the rooms, so she would have no way of taking any with her, and it had been a long night.

He had seen her hiding behind the tree straight away when his torchlight picked out the shine of her dark hair against the pale cotton on her shoulder. It stood out under the bushes and dark colours of the ferns, even though she had done a good job of hiding. He had an eye for detail, which Mr Jack spotted when he first arrived here. It was why they picked him to work in Mr Koh's precious gardens. Mr Jack had drummed the need for perfection into him and it had come in handy this night.

He took care to straighten his face as he rejoined the other men and, breathing slowly and calmly, he looked into each of their faces. No one looked back at him strangely. They were still busy grumbling about the interruption to their night's sleep and worrying about the volcano to think of him and what he was doing. Even so, he stayed on the side nearest the tree, hoping that when they left he would have some influence upon the way they went.

"Got any smokes?" his boss, Mr Jack, asked Kevin, a houseboy from the big house.

"Sure, here you go. You want one too, Jimi?" Kevin grinned and waved the pack in Jimi's face, knowing full well what the answer would be.

Jimi wrinkled his nose and took a step back.

"You know Jimi cares for his body"—Mr Jack spoke for him—"and he's too young to smoke. Anyway, Mr Koh wants him in good shape for…" His voice trailed off. Jimi caught his hardening glance, his eyes cold and black in the shadows.

Jimi stiffened as the other men shuffled their feet and looked down. Looked anywhere except at him. They made a big show of sharing cigarettes and searching pockets for matches. Kevin puffed out his chest and retold tales about his adventures tonight, the others chiming in. Soon they were trying to outdo each other, bragging about who had faced the greatest dangers or seen the most strangers wandering on the mountain. They pointed to the scratches and blood on their skin and clothes.

The talk soon turned to the volcano and speculation of what it might do and when. Jimi looked up at the red, angry sky above the mountain. The volcanic eruption was on Vaui. His home. What was happening over there? Was his grandmother safe? The villagers? How he longed to be across the sea with them.

The sputter and static from Big Joe's walkie-talkie stopped them short. Even as he finished replying to the terse order, the men were pinching the tips of their unfinished cigarettes and ready to go.

"You heard. We head back straight away. No one lost out here after all. Mr Koh wants us back asap, before the guests get up. We go together, over the top." He raised his big hand in the vague direction of the summit.

Mr Jack sighed, Kevin and Ricki began grumbling again about the time wasted and their missed sleep. Jimi hesitated before falling into line with them. What should he do? Mr Jack kept too close an eye on him for him to slip away. And why would Mr Koh say that about the girl? What exactly did he plan to do about the 'no one' who was just behind that tree?

67

he long night was finally over but the sun still seemed reluctant to creep above the horizon, as if contemplating the wisdom of confronting the volcano. Noise from the eruption intensified as Anna neared the peak, thundering rumbles assaulting her ears in sync with the relentless underground grumblings. She scrambled under a leafy frangipani tree as her legs threatened to give way.

The incredible sight of the power of nature laid out before her took her breath away. The occasional footage of a volcanic eruption on a screen was nothing compared to this.

Anna sat cross-legged under the broad leaves of the frangipani, one of many she could see on this side of the mountain. The comforting fragrance seeped into her pores as her gaze shifted from one dramatic event to the next. The sweet aroma from the creamy flowers took her back to the house in Joondanna—to Lucy—and the profusion of blooms adorning the tree outside their front door.

Strange that she'd seen none on the other side of the island. Strange that she was thinking of that and not this. She sighed. She was so tired. Was her mind shutting down, protecting her from what had to be done? She took a sip from her precious water bottle, grateful there had been no more contractions, Braxton-Hicks or otherwise.

Focus, Annalee. Focus. She took another sip, eyeing the few drops left at the bottom of the bottle, and shifted her gaze back to the scenes playing out below. Soon she would be part of this other world of interaction and activity. She needed to take in as much as possible.

The volcano was the catalyst. On an island some distance away, it stood out in stark relief against the pink-mauve dawn sky. A thick stream of fiery-red molten lava oozed down one side, spilling from the lip of a lopsided crater like thick custard pouring from a jug. Clouds of grey-black smoke belched high into the sky, creating an enormous dark cloud. Air currents, resenting the intrusion, sent inky fingers in all directions. White steam and more grey-black smoke poured from fissures at various points around the volcano's sides.

A human drama was playing out in the sea and on the land with a full-scale evacuation underway. Boats of various sizes, heavily laden with people and goods, pushed through a low swell towards the island where Anna was. They were making a beeline for a long wooden jetty set perpendicular to the beach below. Two boats were already at the jetty, a line of people from one trickling away to the beach. The other boat was ready to be secured and begin disembarkation.

Despite her distance from them, Anna picked up the exuberance of the people. Some reached out to help people step off the boats while others ushered groups along the wooden planks where they spilled into the welcoming arms of family or friends who had already reached safety on the beach. Tiny dots of children ran around, weaving in and out of the adults and piles of belongings. Shouts of greeting and squeals of laughter carried up the slope toward her.

Their happiness was incongruous against the backdrop of the erupting volcano. How could they be so joyful after having to flee their homes?

She studied the settlement at the base of the slope. A promontory extended about a kilometre into the sea from the left of the buildings, creating a crescent moon-shaped bay. To the right, what looked to be a man-made groin, constructed of large boulders, extended just beyond the length of the jetty.

A stone wall separated the settlement from the beach, all the way from the groin along the gardens in front of the buildings and disappearing into greenery some distance along the promontory.

A frown shadowed her face as she noticed the wall wasn't the only barrier. Black-garbed figures stood a few steps apart atop the stone wall, their backs to the largest building, their focus on the displaced islanders. A human barrier.

She caught a glint of metal as one turned, and gasped. They were armed with either rifles or sub-machine guns. It could have been a movie set if she wasn't seeing it firsthand.

Guards even stood in the gap in the wall which must lead down to the beach—two shoulder-to-shoulder in the space, another two either side of them but a foot higher, on the wall. Did they expect to be stormed by the families below, who were happy to have survived a catastrophe on their island?

Still, the armed presence didn't appear to have dampened the spirits of the evacuees. From what she could make out, very few of them even cast a glance upwards. They certainly didn't seem intimidated, judging by the cheerful tones reaching her ears.

In contrast to the crowded beach, the impressive buildings and grounds looked deserted. The largest building—was it just a big house, or a hotel?—had a wide verandah facing the ocean. From here, she could just see the verandah's flatter roof and part of a railing at the side. Beyond that, a wide green lawn dotted with beach umbrellas and daybeds stretched to the wall where the guards stood.

Was it too early in the morning for residents or guests? It was difficult to imagine anyone sleeping through the night's eruption and missing this spectacle.

But it was quite a complex. Beautiful gardens and many tropical trees surrounded the white-rendered buildings, tinged pink with the dawn light. She glimpsed tennis courts and a large swimming pool past a line of trees to the left.

Directly below, at the bottom of the slope and well behind the main house, was a line of utilitarian buildings—plain rectangular boxes with corrugated iron roofs, some of them showing patches of rust. A tall hedge of trees and bushes divided them from the 'posh' section. The largest of these buildings, almost directly below her, stood next to an expanse of garden beds planted in neat rows. Vegetables? Two longer, narrower structures closest to the hedge reminded her of cheap motel rooms. Staff accommodation?

Anna glanced at the sun, well above the horizon now. She clearly had to get down there, and fast. Whoever owned the complex were her captors, but the islanders might well be her saviours. They had to be, in fact.

She gave a thankful glance upwards, and a shiver ran along her spine as she realised God was using a volcano and a bunch of displaced people to help her escape. All she had to do now was reach the beach and work out who was who before the wrong people saw her first. Whispering a prayer for guidance and for any help from her 'friend', she inched down the slope, using large boulders, small trees and bushes as cover. This side was less steep than the other and there were none of the gigantic trees with their aerial roots—as if someone had scraped them away and started again.

A sudden violent wave of air pressure overhead with an ear-shattering rhythmic *whomp-whomp-whomp* sent her ducking for cover. Leaves, twigs, and dust swirled into her face as a huge, black helicopter skimmed above. Coughing and spluttering, she clamped her hand over her mouth and nose and squeezed under a rock overhang. When the dust settled along with her pounding heart, she watched the helicopter circle a helipad near the tennis courts as she drained the last drops of her precious water. Swilling the dust from her mouth, she spat into the corner of her top and used it to wipe her face.

At least she didn't appear to be the helicopter's focus. If she was, it would have circled around. Wouldn't it?

The chopper landed and about ten black-clad figures spilled out, each one carrying a weapon. Two other men climbed out and followed at a more leisurely pace. Obviously in charge, they inspected the group who'd lined up a few metres away. By the way he was waving his arms, the taller of the two appeared to be giving orders.

The men shouldered their weapons, turned, and jogged along

the path toward the main building. For a few seconds, they disappeared under trees before re-emerging and crossing the lawn. Half of them stayed at the top of the wall, dispersing themselves between the other guards. The other half headed down the stone steps and onto the beach. Their leaders gradually caught up, but stopped at the top of the steps.

The cheerful chatter from the beach evaporated.

Anna reached the back of the largest outbuilding and tiptoed to the end. After a glance around the corner, she followed the wall along, stopping at the next corner. She listened, risked a quick look, and then sidled around and into a large open doorway. It was a big workshop-cum-gardening shed—although, as sheds go, it was on a grand scale, more barn-like.

She passed long work benches, chock full of tools and equipment; many storage shelves, both lining the walls and free-standing. Why was she even in here? She turned and looked back at the opening. Should she find somewhere closer to the house? But the thought of bumping into one of those guards on the wall beyond it stopped her.

She needed a few minutes' break after the nerve-wracking descent, the adrenaline surge from the helicopter, and, top of the list, her body's need for rest. A few minutes to figure out what to do next. A persistent hum registered and broke through her thoughts. She touched the bench, feeling vibration through its surface. It wasn't the volcano. The sound was higher pitched and more constant. It was coming from the back.

Her eyes widened—tall, rectangular metal cases interspersed

with giant silvery cylinders lined the entire back wall. The fronts had buttons and dials with glowing red or green figures ticking over, some faster than others. Large pipes and wires connected everything, and more pipes came through the wall behind them, with others disappearing into the floor. It must be power generation. Power for the entire island, including the spacious prisons she and the others were kept in, the gyms, the tunnel system and goodness knows what else they did in there. An icy shiver ran up her spine.

A shout sent her ducking behind the nearest workbench. Heart pounding, she inched towards the corner farthest from the door. She made out two voices, but the hum from the generators masked what they were saying—although they didn't disguise a steady rise in volume. They were heading her way.

She spotted a stack of different-sized cardboard boxes as she eased around the corner. Most of them were empty; one contained mulch or grass clippings and another, straw. The sweet, dusty smell of drying grass hit her nostrils. If she could ease a large one out, there would be room to hide. Hopefully, the generator's hum was loud enough to cover her movements. She squeezed in just as one voice rose to a pitch before pausing. A heavy footfall crunched to a stop nearby.

Holding her breath, she shrank back against the wall before the welcome sound of the boot moving off again. A tapping noise and resumed conversation gave her breathing-space. She was safe for the moment. It sounded as if the machines had their full attention.

Through a gap between boxes, she had a narrow view of the corner of a bench, and a little of the passage between it and part of a generator. No one was visible, but boots crunched on loose grit as they moved and she picked up muted conversation now and then. A loud, prolonged hiss followed several raps on metal. A deep voice sounded over the hiss, and Annalee made out the word 'wrench', followed by 'okay' from another voice, before footsteps headed her way.

She held her breath as a booted foot flashed by. The person ground to a halt further along. Metal clinked, and the footsteps returned. As he passed, she got the impression that his step faltered. He didn't stop, but she was almost certain he slowed.

More tapping ensued, the metal squealing in protest. The wrench must be in use. A quick conversation was followed by another prolonged hiss of steam. She heard one of them walking around, more scraping metallic noises, glugging from a thick liquid, and an extended bout of metal clanging on metal. Suddenly, it was silent. Her ears were still ringing when a loud voice barked, "Okay, let's go." She started at the command, but then her brain caught up —the words were English. With any luck, her unknown benefactor would speak English too.

Footsteps faded away. What next? She had no idea what stood between her and freedom and, if someone was on her side, how would she find him?

But then, just minutes later—footsteps. One set, moving cautiously. Slow, deliberate footsteps, masked by the machinery noises after a while until she doubted hearing anything. Suddenly, a boot appeared in the gap.

She squeezed her lips shut over the shriek threatening to escape as the boot pivoted and disappeared. Just as quickly, a box shifted. Anna couldn't stop this gasp and shrank against the wall, digging her fingernails into the palms of her hands. Everything went dark.

Her eyes adjusted to see a large brown eye staring at her.

"Annulee! You Annulee?" he whispered.

"I am. Yes. H-how do you know my name?"

"Annulee." He hadn't answered her question, only repeated her name, as if liking the sound of it. He shifted back for her to see a wide grin, revealing teeth shining white against brown skin. "Annulee. You one brave girl. I help you."

"How do you know me? Who are you? What is this place? Why am I here?"

A shadow flickered over his face at the barrage of questions, and she clamped her lips together.

"I know you, Annulee. Everyone look for you. You one brave girl. Escape from Mr Koh. I help you." His grin returned. He glanced over his shoulder and said, "We go. I take you to Sissy. Sissy help you."

"What is your name? Who is Sissy?" Enough questions. She kept the 'and why do you want to help me?' inside.

With his index finger on his cheek, he said solemnly, "I, Jimi." And with another glance over his shoulder, he said, "Mr Koh, bad man. He kill me pretty quick."

Anna blinked. Had she heard him correctly? Had he said Mr Koh was going to kill him?

He reached out a large hand to her, widening the gap between the boxes with his other hand. As she touched his warm skin, tears pricked her eyes, thoughts of Mishtko and Kay's hands desperate for her help flooding her mind.

As she stood, she risked a look at her helper. He was young, only about seventeen, possibly eighteen. There was a halo of dark curly hair around his handsome face and his skin was flawless. He was taller than her by a head and slightly built, but bulging muscles straining against his shirt sleeves showed he was used to hard physical work. And his care made an impression as he helped her out from between the boxes.

He let go of her hand, took a step back, and twisted his torso as he lifted his shirt to reveal an angry scar running down the side of his lower back. Placing a finger at the top of the scar, he traced the length of it.

"He take… kidney. Soon he take me. My life."

"Your life?" An icy finger reached through Anna's back, as if the scalpel used on Jimi had pierced her flesh. "Why would he want to kill you, Jimi?"

Turning to face her, he clenched both fists together and placed them over his heart, then pushed them towards her. It was Anna's turn to take a step back, her eyes widening.

"He take my life… my heart… soon."

Anna gasped. A clammy sweat beaded her forehead. She clasped her arms across her chest and leant back against the wooden bench, not sure her legs would hold her. "He wants your heart?"

Who was this monster? This Mr Koh? She wanted to wrap her arms around Jimi and reassure him, but what did she know of this side of the mountain? From her own experiences, this man, Koh, was capable of anything. Her stomach lurched and a knotted coil of anger twisted in her chest.

Jimi looked over the shelves to the doorway. With a finger to his lips, he said, "We go now. I take you to Sissy. I help you. Sissy help you. Maybe… you help me."

She put her hand on his arm, aches and pains forgotten. "I will help you, Jimi. You will live. We will both live. I know it."

<h1 style="text-align:center">69</h1>

<hr>

Jimi checked outside before leading her to one of the long, rectangular buildings. At a corner, he motioned for her to stop before he continued. Soon he was back, beckoning her to follow. He paused at one of the doors, tapped softly, but went straight in, holding the door open. Compared to her luxury accommodation inside the mountain, the room was tiny, barely able to fit the single bed, small dresser, and wardrobe. But it smelt fresh. That alone spoke freedom compared to the sterile-smelling confines of her former prison.

"Sissy be here pretty quick. She take breakfast to other girls."

"Other girls? You mean the others in the mountain locked up like I was?"

Jimi nodded his head, eyes solemn. So that's how he knew of her. Sissy delivered the food she had eaten every day.

"How many are there, Jimi? Do you know how many girls are in there?"

He looked away. "No. Many, I think. Sissy know for sure. She doesn't talk much. Safer that way."

Jimi's mention of food made her realise just how hungry she was. She hadn't eaten since the previous night's dinner. Her recollection of that meal and the escape from the room was hazy, as if it was aeons ago. But she was eating for two and right now, a stale crust of bread sounded appetising.

"Jimi, do you think you could get me something to eat while we wait for Sissy? And more water, please."

"Okay, no worries." The expression brought a smile to her face as it slipped off his tongue. She wondered where he had learned it as he took his leave. It was such a common expression in Australia and the matter-of-fact way he'd said it somehow took away a little of her tension. As if he was going to slip out to the take-away store along the road, rather than into the possibility of life-threatening danger.

She sat gingerly on the edge of the bed and examined the scratches, abrasions and bruises, most caked with dried blood laced with dirt and debris from the mountain. There was hardly an unbroken spot visible on her bare skin, and the edges around some of the deeper scratches were looking angry. She needed a shower or bath and antiseptic cream, but there wasn't even a washbasin in Sissy's room. The disparity of how they treated her and the size of this room made her wince. The sight of her reflection in the small mirror on the side of the wardrobe didn't help. She looked a sight with her clothes dirty and torn to match her skin. If Sissy came back before Jimi, she would probably turn tail and run.

Desperately tired but not daring to lie on the bed, she thought about Jimi's revelation. How could anyone dare to exploit, no, to kill such a healthy young man for his organs? And why Jimi? What of the other men from the search party? Was everyone here for the same thing? Or only some of them? And Sissy? She wasn't the only female here, surely. Anna yawned. And how did Jimi's predicament tie in with the women kept prisoner to produce babies?

She started as the door opened and scrabbled to the far corner of the bed. There was no time to hide, even if there had been anywhere. Thankfully, it was Jimi. A woman who must be Sissy followed him through the door. She looked to be about thirty-five, a little plump, and with skin a shade darker than Jimi's. Her dark, wiry hair was tamed into a bun at the nape of her neck. She wore a uniform of sorts, a blue-checked short-sleeved dress with a white collar and cuffs. Her feet sported ankle-length white cotton socks encased in spotless white lace-ups.

Sissy beamed at her from behind Jimi as he held out his offerings. A bowl of rice with vegetables and something resembling chicken. It smelled heavenly. Sissy passed her a bottle of water and a cloth napkin. Although barely warm, the food tasted as good as it smelt, and it wasn't long before she was scraping out the last few grains of rice.

Jimi and Sissy stood near the door while she ate. Between mouthfuls, Anna caught Sissy's changing expressions as her eyes flitted from one part of Anna's exposed skin to the next.

By the time Anna finished, Sissy's eyes were red-rimmed and watery. "You poor, poor, child. You poor, poor chi…" Her hand flew to her mouth, eyes round with terror as the room shook. A deep rumbling sound filled the air.

Sissy stepped to the small window near the door and peered through the corner of a faded flowery curtain. "That volcano going to kill us all." She lifted the curtain higher and stood on tip-toes, eyes searching skywards.

"Mr Koh say we're safe here, but what does he know about volcanoes? He's a wicked, wicked man. Getting punished for the bad things he's done. But we got to leave here, or we'll get punished too." She turned to take in the room. Her eyes bulged with fear as they roved every inch. Every inch except for its other two occupants.

"The good Lord knows maybe I need punishing for doing what I been doing these last five years. I don't know. I don't know." She stopped and drew in a shuddering breath, fingers digging in her pocket where they found a handkerchief. She dabbed wildly at her eyes and sat heavily on the end of the bed.

Anna frowned, opened her mouth to speak, but Jimi got in first. "That volcano on my home. My island." He spoke slowly, emphasising each word. He was staring into her eyes. "I need to help my people. My mam. Who will help her? I need to go there. Mr Koh won't let me go home, but we make a plan. Tanuka say all the people come here now but can't stay. All go to mainland before long."

Sissy eyed Jimi, filling in the gaps. "Tanuka works in the kitchen. Her man is one of Mr Koh's boys. He help on the beach all night and now. Help island people come off boats, get to beach. Make sure they have water, a little food. He tell Tanuka all this. He tells Tanuka the people leave pretty soon. Maybe today, maybe tomorrow. Waiting for boats from Kepolo." As she drew a breath, Jimi resumed.

"Mr Koh has… big men. They not from here." He circled his arms wide. "They from every place. Take care of Mr Koh. Stop people coming here. They drive boats, chopper, have guns."

Jimi explained with a great deal of gesturing that the guards were not only keeping the evacuees on the beach, but also preventing Jimi and other workers who had family on Vaui Island from going down to see them. Annalee was struggling to follow Jimi's rapid-fire speech but she gasped as her tired brain caught a word. What had she missed? Jimi had made fists and was acting out someone using an old style movie camera, as if he was involved in a family game of charades.

"Scientists. Did you say there are scientists here? From overseas? How many?" Annalee was sitting up straight now. The food and water had helped to revitalise her and the threads of an idea were forming.

"Six now, more come, maybe ten, maybe more. Tanuka is not sure." This from Sissy. As she spoke, they heard the rhythmic beat of a helicopter passing overhead. She lifted the curtain a fraction. "That's Mr Koh's chopper coming back, maybe bring more scientists now."

"If that's Mr Koh's helicopter, then whose is the other black helicopter? I saw it land and men who looked like soldiers got out."

"Ha! That's Sergeant Vanuai. He's police from Kepolo, on mainland. He's a big friend of Mr Koh."

"Police." Anna beamed at Sissy. "Will he help us? What do you think, Sissy? Jimi?" She looked from one to the other, the stony looks on their faces not filling her with hope. But she had to try. "The police in Australia help people like us who are in trouble. Could we talk to this sergeant somehow? Tell him our story?" They glanced at each other and then back at her. She wasn't ready to give up yet. Perhaps the sergeant didn't know of Koh's criminal activities. If he represented law and order and she could get to him… tell him about the kidnappings and what was going on…

Sissy snorted, "He's no good. He's a wicked man too. Come here all the time. Party. Party with Mr Koh big time. Brings special friends." Her eyes to the floor, she whispered, "I think sometimes he brings girls."

At the mention of the girls, and the memory of Mishtko who she had left trapped in her luxurious prison cell, a chill ran up Annalee's spine. She wanted to ask Sissy how many girls there were, who they were, how long they had been imprisoned and so much more, but not right now. It was too much for her tired body and foggy brain. She sucked in a breath and squared her jaw; she only knew she would not leave this island without them.

"Okay, if Sergeant Vanuai won't help us, we must make someone else help. The scientists? They can't be Mr Koh's friends, surely?" As Jimi and Sissy looked at each other, she continued. "What about the people from your island, Jimi? I'm sure they will help us, but how can we get to them? We must get to them before they're taken off the island."

"We have to get past Mr Koh's men." Jimi's voice was not hopeful, but Anna wasn't about to give up. There had to be a way.

"Yes. We do. But how?" She tapped her finger on her temple, screwing up her eyes. "What work do you do for Mr Koh, Jimi? Do you work in the house or outside?"

"Outside all the time. I help in the garden, clean windows, fetch this and that. Help Jack Suiy with machines."

"So most of the people here would be used to seeing you in the gardens? Perhaps with a wheelbarrow and tools?"

"Sure thing. Mr Koh like garden neat and clean all the time. No leaves, no twigs, no dead flowers, no sand on path. All sand on beach where it belong." Jimi mimicked another slower paced, deeper voice as he ticked off the orders obviously drilled into him. He ended his list with his trademark wide grin. Anna was glad to see it back.

"What if you carry me in the wheelbarrow around to the front, or the side of the big house near the front? Is there a place we can hide? Under trees or...?" A fresh group of scientists might be a distraction for Koh.

"Yes, yes. Jimi. Japanese garden." Sissy slapped Jimi's arm. "You go there, hide in tea house, plenty bushes. Behind tea house is rocks but a path too, and steps to the beach." Sissy's eyes shone and bulged again, but this time with excitement and hope, her fingers fluttering, her hands coming together as if she was about to clap. "You make sure no one is there first, Jimi. Mr Koh show off his Japanese garden all the time. He is very proud, that one."

"Let's hope they are all too interested in the volcano." With the news that they could move the islanders at any time, Anna was keen to get going as soon as possible. The scientists might help, but would they be willing? Or too caught up with their observations to be of any use? And there were many more islanders than scientists. Safety in numbers. She bit her lip, the image of those armed guards filling her mind. She needed to take the chance. Plus, she wasn't the only one in danger here. There were Jimi, Mishtko and the others.

Jimi stood up and peered around the edge of the curtain. "Okay, I go to plant room, check no one there and come back." Anna smiled at his words until she noticed the agitation on Sissy's face. As Jimi closed the door, Sissy stood up and stepped toward it before turning to stare at Anna. She was shifting from foot to foot and rubbing her left thumb up and down the seam of her uniform, the fingers on her right hand fluttering at her side.

"What's wrong, Sissy? It will be okay, we can do this."

Sissy turned her head and swallowed hard. "No, no. I must go and help in the kitchen pretty quick. Help Tanuka and Bessy cook and prepare food. Big dinner tonight, many guests. I must go before Tito comes or…" The door swung open, startling Sissy into spinning around, her fist raised.

With a deft block to the fist before it connected with his jaw, Jimi laughed. "Whoa, Sissy." He put a finger to his lips and motioned for them to follow him.

Annalee grasped Sissy's hand. "You go, Sissy. Go to the kitchen before they miss you. And thank you. Thank you for helping me." There was no more time to convey how grateful she was for Sissy's help, her kind words, and willingness to put herself in danger. She gave her hand a squeeze and let go as Sissy turned into a path through the trees.

imi was loping ahead, his big strides leaving her in his wake. She didn't have the energy to jog, but caught up in the large shed as he was wrestling a wheelbarrow upright. He lined it with empty sacks before helping Annalee in. By lying on her side and tucking her knees up high around her baby bump, she fitted snugly. He covered up to her neck with more sacks and arranged empty garden pots carefully into the indentations around her body. Finally, he placed garden gloves and hand tools over her legs and balanced a rake and a hoe across the rim.

Annalee forced herself to relax as the coarse sackcloth rasped her skin, irritating the many cuts and scratches. She eased the loose sacking over her face and hair, the dust and fibres at once attacking the back of her throat. Hopefully, she could last the distance without giving them both away.

Wheelbarrows were not built for comfort, and every bump over the worn paving slabs jarred her exposed joints. She was grateful when Jimi turned a corner, the superior path which must be around the big house offering a much smoother ride. The thick covering of sackcloth let in muted light, enough to show when they were passing beneath shade or in sunlight. Unfortunately, each time they were in the sun, the temperature under the sacking soared, with the musty, dust-laden air seeking a fresh assault on her throat and lungs. Anna took in shallow breaths, fighting the desperate need to throw the covering off and gulp in lungfuls of fresh air. It seemed to take an age to travel what must be ten or twenty metres at most. She cursed herself for thinking up the idea at all, longing to stretch her limbs, already protesting at the cramped conditions. Her muscles were hard lumps and, despite the heat, as cold and rigid as the structure she lay in. She opened her mouth to demand Jimi stop when another voice beat her to it.

"Jimi."

Jimi's abrupt response to the harsh command sent the loose tools flying off the wheelbarrow, where they clattered and clanged onto the ground. Annalee stifled a shriek as the barrow's metal elbows grated along the path with a bone-chilling screech. The resulting vibrations reverberated through her frame, setting her teeth on edge.

"What you doin' there, Jimi?" The question was less strident but no less demanding. The seconds stretched interminably as she willed Jimi to come up with a good excuse for his presence on the path.

"Hey, Mr Jack." Jimi's boots crunched as he stepped away from the wheelbarrow. "Mr Koh want me to check the Japanese Garden, make sure all good, rake new lines. He take special guests soon. Show garden. You know..." Annalee imagined the shoulder shrug emphasising the unspoken deference the staff had to the boss's whims and how important the Japanese Garden was to him. Probably more a source of pride to impress his guests rather than a quiet place of contemplation.

"Okay, okay. You be quick then. I need you to help me check plant, fill oil. Need more juice for all these people. Hot water, more shower, more bath..." His voice trailed off, along with fading footsteps.

"Sure thing, Mr Jack." Jimi replaced the fallen tools, emitting a low grunt as he took the weight again. Anna exhaled slowly and waited for her heart to settle. It was barely a few steps more before she felt the tilt as Jimi turned.

"We here," he whispered before rattling onto an incline ending with a bump at the bottom. Unfortunately, it wasn't the end as the wheelbarrow shot up again, Jimi grunting at the exertion. There was a second's pause and then another downward journey, with more bone-shaking rattling before they ground to a halt. The muted light suggested they were under a large tree, or perhaps in the teahouse's shadow.

Jimi busied himself taking the tools then the pots off the barrow, whispering, "Stay still. I look." His boots crunched across a coarse surface before they clumped on wood.

The seconds ticked by slowly as she strained to listen and fought to stay still, her covering of sackcloth once again reminding her of the grazes and scratches on her skin. It twisted ever tighter around her shoulders and neck as if it had a life of its own, closing in on her mouth and nose and threatening to reach down and stuff itself into her throat. Ready to fling it off, she stiffened at the sound of footsteps. Fortunately, Jimi's smiling face beamed at her as he removed the sacks. She breathed in the sweet, fresh air and attempted to climb out.

"Ow." Annalee couldn't stifle the cry this time. "Jimi, I can't move. You'll have to help me." Her feet were lumps of cold putty, feeling cut off below her knees. Jimi scooped her up, his powerful arms easily supporting her the short distance to the teahouse. He deftly slid open a parchment-covered panel with one foot and carried her across the room, gently lowering her to a large cushion. He knelt beside her and massaged her feet as she worked on her calves. She stifled groans as the rush of blood sent in waves of pins and needles.

As circulation returned, she took in her surroundings, realising why the Japanese Garden and teahouse were its owner's pride and joy. She had a nostalgic fondness for this style, perhaps because of the photos from her father's early life and his ancestors' history. The inside of the wooden structure was lavishly decorated, the black lacquered side walls divided into three sections. Full-length woven grass-mat panels, exquisitely painted with traditional Japanese images, filled each section. A majestic crane and golden koi featured on the two nearest the door, with Japanese Geishas, mountain scenes and sculptured trees, gardens and bridges adorning the others. At the far end of the room, a tall, black, lacquered screen concertinaed from one side to the other. It was inlaid with colourful flowers and embellished with pearl highlights and gilt edges. The cushion Anna occupied was one of ten or eleven, evenly spaced around three sides of a long, low table. The tea ceremony guests would face the garden when the sliding doors were fully open. Just one cushion was on the opposite side facing the room.

Her throat spasmed, cutting short her appreciation. Clapping a hand to her mouth, she used the other to mimic her urgent need. Jimi walked confidently to the back of the room and disappeared behind the screen. He returned with a stone beaker of cool water, which she gratefully sipped.

"So far, so good, Jimi," she said, matching her smile to his. But inside, her growing anxiety about what might happen next, and her ability to manage it when she was so tired, was sending waves of nausea through her stomach. All she wanted was to lie on the cush-ions and go to sleep. Thoughts of a warm bath and clean clothes faded compared to her desperate need to satisfy the overwhelming fatigue.

She squeezed her eyes shut and thought of Mishtko and the other women trapped in the mountain. She had to draw strength from somewhere for them. If she couldn't do it for herself, she had to do it for them.

As if reading her mind, Jimi moved to the doorway. "I check path to beach." He disappeared around the panel door. Her eyes blurred as she watched him go. If she stayed where she was, she would be asleep in no time. She flexed her protesting muscles and joints and crept to the door, peering out to the garden.

As in the teahouse, the typical formal Japanese garden with areas of lawn and fantastically shaped designs raked into sections of small pebbles was a cut above the rest. Entirely set in a hollow, the garden had a large, kidney-shaped pond taking up a third of the space. Its surface was a riot of multi-coloured flowers reaching skywards from enormous lily pads. The colours of the lilies and flowering shrubs, even the foliage of the trees, complemented each other perfectly, taking her breath away. She spotted her transport below a large cedar tree on the left side. It stood on a wooden slatted walkway which led to the cutest glossy red bridge, spanning the narrow middle of the pond. The wooden block path continued away from the pond and up an incline, which must have been their entry point.

The sound of water burbling came from somewhere out of sight. A small forest of Japanese maples, which stopped at a tall limestone wall running the entire length of the garden on the near side, hid it. Anna ducked, but couldn't see above the wall. No doubt the house was up there somewhere.

The garden was still and peaceful in the warm, sultry air, with only the rhythmic burbling of the water disturbing the quiet. Even the rumbles from the volcano didn't penetrate this tranquil place. Anna's eyelids felt heavy. She turned back, picked up her beaker and headed to the screen in search of the tap. If she could splash water on her face, it might help her stay awake.

There was a deceptively large alcove behind the lacquer screen, complete with cupboards, sink and a two-burner gas cooktop. She smiled at the idea of the ancient tea ceremony conducted around the long table using all the mod cons hidden back here. Turning the tap on a trickle, she splashed water over her face and neck, appreciating its revitalising coolness. The running water reminded her of how dirty she was. She opened and closed drawers and cupboards in search of a cloth or paper napkins. She might make a better impression on her rescuers if the worst of the grime was gone for her grand entrance.

71

Anna froze at a sudden commotion. With voices getting louder, she shrank against the cupboard, her heart thudding. This was more than Jimi returning. Surely it couldn't be Mr Koh and his guests? Boots clumping across wood and agitated voices answered that question, but it didn't help her fear. She squatted low, jaw clenched.

Jimi's voice became clear. "Okay. Okay I tell you. I look for my people. My gran. I want to help her. Why you not let me go there?"

"You know why, Jimi," a voice boomed. "Why did you come up there? Mr Koh said no. No one goes to the beach. No one goes past the house. Especially not you." Anna heard boots scuffling. "You want to go to the beach? See Mr Koh first." It was quiet for a beat and then, "He's the boss. You. Go. See. Him." Each of the last words was punctuated with a breath.

Anna inched closer to the screen and squinted through the narrow gap between two of the panels. Only Jimi was in sight. Framed in the doorway, he stood side on to the room, looking dejected with his eyes to the floor. His body language displayed disappointment and frustration. If it wasn't for his feet planted firmly apart, as if he was trying to block the other man from entering, his try at subterfuge would be complete.

Unfortunately, his adversary continued advancing, forcing Jimi backwards. Anna saw an index finger poking him in the chest, followed by a beefy black-clad arm. Each poke punctuated his next statements. "You finish your work quick-smart. Then go back and clean up. I want you out of here in three minutes flat. Mr Koh will be down here soon."

Annalee caught Jimi's slight sideways glance and the fleeting expression of surprise as he registered her absence. But the guard was still moving, Jimi almost out of sight beyond the doorframe. The guard was half a head taller than Jimi and more solidly built. His uniform was completely black, and he had a formidable-looking rifle slung over his shoulder. He stopped poking Jimi, lowered his arm and turned to take in the room. Anna followed his gaze, relieved it didn't stop at the place she had vacated at the table. The floor cushion was slightly askew.

He sighed, removed his cap, and wiped his brow with the cuff of his sleeve. "It's hot on that wall. I need a drink. You stay there." He took a step into the room. Anna's heart raced. There was nowhere to hide. And no back door. Only a small window she would never fit through.

Jimi's next word was high-pitched, squeaked out. "Wait… Mr Tray. You betta wait out here. Keep watch. If Mr Koh comes, you can go back real quick. I get water."

Fortunately, the guard listened and stopped mid-step.

"Okay, you go. Be quick about it and don't dirty up the place." The guard turned to face the garden while Jimi strode across the room and around the screen. He took a beaker from the cupboard, filled it with water and left with scarcely a glance at her. She heard the guard drinking thirstily before Jimi returned with the empty cup, gave it a rinse and upended it on the drainer. He looked decidedly grim. Anna flashed him a reassuring smile, which he didn't catch as he left.

The guard barked, "Right, now go. I don't want to see your face again today. You understand?"

"Right, boss. I go so fast you won't see me." Jimi's attempt to lighten the mood was met with silence. Anna heard his footsteps on the wood, the clanking of metal tools against wheelbarrow and then a familiar squeak from its wheel. The guard was no longer visible, but she was sure he was still there. It was so quiet, but she didn't dare move.

After what seemed an age, boots scuffled and sounded against wooden boards before they faded away. She breathed out a sigh, but counted the seconds off for a full two minutes before daring to creep out and risk a look. All was quiet in the garden.

Would Jimi come back? He had done so much for her already. Would he give up now? She couldn't believe that. And she needed his help to get to the beach. If he didn't find a way, it was hopeless. She chewed on her lip, a metallic taste coating her tongue, making her grimace. Besides, if Koh's plans for him were true, he had nothing to lose and everything to gain by coming back.

The time stretched interminably as she scoured the pathways leading into the garden through the lengthening shadows. Then, suddenly, there he was, his face peering from a bush at the edge of the path. He kept to the shadows, his boots in one hand, then he was running barefoot along the path and across the lawn. He leapt up the steps three at a time, landing nimbly beside her.

"We go now." His statement startled her, the wide smile on his face doing little to allay her fears after the episode with the guard.

"How can we if the guard is there?" Annalee had every confidence in Jimi's resourcefulness, but getting past an armed guard was surely an obstacle beyond even his creativity.

"Come on, quick now. This way. You see." He gripped her hand firmly and led her along the walkway and down the steps in the direction the guard had taken, but instead of turning toward the back of the teahouse at the corner, he set out across the neat lawn. They threaded through the Japanese maples until they reached the edge of the pond, which butted up to the high limestone block wall as she'd suspected. The running water she'd heard was cascading from the mouths of three large bamboo pipes set in the wall. Each was a different width, and the water fell musically onto boulders partially submerged in the pond. Jimi stopped with a metre to go, pointed up before putting his finger to his lips.

Annalee frowned as she surveyed the scene, wondering how on earth this would get them out. Surely it was a dead end, unless Jimi planned on having them climb the wall. But he edged closer to it until they were almost below the bamboo pipes. She felt the spray from the water bouncing off the boulders when Jimi turned to reveal its secret. The wall face, which had appeared continuous and solid, was divided, with a narrow passage leading to stone steps, cleverly hidden from anyone in the garden.

Jimi drew her into the passage, released her hand, and turned to face her. A shiver escaped her spine at the difference in temperature in the shadowy passage. But was it that or the realisation that this was it? They were either about to claim their freedom or lose it, and Koh would return her to captivity. When they got to the top of these steps, there would be no more hiding.

Thankfully, Jimi looked confident. "One time Mr Koh come this way… shortcut. Not now… he…" Jimi stopped, his smile fading, a shadow crossing his face. Annalee didn't press it, waiting patiently for him to go on. Time enough for explanations when this was finished. At least she hoped so. With his hands as aids, he changed tack. "House end up there." He blocked the air with his left palm. "Big, big verandah out"—both arms stretched wide. "Then grass lawn." He fluttered his hand across short grass. "Then steps… and beach." His hands descended imaginary steps.

As Annalee drew breath to ask a question, one of the many crowding her mind, Jimi put a finger on her lips. "Best we see. Me first. You wait."

"Jimi…" Anna mouthed, "Be careful," but he was off, taking the first half of the steps two at a time before he slowed and crept cat-like to the top. He squatted below the top entrance, which appeared to be as cleverly concealed as the bottom one. But within seconds, he scrambled back, his face beaming.

"It's my mam. I see her clear. She talks with Mr Koh. She looks so fine. We must go now," Jimi blurted out and grabbed her hand, the need for quiet forgotten.

"Wai.. wait a minute. Tell me more Jimi. Who else is up there? How far away are they from the top of the steps? Did you see any guards?" Anna wasn't so sure one old lady was enough to stop Koh and his henchmen from blocking their bid for freedom.

Jimi frowned, took a breath and relayed what he had seen, again pointing in various directions. "Many people there, and here near house, I think guests. Some there, but most near Mr Koh and my mam. I think mission-ry people from my home talk to Mr Koh with my mam. Come on Annulee, we go now."

There was nothing for it. It was now or never. Anna breathed a silent prayer before following Jimi up the steep steps. Surely, with those who knew him they stood a chance. Didn't they?

Jimi moved aside for Annalee to look. Their vantage point gave a clear view of most of the front of the house. Only the short width of a paved pathway on this side of it separated them. The lavishly furnished, wide verandah leading to the lawn looked crowded. Many more people than she had envisaged. She recoiled at the thought of showing herself, of having to walk past them. She hadn't seen so many people since....

Her head started spinning and she shrank back, sitting heavily on the cool steps. Closing her eyes, her heart drummed against her rib cage, the beat whooshing in her ears. How did she know if anyone was likely to help? To listen to her? Or who was waiting, ready to stop them? And which one of them was Koh?

Her courage was melting away like vapour, now that she was about to come face to face with the monster who had orchestrated all this. She hugged her knees and tried to slow her breathing. Jimi placed a hand on her arm.

"It okay, Annulee. We can do it. I show you." He waited for her to turn and pointed across her shoulder to a large group gathered on the lawn facing the house. "Look there... my mam... see?" he said, obvious pride in his voice.

Annalee ignored the nearby mass of faceless people and focused where he was pointing.

"Yes, I see now."

The group of people with their backs to the beach stood out from a smaller, tight-knit group of black-garbed people facing them. There were about ten or twelve men and women from Jimi's island. The men wore shorts and loose shirts and the women were in colourful ankle-length wrap-around dresses. Jimi's tiny grandmother was in the centre of her group—all islanders bar a white couple standing one on either side of her. They must be the missionaries. His grandmother was waving her arms, pointing and very red in the face as she made her views known. Others in the group added to the discussion when she drew a breath. Annalee couldn't make out what they were saying, but what she saw gave her the confidence she needed. This lively exchange commanded everyone's attention, from the people seated or standing near the house to the guards on the wall. It may be the advantage they needed to get close to their potential allies, without being challenged too soon.

Her heart slowing, not quite back to normal, but at a comfortable level, she scanned across the other groups nearer to the house and closest to her and Jimi. Three men and a woman stood out from Koh's elegantly dressed guests. Likely the visiting scientists Sissy had described. They looked the part. Two of the men sported bushy beards and wore checked shirts with denim jeans and sturdy boots; the other, a younger man, had on a polo shirt and blue jeans. The young fresh-faced woman with them also wore jeans but with a white short-sleeved button-up top.

"Mr Koh." Jimi pointed over her shoulder to the group facing Jimi's grandmother. He added, "Koh's big men," putting up four fingers. Anna frowned as she counted more than five men in that group. Who were the others? Unfortunately, Anna still couldn't make out Koh. It just looked like a mass of black-clothed humanity to her, most of them tall and solidly built. "Police." Jimi pointed out several uniformed men standing a metre apart behind the islanders nearer to the wall above the beach. Thankfully, their weapons were still on their backs.

"Okay, let's do it." Annalee took a deep breath and climbed the remaining steps before she could change her mind, headed diago-nally across the pathway and onto the wooden deck of the verandah. Jimi was beside her in a flash, and she gratefully grasped his arm.

An elegantly dressed woman gasped as they drew abreast and, one by one, heads turned towards them. Anna avoided eye contact, lifted her chin, and willed her legs to keep on moving. She could only imagine what they must be thinking seeing her, a filthy-dirty, bare-foot apparition with a swollen belly barely concealed by her ragged clothes, her skin streaked with dirt and blood, her hair hanging in rat-tails.

The walk took on a surreal effect, as if time slowed to imprint every minute detail in her mind. A dirty pink sky backdrop, domi-nated by the lopsided volcano, oozing red lava and black smoke that distorted the daylight, creating an artificial dusk. The acid tang mixed with iodine and salt air carried on the warm breeze as it crossed the sea, teasing her nostrils. Sulphur caught at her throat, the chemical blend both drying her eyes and making them water. It was as if the entire scene was on fire, and reaching across the water for this refining moment.

Anna registered the startled expressions as heads turned her way; a hand raised to the mouth of a woman seated at a table. Heads moving together to whisper to their neighbours. Frowns on the faces of a tall man and two women they passed close to. Eyes narrowing as they looked her up and down before fixating on her middle. A guard —was it Mr Tray from the Japanese Garden?—moved from her right, his weight shifting as he swung his rifle from his shoulder to his chest before he slowed to a stop. She saw the surprised eyes, the pursed lips of a man at the rear of Koh's group, who jerked back around, pushed through his cohort, and disappeared from view.

Silence spread across the verandah and onto the lawn before them like a wave until it reached those around Koh and the islanders whose faces turned as one. The thud, thud, thud of her heart and the soft pad, pad, pad of her feet and the slap of Jimi's as they moved across the lawn filled her ears. It was as if the entire world was grinding to a halt. Jimi's gran froze mid-word, her finger poised in the air. She stood open-mouthed, her eyes widening. They were but fifteen feet apart now, yet Annalee saw no spark of recognition in her eyes at her grandson's approach.

A voice finally broke the unearthly silence. His voice. The words rose through the air like the ash and smoke from the volcano across the water. Sending tainted and poisonous barbs to assault her ears. Sending her battered senses reeling.

"Ah, Annalee, there you are. We have been so worried about you."

She gasped and stopped, the air fluttering in her throat, threatening to block her next breath. The words were so far from anything she had ever imagined. 'Worried' about her. What on earth? A grotesquely obese man squashed into a wheelchair and dressed formally in a black suit came into view as those surrounding him stepped aside. Rolls of pale flesh oozed around his stiff white collar, meeting the cascade of chins resting on his chest. A moist sheen covered his sallow skin. Grey circles puffed under sunken black eyes. Anna's eyes fixed on the nasal cannula feeding him oxygen, its plastic tube disappearing over his shoulder. He blinked at her and spread his hands wide.

"You will have to forgive me as I attend to my niece," he wheezed out, sucking in shallow gasps of air as he spoke. "As you can see, she is in a certain condition and in need of attention. She hasn't been quite herself since beginning an unfortunate liaison with this young man who was in my employ as an under-gardener. He has taken advantage of her innocence and the position she holds in my family to advance himself beyond his status."

"No!" The guttural groan came from deep inside as her knees gave way. Jimi snaked his arm around her waist, his hand clasping her elbow.

Koh continued, "Annalee ran away to be with him yesterday. We have been searching for her every minute since then."

She shook Jimi's hands off and stood up straighter. "NO. That is not true." Heat coloured her face as expressions hardened. A few sympathetic glances shot in Koh's direction. What could she say to make them believe her? How could she convince them?

"He is NOT my uncle. I have never seen him before today. He

kidnapped me and brought me here. My name is Annalee Tanaka. I am from Perth, Western Australia."

"Come, come, come," Koh said, his voice wheedling and patronising. Nausea built in her stomach. She was going to be sick. "We are very concerned for you, Annalee. You must think about your baby. Let us get you inside. Dr Kessel is waiting for you." Turning to his audience, he added, "It is almost her time. The doctor will examine her to make sure she and the baby are physically sound. Unfortunately, this has all affected her mind, but the doctor will do what he can." He shrugged his shoulders and, with a glance at a man beside him, said, "Rahib and Tak will help you."

As two men made to step out, she put her hands out to block them. "Stop. Get away from me. I won't go with these men. Stop." Turning to the islanders, she searched their eyes.

"It is not true. I am Annalee Tanaka. A nurse from Perth, Western Australia. He is not my uncle, I tell you. I don't know the man. He has kept me here against my will on the other side of the island. *And*"—she raised her hands towards them, her fingers reaching out—"there are other women imprisoned as well. You must help me. Help them."

"You need a doctor, Annalee, my sweet," Koh cajoled. "Let your Uncle Hari help you. Surely you haven't forgotten your Uncle Hari? The times we spent together? Your father and mother, your brother Matthew and my Fraser and Kate? Since a little girl, you played with my Katie. You were so close."

"Uncle... Hari?" She gulped, turning to search his face, finding nothing familiar until their eyes locked. She gasped. There was something in his eyes, but it wasn't from her childhood. She barely remembered her uncle. She was a small child in England when she last saw him. This memory was much more recent. She had seen a likeness to someone else. To... Kay. How? That poor girl dying as she gave birth to her tiny daughter in the mountain, whispering her name... Kay. Kate? Was that Katie? It was incomprehensible. It was monstrous.

"What have you done? What are you doing to me? Who are you?" Annalee's eyes clouded, blackness swirling in from the edges. Nausea bubbled in her stomach, burning the base of her throat.

How could her own uncle be responsible for this, this place of cruelty? Of torture of innocents, of baby farming or whatever it was he did with the babies ripped from their mothers' wombs?

And Kate. His own daughter, her cousin, dying in her arms because of him. It was too much. She was so tired. She swayed further into Jimi, feeling the blackness crowding in.

"No," she said, but her voice was low and weak as the two men stepped closer. She raised her eyes again to the people from Jimi's island, searching for someone, just one person likely to believe her. Her eyes locked on those of the woman next to Jimi's grandmother. Eyes filled with warmth and compassion. She raised her hand toward her.

"Stop!" The woman's powerful voice shot across the terrace. The two guards did just that, spinning around as if reeled in by invisible elastic. One even dropped to his knee as if he were under attack. "This young woman needs to see a doctor, as you say. She is obviously in distress. I am a doctor."

Jenni Wilson stepped forward and was by Annalee's side in a flash, helping Jimi support her weight. She spoke clearly and calmly for everyone's benefit, but her smile was for Anna. "Would you like to see me or this Dr Kessel, Annalee?" The tears in Anna's eyes and slight squeeze of her hand were all the doctor needed from her new patient.

"This is ridiculous. Kessel is her doctor. Our personal doctor here. She must go to him now," Koh blustered. "Sergeant Vanuai, who I am sure you all know, is the senior police officer in this district. He can verify that Annalee is my niece. He also knows the circumstances here. In fact, he is here today to arrest this Jimi Kwaisas for his dealings with my niece." He looked over his shoulder. "Sergeant Vanuai."

A corpulent man in a uniform made to step forward, but stopped. He opened his mouth, thought better of speaking and just stood, eyes bulging, opening and closing his mouth.

The whoosh of rifles sweeping from the backs of the police filled the air, their sights fixed on Koh and his men. The men and woman Annalee had thought to be scientists were suddenly by her side, handguns drawn. More police and several men dressed in civilian clothes began appearing from the house or paths around it, shepherding groups of people or guards before them.

"It's all over, Koh. You are under arrest for kidnap and human trafficking. You've been under investigation for some time. If it wasn't for a volcano and this young lady's appearance, it might have been a lot longer," said one of men next to Anna.

"Vanuai," Koh persisted.

"It's no use calling on him, Koh. Sergeant Vanuai is under arrest. Although very co-operative and talkative these past few days, he has been relieved of his post. His part in your crimes, along with his widespread corruption in other areas, will probably see him spending the rest of his days behind bars."

At this, the sergeant blanched, his eyes bulging further, sweat pouring off his face, his body visibly trembling.

As if awakening from a dream, the diminutive figure of Jimi's gran moved from her spot with surprising speed, shrieking, "Jimi. My Jimi." She threw herself at him and, grasping his free arm with her scrawny hands, said, "Is it you?"

Not waiting for a reply, she raised her face to the sky, "Blessed Jesus, I thank you for bringing my Jimi back to me." And to everyone around, "I tell you he was here. I tell you he was." She began jumping up and down, trying to pull Jimi's face to hers and shouting at the top of her lungs. "My Jimi is come back to me. Praise the Lord! Praise the good Lord! He is not dead. He is not run away from his old mam." Out of breath, she clung to him, sobs replacing her words.

"Mam, my mam." Jimi spoke gently. "We need to get Annulee into the big house. You hush now. Let me do this one thing. I come back right quick." She relinquished his arm to allow him to scoop Anna up but stayed close as he carried her into the house, Jenni Wilson and Agent Pamela Hart following closely. A large group of household workers stood in the spacious sitting room under guard by two more police officers. Sissy took a step forward as they entered.

"Jimi, is Annalee okay?" An officer barred Sissy's way. He gestured with his rifle for her to move back.

Jimi paused and turned to Agent Hart. "Sissy good friend. She help Annulee. She help us now?"

"It's alright, Officer, she can come with us." And to Sissy, "Can you show us to a room suitable for Annalee?"

Sissy bustled forward and led them to an unoccupied guestroom. Jimi placed Anna carefully on the bed and stood by the side of it searching her face, his own pale and grave.

"Thank you, Jimi," Jenni said. "Thank you for looking after Annalee and helping her. You go with Adela, I mean your Mam, and wait outside for us. Annalee is in good hands now."

As Jimi turned to leave, Anna's half-closed eyes shot open. She struggled to sit up, but cried out and sank back, clutching her abdomen. "Mishtko. Mishtko. Get Mishtko." She grasped at the bedsheets, struggling to form the words. Jenni sat on the side of the bed and clasped her hand.

"Tell me what's happening, Annalee."

But "Help Mishtko," was all she managed.

Pamela Hart shot a quizzical look at Jimi, who shrugged his shoulders, but it was a grim-faced Sissy who spoke. "She is in the mountain. She is with the others."

"I'll send someone in to help you, Dr Wilson, while Sissy and Jimi show us the way to this mountain." With that, Hart shepherded them from the room and closed the door.

73

"**B**oss." Jake practically leapt at her as Elaine approached, files of casework heavy in her arms.

"DI Martin is looking for you. He's been in and out of his office half a dozen times in the last ten minutes."

"Right." Elaine frowned as she put the files on her desk. She thought back over the last few days as she approached his door. Everything had been humming along nicely as far as she knew. Still…

She knocked and went straight in. Ross was on the phone but gestured for her to sit. The words 'Wilmott', 'Annalee', and 'how soon', sent her heart racing and she perched on the edge of the chair.

"She's been found." Ross set the receiver down and gave her one of his rare smiles. "Alive and…" The hesitation before he went on to say "well" wasn't lost on Elaine.

DI Martin rotated his screen to show Elaine the email he'd received outlining the details of Annalee's discovery. She gasped more than once, her eyebrows hiking up further each time she read more of the incredible account.

When she'd finished, she opened her mouth to speak then closed it again. She wasn't often lost for words, but this time she didn't know where to start.

"Wilmott?" was all she managed as she dragged her gaze back to Ross's face. His name wasn't mentioned in the email.

"Yes." Ross said, gesturing at the phone. "Finally came out that he was involved." He pointed at the screen. "This Koh wanted the girl. He was one of the principals involved in sending huge quantities of drugs into Western Australia. Various means, but they used fancy launches at times, one of which your Dan skippered. Long story short, Annalee was drugged and shipped out to the island."

For once in her life Elaine felt as if she was floating. The wide smile plastered on her face stayed as she relayed the information to Jake and anyone else within earshot. Her fingers itched to pick up the phone to call Heather Tanaka. It would happen and soon, but she needed a few minutes to re-read the email DI Martin had just forwarded to her. It wasn't all pretty reading, Annalee, as well as the others kept on that island, had gone through a great deal.

But the main thing was, Annalee was safe and well, and in good hands.

EPILOGUE

Annalee smiled at her mother, cradling four-week-old Joshua as they sat in the shade outside David and Jenni Wilson's bungalow. The volcano towering behind the village had ceased activity the night of Koh's arrest, and the islanders were permitted to return three weeks later. Some went back after a few days, confidently believing it was God's will for the eruption to bring Koh's evil deeds into the light and, thus, God who brought it to a stop.

As soon as Heather received the news her daughter had been found, delivered in person by an elated DS Elaine Troy and DC Jake Winters, she had made immediate arrangements to be with Annalee. She met up with Barbara at the airport in Bali and they travelled the last stages of the journey together.

A tearful reunion occurred on the jetty at Peiho—no longer 'Koh's Island'.

Annalee only had to glance at her mother now to replay that scene on the jetty when they had clung to each other after all the months apart. Her heart filled with so much love it took her breath away. She blinked away the tears. Happy tears. And saw tears welling in her mum's eyes too.

"Happy tears." They said in unison. Heather chuckled and planted a kiss on the top of Joshua's head.

With her mum and Auntie Barbara to support her, Annalee had stayed on Peiho until after Joshua's birth, before coming over to Vaui. Dr Jenni, in consultation with a specialist, advised against travelling back to Australia before the delivery. Anna's due date was uncertain, and intermittent bouts of contractions continued until she went into active labour fifteen days after her escape. Joshua made his appearance, screaming lustily and a healthy weight, none the worse for Anna's ordeal.

Now, the extended family group, plus Jimi and his grandmother, were taking advantage of the cool afternoon breeze drifting through the trees on Vaui. Jenni and David, along with Miranda and Liam, had taken their accustomed walk to the bay as the fishing boats came in. They returned, shepherding two people before them.

"Look who washed up on the beach," David said.

Anna jumped up with a squeal and hugged her friend. "Lucy! We thought you were coming tomorrow. And Mick—it's so good to see you."

At that moment, Barbara came through the kitchen door, her granddaughter in her arms. She smiled at the new arrivals.

"And this must be Kay," Lucy said. "She is so tiny. A perfect little doll. May I hold her?"

"She is a miracle. My miracle." Barbara placed Kay into Lucy's capable hands, explaining how well she was doing after her premature birth. Her eyes misted as she swallowed back a sob. The grief of losing her daughter twice all because of her ex-husband's greed and cruelty would take her a long time to get over but, against all odds, the baby had survived. At four months old, she was now almost the weight Joshua had been born with.

Lucy squeezed her arm as they joined the group sitting on the terrace, Mick taking hold of Kay after a nod from Barbara as Lucy made a beeline for Joshua.

"He is so gorgeous, Anna, and he has your eyes," Lucy said as the baby cuddled in to her. "Two beautiful babies. I think it's going to be hard for me to leave this place."

They had learned that the criminal life of Hari Kimura aka Koh had begun even before he left Barbara and his family. His close connection to two brothers he met at college in Japan who had gang affiliations developed into a lucrative international business. Drug smuggling, money laundering and people trafficking were just a few of the activities which financed their lavish lifestyles.

His hedonistic lifestyle took a toll on his health, but he believed that money was the answer and enlisted the aid of several unscrupulous doctors and scientists. Finding a match for Koh's future organ needs led to the suggestion that a close family member would be ideal. This set the stage for Katie's kidnapping and then Anna's. That both of them were taken on the same day, albeit four years apart, was deliberately planned. Japanese Golden Week ends on the sixth of May and in his past Koh had a huge casino win the day after. He termed May seventh his personal Golden Day.

Koh's idea of isolation as a means of control affected Katie's mental health from the beginning. She was just sixteen when kidnapped, but wasn't found to be a suitable direct match for Koh so they artificially inseminated her with genetically altered sperm to produce supposedly perfect offspring. Her confusion, shame and anguish was exacerbated when they took her baby away soon after its birth. Sadly, the child only lived a few days.

She never recovered, growing evermore depressed as the months and years passed. She suffered a further two miscarriages before her last pregnancy.

As Annalee suspected, the events surrounding Katie's death were unforeseen. They brought Anna in as a last resort as no doctor was there. Doctor Kessel, whose medical qualifications were proving difficult to verify, had gone to the mainland to check the health of another kidnapped young woman. Koh's helicopter could have had him back on Peiho in an hour, but he was involved in a car accident, suffered a concussion and was hospitalised. It was three days before he was alert enough to discharge himself.

Koh's illegal trade in harvested organs had begun soon after his move to Peiho. Wealthy individuals around the world not willing to wait for transplant surgery bought the idea that the 'donors' were young, healthy and disease free. Almost all the organs came from young islanders engaged to work there, such as Jimi. He was initially tricked into selling his kidney, ostensibly to save the life of a poor dying child from Vaui. The money promised would go straight to his grandmother for her welfare and his future education. However, one night he overheard a conversation about someone he'd known who had left Vaui for Peiho a year earlier. He realised his friend was dead, like others before him, and that his own life was in danger. Koh wouldn't stop at just taking a kidney.

Incredible and horrifying as that was, the women kept in the mountain had added another shocking revelation altogether.

All were artificially inseminated, a slight consolation for Annalee, marginally more acceptable to her than the alternative. Why they were kept separate from each other was a mystery. Was it to keep them from working together to escape? Or as a cruel measure of control, a way to destroy their independence, to keep them compliant? Apart from Katie and Annalee's familial connection, the other women were strangers, kidnapped from various countries to provide designer babies for those willing to pay. People desperate for a child of their own, or for some like Koh, in need of tissue, cord blood or organs then or in the future.

Annalee had an emotional reunion with five months' pregnant Mishtko and got to know the other rescued women as they stayed on Peiho for some weeks for medical checks and intense counselling. All of them had since returned to their homes or communities with the promise of follow-up support and rehabilitation. Annalee and Mishtko were keeping in touch, with Anna promising she would be there when it was time for Mishtko's baby to arrive.

Many questions remained unanswered as Koh's clandestine dealings began to be revealed, but one of the hardest revelations for Heather and Annalee to hear was that Koh had orchestrated Tony Tanaka's death. Investigators were still tracing the threads, but it appeared that Tony became suspicious of Hari after Katie's disappearance and made enquiries through his contacts in Japan. He had said nothing to Heather, wanting to be sure before taking it further.

And the 'device'? The implants inserted in Anna's and the others' spines were removed easily with Dr Kessel's detailed notes. He had even recorded footage of himself performing the procedure. It turned out that they didn't just provide means of control. They also transmitted data to the research facility in the mountain about each woman's physical condition by monitoring blood chemistry, pressure and temperature fluctuations.

Koh was in poor health and under guard in a prison hospital. He was refusing to speak to anyone. Sergeant Vanuai and several of his inner circle, along with many of the guards from Peiho, were locked up on the mainland. But Dr Kessel, along with two other men, had mysteriously disappeared the night Annalee showed herself. Some records were also missing. Who had fathered the children was a major unanswered question, but DNA testing was underway. Annalee took that news hard but, assured that Joshua was healthy in every way and supported by everyone around her, she was beginning to put it in a safe place in her mind. Most of the time.

As the day cooled, Anna showed Lucy and Mick around the beautiful chapel on the plateau, which had remained undamaged throughout the volcanic eruption. Afterwards, they stood outside its doors, enjoying the view of the island below, before their eyes were drawn as one across to Peiho.

"Have you thought about what you're going to do, Anna?" Lucy said.

Anna turned to look into Lucy's eyes. Her dear friend knew her so well. "About Jamie?" Tears welled in her eyes and Lucy reached for her hand. She knew that Anna and Jamie had been in contact and, although he was concerned and relieved that she had been rescued, things had cooled between them. Jamie had remained in Queensland to support his sister's recovery and couldn't see beyond that for the foreseeable future.

"Not just that, but…" Lucy said.

"I'm honestly confused about him. I get it—what he's been through with his sister and all. But…" She turned away. "Who knows. With everything." She loosed her hand from Lucy's and waved her arm in an arc encompassing the island below and the sea beyond. "I just need time, and maybe without him in the picture… And with the support of Mum, and you guys…" She squeezed Lucy's arm. "To be honest, Luce, I'm not in a hurry to go home. Jenni and David have said they would be happy for me and Joshua to stay indefinitely. I can help run the clinic and lend a hand with babysitting Liam."

"And Peiho Island? What will happen to it?" Mick asked.

Anna fixed her eyes on the very top of Peiho, her face grave. "There's a way to go, but, with the loss of so many Vaui Islanders there, the provincial governor is going to sign it over to the people here to develop. Elders from each of the villages are discussing how they can best make use of it."

She took hold of Lucy and Mick's hands, a warm smile chasing the frown away. "The other side of that mountain is quite the paradise. One day, I'll show you."

ABOUT THE AUTHOR

West Australian author Glennis Paine writes mystery thriller novels and dabbles in poetry and short stories as the inspiration grips. After a career in administration in the health sector she changed direction, teaching secondary students English and Social Sciences before stepping back to allow her passion for writing to come to fruition. She was inspired to write her debut novel, *Butterflies Blue*, after reading a newspaper article on missing persons, and is now hard at work on her second novel. Glennis lives with her husband in Perth, Western Australia, but travels as frequently as possible to visit her two daughters who have flown the nest and live in London.

ACKNOWLEDGEMENTS

I would like to thank my husband, Steve, and daughters, Holly, Alison (dec) and Jessica, for your encouragement which has meant so much over the years. And to my faithful friends who have prayed and walked life's journey with me through the good and the tough times.

To my early readers, Dorothy, Keryl and Sue, special thanks for your thumbs-up which encouraged me to believe others might be interested in this story.

My most grateful thanks to Belinda Pollard, whose wisdom and skilful input in editing this manuscript has been invaluable.

And finally, thank you to the Lord, the master Creator, giver of all good gifts.

9 781764 053204